# City of Screams

Evolution is
running wild.

# CITY OF SCREAMS

JOHN BRINDLEY

CAROLRHODA BOOKS MINNEAPOLIS · NEW YORK

**First American edition published in 2009 by Carolrhoda Books**
Published by arrangement with Orion Children's Books, a division of Orion Publishing Group Ltd., London, England



Carolrhoda Books
A division of Lerner Publishing Group, Inc.
241 First Avenue North
Minneapolis, MN 55401 U.S.A.

Website address: www.lernerbooks.com

Library of Congress Cataloging-in-Publication Data

Brindley, John, 1954–
City of screams / by John Brindley.
p. cm.
Summary: Life already hangs in precarious balance for Phoenix and her family and friends as rebellion bubbles beneath every surface, but when the Adults return, offering desperate acts of salvation, they seem to forget that nature itself is calling the shots.
ISBN: 978–0–7613–3908–3 (trade hardcover : alk. paper)
[1. Evolution—Science fiction. 2. Science fiction.] I. Title.
PZ7.B76874Cit 2009
[Fic]—dc22 2008041165

Manufactured in the United States of America
1 2 3 4 5 6 – SB – 14 13 12 11 10 09

For Jakki

# NATURAL SELECTION

# PART ONE

# 1

Under them, movement . . .

It was traveling with them as they flew across the open plain, the ground a seething mass of green feather and scale, of snapping beak and clutching hands and cracking claws.

Flying above, taunting the young male Green Raptors, Air Agles on the wing. White against the violet sky, they flitted like Angels, with their leader, Gabriel, laughing demonically as the roaring Raptors leapt and fell.

His kind, Air Agles, lived neither in the city like the heavy Ground Agles and the sloping-faced albino Rodents, nor in the countryside like the lizard-legged, bird-faced Raptors. For Air Agles—fliers—flying was like breathing. If they didn't do it, they'd die. They were made for it. Evolution had produced them. They were Nature's chosen ones, the winged beings, the Angels.

Laughing along with them was a single Ground Agle. Evolution had denied Phoenix her wings. She sailed supported by three fliers, soaring with them, laughing down at the snapping rage of the gang of wild Green Raptors below.

"Take me down!" Phoenix shouted out to Gabriel and Jay-Jay, the Air Agles on her left and right.

Gabriel's pale green eyes looked down at the ground.

"Take me lower!" Phoenix cried to him.

Gabriel could have spotted an insect moving far, far below. He could see halfway round the world, over the city to the Rainbow forest, beyond that, across the plains to the mystery of the sea. Gabriel glanced into Phe's face—his eyes could not miss the flight-hysteria on her, the wish to slice through the sky that turned Phoenix round and round on herself every day in the ground-level streets of the city.

"Fly me!" Phoenix screamed at Gabriel. "Show me what it's really like! Fly me down! Show me, now!"

Gabriel looked at Jay-Jay. Together, holding Phoenix by the arms and the back of her plain dress, they looked behind at Jay's Special, Ember, the beautiful Air Agle at the Ground Agle's feet. Ember shook her head. She looked uncomfortable, worried. Phoenix watched Gabriel looking at Jay-Jay. She smiled as they grinned at each other.

"Fly me!" Phoenix was mouthing to Gabriel. If she had wings, she'd never falter, not for a single second. If she had wings she'd be the best, with Gabriel, the ultimate flying Agle.

The descent took Phoenix's breath away. The roaring, flailing green of the huge male bird-lizard people below seemed to rush up at her. They leapt up as she and her fliers plummeted. There was a clutch of grasping man-hands out of the green feathers as Phoenix and her fliers curved away at the last possible moment.

# 2

Earlier that day, Phoenix had looked at her reflection in the bathroom mirror. Her Ground Agle hair was sticking up. When it moved, she felt things through it.

At that moment, she felt sick, but hadn't been. So she put the stick she always used far back inside her mouth. Up came all her food. It still looked like food. That was good. Her eyes went back to the mirror again. Her sensitive hair shifted. What she had felt through it then was nothing but her own disappointment, her anger. She was too heavy, too lumpy.

Phoenix, with her thick-set short legs and chunky arms, would never look like an Air Agle, like Gabriel or Ember, so slim and pale, so sinuous and strong. She could never look that beautiful. She could never fly—unless . . .

Now Phoenix left her stomach behind once again, lifted into the air on Angel wings. "Fantastic!" she screamed at the Air Agles. "Skywards, entirely!"

Gabriel and Jay-Jay laughed. Phe couldn't see Ember at her feet. She could only feel her there. The milk white wings and bodies of the fliers flitted all around as Phoenix watched their back muscles flexing as they flew all round her. It was possible to see the mesh of fine hollow bones branching out from the shoulder blades to support the stretched, semi-translucent skin of the wings. Air Agles were beautiful, every one of them. They had on just frayed shorts and tiny tops, so unlike the plain dresses over the plump bodies of Ground Agles and Rodents. Fliers wore almost nothing in order not to impair their motion. And what movements they made! Such grace and poise. Such strength and stamina.

Phoenix looked into Gabriel's ice-cool green eyes. "Again!" she cried. "Take me there again!"

She was heavy in their arms, she knew. They were light and graceful, she, as Phoenix saw it, heavy and cumbersome. But she loved the feeling of flight so much, the way the Angels looked against the burn-bright sky, flitting and turning, sailing and swooping.

"Again!" she cried once more.

Phoenix felt Ember drawing away, dragging at her feet. She begged Gabriel. "Please, just once more. Please, Gabriel. It's the skymost!"

She knew she'd get to him. He could never resist her, the way she admired what they did, the way she loved what they were. Gabriel believed that being a flier was better than anything. He loved it when a heavy, dark Ground Agle like Phoenix believed so too.

"With me!" he yelled. He led the plummet downwards, taking Jay-Jay and Ember with him. All round them the Angel Agles dropped out of the sky.

Phoenix screamed as the pure rush of adrenaline hit her in the face like the fast-flowing air.

Directly below, the angry Raptors sprang from the ground on their powerful lizard legs. The green of their feathers, the flashing flesh of their heavily muscled arms came at Phoenix as she dropped towards them.

"Faster!" she screamed.

The noise of the roaring Raptors met her with a crunch on the moving air. Phoenix's own sound was drowned as the Air Agles accelerated faster than gravity would have taken them alone. They flew towards the ground, angering the Raptors still further.

At the very last moment again, they turned free-fall into swoop, their bodies arching gracefully just above the clutching hands and clacking bird beaks below. But Gabriel and Jay-Jay, spurred on by Phoenix's screams, had fallen just that much farther than before. The huge arms grabbed for them, for Phoenix as they turned their fall away into rise.

Phe had never felt so frightened, or so excited. The green mass of Raptors churned just beneath her, their hands almost catching her dress. The change from down to up took away the breath like a rush of excitement she might just die of. But behind her, Phoenix felt Ember being forced down even farther by the whiplash effect from Phe's heavy Ground Agle body and legs.

From one side, a huge Raptor leapt up. He looked familiar. Phoenix thought she recognized him. But he seemed to drag her back. Phoenix looked round. The Raptor had caught hold of Ember by the wing. He dragged her down.

Phoenix's feet fell, as she was lifted skywards by Gabriel and Jay-Jay.

"They've got her!" she cried out, but the others couldn't hear. They were too busy flying upwards, away from where Ember had fallen, where she ran and stumbled and fell and was engulfed by the ruffled green of over-agitated feathers.

# 3

Phoenix was whispering to herself in the mirror. "Never thought they'd kill her." She turned and threw herself onto her bed. "Never thought they'd do it."

She couldn't look at her own features anymore. Even her mother had wanted her out of sight. But in Phoenix's eyes, open or closed, was the vision of Ember running from that young male Raptor with one wing torn, the other flapping wildly. Air Agles were not fast on the ground. Raptors were. This particular Raptor was. His name was Spartan. He was their leader. He tore her first.

Young male Raptors were crazily aggressive, but no one would have thought they'd kill Ember like that, tearing her apart in a blind frenzy of hind-talons. Raptors were supposed to protect the city, not kill Agles.

"You drove them to it!" her mother came storming into the room. "You taunted them!"

"It was f— It was supposed to be fun!"

"Fun? That's what you and your friends call fun, is it?"

"No! Not that! Flying! Flying's fun."

"Is it? Is it really? Well, you can get used to being grounded, because that's what you are. You are a Ground Agle. We can't fly. *You* can't fly! Ever! Understood?"

Phoenix looked down.

"You have to understand, because you are what you are. And you're in trouble now. Nothing like this has ever happened before. Do you understand what you've done?"

"I haven't done anything! It was them! It was the Green Raptors. They're savages! They're just killers!"

"No they are not! You taunted them! You made this happen. You—my daughter! And now I don't know what's going to happen. Everything's changed, a murder has happened, for the first time since—since the time of the Blue and the Yellow Raptors, the time of the Adults. And you're responsible! And now I don't know if I'm ever going to be able to trust you again."

# 4

First thing next morning, Totally was bristling into Phoenix's room nose first, twitching nervously. Totally Rodent—Tolly—was like Phe's little sister, even though she was a Rodent. They stood staring at each other for a few moments. Phe noticed, reflected in the deep pink of Tolly's bulbous eyes, how pale and drawn she looked. Her own eyes were dark, brown-approaching-black pits in her wide face.

"You 'kay?" Tolly said. She stood in Phe's room with her ears shifting and her round, frightened eyes bulging.

Phoenix looked away, saying nothing.

"I wasn't allowed in to see you last night," Totally said. "Grandfather's still not back yet." Phoenix's grandfather, a City Councilor, had been summoned to help deal with the crisis. "I just wanted to fly," Phoenix said. "That's all I wanted. Just to fly."

"Then you shouldn't have been out over the plain," Totally said. "Air Agles shouldn't be out there. That's where the Raptors are. That's where they hunt."

"I know that," Phoenix said. "What am I supposed to do about it now? I can't bring Ember back. They killed her."

"But you shouldn't have been there! You shouldn't have been making yourself sick and—"

"Yes, all right! Can you try to make me feel any worse, do you think? Why don't you get going, go to school, where you belong."

"That's where you belong, too."

"Do I?"

"Yes you do!" snapped Totally.

"I'm not sure where I belong anymore."

"Well *I'm* sure! At school, with me, and with all the other Rodents and Ground Agles our age."

# 5

She couldn't look her grandfather in the face. He was an old, old Ground Agle, without the sticking-up hair, without the ability to sense things in the air that Phoenix and the young ones could. He breathed, pacing round her room. "There is an order to things—there must be. It's how we live."

"But why?"

"You know why. We are always in danger. From outside. Something will come for us, one day. Look at the Devastation of the Rodents."

Totally Rodent had lived with them since the Great Devastation. Tolly's parents and brothers and sisters were all killed. It happened everywhere, all at once.

"But that's them," Phoenix said. "A virus attacking—it's just genetics. What's that got to do with me?"

"Everything!" He turned on her. "Don't be so foolish. We have to understand. We must protect ourselves in the future. If we don't understand genetics, if we Ground Agles and Rodents do not study, we are all too susceptible."

"Are we?" Phoenix said flatly.

"Yes, we are. Who are you to doubt it? We need the Raptors to protect the city. Without them we'd have been overrun by blood rabbits long ago. They fight the danger that can be seen, we fight that which can't. We have to be committed to our place in this city. We have to be—no, listen to me! That poor young flier has lost her life. In the whole history of our city community, Ground Agles, Air

Agles, Rodent survivors of the Great Devastation, Green Raptors, nothing like this has ever happened. We never had to make laws, not formal ones, because we never had crime—but this is one! It is a crime—although there will be no punishments. But you must never try to fly again. Do you understand me?"

"That *is* punishment," Phoenix said.

"No, it isn't. It's just the order of things. Evolution made you what you are, there's nothing you can do about it. If we study Evolution, we can find out about ourselves. Changes happen. They are happening all the time. But we mustn't see that poor Agle's death as one of those changes, or we'll adapt to it and start to accept it as inevitable. We must never, ever do that. And you must never, ever try to fly again. Do you hear me, Phoenix? You will never fly again."

# 6

Now there were Raptors on the streets of ASP City. Their lizard-leg talons clicked along the pavements. Their beaked faces looked from left to right. The green sheen of feathers appeared to be almost everywhere.

Phoenix found a female Green waiting outside the apartment block when she left for school with Totally next morning. Greens stalked among the school crowds like feather islands, towering over everyone. Behind Phe and Tolly, claws scratched and scraped along the artificial surface.

"She's following us," Tolly glanced behind again.

Raptor, the language, was taught in all the Agle-Rodent schools. But understanding a real Raptor clicking and swaying and nodding and ruffling was still a very difficult thing. Phoenix couldn't do it, but Totally could.

"Shall I speak to her?" Tolly said.

"No," said Phoenix, "she's following *me*. Don't say anything."

There were no young Air Agles flying over, Phoenix noted, only their Elders with their arms full of food, peering down at her disapprovingly. Then there were so many Raptors outside school, and then no one speaking to Phoenix inside, not even her best friend Sapphire.

They all looked too frightened and confused. Their glances at Phoenix said she was to blame, even when so many of them, especially Sapphire, had been jealous of her friendship with Gabriel. The young Air Agles were the finest and the best. The way they looked, the way they spoke—it was the skymost! They didn't do school. Phoenix didn't want to, not anymore. Sapphire used to say she didn't. But now Sapphie's head was down, along with everyone else's, as the speech tutor tried to teach them Raptor, with so many Greens outside the window as if waiting to be spoken to. Phoenix was sitting next to Sapphire, but still they had not spoken a single word to each other.

Totally was talking in Raptor-speak behind them, getting it all right as usual. There were only two Rodents in the whole class, Totally and a male called Rapacious—Rap—and both were fluent in Raptor. They had a knack for the language and for learning.

"And why," the talk-tutor was asking, in ordinary Rodent, "why is it that we must learn to speak Raptor, and not for Raptors to speak Rodent?"

"Because they have—" Rap Rodent started to say.

The Ground Agle talk-tutor stopped him. "Not you, Rap—nor you, Totally. Let's let one of the others answer, shall we? Phoenix, do you have an answer for us?"

She shifted in her seat. Next to her, Sapphire moved away slightly. "It's because they have a beak," Phoenix said.

"And?" The tutor fizzed at the front of the class, with his head hair prickling. Phe's own hair was undulating over her head. She couldn't stop it. She could feel the agitation of the whole class of Ground Agles, and the two Rodents. The air, as her hair moved through it, was thick and electrified with disapproval, with ill-feeling towards her.

"Phoenix?" the tutor said, trying to ignore her hair movement. "Answer the question, please."

"Raptors can't make our sounds," Phoenix said.

"No," he said, "they cannot make our sounds. But we can make theirs, can't we, Totally?"

Phoenix felt Totally nodding behind her.

"That's one reason why we have to try to understand them. They live outside the city, providing us with protection. We, in turn, give them medicine. That is how our society works. Do you all understand? We must have respect for all other species. Phoenix, do you understand what I'm saying? Do you?"

Then, after the lesson, a lesson in guilt for Phoenix, it was time for midday food. Phoenix would usually pretend that she had brought something to eat from home, while hiding away from Totally who always knew the truth. But today her very own Raptor picked her up outside the door with a nod and a series of clicks. Phoenix was escorted to where the food was stacked by the Elder Air Agles. She was stared at by the Ground Agles and the interspersed Rodents, swooped over by stern-faced Elder fliers and clicked at by foreign-speaking Greens.

Everyone blamed her. She could see it in the flying eyes from overhead and hear it in the rate of Raptor-speak at her back.

"She's the one," she heard them saying, her one-time school friends, as she came into the room where everyone was sitting down to eat. Those closest to her stopped speaking, but Phe could read in the shiver of their hair what they had been talking about. She could see what they were thinking. Even Sapphire turned her back on Phoenix, with her hair sticking up in that same way, as disapproving as the rest of them. Only Totally came near, her bulbous eyes blinking with emotion.

"You've come for something to eat," Tolly said. "That's good."

But Phoenix hadn't any choice. She had to wait in line to collect her food, the fruit and the nuts picked from the Rainbow forest by the young fliers, brought into the city by their Elders. Phoenix had to take the same stuff as every ground-bound bristling Agle and put it in her mouth and . . .

Phoenix looked round the large room at everyone's jaws moving, at the motion of their hair, at their glances. She could hear the food being mashed, masticated in mouths, swallowed and converted into the stuff of Ground Agles, the hefty flesh that would fail to grow even the tiniest of wings. She looked at their thick arms and legs, the density of the flesh round the solid bones that would never, ever allow them to fly. The bile rose in her stomach with a sickening lurch.

There was nowhere for Phoenix to sit. As she moved in one direction, the small spaces between Agles and Rodents disappeared. Their backs were turned towards her. She looked at their food, glimpsed it moving in their champing mouths. Her stomach shifted. Had there been any food at all in her at that moment, it would have come back out.

Phoenix dropped the fruit and the nuts she had collected. Nobody took any notice. Their backs were still towards her as Phoenix ran to the other end of the room and crashed through the back exit at the far end. A single startled Raptor ruffled and click-cried out as Phoenix ran by on her way out of the school grounds.

# 7

With the midday food delivered to the city, Gabriel was at rest. On a roof on the very outskirts of town, as close to the city as the young fliers were allowed, he fanned his great white wings in the heat. "They'll kill you too," he was saying.

Jay-Jay had lost his long-time Special, Ember. She and he had been together always. They were supposed to have been inseparable. "I know him," he said, ignoring what Gabriel was saying. "I know that Raptor. Spartan! I know him, don't worry."

But Jay-Jay's sister, Alice, *was* worried. She kept looking at Gabriel, her every fleeting expression demanding that he do something about this.

"Jay," Gabriel said, "listen to me. We're Angels. We can't fight Raptors. He'll kill you. He'll kill us all."

"I don't care."

Alice's beautiful, imploring face sent an angel-wing flutter through Gabriel's heart. "Don't you care about me?" Alice said to Jay.

He looked away. Jay-Jay had not eaten or spoken properly to anyone since they had dragged him away from the milling mass of murdering Raptors on the dusty plain.

"We have to go," Gabriel said. He knew now that his plan for the Angels to leave the city was right. "We should have gone when I first said it. This wouldn't have happened. We must, before anything else goes wrong. Are you with me?"

Jay-Jay continued to look away. "We're with you," Alice said, for both of them.

One of their Elders glanced over at them. Alice and Gabriel started to eat, their mouths moving as if they hadn't been speaking at all.

"It wasn't our fault," Gabriel whispered, as soon as he thought they weren't being watched. "They killed her—the Raptor Spartan—he dragged Ember right out of the air and . . ." But the Elder opened his wings as if to fly to them. Gabriel looked away.

"We shouldn't have taken the Ground Agle," Alice said. "It wouldn't have happened if we hadn't—"

"It *did* happen!" Jay-Jay snapped.

The Elder flier's wings flapped, his troubled face pointing at the young Angels.

"It happened," Gabriel said, quickly. "So we live with being treated like this, or we go." He glanced at the face of the approaching Elder. "And I say we go."

# 8

The Raptor called out. To Phoenix it sounded like a roar of aggression, just like the young Greens on the plains. Another appeared, ruffled and with shaking head, clicking in front of her. For a moment, Phoenix thought they might want to take her apart, torn like Ember.

But these were protective Elder female Raptors, here to help not to kill. Phoenix ran round the Raptors as they appeared in front of her. She dashed through the streets and down a tiny alley, too small to allow access to something the size of a ruffled Green, even the smaller females.

Phoenix felt dizzy as she ran, weak from lack of food. But her pounding heart and full-forced lungs helped take away the food nausea she'd felt. She sprinted all the harder, to try to feel even better. It didn't work. She was just running away, desperate to see Gabriel again, for the first time since the murder, hoping he at least would still be glad to see her.

Over the alleyway, a pale form flitted. But it was not Gabriel or any of her other flying friends. She had to duck and hide from the not-quite-so-sharp eyes of the Elder fliers overhead.

Gabriel and the others had to be somewhere, just outside the city where the forest crept farther and farther in each year. The city had become quite small, giving way to the countryside that blew potentially poisonous pollen and seeds through the suburban streets until everything was a tangle of lethal snap-brambles and toxic holly. But it was into these overgrown streets that Phoenix ran in a scatter of lizard-birds and sucker-snakes. The lizard-sparrows fluttered on scaly wings past Phe's ears as the snakes coiled sucker-first to attach and to constrict, excreting venom like sour black sauce.

Somewhere in the trees above, somewhere in the outskirts of the city, the able young Angels must be doing what they did—flying! They must be free. All Phoenix wanted now was to be with them, for a while at least. She felt stuck, imprisoned by her need to speak to Gabriel, just to hear his voice.

Gabriel would not blame her for what had happened, Phoenix knew. If only she knew how to find him here, trying to look up into the trees, the sky, without stumbling into snap-brambles and being tied down by her ankles until she lost her life to the plants and insects that would prey on her. She wasn't supposed to be here. It was too dangerous for Ground Agles.

But Phoenix didn't care right now. "Gabriel!" she called.

Here and there were old signs, put up long ago, in the time of the city founders, the legendary Ash and the first flier, Laura. "Adults Strictly Prohibited" the signs said. But they were old and rotten and breaking to pieces, or so rusty they were almost unreadable.

Toxic holly-nettles bristled as she walked along the old road. The odd snap-bramble whipped across at her. The going was getting harder as the undergrowth took more and more possession of the land. Soon there would be nowhere for Phoenix to walk.

She stopped in a small clearing. The sun blazed down between the blue and yellow and violet trees. Everything glowed with sparkling and malevolent color.

"Gabriel!" she called again.

In the treetops flapped nothing but birds and reptiles and their crossed species, but in the deep green and purple bushes ahead, something much bigger stirred. Phoenix hoped it was an Angel, picking low-lying fruit. It wasn't. There were no green bushes. Only purple. The green was from feathers, glistening in the sunlight. Raptor green. So clean and new, so young. So big. So male!

One, two, three Green Raptors turned. They looked at her.

Phoenix looked back at them. She could speak very little Raptor, but their cautious clicks felt like uncertainty. Her hair picked up their signals, signs of nervousness.

"I'm going back," she said, slowly, hoping they'd be able to comprehend the meaning in her Rodent words. Everything about them—their body language, their quietly clacking beaks—spoke of indecision and confusion. "I'm going home," she said to them, walking away steadily.

At her back, Phoenix could feel the increasing distance, the space between her and these near-baby Raptors. They had no will of their own yet, these adolescent Greens still young enough to miss their mothers and wanting the courage of their hunter fathers.

Phoenix walked as steadily as she could. She would not run. It might just jolt them into action, exciting their hunting instincts. It took all of Phe's nervous, heart-rending resolve to move as if with confidence, as if she hadn't seen Ember's wings torn and trampled by Greens as young as these.

But she *had* seen that happen. She had seen the whole thing, brutality in the extreme, instigated by one single young leading Raptor—the one who had snatched Ember from the air, tearing at her dear and precious wing. She could see it now, as if it were happening again, or was about to, as another Raptor stepped alone from the undergrowth into her path. He halted her.

Now Phoenix remembered his name.

Spartan.

Spartan stopped her.

Phoenix stalled, almost crying out.

He stood there, glancing to his right.

Phoenix looked. There was a path through the trees. He was allowing her to make a run for it. He was letting her go.

Phe glanced behind as she dashed between the trees. Nothing came after her. They let her run. She ran like mad. And then she heard them.

Phoenix ran on what was left of an old broken road to where the plains came closest to the city. For some way, the roaring of the Greens had stayed behind her, even getting farther off. But then he was there again—Spartan.

He was very young, about the same age as Phe. But he was the biggest. And he knew it. A single glimpse of his frame, a whisper of his name, and the sight and sound of him would never leave you.

He was still a long way off.

Phoenix faltered. Surely he wouldn't—after what had happened, surely he wouldn't attack again? Would he?

Spartan stepped forward. From the foliage all round him, his Green gang, stepping in line, their great beaked faces swaying in terrible unison.

Now Phoenix could hear them again. They sounded different. That low rumble, that restrained roar. It was horrifying, threatening and raw. Even from here she could see the opaque density of their huge eyes, the nothingness they showed, the no-pity of the plains hunter.

Phoenix backed away.

The Raptors moved farther forward. Their heads went down. Their massive legs flexed beneath the dark green of their scales.

Slowly, deliberately, horribly, they advanced. They had killed an Agle already. And they had got away with it. They had the taste for it. Phoenix could see them savoring it in the clack of their massive, horny beaks, in the meat-eating mouths behind as she turned and ran. The full-throated rage beat at her back.

Down the last few lengths of broken road she dashed, out from between the trees and snapping undergrowth onto the plains. The sound of claw and roar from behind her was as if it wasn't behind at all but upon, up and over her, tearing and terrible.

The sound burst in her ears.

# 9

The Elder Air Agle sat closely supervising the young ones, the tearaways, the flyaways. But if they wanted to take to the sky, these new experts, the Arch Angels as they called themselves, no old Air Agle could stop them. Nothing could.

Gabriel knew that. He sat enduring the disapproval of his Elders, for now. He glanced again at Jay-Jay, gritting his teeth, and at his sister. Alice looked away. She spotted something.

Gabriel saw the faraway focus of her deep pupils, the re-fixing of her pale green eyes. He followed the line of her sight.

Across the plain, almost at the horizon, dust was rising. It looked as if a line of green bushes were moving, rolling through the open countryside. Raptors, stampeding.

But—there!

*There!* A figure alone, running, not in the way a giant male Raptor flashed and stamped, but like someone being pursued, someone really scared.

"Phoenix!" he whispered, focusing in on her distant face. Gabriel was no longer interested in trying to impress the Ground Agle after what had happened. But he could see too clearly the fear on her face. It reminded him of Ember, just before she was taken down and . . .

His wings snapped into full flex and he was thrusting forward, away from the shouts of his Elders left behind on tree and rooftop. "Jay-Jay!" he shouted back, glancing just long enough to see Jay's great wings swooping to follow and then Alice's and half a dozen more pairs of young white-skinned wings. "With me!"

"No!" the Elders shouted. "You will not! Stay! You have been ordered!"

They couldn't see what Gabriel and the others could. The Arch Angels' superior eyesight showed them the fear bristling on the young Ground Agle's head, the terror in her eyes and the blood-lust of the new lead Green, snapping at the forefront of his now out-of-control band of Raptor murderers.

"Spartan!" Gabriel heard Jay spitting just behind him.

Together, they raced out towards the plain with their wings shoving hard against the air whistling under and all round them.

# 10

Then something thumped her from behind, the smash of a fist in the center of her back and Phoenix was down, tumbling over and over onto the hard, dry grass. Huge lizard talons stamped round her, digging into the ground.

Phoenix jumped up again and ran. She managed a glance at the Raptor bearing down over her—Spartan! She was running for her life, madly, while he strode alongside and casually sent her sprawling again with one flick of his wide and scaly leg.

Down she went once more, somersaulting across the plain, landing upon her back with the great new Raptor leader, way ahead of his Green followers, shouting out to the air, scream-roaring his power and his might, reveling in his potential to do her harm.

But just then—a flash! So fast, something flitted overhead. Phoenix hardly saw what it was before a handful of dust blasted into Spartan's face and he stepped back in alarm, scrabbling at his eyes.

As soon as Phoenix sprang back off the ground she felt herself lifted, scooped up, held by her underarms, by hands gripping at the back of her dress, collecting and taking the weight of her hefty dangling legs. A whole flock of formation-flying Angels had her, raising her into the safety of mid-air over her tormentor, Spartan, as he still struggled to clear his eyes. Up she went in an instant, looking down over the plain. She saw Jay-Jay then, flying in like a bullet to crash into Spartan's shoulders, holding onto him by the head, striking at him again and again and again.

Spartan's hands were clutching thin air. Jay-Jay flapped over him, delivering blows that, while they didn't seem to hurt Spartan much, certainly disoriented him. But the other Raptors were arriving on the scene.

Phoenix shouted down to Jay. As she did, two more Angels dropped from somewhere above her, Gabriel and Alice crashing down from on high to gather ever more speed, swooping only at the very, very last moment. Between them, at that same moment, they both grabbed Jay, dragging him off and lifting him clear as a whole small army of Greens stamped and jumped and raged round their stamping jumping raging leader.

"Let me go!" Jay-Jay was struggling. "Let me get him! I've got to!"

"No!" Alice was screaming. "No! Jay! He'll kill you!"

"He will kill you!" Gabriel was shouting.

Spartan raged.

"Please, Jay," Alice was begging. "He'll kill you too. Please don't. Please."

"Don't do it, Angel," Gabriel was saying, as he and Alice lifted Jay-Jay farther away. "Don't—for your sister's sake, at least. Look at her."

But Jay was looking down. He was shouting down. "Next time—Spartan, you and me—next time!"

Spartan, in his swaying, menacing way, was saying exactly the same thing.

# 11

"I was thinking about it before now," Gabriel was saying.

They were perched in the topmost swaying branches of a giant red-leaved tree—nobody named trees or flowers now, as Evolution changed and distorted them into new species every few seasons or so. But this one must have been ancient, as its lower leaves were green, changing color as it went up.

"And I wasn't the only one," Gabriel said, without holding onto the swaying tree. His wings shot out and flicked him into a new position whenever he needed to rebalance. He didn't look as if he ever had to think about it.

Phoenix had to think, though, concentrating hard on hanging on, shifting her body with the sea-sway of the twigs, trying to keep her head on an even keel.

"Most of us," Gabriel said, speaking to Phoenix although not looking at her, "nearly all of us pictured ourselves away from here, living our own kind of life, having more fun. Why not? That's what I thought. Why do we have to stay, gathering food for—for, you know . . ."

"For Ground Agles," Phoenix said, glancing round at the others, the pale fliers relaxed and laughing in the hot sunshine, or Alice talking seriously to a skulking Jay-Jay in the leaves of nearby trees. "For Ground Agles and Rodents."

"Not for Arch Angels," Gabriel said, looking at Phoenix now. "All we do, all we're supposed to be for is collecting. All our flying's only supposed to be for them, never for us. I don't mean you, Phe."

"Yes, you do," she said. She waited for him to deny it. There was a long, long pause.

"So you know," he said, finally, "that we've got to go, don't you? This place, the city, outside it, it's all going to break anyway. Spartan, his kind—what are those young Raptors going to do, protect the city? Can you see it?"

"No," said Phe, shuddering to see only the murderous intention in the beaked and blank-eyed Raptor faces roaring up at her from the ground as the Arch Angels lifted her to safety.

"No," Gabriel repeated. "Why would they? Who are they protecting? Who are we feeding? It's not going to work, not anymore, the city, the society. We don't want it. We want to fly. For ourselves. We want to be free."

"To be free!" It was Phe's turn to repeat now.

"Is all," Gabriel said, with his wings sprouting, flapping involuntarily, lifting him for a few moments in his passionate intensity. "They don't know," he said, "the Rodents, the—you know . . ."

"The Ground Agles," Phoenix said for him. "No, they don't. They don't understand you."

"You do, though," he said, with his beautiful, pale green eyes trained on every last detail of her face. "You know how it is for us to feel skyfree, don't you, Phe? You know why we're going, why we've got to go, don't you? It's high time—it's overdue—all this stuff with Jay-Jay and Spartan—"

"Take me with you!" Phoenix said. "Gabriel, please. Take me, too. I don't want to—I can't stay! Please, you have to! I can't stay without you. Please don't make me."

# 12

"Just tell me what's wrong with her!"

Totally Rodent was watching her foster mother, Phoenix's Female Elder, wringing her five-fingered Agle hands.

"Tell me, Tolly, why would she run off like that?"

"She needs to fly," Totally said.

Her foster grandfather held her thumbless hand. "These needs," he said, shaking his head. "How has she come by such a need?"

"She's . . ." Totally started to say. She faltered.

"What?" Phoenix's mother said. "What is it? Tell me! Tell me right now!"

The Elder Ground Agle held up his hand. They all stopped for a moment, as if pausing for breath. "Now," he said, gently, to Totally, "tell us everything you know, please. We need to know too. Phoenix needs help, doesn't she?"

Totally took a deep breath. "She's—not well."

"What's wrong with her?" Phe's mother stepped forward.

The old Agle tried to calm her again.

Totally blinked, very slowly. "She makes herself—sick," she managed to say, looking at the floor again. "Almost everything she eats she brings back up. She makes it happen, on purpose."

"Why?" Phoenix's horrified mother demanded to know.

"Because of how she looks," the Elder Elder said.

Tolly was glad she didn't have to say it. She could keep quiet now. Her foster grandfather understood. "She wants to look like they do," he went on. "Phoenix wants to look like those young Air Agles. She wants to be thin and fine-limbed and—"

"She wants wings!" Totally said, too suddenly, as Phoenix's mother broke down into tears. "And," she had to continue, "she'll be with them now—or she'll be looking for them. That's all she wants, to be with Gabriel and the other fliers. She's—" She stopped.

"Yes?" Phoenix's mother snapped.

"Yes, Tolly?" the grandfather Agle said more gently.

"She's in love with him," Totally said. "She's in love with the Arch Angel Gabriel."

# 13

She wanted wings, now more than ever. "I'll be stuck here," Phoenix was pleading, "without you. On my own. Don't you see? I don't belong with them, not anymore. I belong with you, Gabriel. With you and the fliers. I do! You must understand!"

But Gabriel *did* understand, better than Phoenix was able to. "We don't know what's out there," he started to say.

"We do though! The forest, the plain. The sea! Is all!"

"No, not all. We'll cross the sea, over the ocean to somewhere else—somewhere new entirely. We don't know how far we'll have to go. It's one thing carrying you for a joyride, Phe. It'll be another getting across the sea to a new place. Think about it—we'll be attacked out there—the vicious seagles flying after us. And we'll be carrying you!"

"I'll lose more weight!" Phoenix promised.

"No! Look at you. You'll make yourself ill. You're ill already. You don't see it. We can't take you, Phoenix. We just *can't*."

# 14

Phoenix wept.

The Angels in the trees all round them looked the other way. Only Gabriel was here with her. "I get how you feel," he said.

"No you don't! How could you? You're an Angel. You can fly. You don't know how it feels to be trapped here, in this place—trapped in the wrong body."

He had been just about to answer that he did know what it was like to be trapped here. But in the wrong body? That silenced him.

She was crying. All was lost. "Gabriel, I thought, you and I . . ."

"You and I?"

"I thought—maybe we were—could be—maybe we were special to each other?"

"Specials? You and I?"

He looked so surprised, so aghast, Phoenix began to feel stupid. "Is it so wrong, you and I? Is it so—"

"A Ground Agle and an Angel?"

"Yes. Why not? We're not so different."

"But we *are*! Phe, I never meant for you to think—you just aren't—I mean, I like, you know, Jay-Jay's sister, Alice. She's—"

"I know! I know! Don't say it! I'm not like that. I don't look like she does. I'm like I am—but it's not long since we were the same. I mean, my Elder Elder says his Elders knew Agles that knew Ash and your Origin of Species, the first flier Laura. In those days, Agles were all the same. They lived outside the city, together. You know the stories. It's not long since then."

"But it is!" Gabriel said, softly but firmly. "Fliers weren't Angels—they weren't like we are. Evolution's working on us. We're better all the time. Look at our Elders. They can't fly like we can, see as far or as well as we can. You and I together? What sort of thing, what sort of baby would we have?"

"Baby? Who's talking about babies?"

"I am. I want to make Angels one day, Arch Angels, not . . ."

"Not what?"

"I'm an Angel," Gabriel stated, unnecessarily. "We're a different species."

"No you're not! You just don't like me like I like you. It's just not fair. Evolution! You love it. I hate it. The way it picks us out and does things to us. It stinks, Evolution!"

All round them, the Angels were taking off from the tops of the trees, flitting into the hot air and falling back down in a flutter.

"See?" Phoenix was saying. "Why you? Why can you fly and not me? Why are you picked out to be . . ."

But Gabriel wasn't listening anymore. He was looking from the flitting fliers through the heat haze to the horizon.

"What is it?" Phoenix asked.

His wings snapped to attention.

"Where are you going?"

But Gabriel shot upwards in a rush of disturbed air, leaving Phoenix to hold tightly onto the small shifting branches under her.

"What is it?" she called, as he flapped down towards her. "What can you see?"

"Look," he said, hovering just over her, pointing to the far horizon.

"What's that?" Phoenix asked, as a plume of distant, dark smoke rose above the far canopy of trees. "A forest fire?"

"No forest fire." Gabriel's green eyes were fixed into the distance. "Black smoke. No forest fire. Something else."

"What else?" Phoenix said, watching the thickening black mushroom billowing over the horizon.

"Don't know," Gabriel said. "But something really, entirely else."

# 15

Totally looked out of the window when she heard the Raptor-roar and then the Agle voices. A cloud of Angels in an arc flew around one hanging figure. Elder Air Agles flapped out on smaller, less able wings to meet them, to remonstrate with them.

"It's Phoenix!" she said.

Totally, with Phoenix's mother and her grandfather, rushed out of the apartment building. The female Raptors were there, clicking and scraping on the crowded street. They looked as if they were about to attack the Angels as they landed.

Phoenix's mother ran at her. "What did you think you were doing?"

"Wait!" Phoenix said. "No." She turned away, looking at the crowd of Ground and Air Agles, the Rodents and the female Raptors. "Listen to me! There's something you need to—"

"What do you mean by this?" Phoenix's grandfather demanded. "You! And you!" He turned to the Elder Air Agles. "You must maintain better control!"

"Please," one of them started to say, as if to make an apology.

"You have to—" Gabriel stepped forward. Totally noticed how his wings were fully closed and settled for the first time.

"And you!" Phoenix's distraught mother rushed up to Gabriel. "If you ever—"

The young Arch Angel cowered. His wings juddered. Jay-Jay, by his side, was already a good couple of meters in the air, along with the half dozen or so others that had landed with them.

"No!" Phoenix shrieked. "Stop! There's something else you need to know about."

"You have to listen!" Gabriel blurted out as the other Angels fell back to earth around him.

"We have to listen?" Phoenix's mother went at him. "I think you young—you fools need to listen, for a change!"

Phoenix let out a scream, so loud and piercing it ruffled through the feathers of the female Greens. "No!—Listen! Please! Please!"

Everybody stopped.

"What is it, Phoenix?" her grandfather asked eventually, speaking quietly. "What's the matter?"

"Just listen," Phoenix said. She glanced at Gabriel as his sharper than a seagle's eyes scanned the hot, blue sky. Then it started.

It sounded like a ticking. It sounded, first of all, like a choir of distant Raptors in unison.

"What is it?" whispered an Elder Ground Agle, with his less sensitive hair elevated and shifting and sparkling, alight with static. "I've never felt anything like it. I've never—"

He stopped speaking. The sound was growing, augmenting, speaking not Raptor but some kind of machine rhythm and rhyme, constantly beating and getting louder and louder and ever more insistent.

"We're too late," Gabriel said, still scanning the expanse of blue between the towering city buildings.

No Angel or Air Agle left the ground now. They all looked up to the sky. The sound was never going to stop: just when they thought it was as loud as it could go, it stepped up and then up again. The air throbbed. Then the air began to move. It was as if a million Arch Angels cavorted in a mass, churning the atmosphere into chaos.

"Too late!" shouted Gabriel.

Nobody heard him. The sky-sound was upon them when a wire, almost too thin to be seen by anyone but the green-eyed Angels, seemed to stretch out from nowhere and attach to a Green Raptor, burying its point somewhere beneath her feathers.

Everyone watched as the Raptor looked down for a moment. A single moment passed before the wire snapped alive and a massive electric current passed visibly along its length and thumped her in the chest. All her Raptor feathers flew out on end as she was thrown backwards with a dusty smack onto the ground and the first of the machines appeared in the spoiled sky.

# 16

It was thought nothing could ever penetrate the protective Raptor ring except another virus or some new kind of pollen. But the ring was dismantled, taken down, shocked into unconsciousness by the current from an electric stun gun.

The air above the buildings was blackened by hundreds of hovering war machines. Storm troopers descended on ropes with the blue smoke of friction burning from their heavy hands. They fell to the ground to join the troops already leaping from heavily camouflaged road machines with more stun guns and automatic weapons and flamethrowers.

"Adults!" Phoenix's Elder Elder had time to say, before he tried to run with her for the safety of their home. They didn't make it and their home was in any case no refuge. The whole city was under siege with every single Raptor stunned unconscious or rounded up and compounded in the countryside and Rodents and Agles confined to their homes. No refuge, no safety.

Only Gabriel and Jay-Jay and the other Angels managed to hold on to their liberty for a little while longer. When the first Raptor went over—the other few Raptors round her collapsing in a quiver of shocked green—the young Air Agles ascended through the blue smoke of the descending storm troopers. They could see the armored plates the invaders were wearing under their array of heavy weapons. Gabriel was the first to notice that these fearsome creatures—these the Elders called Adults—were not wearing their armor: those horn-hard plates were what they were made of. They had huge nail-like panels covering their bodies, as if their flattened skeletons were worn outside. This did not seem to fit with the description of Adults from the Old Tales, the Legend of Ash, the founder Agle, the Hero of their Origin of Species. Those Adults were supposed to have been creatures like Elder Agles, not these shelled warriors, with hard, segmented skin and mosaic faces splattered round pinpoint eyes under helmet-round heads. These Adults were not quite as big as Raptors, but they were much, much bigger than Ground or Air Agles. They dressed as if they were wearing nothing but firearms. Even at rest, they were webbed with straps, cluttered with chunks of well-tended metal, oily-looking but clean. Their great wide faces consisted of plates pieced together with strips of apparently bare flesh in between. Their lips were hard, with a separation strip in the center of each so that every Adult mouth looked to be in four sections. The inside pink of their mouths appeared incongruously soft and too colorful.

Gabriel and the Angels hopped from high window ledge to slanted or flat rooftop and back again, watching what was going on below. They saw the multitude of the invading army take control of the streets, loading the unconscious bodies of the Female Raptors into transport vehicles, sending them away to the out-of-town compounds they had got a glimpse of earlier from the air. The Angels skulked and hopped and brooded high up between the busy street and the sky, between the ground and the air machines, looking down with now-too-acute eyes at the fear on the faces of the Rodents and the Ground Agles and their own captured Elders.

"They're killing Raptors!" Alice said, not because of the flitting electric shock wires but due to the tongues of fire bursting between buildings and the rattle of gunfire and the smashing of windows. For a long time, in the old days, it was said, the city had stood windowless, shattered and broken by Adults dying of Evolution, before the legendary Ash had taken the city from them. Now the Adults were back, smashing the city back into what it was when they last left it.

"No," said Gabriel, carefully. "They're taking control again. It's all been planned out," he said, watching the patterns unfold, the symmetry of the infantry, and the punctuation marks of the flares and the systematic smashing of glass.

"They've done this before. They've done this all before, many times."

"We should go," said Alice. "Let's get out of here."

"I'm not done here," said Jay-Jay, skulking under his wings.

"Yes you are!" Alice snapped. There's nothing more we can do now. Gabriel, it's time."

But Gabriel looked down, far down, through an instant flame, through the lazy smoke as Phoenix appeared for a moment at a smashed window. He saw her look up and then farther up, just before being drawn away from the window by one of her Elders.

The hovering war machines were gathering, almost reflecting the pattern of attack of the ground troops. More and more of the flying fortresses, bristling with guns and flamethrowers, were circling in formation over their Angel heads. More and more weapons appeared, pointing, every one, towards the same point.

Every gun barrel that showed was pointing in their direction as the stuttering air battleships descended and three or four hundred beads of infrared rifle sights homed in on the heat of the Angels.

"Fly!" Gabriel had time to yell, just, before the cannons fired.

# 17

On the street, Phoenix had heard the word, the one fearful sound that had become synonymous with everything a young Rodent or Agle or even a baby Raptor had to fear in the night: Adults! But now the signs Phoenix had seen were gone, trampled into the ground, discarded and disregarded as the Strictly-Prohibited stormed on through.

Phoenix was shoved and jostled with her family back into their apartment when the windows went through and the door was kicked in and several horror soldiers stamped into their little living space and scanned them all. They came shouting, yelling at the tops of their aggressive voices.

"Where are your weapons?" shouted the brutal block of the male Adult farthest forward, thrusting his fearsome black firearm into their faces. "Where are your weapons?"

For a moment, everyone felt too stunned and afraid to speak, hearing perfectly pronounced Rodent language pouring ferociously from the plate-lipped mouth of such a threatening alien presence. Phoenix was the first to find her voice. "We have no weapons," she said quietly, from where she was crouched with her mother and Tolly.

"Where are your weapons!" the Adults screamed louder, growing more and more excited, their smooth flat shoulders hunched, their legs moving and their arms twitching. "Where are your weapons!" with their guns about to go off.

"We have no weapons," Phoenix's grandfather repeated.

"Sir, I'm asking you one last time." The soldier's voice said "Sir" as if he was being very polite and reasonable, holding a gun to another living, feeling, thinking creature's face like that. "I'm asking you one last time, Sir," he said again, as if about to pull the trigger against that face.

Nobody in the room but the Adults understood the word "Sir." The armor plates of the invaders shuddered. Beneath, hardened muscles were prepared, primed and pumped for action.

"I'm asking you, Sir!" came the voice again, from that Adult slit mouth, from the foremost soldier's besplattered fearsome face, from his thickened, hardened head. His dark eyes glinted with menace.

"We have no weapons," Phoenix's grandfather said again, very steadily. "We-never-use-weapons," he said, placing one word deliberately after another, emphasizing the truth of what he was saying.

Phoenix watched with respect as her grandfather's wide-open eyes met and fixed the glint glare of the soldier's pinprick stare. She had never had the opportunity to witness and to admire the old Agle's bravery before.

The soldier seemed to show his respect too, as he lowered his weapon, looking left and right, signaling to his subordinates to begin their search of the place. While the command soldier stood sentry over the family, the others threw open cupboards, kicked against the floor, cracking their unbreakable fists into the walls to check for hidden passages or compartments. In a few minutes, finding nothing, they began to back out, with the commanding officer leaving last, taking a final look at each Agle and Rodent face before him, as if committing everyone to memory.

Phoenix's mother let out a tiny cry as the officer went out at last, leaving an open space where the front door had been.

"Is that what Adults are?" Phoenix asked. Her Elder Elder looked at her. As he did, the whites of his eyes turned to red. The room lit up, fired by the flare blazing up the empty street outside with its light and heat pouring in through the smashed open window.

"That's what they're like," said the old Ground Agle. Behind him, Totally held on hard to Phoenix's mother as the flare-fire died.

Phoenix went to the window. She peered into the street. Armor-plated people, Adult creatures were running in every direction. There were no Agles, no Rodents or Raptors to be seen. There was gunfire and shouts and plumes of filthy orange flame-flowing. Smoke was billowing upwards. Phoenix looked up. There, high above, perched on the edge of one of the highest buildings, were the pale Angels in a line looking down. And there was Gabriel, peering straight at her.

Above him, gathering strength in numbers, the swarm of oily flying war machines homed in, bristling like angry metal, aiming, pointing, purposeful. Phoenix watched as Gabriel looked up, as he called out something she couldn't hear, as the Arch Angels took off in a winged flurry exactly as several machines fired and launched a metal webbing that scooped the Angels up in one and carried them away struggling, their pale wings and limbs tangled with each other and with the oily black mesh of the net.

# TERRIBLE RECOGNITIONS

# PART TWO

# 18

From the cage into which they had been lowered and locked, the Arch Angels were able to see across the square of ruined forest to the periphery of one of the Raptor compounds. Everywhere here stood the blackened stumps of burnt trees. Any undergrowth had been singed away. It looked like the ground had been this bare for a long, long time. So many hard Adult boot-feet had stamped the surface dirt to smooth dust. Campfires were dotted at intervals outside the Raptor and Air Agle cages, with larger and smaller bivouac tents dispersed between the tree stumps. Great hunks of metal were positioned at intervals across this new plain, water containers or huts or weapons stacks bristling like the bushes that had lived here just half a day before.

Gabriel looked up at the metal mesh fixed over their heads to prevent them from flying out. He peered across the open square at the female Raptors as they sat or stood with their flightless broken feathers drooping. They looked deflated now that they had regained consciousness from the powerful electric shocks that had pole-axed them. Gabriel had been expecting to hear a thousand giant roars when he'd looked over and seen the great green bodies dumped on the bare earth. "Wait till those wake up," he'd said to Jay-Jay and Alice. "Gonna be a party!"

But the female Greens seemed so placid now, as if the electric currents had purposely zapped the glands of aggression in their brains. They woke to a changed world, as if they had been transported unconscious to a place where everything had become that much bigger and more powerful than they. Some of the Raptors still slammed for their freedom against the metal mesh walls of their cages, but even they sank back as a battalion of infantry Adults goose-stepped past, heavy with weapons.

Their horn heels kicked up a dust storm as the soldiers, two long lines shoulder to shoulder, goosed up to the compound wires and the foremost sentry unlocked the gate. The Angels had to shift away as the angry soldiers entered bearing arms, shouting and turning to cover one another's back as if they were under attack from their prisoners. The open door was covered from outside and in by more firearms threatening to shoot, and to do it only too willingly.

"Keep back!" the Angels were ordered as they stepped away in alarm. "Keep right back there! I said BACK THERE!"

"BACK THERE! BACK THERE!" so many of the others picked up the battle cry, becoming instantly more aggressive and far more prone to pull their triggers.

"'Kay! 'Kay!" Gabriel tried, once, to placate them, holding up a hand, palm outwards, as he and the others backed their wings against the wires.

"DOWN! DOWN! DOWN!" the ferociously insulted soldiers screamed in his face. "BACK! BACK! Now, DOWN! FACE DOWN! DOWN!"

The Angels crouched as the invading army quivered with anger over them.

"FACE DOWN! Now! NOW!" that first officer screamed from a face full of hardness and harm. He reached forward and grabbed Gabriel by the hair, wrenching his face into the dirt.

"ALL OF YOU!" another screamed at them. "DOWN! FACE DOWN!"

"NOW! NOW! NOW!" they were still shouting over the backs of the Angels as they coughed against the surface dust penetrating into their mouths and up their noses. "STILL! KEEP STILL!"

They could hardly breathe. It was torture, not only with the dust but keeping their wings clasped close to their backs, struggling against the urges to take a deep breath and to make for the air.

"Now!" the officer over them said, ever so slightly more calmly. "Who's in charge here?"

Gabriel wondered, for a moment, if this could be a trick question. He was about to answer, "You are," thinking that this would be what they wanted to hear.

"You winged freaks!" that same soldier said. "Who's your leader?"

"I am," Gabriel said into the burnt dirt. He immediately felt his head wrenched up again by the hair. Two other soldiers gripped him roughly by the wings and hoisted him from the ground.

Jay-Jay looked up. "Don't," he said, fearful for Gabriel's safety.

Gabriel had to watch Jay lifted by his hair, as an automatic weapon was thrust into his face.

"Did you say something?" the leader soldier said, with his face in Jay's, so that Jay-Jay's head was pressed on two sides by weapon and by fearsome Adult face. "Did you speak, Freak?"

"No," Jay-Jay said.

"What?" the soldier whispered terribly.

"No," Jay said again.

The Adult's fist drove like a hammer into Jay-Jay's stomach. He buckled over, his wings flapping outwards automatically. In an instant the other two soldiers had him by the wings and were forcing him down, dragging him out in front of all the others. They pulled him through the dirt, grazing his bare chest and stomach, holding him facedown with a boot-foot hard against the back of his head and on his back between the roots of his wings.

"You will address the Troops of Our Holiest Immaculate Mother as "Sir," every time! Do you understand! DO YOU UNDERSTAND?"

"Yes—SIR!" every Angel said. Not one of them dared ask what "Sir" meant.

The Adult in command looked along the line of prostrated Angel bodies. "Freaks," he said. "Throw this one back," he said, about Jay-Jay, who was flung across in an explosion of rising dust.

"Bring this one," he said, to some of the other soldiers, pointing at Gabriel. "Stay where you are!" he ordered the Angels, as the soldiers backed out of and locked the gates, marching Gabriel across the square and past the other compound where a hundred or more female Green Raptors looked away in confusion and dismay.

# 19

"They were always going to return." Phoenix heard her grandfather whispering to her mother. "This day was always inevitable."

"We don't know why they're here," Phoenix's mother said. "How can we find out what they want?"

"I should speak to them," Phoenix's grandfather said. "As a representative of the Chamber of City Governors I really should—"

"No," Phoenix watched Totally saying, as a window smashed in one of the apartments upstairs and a young Ground Agle voice cried out in pain. "Please, Grandfather," Tolly said, going to him.

When Phoenix and Totally were not much more than babies, the Great Rodent Disorder had begun. The earth shrugged its shoulders slightly and its atmosphere altered once again, turning the weather round. For the first time ever the wind blew into ASP Island from the southwest rather than from the southeast. Evolution ran wild in a world of shifting, unstable conditions. Totally's family all went, so Phoenix's grandfather offered her a home. Phoenix's own father had died some time before, killed by a sucker-snake in the days when Ground Agles still went outside the city to gather food. Now Tolly called Phe's Elder Elder Grandfather, while Phoenix stood aside, watching, worrying about Gabriel, wishing more than ever that she could be with him.

"I must speak to them," her grandfather was saying. Totally cried out as another flame licked outside, exhaling its black acrid breath through the broken window. "Please stay here," she said. Grandfather reached out for Tolly. Phoenix watched.

"They are soldiers," he said. "That means they are trained to perform a function in war and peace. They aren't necessarily bad."

"But you said they're Adults!" Totally said.

"She's right," Phoenix's mother said.

"Adults, yes," he said, going to the open door, "that's why I must speak to them."

"Father," Phoenix's mother said. "Please." But Tolly was moving, going towards the door with the old Ground Agle. "Totally!"

Phoenix's grandfather turned, waiting until Tolly was gently guided away from the doorway. He turned and stepped out.

"Sir!" a stern voice ordered. "Go back in now, Sir! Now! NOW!"

Phoenix could hear the oily clank of chunky hardware, the creak of strained webbing and the boot stamp of military footfalls.

"NOW! RETURN TO YOUR QUARTERS! NOW, SIR! THIS IS YOUR LAST WARNING!"

"I need to speak to your—"

"TURN!" the outside voices screamed, crazed with aggressive intent. "TURN—OR YOU WILL BE SHOT!"

"I am unarmed." Phoenix heard the old Ground Agle's pacifying voice. "You will not shoot me," she heard him say as she felt the too-tight clutch of her mother pulling her, as her mother clung to Phoenix and Totally as if they were the ones under the threat of execution.

"You have no reason to shoot me," the astonishingly calm voice continued outside, contrasted against the battalion of cranked weaponry ranged and readied against him.

Phoenix could hardly bear to listen. The silence out there reverberated with tension, the calm before the firestorm. "Don't let them," she whispered to herself, before whipping free of her mother's grip and running to the door.

"No!" came the scream from behind her. "Phoenix!"

She dashed for the open doorway in defiance. Outside stood her only grandparent facing the firewall of weapons. The bristling arsenal turned on her. Phoenix stopped, suddenly too afraid to speak.

"This is my granddaughter," her grandfather said, quickly. "Her name is Phoenix."

"Take her back in, Sir. Please." A soldier stepped forward. "Take your granddaughter back inside. I'll speak to you." He indicated to some of the over-armed and spiky soldiers to follow him in.

Phoenix, with so many firearms in her face, felt some small relief with the weight of her Elder Elder's warm hand pressing down on her shoulder.

"Please," the command soldier said, back inside their apartment, "please, Sir, do not leave the safety of your home again. Not until you've been given the all clear."

"I'm speaking as one of the City Elders," the old Ground Agle said. "On behalf of my community, I have to request an audience with your Central Council."

"Council?"

"Your Chief—your Commander?"

The soldier regarded him carefully.

Adults' tiny eyes glinted from deep within their block-built faces, through pinpricks of machine light, with the untouchable intelligence like electrical circuitry insulated inside.

"As a City Council Elder," Phoenix's grandfather said, trying to come up with the correct words, "I demand to speak to your Commander-in-Chief."

The blunt, brute soldiers crackled with threat. Their officer waved them down. He looked from the old Agle to Phoenix to the rest of the family. His electric eyes roved back past Phoenix to her grandfather again. "You do not make demands! You follow orders. Is that clear?"

"We need information."

"And you will be given it, in due course. Stay where you are until you are told to move. Is that clear—I said, IS THAT CLEAR?"

"Yes," said Phoenix's grandfather.

"Yes, what?" The officer's eyes glinted with threat.

"Yes, that is clear," said the old Agle.

On the instant, one of the soldiers stepped forward and struck Phoenix's grandfather with a hard, open-palmed hand. The old Agle fell to the floor. "You will say "Sir"!"

"Please," cried Phe's mother, trying to shield her father.

"Don't hurt him," said Totally.

The officer said nothing. He was staring back at Phoenix as she glared her hatred at him.

"Phoenix," her grandfather said, with his voice full of dread.

But Phe couldn't let go. She hated these Adults, not just for the way they would strike out at an old Agle like this, but for taking Angels out of the air, replacing them with black smoke and fire.

"What do you want?" she asked him.

"I want you to stay put," he said. "All of you."

"We will," Phe's mother promised.

"We won't go anywhere," her grandfather said, "not until you tell us to—Sir."

The officer nodded, once, with his deep, dangerous eyes still fixed on Phoenix's face. Then he flicked a command to his troops, just a single slight movement of his head and they backed out, one by one. The officer was the last to leave, stepping backwards out of the door, his hot black gun barrel lingering for just a moment longer than he did.

# 20

Captain Robert FitzRoy tensed and turned. His knuckles clanged on the desk's surface as he leaned forward onto his fists with his huge rounded face thrusting. "I beg your pardon?" he said.

The air here in FitzRoy's office felt like steel in Gabriel's mouth, tasting of gunmetal.

"What exactly," Captain FitzRoy was saying through his rasp-hard lips, "do you mean by that?"

Gabriel had to stand before the desk, before the captain, holding his wings as still as he could—which was not easy. His whole central nervous system steered automatic impulses to the many fine wing muscles, firing them for every possible stimulus, bad or good, fight or flight. Gabriel and the Angels were all flight, no real fight. He belonged in the air. He belonged *to* the air. That was what he had wanted Phoenix to understand, when he first met her. That was what he wanted *everyone* to understand. And that was what he was trying to explain to the soldiers right now. "I mean—I don't mean anything," he said. "It's what we are."

"And you are—say again who you are. Say it once again so that I—that we," he said, indicating expansively to the other Adults in the surprisingly cool room, "can all be sure we heard you correctly. You are?"

"I am the Arch Angel Gabriel," he said.

The saying it was simple. The reaction it got was anything but. Captain FitzRoy drew back as if confronted by a venomous sucker-snake.

Gabriel could feel the drawing away, the shock wave of what he had said shifting through the crowded room. He suddenly felt even more alone, more and more in some kind of terrible trouble.

"It's—I'm—we're Arch Angels," he stammered, trying to understand what was so bad in what he was saying.

"And you are the Arch Angel Gabriel," Captain FitzRoy said. There seemed to be something in it that he couldn't get to grips with.

"Yes," said Gabriel, simply.

"That," said the captain, clashing his lips together, his laser-light eyes darting about the room before bearing down on Gabriel again, "that is blasphemous! Blasphemous!"

"It's who I am," Gabriel said. The Angels flew in an arc and his name was Gabriel. "That's me," he said, with an involuntary twitch of his wings.

"You are a blasphemy!" the captain raged. "Your kind are a living heresy!"

"I don't get it," Gabriel said, nervously, with the feeling of outraged animosity like harm in the air all around him. The urge to fly away from it was too powerful, and his wings snapped outwards and attempted a single flap before he could bring them back under control.

"Restrain the Mutation!" Captain FitzRoy ordered. "It offends decency to be shown these distortions, these flaps of disgrace. It should be hidden, this abomination!"

Gabriel was forced to suffer his wings and his arms to be dragged behind him. His head was being held firm by his hair, so that although his body was tilted forward, his face was up. His keen green eyes were fixed into the mesmeric distance of the Adult's electromechanical gaze.

The captain's face approached across the table, appearing to grow wider, deeper, harder. Up close, it appeared to have been manufactured by some kind of synthetic process.

"And out of the ground—" Gabriel smelled the captain's Adult words driven directly into his own face "—the Lord Genome formed every beast of the field, and every fowl of the air; and brought them to the man to see what he would call them—and now I have seen I will call you—what should I call you? Angel?" And he shook his head very slowly, very like the old Raptor signal for aggression. "You were never that. And I never want to hear you, or any abomination like you, use those words. Never again. Do you understand what I'm saying to you?"

Gabriel tried to nod. He had missed so much schooling through his irresistible urge to fly free that he knew very little about Evolution. His hair was wrenched harder, dragging his head back.

"You know what to say!" another Adult snarled into his left ear. "You have been told what to say—say it!"

"Yes—Sir!" Gabriel said.

The other Adult did not relent his grip on Gabriel's hair.

"Now," Captain FitzRoy said, with serious deliberation, "Genome has chosen fit to show us this—this Anti-Angel—yes. You are Anti. Anti-Angels, Anti-Genome and Anti-us. Your name, from here on, is not Gabriel. It is Stigma, for you are winged and marked with the sign of the Devil. Your name is Stigma and you are Anti. Tell me your name."

But for a second, for less than that, Gabriel was unable to respond.

The captain's hard-baked hand whipped Gabriel on one side of his face.

"Your name!" the glint-eyed Adult shouted into his thumped face.

"Stigma," Gabriel said.

Before he could think to say any other word, Captain FitzRoy's hand landed even harder on the other side of his face.

"Stigma, Sir," Gabriel said, with tears of pain and humiliation rolling down his cheeks.

# 21

"Don't," Totally said.

"I will," Phoenix said. "I'll find out what they've done with Gabriel and the others."

"Then what?"

"I don't know. Something, though. I can't sit around here and do nothing. It's not right."

"We have to wait," Totally said, with that look of sheer worry only a Rodent face could create. "Grandfather says."

"When did I last care what anyone says?" Phoenix said.

"You always care what Gabriel says and what he thinks."

"That's different!"

"You two!" came the call from downstairs. "Come and eat."

Phoenix looked at Totally. "Don't you say anything," she said.

Totally blinked, slowly.

"No," Phe said, "I mean it. If you say anything, I'll never trust you again, I swear it."

Tolly blinked again.

"Promise me?" Phe said. "Tolly? Don't you say anything about what I said, will you?"

Totally shook her head, sadly.

Phoenix took another long look at the worry on her foster sister's face. "Come on," Phe said, getting up off the bed and going out. But as she rose, Phe stumbled slightly. She was feeling light-headed, dizzy through lack of food. Most of the time she felt like this now. It comforted, in some strange way, as if it was telling her she was losing some of her Ground Agle bulk, becoming a little more like an Angel every time.

Food was laid out. Phe's mother and grandfather were already sitting at the table waiting for them to start their meal. This was not what usually happened, everyone assembled together like this. But here they were, as on a very special occasion. Phoenix faltered at the door at the sight of all the food. She noticed her mother and her grandfather watching her closely.

"Sit down, you two," her grandfather said, indicating the two empty chairs at the table.

Phoenix wanted to take a look at Totally, but she felt the other eyes in the room fixed firmly on her. She sat and swallowed, as if her mouth was already full of stuff she did not want to eat.

"I want to talk to you," her grandfather began the meal by saying. "Both of you. Listen carefully to me. You must not do anything silly while the Adults are here. Do you understand me?" He was looking from one to the other, Phoenix, then Totally. "Tolly?" he said.

"Yes, Grandfather. I understand."

"Phoenix?"

But Phe's eyes were still fixed on all the food laid out on the table before her. Never had such a meal been prepared in their house, on any occasion.

"Phoenix? Do you understand what it is I'm saying to you?"

"Yes," she said.

"And you promise me—and your mother—that you won't try anything silly—that you'll do as you're told? It's important, Phe. You must promise me."

She nodded. "I promise."

Phoenix managed a glance at Totally, who was deliberately looking the other way. Her grandfather was speaking to Phoenix as if Totally had already told him what she'd just been saying upstairs.

"And you, Tolly?" the old Agle said.

She promised him, faithfully. Phoenix did not feel nearly so sincere.

"Now let's eat," her grandfather said. "We're going to need every bit of our strength."

"That means you, too," Phe's mother said, leaning forward. "You need your food."

"Let's just enjoy the meal together," Phe's grandfather said, patting her mother on the back of the hand.

"Yes," her mother said, still staring at Phoenix, "and when we're finished, we will not rush off before we've had the chance to digest anything."

Totally was still looking the other way as Phoenix glared at her. She wouldn't want to admit telling tales, but Phe knew her foster sister had told them how she had tried to make herself lighter for flight and how she hated herself for being as she was, as *they* were, her thick-set ground-bound mother and grandfather.

"Eat, Phoenix!" her mother ordered, as if food were the most important thing in the world.

Totally risked a glance up, with a placatory look on her face. Phoenix caught the look and killed it. She would never, ever trust her foster sister again.

# 22

Captain Robert FitzRoy looked away with disdain. "Fasten this thing's hands, and his, his—flying flaps. I will not be insulted so."

Gabriel looked to the floor. Adult feet clanged on the metal ground all round him. His bruised face hurt from being swiped by such hard hands. His shoulders and back ached where his arms were pulled so far forward and his wings dragged so far back. He wondered through shocked tears what he could have done to offend, to insult these Adults without even speaking. All his life everyone had lived wary of the return of these strange beings, the frightening and destructive enigma at the heart of the stories of the legendary Ash. Now, as in the tales of the old city, the Adult words were so full of meaning and menace, bringing importance and a sense of dreadful values into the ordinary and the long accepted.

Like Gabriel's wings: the most powerful and beautiful attribute, the meaning of life for an Angel—now he had to suffer huge metal clips to be attached, holding the wings together behind. His hands were secured in front by a plastic band that clicked tighter and tighter until his wrists and hands tingled and his skin was pinched paper white.

"Now," Captain FitzRoy said, "before you are taken away, do you have anything to say in your defense?"

"Defense?" Suddenly his ear met the wall, or rather the wall of a hard Adult palm crashed into the side of his head from behind. Gabriel thought he heard a great sound coming at him from the right, smacking into him, throwing his head to the left.

"Do not question the captain!" a voice bellowed as the other noise receded into pain.

Gabriel stared at the metal floor, saying nothing.

"I should have thought," Captain FitzRoy said, "that a few words of contrition would not be out of place, at this moment."

He stopped speaking. Gabriel heard the silence ringing out loud against his unbalanced ears. He hadn't understood the captain's words but knew from the swirl of the silence that he was expected to say something. "I'm sorry," he said, thinking that this might be the right thing to say.

But another wall slammed into his ear from the other side. Gabriel's head rocked. "I'm sorry—Sir!" he said.

"Now then," Captain FitzRoy said, speaking into Gabriel's face, "now then, Stigma."

Someone wrenched Gabriel's head back up to face the captain. An uprush of contempt came bubbling into Gabriel's eyes from his Angel heart. He tried to hide it but the captain's intelligence glinted in his deep dark eyes, capturing Gabriel's opinion of him and holding it, hard.

"Well," the captain said, breathing in massively, "we shall see, Stigma, we shall see. We have a new enemy, gentlemen," he said, speaking to the room of soldiers without looking away from Gabriel's face.

Gabriel tried to change the look in his eyes, to hide his feelings. He felt sick with fear and worry for what the Adults might do to all the Angels, not only himself. "I'm sorry, Sir," he said again, trying to bring his wide green eyes in line with what he was saying.

"I'm sure you are," Captain FitzRoy said. "Or at least, you will be."

Gabriel was very well aware of the menace in these words as he swallowed down what was rising in the acid churning of his stomach.

"You, Stigma," the captain said, "are going to be taken to another office. You will be in the presence of the Holy Commander. You are very privileged. You will not speak. You will not look up unless specifically instructed to do so. Do you understand?"

"Yes, Sir!" Gabriel said straightaway, still fully expecting another wall-whack to one side of his head or the other.

Captain FitzRoy registered Gabriel's flinch with a glint of pleasure. "Take him," he said, as the soldiers clumped to attention, dragging Gabriel through one door to another room, then out across a grid bridge above the military encampment and into another cool cube, a bigger office with carpet on the floor and wooden furniture.

All the way over, Gabriel kept his eyes fixed to the floor, peering through the metal mesh of the bridge over which they passed, looking down onto the hundreds of foot soldiers booting around on the ground. For Gabriel, this view was not from far enough up. He ached for the air all round him, for the feel of the force of it against his wings as he soared and swooped. So soon, he felt as if he had lost so much. Some secret tears fell from him and dropped through the grid onto the unfeeling head-plates of the soldiers below. They would never know.

In the other office, Gabriel was manhandled into position before a big wooden desk with his head lowered, forced ever farther down from behind.

"The Mutation, Sir!" Gabriel heard Captain FitzRoy announce.

"Oh," another, different kind of voice said. "Oh, I see. Release the—the—"

"Release the flight flaps," Captain FitzRoy said.

Gabriel felt the huge metal clip being removed from his wings. Automatically, they opened and flexed as soon as they were freed.

"Oh," said the other voice, with disgusted surprise. "And, let me see the face of the thing."

Gabriel's head was jerked up. He had to look at the commander. He opened his eyes. It wasn't at all what he expected. Instead, he found himself looking into a small face, with softer plates that seemed to still to be forming from the skin around them. The eyes were bigger in proportion. Gabriel did have to look up to see this face but only because this little Adult was standing on top of the desk looking down at everyone else in the room.

"What is this thing?" the voice of the commander said.

Gabriel could hear it now—the higher pitch, the ring, the sound of extreme youth. This Adult was still a boy. A boy Adult!

"Calls itself an angel," Captain FitzRoy said. "Look at this." And he span Gabriel round to show the commander the roots of his wings. "It can actually fly using these. And this one calls itself the Arch Angel Gabriel."

Turned away from the commander as he was, Gabriel had to stand trying not to look at any of the soldiers as they crowded down on him. He waited, trying not to tremble as something touched him where his wings were fixed to the extended scapular bones of his back.

"Mummy!" the Adult's boy-child voice cried suddenly. "Mummy! Mummy! Look!"

"You will not move a muscle," Captain FitzRoy growled low into Gabriel's ringing ear. "You will remain perfectly still."

"Mummy! Mummy!" the voice cried out. "Come and see. It's horrid! Come and see!"

Gabriel heard the door open behind him. As it did, the entire room full of foot soldiers lowered onto one knee with their heads bowed. After the sound of the movement of leather webbing and armaments shifting, the room fell silent. Gabriel waited. He was the only one, as far as he could see, still standing.

"Captain FitzRoy," another voice said, "what is the meaning of this?" This voice was different again: female, older, strong and certain, accustomed to giving orders and expecting them to be obeyed. "Captain FitzRoy," she said, "rise, speak."

"As I explained to the commander," the captain said, "this one calls itself the Arch Angel Gabriel."

"Does it, indeed?" she said.

"I have renamed it Stigma. And its kind are Anti. This," he said, stretching, Gabriel could see, towards the Angel wings, "is the mark of the Devil."

"It's horrid," the boy Adult, the commander shuddered. "Mummy, it's horrid!"

"Let me see its face," the female's voice said. "Turn it towards us."

The captain turned Gabriel. Gabriel's eyes roved over the kneeling troops, touched upon the boy Commander's waist and alighted on his Mummy-Mother. She couldn't have been very much bigger than her son, with wrinkled skin between her pale thin plates. But her eyes were the deepest, the sharpest, the most electric yet. In her hand, she carried a stick, an ornate, black-and-white wand. She appeared as if she were about to perform a magic trick.

"I await your orders," Captain FitzRoy said.

Gabriel waited in silence, struggling to resist the urge to take another look at the mother of the little Commander. He gazed steadily at the floor, aware of the electric eyes scanning him.

"So," the female Adult's voice said, at long last, "tell me, Captain Owen, what is your opinion?"

Gabriel glanced up, aware for the first time of another officer in the room, another Elder Adult wearing similar arm and weapons insignia to Captain FitzRoy's. The new captain cleared his throat.

"Madam," his softer, more measured voice said, "I have no opinion on Mutations. But I do believe that incarcerating certain—segments—of a community is not the best way of maintaining the peace. These—abominations—are taken to be—mistakenly—new species. They are accepted here. I have always found it expedient to explore the consequences before taking such actions. It is my opinion that we should be more—circumspect?"

Gabriel frowned into another long pause. He had hardly understood a word that Captain Owen spoke, but he thought, he hoped, they sounded more kindly than those words spat out by Captain FitzRoy.

"Circumspect, you say?" the female voice came.

"You say circumspect?" whined the boy Adult.

"Certainly in the initial stages," said Captain Owen.

"Show me the thing's flying flaps again," the female ordered.

Gabriel was turned again. He heard the little Commander give another frightened cry.

"How can we allow such an abnormality?" said the female Adult.

"How can we allow such an abnormality?" said her son.

"We cannot, Sir," said Captain FitzRoy, very quickly.

"They must be constrained, must they not, Captain FitzRoy?" she said.

"They must be constrained, must they not?" said her son.

"Yes, Sir," said that Captain.

"How many are they?" she said.

"How many are they?" said he.

"At this moment, we cannot be sure. They are a minority. They will be controlled."

"Forgive me," said Captain Owen's softer voice, "but I believe these—these wretched things are responsible for delivering food into the city."

"I can manage that," said Captain FitzRoy. "Or Our Holy Commander will be obliged to suffer the sight of these flying things over and above him."

"It offends our sight," she said.

"It offends our sight," said he.

"Remove the abomination, Captain," said she.

"Remove the abomination, Captain FitzRoy," the boy commanded.

"Yes, Sir," said the captain, drawing Gabriel away roughly.

Gabriel looked at Captain Owen. The kinder Captain was looking down.

"It's too horrid, Mummy," Gabriel heard the boy saying, as the kneeling army snapped to, with so many metal implements clattering to attention with them as so many rough hands held Gabriel's shoulders, dragging back his wings and reapplying the heavy metal clip that held them hard together in the middle of his aching back.

# 23

"Don't!" Totally cried.

"If I want to, I will." Phoenix held the sick-stick she used to induce vomiting, as if threatening the young Rodent with it. "It's my body. I'll do as I please."

She had just devoured the biggest meal she had ever eaten, to prove she could if she wanted to. Now she was showing Totally that she could still do whatever she wanted with her food, even long after it had been eaten.

"I had to tell them," Totally wept, with the downy white fur on her pale face flattened and wet. "You aren't going to make yourself sick anymore, are you?"

"What if I am?"

"I'll have to tell."

"No, you won't. You won't tell anybody anything, not anymore. Because you won't find out. From now on, you keep your distance, and I'll keep mine. But I will tell you this much. . . . I'm not going to be sick, this time. That's all you're going to know about what I'm going to do."

"Phe, don't. Don't do anything silly. You promised."

"Yes, like you promised to keep my secrets."

"That's different. I was trying to help you. You needed help. You still do. Let Grandfather—he said it'll be all right. You need him to—what's the matter?"

Totally had noticed the shimmer of Phoenix's sensitive hair as it bristled across her head. "What is it?"

"Wait. Something—hang on."

Totally's ears moved, listening hard for sounds as Phoenix felt the air, filtering it for the radio frequencies of others' emotions.

"Outside," Phe whispered.

"I can hear them," Tolly whispered back.

They moved to the broken window. Both had promised their grandfather they would stay away from the smashed frame. Both abandoned their promise. They looked out and down into the street below. Nothing happened. But they both felt and heard that something soon would.

"It's him," Phoenix said, softly, just before a procession of soldiers stamp-marched a prisoner round the corner. Gabriel was being escorted through the streets, his head down, his hands tied in front by a big plastic band. His wings were fastened cruelly together behind, held by a big black clip. Around his neck hung a sign: "I AM STIGMA. IT IS BLASPHEMOUS TO FLY!" The writing on the sign was so large it could be read from three floors up. It was possible to see the expression on Gabriel's face—no, it was impossible *not* to see the fear and hopelessness he was suffering.

"It is blasphemous to fly," Totally quoted. "What does it mean?"

They watched Gabriel marched past. Just before the procession turned a corner, one of the soldiers lashed out and caught Gabriel on the side of the head. They had to see Gabriel's head jerking to one side.

"Whatever it means," Phoenix said, "it doesn't mean it's going to be all right." She looked straight at Totally. "No matter what Grandfather says."

# 24

"Hear this," called an amplified voice from the street below, "all dwellers in this section of the city. There are plentiful supplies, so do not concern yourselves. Take what has been left here for you now and make your way immediately, and I stress, *immediately,* to the city center, to the grounds of what you call the Royal Palace. There, you will be addressed by the Holy Commander. Everyone must attend, *immediately.* Anyone disobeying this order will be dealt with most severely. That is all."

Phoenix looked out of the window with her grandfather. A vehicle, like a small open armored car, moved on down the street repeating the message again and again.

"What do we do?" Phoenix's mother said.

"We do exactly as they say," her grandfather said. "We do exactly as we're told, for now. We have to find out precisely what the situation is." He looked at Phoenix. "We go. And you give the same message to everyone you meet—keep your head! And you, Totally. Tell your friends. There will be no foolishness." He looked hard at her, then back to Phe's mother. "Come on," he said, "we must go now."

Ground Agles and Rodents were pouring from the apartment blocks. In the street, packages were stacked.

"Supplies," Phoenix's grandfather said. "They've left us food and water."

"What sort of food would these—Adults!—what would they leave us to eat?" said Phe's mother.

There were guards, armed Adults keeping their distance, just watching.

"I don't care what sort of food it is," Phoenix said. "I'm not eating any of it."

"Yes you are!" her mother said, taking her by the arm. "This is all there is now."

Phoenix shook herself free. Her grandfather turned away from her. "Tolly," he said, "you try some of this. Look, this food—I think I know what it is." He nibbled the corner of a slab of brown stuff he'd unwrapped. "You'll enjoy this."

Phoenix stood watching with a disgusted look, while her mother cringed as Totally took a small bite. She seemed to have to think about what she was tasting before her expression cleared. Rodents could not smile. The structure of their faces would never allow it. But the unexpected pleasure that Tolly felt was still obvious in her eyes and in the way her body swayed. "Oh, it's—it's—"

"It's chocolate," the old Agle said. "The Adults brought it here once before. I heard about it. Try some," he said to Phoenix. She didn't say anything. Her family thought she was looking at Totally's face, but she was staring at what she could see coming their way.

There was a roadblock of green, a feather and scale barrier moving forward, distributing its color here and here and here among the families on the street. Behind Totally as she swayed in the Rodent bot-blag expression of pleasure, immediately behind her, a giant Green Raptor swayed, expressing entirely another emotion.

"You'll try it!" Phe's mother was saying to her. "You will eat some of this food."

But still Phoenix was silent, staring.

Her grandfather looked round.

The huge Green clacked in his face.

Totally turned and backed away. Her foster mother took hold of her.

The Green swayed. All round them similarly swaying very young male Raptors confronted the families, clicking over them, their feathers threateningly ruffled with newly unleashed hatred.

Phoenix's grandfather looked towards the Adults. But the Raptor bore down on him, towering over him, with its great horny beak clacking almost into the old Ground Agle's face. The Adults stood away, allowing this to happen. The Greens were all huge, all extremely young, male and madly aggressive.

Phe's grandfather tried to click-talk. The young Green rumbled from somewhere deep within its throat.

"What's he saying, Totally?"

"She has to eat," Tolly said, quietly.

"What?" said Phe.

The Green swayed towards her.

From across the other side of the road, an Adult voice let out a burst of ugly laughter.

Phoenix felt her mother's hand holding hard onto her arm. "Eat it," she said, quietly.

"No!" said Phoenix.

The Green swayed harder. His feathers rippled as he looked away for a moment, across the road to the laughing Adults. He swept back, with his great, murderous roar striking Phoenix in the face. His beak clacked and his claws scraped against the surface of the road. Phoenix's mother let out a cry of fear. Her grandfather moved to help her. The Raptor lashed out with one lizard hind leg, just missing the old Agle but slicing through a metal water container, which burst in a deluge.

"Stop it!" Phoenix cried out. She took another slab of the chocolate stuff and crammed her mouth. She chewed. The sweetness flooded her.

"Look here!" she shouted up at the Raptor, showing him the melted mess in her mouth. She swallowed down as much as she could in one go, showing him inside her mouth again.

The giant Green swayed over them all. There was no protection, for any of them.

"Move them along!" the Adults were shouting, showing the Raptors which way they wanted everyone to go with a swing of their ever-present firearms.

"The Royal Palace!" they pointed with a gun.

And Phoenix spat brown on the pavement, promising herself that she would never suffer the oversweet, cloying fat flavor of chocolate in her mouth, ever again.

# 25

This wasn't the first time Phoenix and Totally had been in the grounds of the old Royal Palace, now used as the City Council Chambers. As an ASP City Elder, Phe's grandfather had taken them there with him, often. Once, Phe and Tolly had been shown the room, the legendary place where the fearful Raptor leader, King Talon, had fallen and where Ash the ASP champion, founder of the City community, had been badly injured. Totally had been enthralled to see it, but Phoenix hadn't been so interested, with her head filled, as it always was, with flight and fliers.

"It all seems spoiled now," Totally said, looking at the great house from within the overcrowded grounds.

"It's full of equipment," Phoenix bristled, "electrical stuff. I can feel it all, buzzing." She, like so many of the Ground Agles here, stood taller with the effect of static electricity generated from inside the Palace.

"This is the Adults' headquarters now," her grandfather said, staring at the tall blank windows of the huge, impressive house.

On the roof, on the roofs—for there were many corners up there—stood larger than life stone effigies of fliers, stone Angels about to take off. On the ground, under armed guard along one side of the Palace, Phoenix glimpsed between the Adult weapons and excited Green Raptor feathers, a triple row of grounded Air Agles with their wings back and their heads down. It looked, for a moment, as if the stone effigies had fallen from their perches on the roofs and had been collected and reassembled haphazardly.

Phoenix was about to point out the broken Angels to her grandfather when a piercing electrical whistle burst into their ears, ruffling at very high frequency through the oscillating hair of the Ground Agles.

"Now hear this," a voice came through as the shrill whistle of electrical feedback faded.

Phe's mother pointed to the raised entrance of the Royal Palace at the top of the stone steps.

"My name is Captain FitzRoy," an Adult officer was saying, speaking through an amplifier. His expanded voice came from every direction out of several speakers all at once. "And this," he said, indicating another officer like him on a lower step, "is Captain Owen. We are responsible for patrolling every sector of this city, and I thank the Lord Genome that we have been given the opportunity to safeguard this strategically important border. Yes, let us give thanks, before you are addressed by the Supreme Commander of the Troops of the Truth of our Holiest Immaculate Mother." And he paused, looking out over the crowded grounds of the old Royal Palace, as if waiting for the Agles and the Rodents to give thanks of their own.

Phoenix looked around as the Elders shuffled uncomfortably. She glanced at her grandfather as he stared at the captain on the steps.

"Your lives," Captain FitzRoy went on at last, breaking the discomfort of the humming, amplified silence, "should soon get back to normal. We are not here to cause you undue disruption.... But we are here to protect you and to bring you salvation." He paused again, as if to allow his words to sink in.

"There is probably much good here," he said, "and we are hoping to be instrumental in preserving and extending the good and helping to eliminate the evil." He stopped speaking at that moment as the other officer, Captain Owen, stepped up and whispered something to him. He nodded.

"You will now," he spoke out, "be addressed by our Supreme Commander. His word is the Holiest Mother's Truth and must never be interrupted. You will all bow your heads," he said, looking out. He waited.

Phoenix glanced again at her grandfather. He was still staring wide-eyed at Captain FitzRoy.

"You will all bow your heads!" bellowed the captain from the steps. The soldiers all round clicked their loaded guns and the Green Raptors fell out at this signal, going among the crowd, clacking out a warning.

Totally told Phoenix what they were saying.

"Heads down!" they rattled, stalking like plains hunters among a herd of prey. "Heads! Now!"

And so many thousands of Agle and Rodent heads lowered, interspersed by the wagging tops of snapping Raptors. Phoenix felt the tension in the air, as if something was about to snap, something terrible about to start happening.

# 26

"Look up!" came the order from Captain FitzRoy. "The Commander of Our Mother's Holiest Truth!" he announced, as a small Adult waited for the microphone to be adjusted to his height.

Behind this boy Adult, curtains had been hung at the open doorway to the big house. He glanced back and said something before stepping forward to speak out. He looked only about half the size of Captain Owen or Captain FitzRoy, but they had both knelt to be on or just under the same level as their Commander. Every other soldier stayed three or four steps down from the top, keeping their heads low.

"There is only one Lord Genome," he said, with his grey mouth too close to the electronic microphone. The amplifiers shrieked out an appalling whistle. Ground Agles covered their ears. Phoenix let out a little cry of pain. A massive Green Raptor looked over. Phe felt her mother move closer to her side.

"There is only one Lord Genome," the little Adult said. "There is only one True Way. Ours is the way of the Truth," he said, staring out over the top of the crowds around the steps, glancing back at the curtains behind every now and then as if for reassurance. "We are the One True Way!" he boasted, looking, at that moment, straight at Phoenix.

She shuffled, disconcerted by his unquestionable certainty and his stare.

"Genome's Truth, His Will is done, His Word affirmed anew through Our Holy Immaculate Mother. Genome made us in His

Image. You, our subjects, are not of Genome's True Image—you are inferior. But confess you your sins and you may be redeemed from your dread path downwards into the shadow of the valley of death. You should fear Evil! Confess, and you shall receive absolution! Confess, and you shall be redeemed from the tidal change into the evil that is Mutation!"

He looked about, this boy, with lit eyes that reflected the sun as if from pointed mirrors focused with fire. Phoenix couldn't take her own eyes away from him. She and everyone around her stood transfixed, as if in a daze of horrified wonder. She waited almost without a breath as he paused for a very long time. His words were not fully understood, certainly not by Phoenix, but she was as fascinated to hear him continue, as she had been to look into the open wound when she had accidentally gashed her knee some months ago.

The boy Commander's mouth opened like another raw wound. "We will show you," he said. His mouth clamped closed. He said it again. "We will show you the way to absolution and to salvation. You have one chance to understand the—the—"

Phoenix could see the light flickering in his eyes. No, he was blinking. His mouth was opening and closing. No, he was speaking. He had leaned backwards towards the drawn curtain behind him and was whispering to some unseen influence situated behind.

"You have this one chance," he came back saying, "to understand the error of your ways and to begin to rectify them. Those of you who can. For some it is too late—too late!" he yelped, looking towards Captain FitzRoy.

As if he had been given a direct instruction, the captain signaled to the foot soldiers and Green Raptors, ordering forward the young Air Agles in a straggling triple line out from the deep shadow of the

Palace building. Gabriel was driven forward first. There was a gasp from the crowd as the sunlight showed the bruised and battered cheeks and shoulders of the young Air Agle with the sign round his neck. "I AM STIGMA!"

The Angels were brought from the shade into the sunlight in disgrace, each one bound hand and wing, in front and behind by big plastic brace and spiteful metal clamp.

Standing over all the young fliers, but over Jay-Jay especially, *ruling* over him, ruffled with Green pride, the biggest, the cruelest beaked predator from the plains—Spartan!

"Behold!" the quivering commander crowed. He fidgeted up there on the top of the steps in front of a heavy drape, behind a humming microphone, shifting from foot to foot.

Spartan preened and paraded, glaring out over the heads of the crowd, turning and clacking, as if laughing into Jay-Jay's red and angry face.

"Rejoice!" the commander's voice screeched, becoming more high-pitched than ever. "The evil resident among you will be restrained. This—" he squirmed, peering down, looking far right through to left at the straggling lines of young Air Agles "—this is sin personified. This—the Devil-emblem of wings—is evil made flesh."

"No," Phoenix heard her grandfather say by her side, but too quietly for anybody else to hear. "No."

"Confess and you shall receive absolution!" the commander wailed. "Unless you are beyond, unless you are of this basest flesh, unless you are—you are tainted!" he screamed.

And as he screamed, Phoenix's eyes caught Gabriel's for a moment. For that moment she caught a glimpse, a fleeting feeling, just the merest flavor of his shame, his sense of guilt through the hurt in his eyes. A moment was all it took to tell how unbearable it was, for Phoenix, who was receiving Gabriel's shame secondhand. For him, the weight of it all and the sign round his neck dragged down his head, his face to the ground. For her, it was as if her head was weighted too, dragged down by his shared emotions.

"Even then," the powerful boy crowed from his podium on the steps, "even abomination must learn its errors if the world is to be rectified, if the tide of change into distortion is to be reversed and the world is to be—the world is to be—the world is—"

Again, the commander returned to the drapes at his back as if for instruction, as if to collect the correct words to be delivered with a higher- and higher-pitched frantic voice.

"If the world is ever to be pure again, the sinners will be made contrite and then eradicated! Eradicated! Look on this now!" his voice screeched.

Gabriel's head hung lower. The Angels were tied and they were contrite. As Phoenix looked through the strangely silent crowd, with not one of the hundreds of babies there murmuring a single sound, feeling the disgust of the armed Adults and the new bruising hatred of Spartan and the young male Raptors, she began to understand, or to feel, the meaning of the word *contrite.* And then the word *eradicated* came to her, suddenly, like the clutch of a down-driven emotion.

And then Spartan's eyes were upon her, fixing Phoenix to the spot.

It was a day of terrible recognitions.

# As the Sparks Fly Upward

# Part Three

# 27

After an afternoon and long evening of subdued tension, with Ground Agles and Rodents confined to their houses, after a night of such broken, threatening sleep that tired her more than wakefulness, Phoenix had to go back to school.

The Raptors were on the streets, as before. But now the Greens were bigger, far more aggressive, snapping happy with no sign of a female Raptor anywhere.

Phoenix kept expecting the next clacking, swaying Raptor face to be that of Spartan, coming for her. She walked quickly to the schoolhouse with Totally, both keeping their heads down. The young male Raptors clipped into any faces turned towards them. The Adults scattered here and there looked on impassively. It was as if the city streets had been given over to the young male Greens.

Phe's grandfather, looking out of the window that morning, had said that this wouldn't last—that he and the other City Elders had been allowed an interview with Captain Owen early that morning and that he had assured them that things would soon get back to normal. "Contingency plans" was what Grandfather had said the captain had called them.

"What does it mean?" Phe whispered to Totally, as they passed quickly through green-lined Raptor avenues. "What's a 'contingency plan'?"

But Totally hurried on through as young frightened Ground Agles were dragged from their friends and isolated and screamed at in full Raptor rage. Right into the entrance doors of the school buildings, the Raptors kept them under their control. Only the too-small doorways prevented them from snapping and slapping all the way into the classrooms.

Phoenix and Totally ran into the building, breathing heavily with relief. But inside, the Adults were waiting. The corridors were lined with armored faces, bristling with oily, wet-look weapons. Any conversations breaking out with the relief at leaving the Raptors behind outside ended almost as soon as they had begun. The Adults did not speak. They did not need to. Their unliving, cold-spark eyes and their almost alive armaments said it all.

The Ground Agles and the Rodents quickly made their way to their first lessons. As soon as the tutor entered the classroom, Phoenix threw up her hand to ask the question that had been burning in her mouth all the way to school. "Where are the fliers? What have they done with them?"

But the armed sentries behind stood to greater attention. The clicking of firearms being cocked at the back of the room was not unlike the threat of Raptor-speak in the streets.

Phoenix glanced round, with her pulse rising wildly. She was as nervous as everyone else there, but she had to ask—she had to *know.*

The soldiers were ready to advance. All over the classroom, heads were diving down. Next to her, Phe's silent one-time friend Sapphire ducked below her desk and crawled away to an empty space.

"That's not why we're here," the tutor was saying, looking past Phoenix's drained face to the advance guard with the lights deep in their eyes blinking on and off like warning indicators.

"Why aren't you allowed to ask them?" Phoenix pleaded.

"Keep control here!" shouted one of the soldiers at the tutor.

"Phoenix," the tutor said, moving quickly towards her. "Phoenix, sit down and be silent." He placed a hand on her shoulder as she collapsed back into her seat.

Through her hair, on her skin and in her mouth she could feel and taste the tutor's dread. She looked around the subdued room. Sapphire sat as far away as possible. Totally shook her head at Phoenix, blinking her big slow eyes. Totally's Rodent friend Rap shook with nervous tension.

Today the tutor's lesson seemed to be about how scared they should be feeling. And so it began, this first lesson in fear, and the shame of being afraid, still under armed guard. All over the city, Phoenix knew, Ground Agles and Rodents were being held silent.

She glanced round again at her classmates, all Agles but Totally and Rap. On every spiky-haired head, the feeling of threat undulated, saying what they were not allowed to.

From the front of the classroom, facing his students and the back wall of weaponry interspersed with Adult faces, the tutor started to speak. His voice came out uncertainly, although his hair stood and shrieked in that Ground Agle way.

"Today," his small voice stuttered from his frantic head, "today—this morning, we will be talking about the comparative rates at which species evolve around us, with respect to how it would have happened during some of the prehistoric periods identified in the strata of mineral deposits."

It was a long sentence, spoken nervously, with his small voice fading, his mouth tightening as if gripped by sudden, irresistible thirsts. He finished his introduction and looked out across the class. But not to ensure that his pupils understood what their lesson was to be about—he paused, as if for some kind of Adult approval, or at least to avoid disapproval. There was no reaction from the back of the class, so he went on.

"In the past, the evolution of species was something that happened over thousands, tens of thousands, or even millions of years—"

"But what does it benefit you," came a female voice from the back of the classroom, "to talk of millions of years?"

The whole class turned. Phoenix hadn't noticed that some of the Adults were female. She had only noted the near-metal plates of their skin, the gleaming gunmetal of their assault weapons.

"It is," the Agle tutor started to say. He stopped, unsure of himself. He looked at the class, as they looked to him. "It is what we—through the study of geology and nuclear physics—through Evolution we understand the world—and our place in it."

"Then it is a gross misunderstanding!" The female Adult lurched forward, clumping between the desks. "A million years? More? Who are you to know such things? This length of time is beyond the world. It is before the world, before time itself began."

"No," the tutor tried to argue, "the world is thousands of millions of years old. The universe has been here for billions of—"

"Billions?" A male Adult launched forward now, as if to defend by attack. "How are you appointed to express such time periods, such Genome-known expanses, in your ordinary, mortal terms?"

The tutor looked at his class. They had been looking to him for guidance, protection—now he seemed to be asking them for the same.

"You talk of billions of years," the Adult soldier stepped up to the front.

From the rear, his backup surged like the next wave of his attack. "These billions of years that you account for so simply, they are fundamental to your system of beliefs, are they not?"

"My," the tutor stammered. "I'm not—not talking about a—belief system as you call it."

"Oh!" the soldier exclaimed. He had driven even farther forward so that his hard face was pushed into the tutor's. "These billions of years—they are documented, are they?"

"Well," the tutor's voice was fading out, "in a way, they are documented in the strata of the rock formation and in the—in the—"

"Here," the soldier stated, "is documentation!" He reached behind, where the female Adult handed him a book. "This," he said, holding this book in the tutor's face, "is the Truth documented!"

He turned to the class. "This is the Book of Truth," he announced. "It is ancient Holy Scripture, Genome's own words spoken through his prophets, promising salvation and life everlasting in the hereafter. Because the Truth it reveals is timeless. Timeless and unquestionable!"

Phoenix took her first really close look into the eyes of the Adults. They were so small, so deeply contained inside the large head. By this soldier's side, Phe's tutor's eyes shifted nervously, focusing and refocusing from the front to the back of the room. But the Adult black beads next to him simply pointed, as if directing dark rays out and not collecting colored light beams in. He opened the book and read: *"And Genome created man in his own image, male and female he created them."*

The Adult eyes blinked out. His mouth moved, very pink inside. But the sound of these words seemed to be fired on the black beams from those eyes, from the single spark of certainty contained and indelible inside that over-evolved hard head.

Phoenix wanted to duck behind her desk to avoid those blackened spoiling eye-pits, to get out of the frontline attack of those words.

"And Genome saw everything that he had made, and it was very good. And there was evening and there was morning, the sixth day. And the heaven and the earth were finished."

Phoenix felt she should say no to this, as her grandfather had said no on the grounds of the Royal Palace the day before. But he had spoken too quietly to be heard then. And now the tutor was silent, as if ashamed, and Phe's classmates were sorry for him and for themselves, with their heads hung, with nobody but the Adults having anything more to say.

"It is not your fault," the Adult with much more to say went on, turning to the only one looking at him. His eyes stabbed at Phoenix, before moving onto the next in line and the next, waiting until they each acknowledged his authority with a glance before looking away again. His stare pinned them individually, fixing their opinions under his, beneath his.

"That you have been contaminated by these ideas," he continued at long last, "is no fault of your own. How could you know, unless the Word of Truth is brought to you?"

"You!" He stabbed the word at the tutor, whose face fell. "You and your blasphemous teachings have given the Devil free rein here. You," he said, closing in on the closing-down Ground Agle tutor, "are the one to be condemned, not these defenseless innocents in your charge. Yours is the crime of teaching in contravention to the Word of Our Lord Genome. You must not be allowed to corrupt this potentially civilized society with your filth any longer."

"Take him away!" he pronounced, watching while the tutor, somehow deeply shamed, was led away by the female Adult with two other males.

Phoenix appeared to be the only one watching him go. Her classmates, with their averted eyes, could not bear to watch. She glanced over at Totally; Tolly gave her that look—the one that said, Don't—the one that always pleaded with Phoenix not to try anything.

Phoenix looked back at the Adult standing alone now at the front of the class.

"Now," he said, with his hard lips clumping together.

Phe tried to get a fix through her sensitive hair on how he was feeling, to get an idea of what he, he and all the others of his kind, were like inside. But there were no emotions to be picked up from outside him that way. He gave nothing away, being so self-contained within his horny, armored skin. All round him, round each of them, these Adult beings, a dead and stifling nothingness, taking, always taking, and giving nothing out in return.

Phoenix glanced towards the open door through which her tutor had been led. He was nowhere now. He, like the Angels, had simply disappeared.

# 28

"We have to find out where they are!" Phoenix was saying, over their food. The table was laid over-sumptuously again.

"They took the teachers away," Totally said.

"Why?" Phoenix's mother asked. She was looking at Phoenix's grandfather. "Why take away the teachers?"

"It's because of the lessons they gave us instead," Totally said, as the old Agle kept his silence.

Phoenix was staring at all the food. "I'm not eating that!" she said, pointing to the pile of chocolate pieces on the plate in the center of the table.

"Yes you are!" her mother snapped. "Don't you start on any of that not-eating stupidity of yours. Don't you dare! Eat!"

Phoenix grabbed handfuls of fruit. "No chocolate!" she said, before cramming her mouth.

"But we must eat it," her grandfather said. "We have been given it to eat. We must do that."

"Why?" Phoenix's crammed mouth spluttered rudely. "Why *must* we?"

"Because we have been given all this," her grandfather extended his hand across the full table.

"Then we can give it back, can't we?"

"No!" the old Agle shook his head. "Please—there's nothing more to be discussed. You don't understand what's going on here."

"Don't I? I understand our teachers were taken away. I understand the Arch Angels were—"

"Don't call them that!" her mother almost shouted at her.

"Why? Why not? Because the Adults have kindly given us food? Because they've taken away our teachers and our friends? Because they're giving us lessons about Genome making the world and everything in it? Because we were forced to kneel down and bow our heads and beg for our lives to last forever? Is that why?"

"It's only for now," her grandfather said, trying to calm and moderate his voice. "It won't last."

"No?" snapped Phoenix. "Won't it? With all their talk of eternal life? It won't last? Eternal life? With them, with Genome? What's the point of eternal life? What's the use of that—and all this—if nothing ever ends?

# 29

Penned in by thick wires, the fliers' hands had been cut free of the plastic bands that bound them. But their wings were still clipped, held together behind their backs.

Gabriel stood on his own, looking out. He watched as the female Raptors were removed from their own cage and taken away in trucks. With the dominant females out of the way, the young males preened in the hot sunlight, roaring up at the sky, where no Air Agle, no Arch Angel could bear to look.

Stalking round outside the cage of Angels, the Raptors clacked and stamped. Dust flew from clawed feet. They were masters of the Angels now, or so their roars insisted.

Gabriel had been watching out for Jay-Jay. He told Alice not to leave Jay's side. Gabriel swallowed hard against another uprush of fear and anger. He stood looking out through the mesh of thick wire at Raptors dancing in the dust. There were a few Adults dotted here and there watching from a distance.

Clamped behind his back, Gabriel's wings were hurting, flexing against the pull of the cruel black cleat holding them together. He glanced at the young fliers, the paleness of their intense pained faces. They couldn't be constrained much longer without harm. An Arch Angel would die of not flying.

Gabriel swallowed once again as he watched a convoy of trucks appear, clearing a path through the war-dancing Greens.

"What's happening?" Gabriel heard Alice speaking very close to him. "Is that what I think it is?"

But Gabriel could make no answer. All he could do was watch as the convoy drew up nearby and the trucks were unloaded and the cargo driven to stand in ragged lines along the front of the Angels' cell cage.

Then Jay-Jay was by Gabriel's side, trembling with rage. "That's my Elder—and my Elder Elder!"

The Elder Air Agles huddled outside did not have their hands bound or their wings clipped. But they were marked, red sore or darkened in patches by bruising.

"What have they done to them?" Alice was saying.

The Arch Angels were all on their feet now, gathered together at the front of the cage. A face, an Adult splatter-mask that Gabriel recognized immediately, was being transported to the scene in his own little camouflaged vehicle with a driver. Captain FitzRoy leapt out, stamping to the front of the Angel enclosure.

"Back!" he roared. "NOW!" He indicated to the nearest soldiers. Two of them reached out with some kind of metal rods and just touched the bars of the cage.

An electric shock shot through the nearest Angels, lifting their hair and throwing them backwards. Gabriel pushed the Angel crowd away from the danger.

"Now!" the captain turned to the Elder Air Agles. "You senior—you seniors. You can all fly. Indeed, you must. You are collectors of food, I understand. That is your function here. You must continue in that."

"No," Jay-Jay said, into Gabriel's ear. Gabriel turned and touched him on the arm.

"In fact," Captain FitzRoy continued, "your efforts must be increased, as now there are many more to be fed and fewer to collect. Your young people—your youngsters here, you see, will here remain. So you will bring food for—"

"Don't do it!" yelled Jay-Jay.

Alice tried to silence him.

For a moment, Gabriel was going to keep Jay-Jay down as well. But then he saw the look of defiance in the young flier's angelic face. Jay had hatred written there for everyone to see, inspiring, leading his leader.

"He's right," Gabriel said to Alice. He turned. "Don't do it!" he shouted out to his Elders.

"Fly away! Don't come back! Don't help them. None of us will. Don't do as they say. We're the Angels, not them! Go! Fly! Now! Take to the sky!"

The Adults came booting into the cage as soon as the door was unlocked. The stun weapons crackled and the shocked, electrically frozen Angels fell, quivering in the dust. Jay-Jay was struck in the chest and went down gasping. Alice was dragged away by her hair.

Captain FitzRoy marched into the Angel compound to grab Gabriel by the "STIGMA" plate still strung round his neck. He dragged the leading Angel out before the shocked and pale, battered and bruised Elders, swinging and flinging him down into the dust. The two or three Elders that made a move forward were beaten back by the butts of automatic weapons.

"THIS!" the captain screamed. "This is why you will do as you are told!" And he indicated to more soldiers that Gabriel couldn't see from where he had stumbled onto the dry ground. But then he could see the opening the soldiers drove between the Elder fliers and the thing that followed on through.

Gabriel could not miss this—the size of it, the color and the sound of its grumbling low throat roar. The most massive Green Raptor swayed through the opening gap in the crowd round Gabriel and stopped, with its great cloudy-eyed beaked head-threat swaying from side to side.

Spartan.

Gabriel looked up.

The great Green Raptor stood and looked around, growling mad. His face fixed onto the flier at his feet. His huge eyes clouded still further. The grumble roar in his throat sounded like terrible and dreadful hunger.

"We'll fly for you!" Gabriel could hear the Elders calling out, begging for him.

"Let him go, please!"

But Gabriel knew that even Captain FitzRoy could not stop this thing now. He knew this Raptor in particular, was, at this moment, almost unstoppable. Spartan lifted his huge head. He looked up to the sky and let out his full, unrestrained roar. Gabriel could feel it reverberating through his chest. But he could also feel that the clip on his wings had come loose when he was thrown to the ground.

He had only one chance. Spartan was going to kill him. Gabriel had to fly.

# 30

His wings snapped to. Even in great danger, Gabriel felt the thrill of flight. Flexing his back muscles was like suddenly being able to breathe again. He leapt up, wings out, reaching for the high free air. But Spartan leapt with him, dragging him down by the heel in the way he had hauled Ember to the ground before tearing her wings, giving permission to his followers to take her to pieces. Gabriel was brought back to earth in the same way. His wings flapped to no effect as the huge Raptor scrambled at him, as the razor beak sliced through the air in front of Gabriel's face.

He cried out. All round him, his Elders and the Arch Angels were screaming. But Spartan's attack roar drowned them all to nothing.

Gabriel saw only feathers and scales, clouded eyes and dreadful beak. He was about to be torn by Spartan, split apart, his precious wings ripped from his back. Then, suddenly, there were hands, Angel hands covering Spartan's eyes. Suddenly there was another pale figure attacking the Raptor from behind.

Jay-Jay had run from the cage as the Adults and the other Raptors were all watching what was happening to Gabriel. Jay had run out and leapt screaming onto Spartan's back.

"I'll kill you!" he was screaming. "I'll kill you, you murderer, you filthy meat-eating scum!"

Jay was pulling at Spartan's head feathers, clawing at his face. The great beak was cracking closed again and again in front of Gabriel's eyes. Round and round they span, with Jay's and Gabriel's screams sounding out between Spartan's giant Raptor roars, the heart-attacking rage of his war cries.

Gabriel hit Spartan on the beak and almost broke his hand. He scrabbled at the Raptor face in front of him. Jay-Jay's hands were still over the clouded eyes. Then he went over, this hugest of young Raptors, crashing into the dust with his feathers flying. Gabriel and Jay thought they had taken him down, brought him to the ground.

But as the two Angels leapt up, they saw the electric stun guns that had knocked Spartan senseless coming for them. Gabriel just had time to flap his wings, Jay-Jay time for one more kick at the Raptor face at his feet, when the electrical charges were released again and they too thudded down, paralyzed.

Every muscle in Gabriel's body flexed at once and stayed like that, pumped hard and stiffened, so that as he dropped onto his back, onto his wings, he looked and felt like a fallen statue from the roof of the old Royal Palace. He writhed on the ground as the stun effects began to wear off. He looked round at Jay-Jay also writhing and at Spartan being given another heavy jolt to keep him down.

Gabriel felt himself being hauled up by the metal plate still clanking against his chest. Captain FitzRoy dragged him before the Elder fliers as they stood shocked, ringed in by a barricade of weapons.

"So!" the captain called, swinging Gabriel round by the neck chain. "This!" he shouted out, dragging Gabriel to his knees. "This anti-Genome, this mutant abomination, calling itself an Arch Angel, is the worst of you—but we do not consider yourselves superior to your Devil offspring. You can all fly—that is your sin! But sin you must. Do not commit sin still further by thinking to shirk your responsibilities towards these you have made from your own tainted flesh. We shall count you all out and count you all back in. For every individual failing to return, five of these will die. This!" he screamed, pulling at the plate round Gabriel's neck, dragging the Arch Angel leader along the ground. "This is STIGMA! You are all stigmatized, you are Legion, and we shall count the number of the beast through you. Fly! You Devil-spawn, fly!"

# 31

Phoenix woke, unable to quite believe that she had fallen asleep. Always eating so much didn't seem to give her any more energy. It tired her, sending her to sleep when the sun had not yet set.

Waking with a start, it was still light outside. There was no sound to disturb her, but a feeling of anguish filtering through Phoenix's hair had her sitting up startled on her bed, listening carefully.

Going out onto the landing, Phoenix could feel where her mother was, sitting worrying in her own room. There was nothing unusual in this, not now, except for the level of her mother's near despair. Phoenix was about to knock on her door when she heard a voice from downstairs. It was an Adult voice, one she thought she recognized.

Creeping to the bottom of the stairs, Phoenix hid under the unhinged door that was leaning against the wall. She could not see into the room but could hear her grandfather as he spoke to someone.

"But teachers?" he was saying. "Why take the teachers?"

From where Phoenix crouched under the torn-away door, she could hear the creak of weapon straps, the shift of small arms, the stamp of soldiers against the floor of their little apartment.

"Your teachings are blasphemies," she heard the voice of Captain Owen say, but without anger. "You teach about millions or even billions of years—when Genome's creation is itself only just over six thousand years old."

"But that's not—" Phoenix's grandfather started to say. He stopped as soon as the soldiers stationed all around them clenched to closer attention, straining into near action. Phoenix heard the threatening shift of muscle and hardware.

"Stand down!" ordered Captain Owen. "I said—stand down! At ease, all of you. In fact, leave." Not one soldier moved. Phoenix would have heard them. "That *is* an order. Out, all of you."

Now Phoenix could hear them shuffling into the hall outside, three or four or five foot soldiers reluctantly stepping away.

Captain Owen waited until the last one had stomped out of the apartment through the other open doorway. Alone with Phoenix's grandfather, the officer took a great sigh of a breath.

"Your teachers have been taken," he said, pausing there. "And your science investigators and a great deal of you City Elders."

"And the Angels," said Phoenix, before she could stop herself. She froze, trying to huddle smaller behind the door.

Her grandfather appeared over her, frowning with disapproval. "It's just my granddaughter," he said.

"Please, allow her in," Phe heard the captain say.

She was keeping quiet now, with Captain Owen's curious gaze concentrated on her, standing next to her disapproving grandfather. The captain's eyes were locked with hers for a long while, before he turned his attention back to the Elder Agle.

"You have lived for too long," he went on, "in a society of—let us say you have been tolerant—too tolerant. You have made the gravest errors. First and most surprising of which is your acceptance of Mutation. You talk of billions of years and you tolerate Mutation. Indeed, you seem to welcome such change as part of a process. You imagine that your Evolution has a purpose and intelligence, that it can design superior beings using nothing but earthly, mortal processes. This is a lie. It is entirely un-Truth. It is a blasphemy against the world of Genome, our Creator, our eternal rest and our peace."

"Peace?" Phoenix heard her grandfather stutter out. "You speak of peace?"

"Yes, Sir! I speak of peace. That is the peace following the defeat of evil, the defeat of the un-Truth. Genome is the Way and the Light. If we must fight for Him, then so be it. We will fight. It is a good fight and one in which we are assured of victory. Genome is on our side. You—you people—you and your mutations living here—you cannot appreciate the danger you are in. When Genome made us in his image—"

"But we aren't like you!" Phoenix interrupted him. Her grandfather's hand landed heavily on her shoulder.

"No," the captain said, with his eyes directed at her, "and that you must learn to live with. Genome made man in His image—you have strayed, but not too far, if only you can repent. With repentance and just humility, you too can achieve a certain level of enlightenment. We will show you. We will teach you. Your own misguided teachers will be retrained and rehabilitated."

"But why take our Elders and our scientists?" asked the Elder Ground Agle.

"Some of your Elders, as you call them, have been taken into custody by Captain FitzRoy. His methods and mine are—well, we differ in our approach. It remains to be seen who will prove the most effective."

It was here that Phoenix sensed something. Most of the time Adults were surrounded by the negative, sucking energies of disgust and hate. But at last Phoenix picked up the flickering frequency of some other signal. Her grandfather felt it too—it was something like fear. Phe's bristling senses told her that Captain Owen was in fear of Captain FitzRoy, or of what Captain FitzRoy might do.

"And our scientists?" Phe's grandfather tried to move the captain away from that which frightened and disturbed him.

"Your science investigators, yes. We are interested in certain technical—expertise. You have some knowledge, some extensive knowledge it seems, of the principles of nuclear reaction. Fusion and fission."

"We understand the principles. As a society we are interested in understanding. We use our understanding to explain the world—"

"You do not explain the world! The world is inexplicable. You describe a technical process, a method of releasing, harnessing great energy."

"We will make no bombs," said Phe's grandfather.

"No," the captain said, "and we are in no need of such bombs. We are the keepers of the Revelation Element."

"Revelation Element?" Phoenix spoke up again. Her grandfather gripped even more tightly onto her shoulder. But the old Agle still faced the captain, expecting the question to be answered.

"You have no need to know what that is," said Captain Owen. "Just rejoice that we, through the Holy Mother, are keepers of the Revelation. Just understand that it is infinitely more powerful than any nuclear bomb. We have no need to exploit such technology—but our enemies might. If they have this knowledge and we have not—then—it is perhaps to their advantage. We will work with your scientists to understand. But they—so far—have seen fit to supply only misinformation. They contradict one another. They lie to us. It is a sin. They will stop it. You, Sir, should be instrumental in coordinating our efforts with your own. Only in that way will you discover the liberation you'll need in which to seek redemption. Will you help us, Sir?"

Her grandfather, saying nothing, appeared to be thinking about it.

"But what about the Angels?" Phoenix tried to whisper to him.

The captain chose to ignore her, concentrating on the face of the Elder Agle.

"The Angels!" she hissed.

"Phoenix," her grandfather said, with his eyes fixed on the captain's. "Be silent."

"But they have to let them go!"

Outside the broken door, the automatic weapons clattered to attention with the eavesdropping army.

"Stand down, I say!" shouted Captain Owen.

"Please let the Angels go," Phe said.

The captain's eyes swept towards her.

"You must try to forgive my granddaughter," Phoenix had to bear her grandfather saying. She did not *want* to be forgiven—there was nothing *to* forgive.

The captain nodded, once, slowly.

"My granddaughter is impetuous. She believes herself to be in love with—"

"What?" said Phoenix. She flexed her hands.

"In love?" the captain said. He looked at Phoenix again. "Genome is love," he said. "That is all. You will be taught the Truth. Genome is love. You will soon learn that lesson—all of you."

# 32

Gabriel and Jay-Jay were lying in the dust inside their enclosure. Elder fliers dropped food through the wire mesh on top of the cage.

"I'd have killed him," Jay-Jay was saying. He was cut and grazed and bruised all down one side of his face. Gabriel's body was damaged in a similar way. The STIGMA plate hung heavy against his chest. It hurt when he breathed.

Alice was crying over them. "Please be careful," she said. "Please. I don't know what we'd do if . . . I just don't know!"

"It's all right," Gabriel tried to settle her.

"Spartan!" Jay-Jay spat out the name. "SPARTAN!" he screamed out loud, sitting up.

Outside, never very far away, a group of Green Raptors looked up and over at the Angel cage.

"Where is he?" Jay-Jay shouted. Alice tried to take hold of him. Jay shrugged her away, jumping up. "Spartan! Where are you?"

And then he was there. He was always there. Jay-Jay and Gabriel knew it. All the young fliers did. Spartan was there, full of feather and hard of scale and claw and serrated beak. And then he was *right* there, launching himself from the middle of his band of Raptor brothers, crashing into the sidebars of the Angel enclosure.

In that same moment, Jay was over at him, a much smaller, fainter figure against the huge Raptor form. But Jay-Jay wanted to fight him. "I'll kill you!"

He wouldn't. Jay would be killed.

Gabriel jumped at Jay, dragging him away. The Angels gathered in an arch round Gabriel as he and Alice held Jay-Jay down. The Raptors, Spartan's raging hoards, at the same time had leapt with him onto the top of the cage. Their heavy claws gripped and ripped at the bars overhead. The noise was almost unbearable, the roars, the Angel screams, the crashing of the thick steel mesh.

Gabriel held tightly onto Jay-Jay and Alice. Jay still struggled to get to Spartan. It would be suicide. Maybe that was what Jay-Jay really wanted now, now that Ember was gone.

"Don't go, Jay," Gabriel said. But nobody heard him above the noise. "Don't go!" he said, holding his friend ever tighter. He looked out of the compound as the Adult soldiers gathered with ready stun guns. At their head, Captain FitzRoy stood looking over. Gabriel watched him wave his troops down.

FitzRoy gazed with curiosity at the wrath of the Raptors for a long while, while Gabriel watched him.

Then Gabriel found himself eye to eye with the captain. He wanted to look away, but couldn't control his loathing for this Adult-thing, for all the Adult-things and their weapons and their certainty and their power to cage and control and, someday soon, to kill.

Captain FitzRoy accepted the hatred from Gabriel's eyes. He'd seen it before. He shimmered with self-satisfied humor, glancing up at the Green fury on the top of the cage once more.

Gabriel watched him glance up before Captain FitzRoy looked back at him for a few moments more, in which to nod, as if to say, "One day, Stigma—it's coming!" and turn, and walk away into the setting sun.

# 33

Totally opened her eyes. She usually slept so soundly, switching off almost as soon as she got into bed, switching back on again in the morning, refreshed. Now her eyes opened on her for the twentieth or thirtieth time that night. Every time she thought she had heard something disturbing. She had—the scrape of Raptor claw, the click of Green talk from outside.

Nobody in this city but Green Raptors spoke at night. There was nothing to say, with the night too silent and moonlit for anything other than what would sound like conspiratorial whispers. Better by far, as Totally's foster grandfather said, to keep quiet until the time came again when there would be better things to say. But when would that be? And what would be better to say, after everything that had happened here in this city? When everyone felt so ashamed of being so afraid?

So it was fear then, waking Totally time and time again all through the sharp clear night.

No—it wasn't. Not this time. There was a noise—in the house!

Again. Someone moving. Totally's foster mother or grandfather?

She listened out even more carefully.

A door opened. The front door of the apartment, gently opening, closing again.

Totally just about managed to hear it. She scrambled out of bed to peer out of the window. The streets were blanketed in silver light. All the shadows were short, where the moon was hanging high, immediately above the city.

A Green Raptor scraped up the pavement and disappeared round the corner.

Totally waited. Nothing moved. The moon seemed as if it were stuck, or hung up by hand, a lantern to light the curfew.

Then she saw it. A flitting movement, a dash from one short shadow to the next.

"Oh no!" Totally whispered, rushing from window to wardrobe, throwing on the first of her dresses that came to hand and dashing out of her room.

# 34

The moon was high and bright, casting only short, dense shadows. Phoenix was glad that the sky was clear and the night illuminated. Without this light, the big eyes of the Raptors would give them one more massive advantage over her. As it was, she'd try to see them before they caught sight of her, if she kept to the short shadows, sticking to the sides of the buildings.

Now Phe was glad she had starved herself for all that time. She was much thinner than most Ground Agles, the young ones especially. Tonight, pressed into a shadow against a wall, slipping through the city streets, she felt that the sickness she had induced so often had achieved its true purpose after all.

She turned a corner. Scraping towards her, a huge Raptor shadow in the moonlight. Phoenix squeezed back farther against the wall and watched him kick by, talking to himself.

The street-guard Raptors were the very young ones, Phoenix knew, the reckless and the foolish, puffed up with their ferocious sense of power. There was no doubt that the Greens were getting bigger, generation by generation. This one, very young as he was, was huge. Phoenix felt her heart banging so hard she thought he was going to be able to hear it he was so close. But he was too engrossed in his own click-talk, whatever he was saying to himself.

Phe breathed out. She was shaking. She had seen what Raptors could do, when Spartan had dragged poor Ember out of the air. She felt sick. But now she didn't want to be. Phoenix needed her strength. She had seen, perched in that tree with Gabriel, where the Adults had been burning the forest away and erecting cages. Somewhere, in among all that, the Arch Angels were being kept prisoner. Gabriel would be there, locked up, unable to fly, with that cruel metal plate round his neck.

Phoenix trembled with anger just to think about him that way, with that pitiful look on his face she had seen as they paraded him through the streets. And Captain FitzRoy, on the steps of the Royal Palace, using words like *eradicated.*

Again, Phe felt her pulse beginning to race. Eradicated! It meant... all it meant at the moment was that she had to get through these streets unseen and make her way to that dreadful burnt plain and find the Angels. She ducked down behind some old bins tucked into a dark corner. Three Raptors came and stood only two arms' lengths away. She could hear what they were saying. But she couldn't understand them, just as they could not begin to comprehend her.

Just like Captain Owen, looking at her in the way he did, ridiculing her feelings. "Genome is love," he said. He was just as far away from her, from even beginning to understand her, as were these lizard-legged birdbrains stalking away into the silver streets.

Phoenix dodged away, flitting from shadow to shadow. It felt like hours before she was able to work her way out of the old city and into the iron-and-tin town that the Adults had erected. There was no forest left between the city and here, as if all this was part of the city now.

For a long, long time she scrambled from wall to wall, avoiding the lights leaking from the windows where the Adults seemed to want to avoid ever being in the dark. Some of the words they had been repeating at them in the classrooms all day kept coming back to Phe: "And the earth was waste and void; and darkness was upon the face of the deep."

Darkness, waste and voids . . . as if the night was horrible, something to be kept away, to be destroyed by synthetic light if at all possible.

Phoenix hid by a stack, a bristling bush, of piled-high weapons. She squatted watching an Adult appear at a lit window to direct with gestures the stalking Raptors on guard even here. The Adult did not want to come outside. The Raptors roamed where they wanted, ruffling their feathers and clicking to themselves or at each other.

The moon was lower in the sky now. There were more shadows to hide in. Phoenix ran from place to place, searching. But the Adult town was so big. There were huge expanses where no one lived and nothing moved but the odd lost crawling creatures with piercing night eyes. They scuttled away from Phoenix's feet.

She turned a corner between great metal containers, moving into the moonlight.

She stopped.

Two Green Raptors turned as she appeared.

Phoenix dived back into the darkness. She looked round to check the shadows before running back the way she had come. But the Raptors were crashing round the corner at her, two huge young Greens with their feathers flying and their big beaks clacking.

Phe drew back farther into the corner of the metal containers. She watched the Raptors clump to a halt. She tried to hold her breath. They were so close Phoenix could smell the feather-oil scent of Raptor on the air. If they found her here, they would tear her.

Phoenix held her breath again and clenched, closing her eyes. They were so close, almost treading on her toes.

She opened her eyes. The Raptors were looking for her—but on the ground. One Green's face snapped towards her, looking down at her feet. He had seen her, even in the almost pitch darkness of her hiding corner.

He raged forward.

Phe clenched harder. Her eyes closed. She waited to be dragged out, to be held by hand and torn by talon and beak.

But nothing happened.

She opened one eye. The scrabbling Raptor ran around, raising the dust, trying to catch the little creatures, the night rat-lizards running from under the metal boxes. Once caught, the little creatures were clawed open and then crunched by beak and swallowed down with as much relish as Tolly had shown succumbing to the sweet enticement of the Adult chocolate. Phoenix looked on with disgust as the Raptor pair moved down the aisle between the containers, catching and crunching their morsels as they went.

She ran the other way, dodging in deep shadow until she saw what she had been looking for—the cages. Huge prison cages. Most were empty, waiting. Ready for prisoners. But one was full. Fallen Angels were lying everywhere inside, everyone with their fantastic young white wings clipped. They lay sleeping on their sides, these beautiful pale beings, with the taut-skinned wings sticking out like sails from their backs.

Phoenix stopped and looked. The pattern of the Angels lying on the ground, the huddled body, arms and legs, with the white sail resting on the baked brown soil—the whole image was so spectacular, the Angels even more beautiful than she remembered. She just wanted to stay where she was, still hidden in the darkness, to watch, while the moon silvered wings and bodies to gleam and shine, making a mosaic on the ground of their prison.

# 35

"I've got it!" Gabriel hissed into Jay-Jay's ear. "We dig! We dig a hole, right next to the edge. It doesn't have to be big. Just enough to squeeze under."

"Just give me one chance," Jay-Jay said, with Alice asleep by his side.

"I know," Gabriel said. "I got to fly. I'll die, kept here like this. Come on. We dig. You and me. Keep it quiet. It'll be dark for a good couple of hours yet. We'll get out. All of us, one by one."

They had only their hands. Angels were not particularly strong in their arms. They carried food through the air a little at a time. But the dusty soil was baked and crumbly. It gave way to their fingers and soon they were about half an arm's length down into the ground.

"We don't need much deeper," said Gabriel. "This is too easy."

"Too easy," said Jay, flatly. "This was never gonna happen, not like this."

Gabriel knew what he was talking about by now. His fingers had hit on what Jay's had felt just before him. Not far down below the dusty surface, steel bars. The bottom of the cage was concealed underground.

"We're caged in," Jay-Jay said. "Right from the start. We're never getting out."

"Don't say that," said Gabriel. "We will, somehow."

"You will," whispered a voice from right beside them, from outside their prison bars. She was crouching there outside the cage close to Gabriel, trying to put her hand through the thick steel mesh.

"Phoenix!" he shined, with his face lighting up.

"I'll get you out," she was smiling back at him, looping her fingers over the bars.

He touched her hand. "But how? How did you come here?"

"I came to get you out. Hello, Jay-Jay," she said. But Jay just stared. "What is it?" Phoenix asked, as Gabriel looked up, with a similar look and Jay shouted as if into her face:

"Filthy murderer!"

# 36

She just had time to turn before the terror was on her. Phoenix screamed as Spartan picked her from the ground with one hand and slammed her back into the bars of the steel cage. Her scream stopped dead. The air was smashed out of her. She hit the back of her head. His frantically clacking razor beak tore at the air in front of her face. But Phoenix saw the slender hand of an Angel stretch through and grab Spartan by the head feathers, just before a handful of the soft sharp soil spattered into his Raptor eyes.

Spartan bellowed out in pain and rage.

Phoenix found herself dumped at the foot of the cage. She just managed to roll clear before the great lizard legs in front of her leapt into the steel bars.

Jay-Jay and Gabriel were grabbing at the great Raptor's feathers, scratching at his eyes. Their shouts were drowned out by Spartan's terrible cries. He crashed again and again against the side of the compound. All the other Angels were suddenly awake, dashing to help fight the Raptor.

Phoenix scrambled farther away. The Raptor roars were coming at her, as if from every direction, thumping her head from one side, from the other. Almost too late, she saw them—the other two, the hunting Greens with their mouths full of little crawling creatures. Only now, their mouths were full of dreadful sounds as they dashed down, a mass of feather and flying talon blade.

Phoenix ran.

The Raptors, flying by her, crashed at the bars to help their leader. The force of the two of them hitting home together rocked the cage and knocked the Angels, sending them falling backwards onto their wings.

Phoenix glanced round. The Angels were back at the bars of their prison, yelling and screaming at Spartan and the other two. But the Raptors were running, their huge green legs muscular, scales and talons glinting in the cruel moonshine. The Raptors raged towards her. In the lead, Spartan. He knew where she was. He wasn't looking for any scuttling creatures to eat. He was hunting Ground Agle.

Phoenix had to keep on running. She made it to the end of the long corridor between stacks of containers, turning the corner into naked moonlight. She was met with another wall of Raptor roar, a sound that slapped her back, hitting her in the face. There were more—a group of five or six, responding to their leader's battle cry.

Phoenix rounded another corner, dashing into the next aisle between the metal boxes. Behind her, right behind, the giant Raptor leader raged. Behind him, eight, nine, twelve, twenty excited Greens puffed up and pounding down upon her, came at her like the murderous gang going at Ember that day on the plain.

They were so fast! Phoenix could never outrun them. She had to make the next corner, to turn and to turn again. She'd be maybe quicker, sharper when dodging and weaving and—

And nothing.

# 37

There was a moment, time enough to feel the shred of tearing beaks across her back and up her arms, hacking at her neck and head. But in that moment, Phoenix felt herself falling, her legs pulled from under her. She lumped down onto the soil. It felt as if the Raptors wanted to drag her away before pulling her to pieces.

She was still screaming as the soil slipped under her, or rather she over it, as something dragged her to one side. Phoenix found herself slipping through a gap under one of the containers, disappearing down what appeared to be a hole.

Raptors flew in at her. Spartan raged into her face, but from thankfully just too far away to let him touch her.

She was falling. The arms of the Raptors were clutching for her through the entrance of the hole into which she had slipped. Or into which she had been pulled.

The hole was too small to allow a great Raptor entry. They screamed and scrambled to get through, but Phoenix, still falling, slithering quickly down a stony slope, fell too far away for them to reach her.

She turned to take a look down at the space into which she was now dropping. But the hole was too small and the rocky side struck Phoenix behind the ear and knocked her almost senseless.

As if whirling and tumbling through just dizzying air, Phe fell to the bottom of what felt like a well. She lay breathing, gathering her senses, beginning to wonder what could have happened to her.

A face appeared, softly glowing in the gentle light. The moon seemed to be creating a strange glow, low but warm, shadowless but somehow shifting, moving, changing the emphasis of the sloping pink and white features gazing down at her.

"Totally!" Phoenix finally found voice to say. "What happened?" She tried to sit up, only to find out how dizzy she was. Phe fell back. "Tolly—what are you doing here? Where am I? What is this place? How did you—"

Totally put her slight hand over Phe's mouth. "Enough. You're in the runs."

"The runs?" Phoenix sat up, rubbing at the back of her head. A lump was quickly forming. "What runs?"

"The rat runs. Tunnels under the city, running right out into the countryside. They're secret. Nobody's supposed to know about them. Not even me. And you are such an idiot."

# 38

"Such an idiot! What did you think you were doing up there?"

From the length of the slope down which Phoenix had slipped, she knew that she must be a long way underground.

"Answer me, you absolute idiot!" Totally was almost crying into her face. "You could have been killed!"

Phoenix's heart was still thumping as if about to burst. Her mouth was opening and closing, but nothing would come out.

Totally stood before her, breathing almost as heavily, watching Phe looking round at the shifting, wavering moonlight effect as it came and went, fluttering by, lights on the wing.

"They're called fire-butterflies," Totally said, a little more softly.

Together they watched the huge and glowing, incandescent creatures playing at lighting up the dense air.

Phoenix looked up the long slope of the hole leading back to the Raptors. "I've got to go back!" she said, suddenly trying to get up. The ceiling was too low. Totally could stand, while Phoenix hit the top of her head.

"You really are an idiot," Tolly said. "Don't you get it? What would have happened if I hadn't followed you?"

"You followed me all that way?"

"No. I didn't have to. I just had to know in which direction you were going. These tunnels go everywhere. But listen, if I hadn't been here—"

Phoenix hugged her foster sister. "Thanks, Tolly."

"Yes, fine," Totally said. "But now we have to go home."

"But . . . the Angels!"

"We have to go home!" Tolly said again. "Come on," she said, shoving Phoenix, "I'll push you all the way, if I have to."

"'Kay! 'Kay! Stop! I'm going, see? I'm going home. For now."

Totally didn't say anything else. The fire-butterflies flitted everywhere, lighting up the chalky corridors.

"But—this place!" Phoenix said, incredulous.

"My Elder Elders built all of this," Totally told her, as they scrambled through.

"Before I was born, all Rodents lived underground, you know that, from the old stories. Well, this was where, down here. Thousands of us, before—well, you know what before. These rat runs lead to—I'll show you."

Phoenix was ever more astonished as the tunnel they were in, growing bigger, opening out as they went, suddenly gave way to a vast echoing subterranean space. It was like a massive, majestic hall carved out of the soft rock, bigger by far than any room in any big house that Phoenix had ever seen.

"At one time," Totally was saying, looking out across the expanse, "this whole thing would have been full of Rodents. We would have been here, in all the rat runs, living in all the other rooms off the runs that you haven't seen. This place is vast. It goes everywhere. Once, we were really something."

Phoenix was silent, awestruck. The fire-butterflies fluttering on every level glowed with soft light, so that the cathedral space seemed to shift and shimmer, always changing, darker and lighter patches interchanging, falling and rising, moving round, approaching and tending away into the fading, hazy distance.

"It's so—so . . ."

"Beautiful?" Totally said.

That wasn't a word Phoenix used very much, apart from when she was talking about the Angels. But, yes, this place was beautiful. And Tolly looked beautiful in it, with tears falling from her huge pink eyes.

"I didn't know," Phe said.

Tolly brushed the downy thin fur on her face. "No, you didn't. How could you? Grandfather and the City Elders meet here sometimes. It's supposed to be kept secret, for emergencies only."

"But how come you know about it?"

"I've never forgotten. I was born here. I remember it all."

"All of it? How?"

"I meant I remembered it was here. I come down here sometimes—often. When you're out. I love this place." They stood for a moment more watching the shimmer of the fire-butterflies. "It's time to go," Totally said.

Phoenix was still looking around, studying the walls and the corners and the ceilings as they pushed on through.

"You'll never remember the way back," Totally said.

"Maybe not. But I'll find *a* way back. I have to."

"No, Phe! You mustn't. It's too dangerous. They'll kill you next time—Phoenix, if I think you're up to something, I'll do what I have to do to stop you."

"Oh yes? And what's that?"

"I'll tell Grandfather for a start. I'll tell Captain Owen if I have to—"

Phoenix stopped and turned to face her foster sister. "You'll tell *them*—you'll tell the Adults? I don't believe you'd do that—not that!"

"Grandfather says Captain Owen's a reasonable Adult. I'd tell him, to stop you killing yourself, because that's all you'd do. You'd only end up killing yourself—and a whole lot of Air Agles too."

# 39

At breakfast next morning, Phoenix was watching her mother and grandfather very carefully. She didn't yet know what Totally might have told them about last night. But other than the permanent worry look on their faces, Phe could see or feel nothing out of the ordinary. Worry was ordinary now. It came of not knowing what might happen next. They all felt it, Phoenix and Totally included.

Breakfast came and went, with Phoenix eating as much as anyone her age and size, chewing quickly and nervously, without bothering to try to bring it back up afterwards. She had stopped thinking about her body shape and how heavy she was. There were too many other worries bearing down on her, too much suffering everywhere to allow her the luxury of such self-pity. Phoenix needed all her strength to fight back.

She needed more sleep too, but that would have to wait until... who knew until when? Who knew anything in this Adult world now? Her mother? Her grandfather and the City Elders? Phoenix knew a whole lot more than they did now—a whole lot more!

"I've hardly slept at all," Totally was saying as they went downstairs. "I kept thinking about you. I kept thinking about those Raptors coming at you. I kept thinking of him, of..."

Totally did not finish what she was saying as she and Phoenix came out of their building. She was about to say she couldn't help thinking about him, the leader, the biggest, the fiercest Raptor—she couldn't help thinking about—

But she stopped.

Phoenix halted with her. They stood out there on the street together, some ways from the doors of their home. Malingering in the shade of their building, a Raptor, waiting for them as before, ready to follow them to school.

Spartan.

He was there, for who knew how long, towering in the shade, waiting. He placed one sharp and pointed claw in front of the other, as if ready to walk after them. There he stood, stock-still, staring at them, but imperviously, unaffected by them or anything around them.

"Oh, no," Totally breathed.

Phoenix turned away. "Walk!" she said, moving off towards their school. She felt almost faint with fear.

Spartan had shown none of his usual aggression so far, but Phoenix did not need to be shown. She felt it needling into her scalp through her hair. Even without that, she needed to know nothing more than the fact that he was here, that he knew who she was and where she lived.

"Just walk," she hissed at Totally. "Don't look round!"

Too late, though. Tolly looked. She couldn't help herself. "It's him!" she whispered. "You know who—he's following us—Phe, what have you done?"

# 40

It was the air around him he loved so much, the movement of it, the shifting, forceful fluidity under his wings as he slid on the morning thermals towards the distant horizon. He loved the changing perspective of the ground below, the colors as the sun climbed higher, as he, with it, ascended into its glory.

Then they grabbed hold of the plate on its chain round his sore neck, and Gabriel was dragged out of the sky. Pulled upwards, not dragged down by the STIGMA sign, hoisted and clattered out of his late sleep, Gabriel let fall his dreams of flight.

Jay-Jay, making a move to help him, was beaten down in an instant.

Gabriel tried to speak to him, to signal to the others as they were kicked and knocked back with the butts of weapons to clear the way. Gabriel knew that Jay and so many of the other fliers couldn't take too much more of this. He wasn't sure of himself, either.

The Adults shouted directly into his throbbing ears. His head was about to explode. They led him to a waiting truck and threw him in a cage in the back. His shoulders were aching and his head, but his back, where the restrained wings pulled at him continuously, was where he suffered most. Even the plate and the chain round his neck rubbing him sore, his skin weeping, even the shame of being labeled in this way was nothing compared to never being allowed to take off and fly. He didn't belong here! Why could they not see that, these Adults?

They couldn't seem to see anything. They seemed blinded, throwing him into another cage, dragging him back out after a bumping and lurching journey into the city, shoving him up the steps of the Royal Palace. Full as it now was with equipment and implements of war, this great house was twisted and distorted to suit the blindness of purpose now throwing Gabriel to the floor. They forced him, the blinking but blind Adults, to clasp his hands in front of his face.

"Beg for forgiveness," said a strangely softened voice.

Gabriel took a glance up. In front of him now, the next Adult wore long, flowing robes with elaborately embroidered patterns all in cream and deep mauve and laced with golden thread. On his head, a high and fancy hat. At any other time, anywhere else, Gabriel might once have found this sight hilarious. How he and the other Angels would have laughed. Now he cried.

"Even you," the soft, seemingly kind voice floated and filled the air, enveloping Gabriel, imprisoning him as effectively as the soldiers' threats and weapons thrusts, "even now, with the marks and mutant distortions of the Devil on your body, you can seek and find forgiveness and a kind of absolution. If only you will take Genome to your heart and swear," and a big black book was thrust into Gabriel's face, "by all that is Holy, that you renounce the Evil One and his practices forever."

# 41

For some way they walked on in silence, while immediately behind, so close, his cruel talons trailing, scraping—Spartan.

Phoenix glanced at Totally, once, twice. She could feel everything—beside her, her foster sister's dread, behind, *him*. Phe could feel him in her hair, with every vibration of the air in the high-tension frequency of fear.

Then he spoke. Spartan's ratchet throat rattled with threat and dreadful promise.

"What did he say?" Phoenix whispered, knowing how fluently her sister spoke Raptor. "What's he saying?"

Spartan clipped after them, moving faster. His big, beaked head appeared, rumbling out a low, controlled growl.

"He's going to get you," Totally had to say, hurrying on. Spartan was at her shoulder. She was speaking to Phoenix, staring ahead, trying not to look into the Raptor's face. "He's going to—no, I can't!"

"Tell me!" Phoenix demanded.

"No!"

They were rushing along, alone in the crowded street, almost running away. But Spartan passed them in two strides, halting them. His arms were out, his huge hands spread. His wagging head swung from one side to the other, from Phoenix to Totally and back again.

"Tell me!" Phoenix screamed, as if back at the Raptor, asking Totally.

"He knows it was you! He's going to—he's going to do things!"

"What things?"

"Nothing can stop him—he says nothing can stop him. He says—he says he'll do it—things—at any time he feels like it!"

Phoenix was watching what Spartan was saying as Totally was telling her. She couldn't look away from his great swaying head, the clack of that fearful beak, those storm-clouded eyes.

"He's going to kill you," Totally said.

# 42

"Do you renounce the Evil One and his distortions to your body? Do you truly take Genome into your corrupted heart?"

Gabriel, on his knees, struggling to suppress his every flight reflex, blinked back his tears. "I don't get it—I don't know what you want."

"I want only to help you. Renounce your pact with Evil!"

"What does it mean?"

"It means absolution, salvation. Just renounce him—admit the evil of your distortions. Admit that to fly, to use your distortions in the way you do—admit the evil and the Evil influence in what you do and are able to do. It is a terrible, monstrous thing, this flight of yours. It is of the Devil. Renounce it, and you will be saved!"

Tears were rolling down Gabriel's face.

"Renounce flight! It is evil, blasphemous. You must now absolve yourself of the corruption of your mutation from Genome's Holy Creation. Admit you are of the Evil One. Confess your sins! It is your only hope."

Gabriel's head was down. His tears were falling. He looked up. He would have loved to look up and see the sky, his own open endless homeland, but could see nothing farther than the Adult ceiling, the top of the box into which they liked to trap everything and keep it down and under control.

"Give up!" the fantastically dressed but angry Adult insisted. "Flight! Give it up for good! Absolve yourself. Deny flight! Deny the Devil! Deny! Deny! Deny!"

"No!" he screamed, the Angel on his knees, crying out. "No! Flight? Never!"

"What, never?"

"I'm an Angel!"

"No! That is a blasphemy!"

"No! I'm an Arch Angel!"

"Blasphemous sinner!"

"No! Arch Angel Gabriel!"

"Black Sin!" the robed Adult shouted, lashing out with another hard-palmed hand. The softness of his voice had long since given way, finally replaced by the next knock to the Arch Angel's face, splaying him sideways.

Gabriel, from the floor, struggling, tied wings slapping down again and again, cried out. "I'm the Arch Angel! I'm Gabriel! I'm made for flight!"

"You are Stigma!" the Adult rushed to bellow down over him. "And you are made for Hell, which is where you belong! I can do no more here!" he turned and called.

From the other end of the room, from a hall-sized curtained-off space, the small-sized Adult and his Mummy seated high on elevated, elaborate chairs, were carried in by a squadron of soldiers. With them, the captains FitzRoy and Owen.

The procession filed out and the robed Adult bent his head, lowering his eyes. Two soldiers rushed to force Gabriel face down onto the floor.

"I have done all I can," the robed one's voice had flopped back into steady softness. "Our Holy Office is negated by the corruption of the Mutation. His is Stigma, indeed!" he pronounced, pointing down at Gabriel.

"Captain FitzRoy," the female Adult said, from the movable throne by her little son's side, "the priest has made you correct, I believe."

"I believe so, too," he said, that captain, slipping a glance towards the other, the captain Owen, standing keeping to himself a little way off from everyone else.

"He is Stigma," FitzRoy said, without looking down at Gabriel, who was looking up at him.

Gabriel could see a look on that Captain's face. The smugness with which he had sneered at the other captain still lingered there, as if it would never now need to go away again.

# 43

All round them, young Ground Agles and Rodents ducked and ran. The other Raptors on the street took up their leader's roar. The broken window frames rattled their rage into the damaged buildings.

Totally tried to run away from Spartan—he, scraping forward, went for her.

"No!" Phoenix shouted. She moved towards Spartan—he, with one swipe of his arm, knocked Phoenix to the ground. With the other arm, he reached out and collected Totally, holding her by the back of her dress, lifting her into the air. Phoenix jumped back onto her feet.

The great Green Raptor turned full circle, with the little, terrified Rodent held high. He snapped, he wagged, he shouted out. The air was thick with Raptor roar, as if it were a solid thing, impenetrable and permanent.

Phoenix dashed at him. He dropped Totally to the ground and swiped at Phoenix, knocking her down. Spartan leapt, crashing down over her. She looked up past his massive green-scaled legs, his overinflated body, his head feathers, to his face. Through the screams, Spartan roared horribly. The other Raptors took up the call to drown out the Agle protests.

Phoenix had to look into the huge Raptor's always-open eyes at the reflection of herself on the ground. But his head veered away, snapping left and right at the Elder Agles as they approached protesting. He forced them to back away, before taking one last swaying look at Phoenix, on the ground, at Totally, on the ground.

He stepped away at last, slowly, treading down onto his claw-toed feet almost delicately, but with huge and violent pride. Every step he took, each slow scrape of claw on concrete, affirmed his confidence. His one last glance round at the terrified Tolly and Phe promised action, soon.

# 44

They went to school. There was nowhere else to go, no other escape from the terror of the streets. They wanted to feel safe, in their familiar classroom with teachers and friends. But an Adult in strange robes and a tall hat presided over their lessons in school that day. Phoenix and Totally and their classmates were told this figure, this priest-person, was their father. That was what they were supposed to call him, if ever they were allowed to speak in his presence—Father.

Several times during the day, the whole school was assembled, the students forced to fall to their knees while the cream and mauve-robed priest sang-spoke strange words over them.

"In the name of the Father, the Holy Immaculate Mother, keeper of the Revelation, and the Sacrosanct Son, forgive us our trespasses."

Nobody in ASP City knew what trespass was, it wasn't something that happened there, but they had to beg forgiveness for it.

"In the name of the Father . . ."

"Which father is that?" Phoenix asked at one time, thinking that it was a reasonable question. For saying that, she was hauled out to the front to be shouted at and intimidated:

"Who are you to question the Word? On whose authority do you think you speak, when you question your Lord and your Maker?"

Then after school, on the way home, speaking rapidly between the clacking raps of Raptor, Phoenix hissed at Totally, "There's no stopping this. How could Grandfather or anyone ever talk to them? Everything we say insults them."

Totally had been limping from where she had been thrown to the ground that morning. Her pain was wearing off a little now, but not her fear. She had hardly spoken since the attack.

"They'll never go away now," Phoenix was saying. "They'll never let the Angels go. They'll never leave us alone."

"Oh, no!" said Totally.

Phoenix looked at her. Totally was staring up the street. Following the line of her sight, Phoenix soon saw. "Keep walking!" she whispered. "Don't stop. Don't let him see our fear."

Spartan stood there. He did not move, watching them without speaking, threatening them once more with his massive and imposing presence.

"What shall we do?" Phoenix said, as soon as they turned the corner out of his sight.

On the very next corner, the giant Green stood set in position, like a statuesque representation of threat.

Totally was shaking. So was Phoenix.

But Spartan was set steady, a rock-solid statue on every corner, every step of the way home.

# 45

"Don't tell him!" Phoenix was saying, still shaking, staring at Totally. "Don't tell Grandfather anything. You'll get him killed."

They were in Phe's room now. Tolly was still shaking too, shuddering, wracked with fear.

"He's too old," Phoenix said. "He can't do anything. He thinks Captain Owen is reasonable, but Captain Owen doesn't stop the Raptors, he doesn't stop Spartan roaming the streets, doing as he likes."

"But what can we do?" shuddered Totally. "What can we do?"

"There's only one thing we *can* do," said Phoenix. "We have to get the Angels out, there's nothing else for it. We get the Angels out, they'll fly away. If we get them out, they'll have to take us with them. Are you with me?"

Totally looked horrified.

"Because," said Phoenix, "if you're not with me, I'm going on my own. They'll never let the Angels go, and I don't think Spartan's ever going to leave us alone now. I can't stand this, Tolly. I have to get away. Please help me."

Phoenix stopped and waited for an answer. Totally felt too afraid to speak. Phe went to her and put her arms round her.

"When?" Totally whispered.

Phe looked into her face. "Tonight," she said.

# 46

As soon as they lifted the drain cover, just a couple of blocks away from home, and dropped into the deep shaft that led to the old subterranean Rodent world, their way was lit by the flitting fire-butterflies. The air down there was as warm as the butterfly light, never too hot or too cold.

"I'm not so sure about this," Totally was saying once again. "This is stupid. We don't even have a proper plan. How do we get them out of the cage?"

They were ducking through the narrow runs. Phoenix, the bigger of the two, had already knocked her head on the low ceilings. Afraid as she was, as afraid as Totally was making her feel, still she was fascinated by the look of sandstone walls, the way she could still see where they had been carved, gnawed away by those ancient Rodents.

"This place," she said, as they entered one of the many small halls, old meeting places, "this is so—it's fantastic!"

"Yes," said Totally, "but how do we get them out of that cage? How do we do that? I don't think we should. We don't even have a proper plan."

"Stop saying that! We'll think of something."

Phoenix was still looking about in wonder. But the truth was, she really did have no clear idea of how they were going to get the Angels out. She had just some vague image of finding out where the keys to their cage were and stealing them.

"Don't you wish," she said, still trying to distract Totally from questioning her, "that Rodents still lived down here? It seems such a waste."

"Yes," said Totally, dashing on through. "Yes, that's all—" And then she stopped. Fire-butterflies with huge wingspans fluttered round her, the motion of their light shifting the expressions on her face.

"This is going to kill Mother," she said.

Phoenix halted with her. "We have no choice," she said.

"No," Totally said, suddenly, "not we. Because I won't be going with you."

"Tolly, you can't..."

"Yes, I can. I can stay. I'll be all right."

"But what about Spartan?" Phe said. "He'll come for you."

"It's not me he wants. I doubt that Spartan could tell one Rodent from another. I'll tell Mother what happened. Besides, what would I do away from here?"

For a few moments, they stood together, letting the fire-flight of butterflies move the shadows of their faces.

"This way," Totally said, to break their silence. "Come on. We have to hurry if we're going to go through with this madness."

Phoenix had never felt so confused. Not only was she frightened, but she was saddened at the thought of leaving her family behind. At the same time, she was excited. She was going to get away, to be taken away, as she'd so wanted, by Gabriel and his Arch Angels. But still she did not know how to release them from the cage.

The rat runs were long and always sloping. Their footfalls bounced back at them, echoing the emptiness. It sounded as if more than just the two of them were running through, as if they were accompanied. As if Totally's ancestors still ran through the corridors to the great Rodent Hall, as they had once, long, long ago.

# 47

Coming up between the military metal box containers, Phe and Tolly could hear the Raptors scrambling after their small morsel prey in the next aisle.

"If they spot us," Totally whispered, "stay by me. I'll find another entry hole into the runs."

Almost immediately they had to fall back into the deep shadows between boxes. A hunting party of excited Raptors came clicking and diving round the corner. Rat lizards were scuttling to and fro across the moonlit aisles. A huge hungry Green fell onto the floor at Phoenix and Totally's feet, bouncing up in front of them with the struggling creature squeaking in its beak.

They had to stand, so close the Raptor could have reached out and touched them, watching the horrendous hard beak working, crunching as the rat lizard disappeared in bits into the hidden mouth. The Raptor stood on his own for a few minutes, savoring the flavor of his snack. His horny beak opened and closed a few times, almost as if he were licking his non-existent lips.

"Ugh!" Totally exclaimed, as soon as he had stalked away, still looking on the ground for more to eat. "They are disgusting!"

"Come on," Phoenix said, moving off, trying not to think of Spartan's beak.

They moved through the alleyways until they peeked out across an open field of dust at the Angel cage in the moonlight. Phoenix could feel the blood thick in her pressurized veins. Her breath became much harder. So did Totally's. "This is it," she heard Totally whisper. "There they are. What now?"

"Now we find the keys," Phoenix said. "Over there, look, where the lights are on."

"Be careful!" Totally hissed as Phoenix sloped out into the open, like a moving shadow in the moonlight.

But the Raptors were all hungry, living, as they were here, only on the bite-full morsels they could catch on the ground. The Greens were used to hunting the large plains animals, gorging themselves on fresh, bloody meat every day. Here, they must be constantly hungry, forever watching the ground for any crunching creature, however bony and dissatisfying.

Phoenix and Totally were able to dash through the patches of open moonlight until they reached the safety shadow of the wall of a hut. Together, one either side of the lit, open window, they peeked through.

He had his back to them. A single Adult. He turned. "So," he said, as if speaking to the two at the window.

Outside, they ducked. They listened. The voice continued. Phoenix and Totally approached the window again with one eye each.

"Thank you," he said, as if looking at them, "for coming all the way over here at this time of night." Captain FitzRoy clasped his hands behind his back.

Moving away from the window, another Adult figure, dressed very differently, approached the captain. "I understand," the priest-person said, the one the Agles and Rodents were forced to call Father, still in his robes, "I understand the need for discretion."

"We understand each other," the captain said. "Whatever we say together goes no further than this room. But I need to understand—

or rather, I need to know where you stand. These people—these Mutants—I hope you can tell me how Our Holy Ministry defines these—these abominations. Can you?"

"Well, of course," the Father said, "the winged ones—they are the Devil incarnate. They can never be allowed to flourish. In the name of Genome, we must find a way of, let us say, purifying and cleansing the earth."

"Yes, yes, of course. But what of the rest of this society? You have had time to see and try to teach them. What are they?"

"Yes," he agreed, the priest-father, looking away as if that were answer enough to all the captain's questions.

But outside, Phoenix and Totally needed to hear more. They had to hear what they were, to the priest, to the Holy Ministry of the Adults.

"I have prayed," the priest went on at last, looking back at Captain FitzRoy, "I have knelt and prayed for many, many hours on their behalf. They do not appreciate it. They cannot, I'm already sure, ever accept the love of Genome into their hearts. They are too corrupted. Their bodies, even without wings, are blasphemous distortions of the Way and the Light. They believe in Un-Truths, terrible stories of Evolution holding sway—that is, holding power over the face of the earth, even over Our Lord Himself. Everything they say and do contradicts Genome's teachings, contravening His Laws. These creatures are the work of the Devil."

"And they must be expunged?" the captain asked.

The priest nodded. "They must be expunged."

"All of them?" Captain FitzRoy was asking.

Still nodding, the priest agreed. "Every one of them."

"Including those disgraceful Raptors?"

"Every last one," the Holy priest-person said, with nodding finality.

# 48

They ran away from the talk of expunging and all it meant. Dodging from shadow to shadow, Phoenix and Totally ran towards the Angels.

"You heard them," Phoenix was saying. "You know what it means!"

"Yes," Totally agreed. All her doubts had evaporated now. "It means we have to get them out."

They ran into the shadow of a huge bristling mound of hardware, one of so many stacked across the new open plain. Totally was panting, breathless. "We have to get them out. And you have to go, all of you, to get help."

"Help? Where from?"

"From anywhere. Phoenix, none of us will survive these things, these Adults. You heard them—*expunged*! It means 'eradicated.' It means—"

"Murdered," said Phoenix. "That's what it means."

"That's what they're like. They think they can do that. They think they have the right."

"Genome gives it to them," Phe said.

"Yes. I don't understand how, or why, but this Genome of theirs, it lets them do what they like. It gives them permission. There has to be help, somewhere in the world. There has to be a way of fighting back against them—there has to be, or we're all lost."

"But we still don't know how we're going to get the Angels out," Phoenix said.

Totally looked at the bristling bush behind which they were hiding. "I think I know a way," she said. "Do you know what these are?" And she laid her four-fingered hand on the stacked, purposeful-looking heap of equipment.

"No," said Phoenix. "It's their stuff. Adult stuff. Stuff to do harm with."

"Exactly," said Totally. "Now, you go over to the Angels. Get them to move as far back from the door of the cage as they can. On the ground, down, as flat as possible. Then come back here."

"We're going to use this stuff," Phoenix said, looking incredulously at the piled-high, moon-reflecting hardware. "We don't know how."

"I do," said Totally. "I've watched them attacking in the streets. I've seen what they do. But I can't do it," she said, holding up her thumbless hand. "Now go, hurry! Get the clips off their wings. Run!"

She watched Phoenix safely cross to the cage of the Angels. Totally was close enough to observe the reaction of Gabriel, the excitement on his face at seeing Phoenix, the way he dashed to the edge to be close enough to touch her. She could see how Phoenix touched him back. Gabriel was relieved to see her, excited that she must have found ways of getting here—and desperately hopeful that Phoenix might give him a means of escape. But Totally could also see how desperate Phe was for the Angel's touch.

Phoenix was outside the cage, but her need to break free was just as great as Gabriel's. For a moment, for the little time left to think and feel, Totally felt something for her foster sister for the first time ever: Tolly felt sorry for Phe.

Then there was no time left. Now it was all effort and drag, pulling at one of the heavy, shoulder-held weapons, finding out how to open it, scrambling over to the next pile, selecting one of the over-sized bullets and tipping it out of its wooden case.

Tolly had to roll the ammunition across a moonlit gap to the massive gun. She had to maneuver the shell into place inside the weapon. When Phoenix returned, Totally showed her how to hold it as the soldiers had, looking down the big barrel at whatever they wanted to damage. Totally had seen their fingers working on the triggers.

"There," she hissed. "Aim it at the front of the cage, then press that, squeeze that, there. Squeeze it!"

"I am!" Phoenix was hissing back. "Nothing's happening. It doesn't work."

"Show me," Tolly said. She found another catch at the side and clicked it into a different position. "Now try . . ."

But even as she said it, Phe squeezed and they were both blown tumbling backwards as everything exploded and the secretive night disappeared in sparks and fire.

# 49

Phoenix felt the smash in the shoulder. She was vaguely aware of a fire-butterfly wending from them before she hit the ground.

Wham!

The shock wave through the air punched them. Phoenix and Totally were rolling along the ground.

At the cage, a ball of fire and whistling sparks of shrapnel winged away in every direction. All around, metal red-hot missiles thumped into the ground or ricocheted, spiraling away with a screaming whine.

Phoenix jumped up, dragging Totally with her. "We did it! We did it! Come on!"

Half the cage was missing. Some of the Angels were crying out. They were wounded, hit by the hard flying pellets of metal.

"Now!" Phoenix was screaming at the opening. "Now! Gabriel! It's time!"

But he was rushing round, encouraging the injured to their feet.

Phoenix and Totally stood back as the Angels went for the gap, running to free their wings into the unrestricted air. The uprush was like a whirlwind, picking up the scorched soil. But then the sound of Raptor roar overcame the beat of wings, the whoosh of the Angel wind. Then the battle cry of the Adults came, as if carried on Raptor roar, the whole cacophony built of sound-harm.

"Gabriel!"

But he was there, in the last possible moment, with Jay-Jay and Alice. Phoenix felt Totally grip her arm once, then Totally was gone. Gabriel was there, and he and the Angels were lifting Phoenix with them as they flapped precipitously upwards, leaving the ground a whirl of dust and churning Adults and Raptors, trying to protect their eyes.

A shot rang out. An Angel fell.

"Go!" Gabriel cried. "Go! Go! Go!"

Phoenix looked down. Out of the milling crowded confusion on the ground, one small Rodent figure dashed, unseen, into the safety of the shadows. There it disappeared.

With Gabriel on one arm, Jay-Jay on the other, Alice at her feet and Totally back inside the impregnable rat runs, Phoenix started to almost feel safe herself. One or two shots rang out, whistling past them into the night. But their attack, the escape had been too sudden.

"They'll never catch us!" Gabriel cried, looking down at the carnage below. "We fly—to the sea!"

"We'll get away!" Phoenix cried back at him. "At last we'll get away!"

But then they turned around in the air. Phoenix was confused. They seemed to spin, to start to turn back. She looked away from Gabriel at Jay-Jay. He was spinning them, turning to look back.

"Jay!" Phoenix heard Alice screaming from behind. "Jay! No!"

Phoenix felt her arm released. She fell, flopping down on one side. Her head was hanging. Now she could see it. Now she could see him. Jay-Jay had seen him.

Alice still screamed, "No!"

Spartan!

Above the noise and chaos, he stood and roared. The sight of him, the sound! With his great, enraged head lifted, he bellowed up at the flock of Angels lifting away from the earth.

Phoenix was spinning. Then her legs fell. Jay-Jay had fallen away, dropping from the rapidly forming arch pattern, diving back, suddenly, madly. Alice fell after him, screaming after him.

Gabriel was calling out. "Jay! Jay-Jay! Leave it! Please! Leave it!"

But now they were falling too. The weight Phoenix had always hated was dragging them out of the sky. Above them, the Angels broke formation and were scattered. Everything started to fall—but nothing as fast as Jay-Jay with Spartan's battle challenge aimed directly at him, roaring in his face. And Jay caught everything Spartan threw up at him, flying back down in front of all the other Angels. Jay-Jay fell as fast as the big bullet had left Phe's shoulder cannon minutes before.

The giant Green Raptor steadied himself on his hugely flexed legs, hands up, arms pumped, head high, horn-hard serrated beak primed. Jay-Jay turned at the very last moment, going in feet first. Spartan, not expecting that, caught the Angel's heels in his face. He stepped back a pace, two. No more. Jay came flying off him like a piece of ricochet shrapnel. Alice screamed after him. The other Angels swooped and lifted, taking on some of the other Raptors while the Adults ran to their bristling bushes of weapons. Gabriel and Phoenix fell to the ground a little way from the main body of action.

"Stay here!" Gabriel shouted, flying straight off. Phoenix could not stop. She started to run. But something grabbed her, halting her before she could get going.

"Don't!" Totally was shouting in her ear.

Spartan launched himself talon-first at Jay-Jay where he had tumbled to the ground. But Alice was flitting over him and then Gabriel swooped to slap him across the eyes. Spartan screamed. Jay was up and flying.

More shots rang out. Angels dropped, thumping down onto the ground, broken, gone. Phoenix watched them fall. And now Gabriel was flying for Jay-Jay, but Jay was lugging up a piece of twisted metal from the corner of the cage. Spartan raged at him again. But Jay leapt, flying up, then down, bringing his metal rod swinging straight into Spartan's face.

The great Green fell. Gabriel tried for Jay. So did Alice. He, hanging still in the air, threatened them with his metal weapon. Spartan was struggling to his feet. The other Raptors stalled, watching silently. The shots stopped. The Adults halted with their ready weapons still and silent.

In the air all round, the hovering Angels stood low in the sky, wings flapping.

"Jay! Angel!" Gabriel cried out. "Don't do it!" But just below him, Spartan, back on his feet, challenged Jay-Jay, blaring straight up at him. Jay stalled, for just one moment.

"Please—Angel!" pleaded Gabriel.

But Jay-Jay was gone.

Spartan leapt up for him as Jay swooped in. The heavy iron bar caught Spartan across the shoulders, but he caught Jay. Down they went. But Spartan was up again. He stood over Jay. Gabriel swept across his face, followed closely by Alice. Spartan looked up. Then he looked down. Jay-Jay had leapt, he had flown at the Raptor, head down, holding the iron bar before him.

Phoenix had seen it all. She watched Jay fly at Spartan with the metal rod. She inhaled sharply as the metal seemed at first to miss Spartan. She held her breath. The bar had not missed. It had entered. It appeared on the other side. She watched Spartan look down at it. He looked at Jay once more. His great beak clacked, twice, three times.

Spartan toppled over. Everything stopped.

The Great New Raptor Leader dropped facedown onto the blackened ground with the iron bar sticking out of him.

Jay stood quivering, the Angels hovering.

There was a moment's silence. Then it was broken. An explosion. Everything, everywhere, seemed to blow up, all at once.

# 50

Cannons fired. From every location, a flare, a rocket carrying the steel mesh nets for trapping Angels.

"No!" Totally screamed as Phoenix tried to start towards Gabriel. "Come with me!"

The nets had fallen. Gabriel, Jay-Jay and almost every other Angel had been brought down, struggling. A few escaped, but the other Adults were waiting now, ready to pick them off, shooting them out of the air. They fell dead in a puff of funereal black ground powder.

Totally's hand closed over Phoenix's mouth to stop her screams. "With me! Now!" She dragged her foster sister back to the depths between the boxes. Phoenix went to struggle forward again.

"There's nothing you can do!" Totally shouted at her. "We have to get away. Phe, please, listen to me. We'll think of something else, I promise. Come on. Quickly! Just through here."

As they dropped into the Rodent hole, Phoenix tried one last time to struggle to get back to Gabriel. But the sides were too steep, too set against her and she knew it was hopeless.

# 51

Very early next morning, a crash brought an abrupt end to any fitful, unsatisfying sleep.

"Out!" the Adults' voices ordered, hugely inflated with aggression. "NOW! ALL OF YOU!"

Phoenix and Totally were glancing at each other, frightened speechless that the Adults had found them out. But outside their apartment, doors were being kicked open everywhere, families ordered out of their homes onto the Raptor-lined streets.

"What's wrong with them?" Phe's mother was asking her grandfather. She was looking at the Adults, at the Raptors, the agitation they shared, their nearness to violence.

"Wait and see," the Elder Agle's calm voice came, as he tried to reassure them all. Phe and Tolly, glancing at each other again and again, did not look or feel assured.

A car was moving slowly down the street. From it, Captain Owen's voice bellowed through a loudspeaker. "You will make your way to the grounds of the Royal Palace, immediately. Do not stop, do not collect any belongings. Go immediately to the Royal Palace. Go to the grounds of the Royal Palace, immediately. Do not . . ."

And so the armored car passed, issuing the order to move without a word of explanation.

When nobody did immediately move, the Raptors closed in, more puffed up than ever, with their heavy heads swaying. A few shots were fired somewhere up the street as one giant Green flicked out with his diamond talons and a Ground Agle fell down cut and bleeding.

"No!" cried Phoenix's grandfather, moving as if to help the injured Agle. "What *is* this?"

"Grandfather!" Totally said.

The Raptors were moving in. The Elder Agle was glaring at them as they tried to guide him away. "What's happening?" he was saying. "What do you know about this?"

Phoenix had already decided, on Totally's insistence, that she would tell their grandfather everything and let him decide what to do. But it was barely dawn and everywhere Agles were under attack. The Greens, it seemed, no longer had to control themselves. They lashed out. They roared. Their frightening feathers were rising up. Agles and Rodents were knocked down but forced to get straight up and continue on along the crowded pavements. The whole city was on the move, closing into its center, falling towards the Palace while the Raptors thrashed and clipped and slashed and the Adults screamed into faces and thrust forward with loaded weapons. One young Rodent caught the butt of an automatic rifle on the side of his head.

"No!" cried Phoenix and Totally together, as their grandfather made another move towards the injured, crying Rodent.

"What have you done?" he asked them again, looking closely at the look of knowing worry written in their faces.

"Done?" their mother said, her face pale and shocked. "Done? Have you done something? Phoenix? Totally? Tell me! I can feel it! What have you done?"

But the Raptors flailed towards them, tuning into Phe's mother's agitated voice. They moved on quickly, quietly.

Phoenix tried to avoid the looks from her mother and from her grandfather. Once she exchanged another glance with Totally, but their guilty expressions were caught by mother and grandfather both, and held as if for further interrogation later. Phoenix could already feel the weight of the questions she would have to answer, the responsibility she would feel.

Nearer and nearer the Palace, the Raptor fury and the Adult anger were being allowed freer and freer rein. In the heat of the rising sun, the Ground Agles and the Rodents were being forced to run through avenues of furious Raptors interspersed with islands of armed Adults striking out at will. The roaring and shouting and the screaming were almost unbearable.

Phoenix had caused this. She would have owned up there and then, if only stopping here might mean being listened to and heard and not attacked, like the poor Ground Agle mother trying to protect her little screaming daughter and catching an Adult fist to the side of her face and a slash on the arm from another curved cutting Raptor talon.

She fell, this Agle mother, with her baby child crying over her. A great Green was upon them in an instant. He was going to take the little one in his beak. Phoenix's family could see what was about to happen.

Phoenix had caused this. She ran to help the mother and child. But her grandfather was there before her, quickly collecting the mother from the ground. He thrust the baby at Phoenix just before the Raptor cracked him about the back of his head.

Phe's mother cried out. She too was hit. Totally took hold of her with her thumbless hands and ran. They all ran, Phoenix with the screaming Agle child, her grandfather with the child's mother, Totally with her foster mother, tearing down the final avenue of screeching, roaring Adult-Raptor cries and threats, into the huge open gates of the old Royal Palace.

Inside, it was hardly any better. The same angered Adults and enraged Raptors were herding Agles and Rodents, driving them all closer to the steps of the Palace. There, as before, the microphones and the speakers were set up, ready for another announcement. But this time there was no curtain, no lowered microphone for the little boy Adult to speak into. Instead, Captain FitzRoy stood on the top step by himself. Below him, the robed priest stood in his flowing finery with Captain Owen.

Captain FitzRoy looked out, watching with fierce, glittering intensity as his own troops and his favored Raptors drove everybody closer and closer in, pushing them one against the other so tightly it was difficult to breathe.

The heat was intense. Parents held their children as high as they could into the air. Phoenix and many others saw a crying child held high to breathe, knocked flying over the heads of the crowd by an insulted Raptor. The screaming baby had to be passed back slowly to its father, who barely managed to silence its cries.

But all round them, the cries died. The Palace grounds fell silent. Through the heat, through the used air, the Agles sensed the hostility in their antennae hair. But now the Rodents felt it too, as the atmosphere was thick and intensely heated with anger and aggression.

Nothing happened for a long while. For a long, long while, they had to stand in the soupy atmosphere. Then, as before, a ripple passed through the crowd as the young Air Agles were led out without their Elders. Now they were manacled, chained together. Now they were more bruised, more abused.

Gabriel carried great dark marks down one side of his face. He still wore the metal plate. Jay-Jay, chained to Gabriel, looked up suddenly. Another ripple of shock passed through the crowd.

Phoenix had to put up her arm to place a hand over her mouth. Otherwise, she would have cried out. Jay-Jay's face—one eye was closed entirely, his mouth hugely puffed out and distorted. Some of the hair on one side of his head seemed to have been dragged out, showing a red and swollen bald patch.

"You!" Captain FitzRoy's huge voice thumped out of the speakers in the trees and fixed to the front of the great house. He stopped. It was as if he was addressing Phoenix directly. But then she realized that everyone there felt like that.

"You have been brought here again," the captain went on. "But this time, the circumstances are different. Very different! These are difficult times," he glowered, looking out across the crowd. "Dangerous times! Yet you are privileged people—ungrateful but privileged people. Here, this morning, you will have the honor of being addressed by Our Supreme and Holiest Immaculate Mother, Keeper of Genome's Own Revelation. You will—be in no doubt—show penance and gratitude. You will show humility! You will bow your heads!"

He stopped. Nobody moved. They didn't know his last sentence had been a command.

"You will bow your heads!" The loudspeakers blared, initiating the angry action of the troops and their servant Raptors.

Every eye fell downwards, looked at the back in front. They waited until the clamor-shout and Raptor-roar faded. Then still they waited, on and on, for whatever would happen next.

Phoenix felt the blood coursing through her face, beating in her ears. Her hair wavered in the harm of the atmosphere, picking up fear, picking up pain. When she directed her feeler-head of hair towards the surviving Angels, the anguish she felt knocked her back. Her head came up.

"Look up!" Captain FitzRoy's voice came, as if he had been awaiting Phoenix's signal to say it.

Now everyone was looking at what Phe was seeing. At the top of the steps, with Captain FitzRoy stepping down one lower, the boy Adult peeped, cowering behind the female Adult. This must be the Holiest Mother of the commander, Phe realized, revealed from behind her curtain, hiding her son's fear, but badly. He quivered, shivering behind her beautifully flowing dress.

The Immaculate Mother stepped up to the microphone. In one hand, she carried an ornate, black-and-white wand, which she waved, as if casting a spell over the crowd. "We have been magnanimous!" Pause. "We have been charitable!" Pause again. Another wave of the wand. "We have endeavored to bring long-term peace. We have been repaid with violence. Violence that endangers the lives of everyone. A great Raptor ally has been slain as a result of acts of terrorism. We will never, ever stand idly by and allow terrorists the liberty to endanger us all."

At this, the boy Adult cringed farther into the deep folds of his holy mother's loose dress. His whimpers were magnified and broadcast across the land.

"By Genome, we will not allow this!" the mother spoke on. "By Genome, our army, the good soldiers of Our Holy Ministry, our supreme Captain FitzRoy," she almost shouted, halting, glancing at, but not mentioning, Captain Owen, "will not allow this—not in our lands, in Genome's own country. You will learn a lesson, here, today. Genome is love—and, by all that is holy, you will learn to love him! Captain FitzRoy!"

# 52

Gabriel looked from under his lowered brow at Captain FitzRoy as he stepped up to the Holy Mother and kissed the wand as she held it towards him. He took back the microphone. Gabriel saw the look of triumph on FitzRoy's face as he glanced down towards Captain Owen. Gabriel shuddered.

Next to him, a tear dropped from the swollen cheek of his best friend. Just behind, he felt Alice shaking, trying to resist the urge to hold and comfort her brother.

"Genome is love!" FitzRoy repeated. On his right hand, the priest-person nodded savagely.

"Love is worth fighting for," FitzRoy went on. "Insurgents are acting under cover of darkness, working to undermine our Great Ministry. By all that is holy, Genome will be victorious! We will never negotiate with terrorists!"

He nodded, as at Gabriel. The soldiers sprang into action. They unlocked and took Jay-Jay. They held Gabriel and Alice. They threatened every other Angel who even thought of moving.

"This land will be cleansed!" Captain FitzRoy announced, as the struggling Jay was shoved up the stone steps of the Palace. At the top, he was held, with his back to the crowd.

"This," FitzRoy said, as Captain Owen looked away, looking down, "is the true extent of your sins. These," he shouted into the too-loud microphone system, as Jay's wings were unclipped and held out, fully extended by the soldiers on either side, "abominations affixed to the body, are the Devil incarnate! You insurgents, you terrorists that believe these are worth saving, are the Devil's advocates. You are the agents of corruption and decay. Neither you nor we can be truly cleansed until we rid these lands—these bodies—of these terrible, terrifying afflictions!" And Gabriel watched him signal to the priest to take his place beside him, at the top of the steps next to Jay-Jay.

The Arch Angel they held there, wings opened wide, head up, feet together as if fixed, nailed into position, was looking up at the open, wide and free sky. Two soldiers stepped up and stuck needles into Jay's back, one either side.

Gabriel looked up too. "Don't let them," he whispered. "How can this be allowed? How can this be allowed to happen?"

53

Phoenix listened without understanding most of the words Captain FitzRoy was using. But she sensed their meaning. She kept feeling her grandfather, her mother, and Totally holding onto her. She watched them hustle Jay-Jay up the steps, holding him out like that. She cried as she saw Jay stand tall with his head up, his face fixed to the sky as they jabbed him with hypodermic needles. Phoenix, for a moment, looked up too. She saw a movement on the roof.

But down below, the priest in full-flowing garb had stepped up and was making a sign. He was being given something that had been handed to Captain FitzRoy by a soldier. The priest held and blessed a bayonet, a rifle blade from the end of a gun barrel. It glinted in the malevolent sunshine.

"The Number of the Beast!" announced the priest, as the hypodermic soldiers either side of Jay held out his wings ever farther, harder, tighter.

"No!" Phoenix breathed.

"Blessed are the pure in heart," the priest incanted, stepping up to Jay-Jay.

Jay couldn't see what was about to happen. Everyone else could. The mirror-shiny, sharp slender blade, lifted, glinted. The robed priest stood prepared, in the love of his Genome god.

Phoenix could not stop her voice any longer. "No!" she cried.

From the roof, an Elder Air Agle dropped. He looked, Phoenix could see straightaway, like an older version of Jay-Jay, with slightly heavier body and lesser wings. Jay's Elder flew down, swooping low across the crowd, over the soldiers and the Raptors towards Captain FitzRoy and the trinity of priest, Holy Mother and Son. He came in low. The Raptors leapt for him. They missed. He was too fast.

A shot rang out. He was too slow.

In he flew, falling, crashing into the front of the great house, breaking down onto the ground where Jay-Jay could see him lying lifeless.

"Don't!" Jay screamed, struggling against the soldiers either side.

"No, don't," cried Phoenix. Cried Totally. Cried the families, all of them, the Ground Agles and the Rodents. "Do not!"

But the holy priest stepped farther into Jay's forced-wide wingspan and he—in the name of Genome—slipped in easy with the hardened, over-sharpened pointed rifle knife—and in the name of their god he ripped right through the tendons of the wing close to Jay-Jay's back and it came away from him, held up in triumph by the Adults, by order of their Captain FitzRoy.

The crowd tried to scream the wing back on. But the Raptors beat them down in sound and in fury and the priest sliced again and both wings, both—in the name of Love!

And Jay's head hung for the first time as his back bled in two huge red running tears and his fellow Angels cried and fell fainting and almost died at the sight while the son beside his Immaculate Mother squirmed and hid, but peeked and glinted with glee.

"Don't forgive them!" Gabriel roared, calling out to the crowd. "Don't forgive them for what they do—they know exactly what they do! Never forgive!"—crying out, before the butt of the nearest rifle caught him and battered the Arch Angel Gabriel to the ground.

# CITY OF SCREAMS

# PART FOUR

# 54

"What did you think you were going to do?" Phoenix's mother's eyes were wild with anger from fear.

"We did what we had to do!" Phoenix screamed back at her.

Her grandfather was standing between them. Totally was crouching over the other side of the kitchen, as if hiding behind the table.

"Yes!" screamed Phoenix's mother across the gap between them filled by her grandfather. "Yes, you did it all right! How many have died because of what you did? A Raptor? Air Agles! And that young one's wings!"

But Phe's screams were the loudest now. She had to let it out. "Don't tell me! I know!" She was crying, hitting herself on the sides of her face. "Don't tell me!"

"Enough!" yelled her grandfather, catching hold of her. "That's enough!"

"It's more than enough!" Phoenix's mother still screamed like the city. "Much more!"

"Stop!" the Elder Ground Agle ordered them. "Right now! Stop this. This is not what we should be doing."

"Tell us what to do then!" demanded Phoenix. "Tell us what to do about all of this! You're the City Elder! You're the responsible one! Why can't you make something happen?"

She was raging into her grandfather's face. Phoenix's mother was trembling and speechless. Totally tried to hide, covering her ears with her four-fingered hands.

"You've just let this happen!" Phoenix shouted at the old Agle. "You gave in! Right from the start! The City should have acted—fought! You never did anything! You might as well have stood Jay-Jay up and cut off his wings with a knife from our kitchen for all your—"

The slap rang out. They all felt it. Phoenix was knocked back. The room rang with the sound of the clap. Phoenix collapsed. Her grandfather stood, shocked and speechless. He had not hit her.

Phoenix's mother collected her, falling to the floor with her. Her mother had lunged across and struck her, for the first time ever. And now they held onto each other, rocking, crying, trying to find some strength from somewhere, from giving or receiving a slap, from anywhere, to get them through this.

The Elder Ground Agle stood alone, looking down on his daughter and his granddaughter. All his life he had been reasonable and kind. And now he was wrong. Reason and kindness were mistakes now, fatal errors he had made time and time again.

Phoenix could feel him standing over her and her mother. She could feel the throb of her cheek from the slap, but her grandfather's pain was greater. Every hair follicle on her head was a piercing prick of the sharpness of his emotion. She had attacked and hurt him. But at the moment, the screaming moment in her mother's arms, Phoenix couldn't help but think that he deserved to feel like this.

She could not clear her head of the image of Jay-Jay collapsing onto the Palace steps with his wingless, hopeless back covered in blood. Phoenix still felt dizzy and sick as she thought of the military doctor-soldiers rushing to stem the blood flow from the injured Angel, while the other soldiers held up the severed wings, holding them out, one wing, the other, with that dreadful, horrifying space in between.

"We had them free," Phoenix found enough of her voice to say, as her mother held her on the kitchen floor. "We had them out and flying away. It would have worked. We were going to fly with them to—"

"I could have stopped this," her grandfather said, only now able to respond to what Phoenix had accused him of. "You're right, I could have—"

"No!" Totally said, suddenly. "No, Grandfather! Captain FitzRoy and the priest—we heard them. From here on, there's nothing they won't do to us—every one of us!"

Nobody said anything. Through the silence, from far away, a very young Ground Agle cried.

Phoenix winced as her mother spoke. "What did you hear? Tell us what you heard."

"Captain FitzRoy, the priest, all the Adults—Genome," Tolly said, "Genome—Genome hates us!"

The Elder Ground Agle, looking older by the moment, stood numb, disembodied, hopelessly lost.

"Genome is love," Totally said. "But he's hate, too. That's what he is—love and hate. But mostly, he's hate."

# 55

Some of the Angels were dead, shot down out of the night sky, gone, forever.

Now Gabriel had to watch as his best friend Jay-Jay wished he were one of them. Gabriel, as leader of the new fliers, should have something to say to him—but what could he say? What possible words could Gabriel find as, wrapped in sodden, browning bandages, Jay threw himself away from Alice again, towards the bars of their new cage?

Outside, held at bay by a cordon of stun-gun-equipped Adults, the leaderless young Raptors milled in green chaos, raging and ripping, occasionally tearing at one another in their mindless anger and frustration. They wanted nothing more than to get inside the cage at the Angels, at Jay-Jay, to tear him limb from wingless limb.

Jay threw himself. He cracked against the steel cage. He fell, Alice and the others covering him as he crawled and curled and cried, as he wished he'd died, as Gabriel looked on, unable to speak.

Stigma—so said the plate at Gabriel's breast. At first, he had not understood its meaning, but the nameplate seemed more and more to define him, as if he was growing into the meaning of the word, as if he were all the while a stigma and had only to be shown the word to become it. Everything he had gloried in being, his mastery of flight, his skymost life, was the cause of harm and shame and ruin.

What could he possibly say to Jay-Jay but sorry? How could he be sorry enough for Jay's wings, for the rest of Jay's flightless life? Gabriel knew there was nothing to say now.

# 56

There were no Raptors on the streets. All day, looking out of the window, waiting for a sign of what might happen next, hoping for a glimpse of hope, an Agle wing in the sky, only Adults appeared. More and more of them. No other species were free enough to be out there.

From time to time a vehicle with a loudspeaker cruised by. "Stay in your homes! You are ordered not to leave your houses! Stay in your homes!"

So they stayed, everyone, in the headache of their houses, in their fearful flats in the screaming city. It seemed to last a week, that day of still and stifling heat. Totally came into Phoenix's room for a while. They sat in silence, as if waiting, watching the sun, the angle of its rays sloping through the window. The air was dusty, full of motes from the activity outside, the military marching, the vehicles, the sentry posts being erected at regular intervals along the street.

In the end, with the sun still lighting up the encroaching street dust in Phoenix's room, Totally left, without a word. They had not so much as glanced at each other. They were too full of hurt, guilt, helplessness.

Right up until the sun finally set, the noise of the military on the move clattered and crunched and crashed outside. Now this was full-scale occupation, the complete control and oppression of one community of species by another. When the sun disappeared it seemed to just be resurrected, but flittingly, the city lit with powerful moving lamps and lasers. Spotlights strafed the pavements, picking out the corner hiding places, piercing the doorways and beaming in through open windows. If Phoenix dozed a little, the light entered her room to infiltrate even her eyelids. Eyes shut, it was like facing the sun at dawn. Eyes open, the room was blindingly illuminated, like being inside the heat of a fire. The spotlight would then move away, onto the next apartment, leaving Phoenix blinking, eyes watering, open or closed.

Her eyes were watering, but she was not crying. The tears still came, as if they were never now going to stop. She kept seeing Jay-Jay again, being held there, while that priest glinted towards him—only it wasn't Jay any longer, in Phe's mind's eye. She kept seeing Gabriel being held. Gabriel looking up to the sky.

"Don't forgive them!" he had said. She saw him being cut. Phoenix would never forgive them. Tears came, continuously. Eyes closed, eyes open. Closed. She might doze for a while. Every time she did, the light came flooding back in. Eyes open.

And there, in the spotlight, a darkened figure, standing by her bed.

"What is it?" She leapt.

The light moved on, leaving her mother looming over her. "It's your grandfather."

Phoenix blinked away her tears. She rubbed her eyes. "Grandfather? What's happened?"

"He went out," her mother said.

"Out? Where?"

"I don't know. He went out after dark, hours and hours ago. You've been out at night. I thought you might know where he went. He was disturbed, after what you said to him. I've never seen him like that. I'm so worried about him."

"But what did he say?"

"He said the time had come to act. He was going to try to call a meeting of the City Elders, those not already taken. Where? Where would they go? Where would they meet?"

Phoenix didn't have to think about it. "There's only one place," she said.

"Is there? Where? Tell me!"

But Phoenix was up and in her dress in seconds.

"Phoenix, what are you doing?"

"It's my fault," Phe said. "I'm the reason he went. If I hadn't accused him of doing nothing!"

Then Totally was at the door of Phe's room. "I should go," she was saying, immediately understanding what was going on.

"Nobody's going anywhere," their mother was saying. "Phoenix!" But Phe was already crashing out of the door past Tolly. "Phoenix!—where's she going?"

"The rat runs," Phe heard her foster sister saying to her mother as Phe ran out of the apartment and down the stairs to the street. Tolly looked out of the door.

The rising sun picked her out, striking her in the eyes like another angry Adult spotlight.

# 57

As soon as the sun came up, the Adults were there, coming for them. A dozen or more Raptors had to be electrically stunned, zapped with the quick but massive crack of released charge. They fell quivering onto a kind of bed of their own feathers, their hands and arms flexing, heads rolling as if in an epileptic seizure.

The Angels watched the Adults coming towards them against the new day's sun. They were ordered into the center of the cage, there to crouch and wait without moving.

Gabriel and Alice had to drag Jay-Jay with them. They had to force him down. He was weak and sweaty but wanted to fight, Gabriel knew, to the death. Alice knew it too. She tried too hard to hang onto her brother. But Gabriel, holding Jay down with him, tried to imagine what it was like to go through what Jay had suffered. He tried to imagine losing his own wings. How could he live without them? And now the Adults were coming for them. They were looking, searching, sorting the Angels, shoving them aside one by one.

Gabriel knew what they were looking for. He stood. "Here I am," he said.

Jay-Jay stood swaying by his side. Then Alice with them.

The soldiers pulled them away, Gabriel, Jay-Jay and Alice. They ordered the other Angels to stay exactly where they were.

Outside the cage, the Green Raptors stormed towards the three Angels, towards Jay-Jay. The stun guns zapped and Raptors fell in heaps, but still they kept on coming.

Jay would have brought them on. His sister cried to him. "Don't you forget me!"

Gabriel kept a hand hard on Jay's arm. He was afraid. But he too would rather have braved the onslaught of the Raptors than face the prospect of the blessing of the priest with the blade.

The Adults hustled them through, leaving behind a trail of stunned and twitching Raptors fighting on the ground against the involuntary flexing of their own muscles. Up ahead, an armored vehicle with its back doors open and its engine running. Gabriel had known, ever since he'd first set eyes on the Adults, ever since he'd first smelled the burnt air of their military machines, that this kind of force would never end. He considered turning suddenly, running back to the Raptor gangs raging behind them, launching himself into the welcome of their honestly aggressive tearing talons. At least the Greens did what they did out of simple hatred. At least they didn't confuse things by offering peace and safety while bringing war and danger. Young Green Raptors promised harm and brought it. They never talked of Love and Forgiveness. Raptors and Angels were similar now, in that they forgave nothing.

Jay-Jay stumbled at the open door of the truck. He was too dazed and too weak. But one of the armored Adults caught him before Gabriel could.

Alice went to help defend Jay from this latest attack. But the Adult held up her hand, helping Jay into the vehicle. There, in the back, was a bed and some seats. Jay was taken to lie on the bed, Alice and Gabriel invited to sit. Another Adult, an unarmed male, stood over Jay-Jay with a syringe, squirting some kind of thick liquid into the air.

"No!" Alice leapt forward.

"Leave him!" Gabriel stood, reaching for the syringe.

The Adult stepped away. "This will help him," he said. "It's an antibiotic and a sedative. He needs to rest."

"You leave him alone!" Alice almost spat in the Adult's face.

Jay was sweating profusely, looking away into the distance at what he alone could see.

"He'll die if I don't," the Adult said. He waited, glancing at Gabriel.

Gabriel took Alice and held her while the needle was stuck into Jay's arm and the liquid disappeared. "Does it matter if it's poison?" Gabriel whispered into Alice's ear. She glanced at him with loathing.

The Adult jumped out of the truck and closed the door behind him.

"Does it matter if they poison us all now?" Gabriel was still speaking into Alice's offended face as the engine started. "This is what they'll do to us," Gabriel said, touching Jay-Jay's arm. "All of us."

The armored vehicle started off and they stumbled. They grasped each other.

"We're never getting away now," Alice whispered, "are we?" Her face was pressed against the metal plate on Gabriel's chest.

Gabriel did not want to say it. They were never getting away. The Adults could do what they liked to them.

"We'll never fly again," Alice cried.

"No," Gabriel had to say, holding her close. "We never will."

Alice felt as if she were about to collapse. "You're right about the poison," she whispered. "Let them poison us. I'd rather die than . . ."

"So would I," Gabriel said. "I'd much rather die."

# 58

She tried to run unnoticed through the low morning sunshine, but the spotlight of the dawn pinned her down, along with the guns that bristled towards her, gleaming with oily threat.

"Move and you will be shot!" The Adult voices rang out.

"'Kay!" she called back, with her hands up in the air. "'Kay! Please don't fire!"

"One more move and you will be killed!"

"I won't move. Don't shoot! I'm looking for my grandfather. And I need to see Captain Owen!"

"Stay right where you are!"

Whenever the Adults ran at someone, it seemed as though they were about to run right through, to trample them into the ground. Phoenix stood as still as she could as four of them crashed in on her, treating her, one little female Ground Agle, like some kind of secret weapon.

"Down! Down! Down!" they raged, pulling and pushing her, forcing her face down on the ground. "Hands behind your head!"

They searched her, quickly, thoroughly. Two of the four grabbed at her, lifting her to her feet.

Phe's face was full of the dark armored features of the enraged Adults as they attacked her with their voices. "Please let me see Captain Owen!" she cried up at them.

"Don't speak! Don't you speak!"

"I know Captain Owen! He will want to see me, I promise. Please take me to him. Please. Please!"

They drew back from her. Something had stopped them. Phoenix had squeezed her eyes closed, pleading against their shouting, dense and dreadful voices. Then she felt the release of pressure through her hair as they fell silent, as their faces shifted away from hers.

"That's enough!" a voice said.

Phoenix recognized it. She opened her eyes. Captain Owen himself stood over her. Phe could feel other emotions emanating from him, as if this were no Adult standing there. As if Captain Owen were now some kind of other species entirely.

"You are Phoenix," he said. His calm voice helped settle Phe's Agle hair. She felt that she would be allowed to look at him.

"You've remembered my name."

He nodded.

"You must remember my grandfather?"

Captain Owen didn't reply.

"I know you do," she said, because she felt he did, through her scalp, through what she could see in his face.

"Where is he?" Phoenix asked, quietly, afraid of what the captain might have to tell her. He told her nothing. But she could read him, sense meaning in his unspoken words. "I have to find him," she said.

Captain Owen let his gaze linger on Phe's face a moment or two longer. Then he nodded, once. "Let her go," he said.

The soldiers round them looked at each other. Captain Owen nodded to Phoenix again, for her to go.

She turned, easing between the hard-bodied, motionless torsos of the bemused soldiers. Phoenix walked slowly away from them.

Some steadily increasing, uneasy feeling, some negative undulation through the roots of her hair, warned to expect a shot, a bullet in the back.

Captain Owen was coming after her. After him, his troops. As Phoenix passed down the street, past more and more sentry posts, the battalion of military personnel gathered behind her. Every one of them, with the exception of Captain Owen, was heavily armed, grim-faced and itchy-fingered. Every one of them, with the exception of the captain, would have shot her in the back. One of them still surely would, if she didn't find her way out of this, very soon.

She shouldn't have run. Phoenix knew she shouldn't have, but the urge was too great, the threat-sense through her oversensitized scalp too like the crawl of a thousand pin-footed scorpion beetles.

A shot rang out—*the* shot, the one she had been anticipating. The bullet intended for between her shoulder blades whistled by her ear. Phoenix looked back. Captain Owen had the soldier by the firing arm, wrenching the rifle from him.

"Let her go," she heard the captain say as Phe ran round the corner out of sight to raise the metal cover of the hole in the ground that led to the old city sewers, onto which the rat runs had been built.

# 59

Alice was tending her brother. "I don't think he's dying," she was saying. "He's breathing more easily now. He's resting."

Gabriel was sitting on one of the seats in the back of the truck, leaning forward to allow for his clipped-back wings. He was gazing at the floor.

"I think he's going to be all right," Alice said.

Gabriel glanced over at her. So often, he had wished for more time alone with Alice. Now, effectively, with Jay-Jay in some kind of drug coma, they were together in a room of their own. But all Gabriel could do was to stare at the floor. "What does it matter?" he said.

"He's still my brother," Alice said. "It's still Jay-Jay, your best friend."

"Yeah!" Gabriel jumped up. "Oh, yeah. That's his face all right. And when they come again, when they take my wings, and yours, will we be us—will we? We should just—we should fight them!"

"Yes," Alice said, looking down at Jay. "Yes, we should."

"Even if they kill us all, we should fly in their faces. And we will, now—right now! When they come for us. They'll take our wings. We fight back, yes? Jay knew. That's all he wanted, in the end. So we do it. We fight, we fly, we die. Yes? Alice? We fight, we die, but with wings on."

"Yes," Alice said.

# 60

It was far too dark. Something else had changed.

Phoenix stumbled down the last few rungs of a metal ladder. On the floor at her feet, straightaway, the flattened, barely glowing wings of fire-butterflies. There were so many, all lying opened out on the ground that Phe, stepping forward carefully, still had to tread on them. Their brittle bodies crunched underfoot.

She turned a corner, diving into the first of the proper runs. Here too, the huge butterflies glowed weakly, fading out on the carved floor. None flew, not one. Everywhere she went, ducking through the carved-out corridors, the golden glow of the place was flattened, splayed and spoiled underfoot. There was only just enough light left by which to see her way.

As she went deeper, Phoenix started to become aware of something else—a smell. Before, with Totally, the rat runs had a slightly sweet aroma, as if the rock walls were infused with the juice of fruit. Now, with the flattened butterflies cracking like empty shells, this place, the smell of it—it reminded Phoenix of... Adults! It stank like they did. Or more like their weapons, their metal, their vehicles. Yes, as she breathed in the burnt oily air, she was reminded of the blue smoke issuing from the rear ends of their cars, their trucks and armored fighting machines. The deadened rat runs smelled just like the exhaust fumes that Adults seemed to love so much they produced them everywhere.

Everywhere? Here?

Had they found a way of getting down here? Was this why the place now reeked of them? Had they come down here to kill all the fire-butterflies? Why would they? How could they? Adults were too big. They'd never make it through the little tunnels.

Unless—unless they had found out about the runs and filled them with their smoke? The vile stench down here now seemed as if it would kill everything... *Everything*?

Phoenix ran. She hit her head, scraping her arms along the rough-hewn walls. She dashed downwards into ever-deepening tunnels, running towards the bottom, the old Central hall of the Rodents, where Totally had told her that the City Elders still sometimes met. It was supposed to be a secret, for emergencies only. And this was an emergency!

"Grandfather!" she screamed out, falling into the darkened and gloomy expanse of the Great Rodent Hall. "Grandfather!" she screamed again. Phoenix's own voice echoed back at her from the far shadows. "Grandfather!"

"Please answer me!" But the only answer: "Please answer me!"—as if she were mocking herself.

She ran, crunching across the butterfly floor, looking everywhere. As she stamped, dead fire-wings sent specks of failing light sparking round her ankles.

"Grandfather!" Herself, in reply: "Grandfather!"

Then she stumbled. She fell onto something—someone!

She scrambled away, straight into another. Then another.

Agles. Their bodies. Old Ground Agles, lying on the ground. They were dead, every one of them.

"No!" she screamed.

# 61

The back door of the truck opened. As soon as it did, Gabriel flew out, followed closely by Alice. They had both dragged away the clips from the scabs on their wings. Gabriel had taken off the Stigma plate once and for all. Now he lashed out with it on its chain, lunging for the face of the nearest Adult.

The truck had backed into a huge room, one of the Adults' metal box houses, but bigger, with smaller cars parked here and there.

Gabriel and Alice flew into the roof as the Adults backed away from his flailing Stigma sign. They let out a cry of near joy, at the feel of their wings working. They were flying! It was all they needed. Flying, for them, was fighting. This was the fight they were going to put up, to the death.

They turned round and round in the air, circling each other, Gabriel and Alice, Alice and Gabriel, very quickly realizing that they were trapped in the vast expanse of the metal warehouse, or hangar. Still, they were in flight. A freedom of sorts, just to be in the air, flexing the muscles of the back and neck, allowing the instincts to take over.

But then—a crack!

*Crack!* And Gabriel saw Alice falter, almost as though she had stumbled in mid-flight. He just had time to look down at the soldiers with their guns before the next crack rang out.

Getting shot was not nearly as painful as Gabriel had imagined it would be. It stung, a lot. It made him dizzy, but not quite straightaway. He had time to watch Alice fall, or more like glide to the ground. She swooped, then staggered onto her legs before finally collapsing.

Gabriel flew after her. But his body was shutting down. He too took a tumble as soon as his feet touched down. He fell onto his knees, with his wings hanging limply, spread out on either side of him.

Falling forward, he started to crawl towards Alice's body. She lay, already lifeless. The life was draining away from Gabriel. He clawed at the ground. Alice's restful face was not far away from him. But he couldn't make it. She was fading out. She was sliding away, as the world went, slipping from under him.

# 62

He was gone from the world. Forever.

"No!" she screamed.

"No!" Not her echo. Phoenix, screaming again, again. "No! *No!*"

"Grandfather!" She held him close. "Please, please don't! Not this! Not this, not now!"

Then even the echo died. Nobody said anything to Phoenix. There was nobody with her. Her grandfather lay among the fading fire-butterfly bodies, looking up at nothing. Nothing looking at nothing.

Just Phoenix left here, trying to breathe. She sat rocking, shocked and dazed. The air still stank of Adult, of machine-burn, of exhausted particles. From some subconsciously remembered school lesson, the words *carbon monoxide* came to her. It was poison.

Captain Owen! He had let her go. She should have realized he had let her get away for a reason, knowing she would come down here and find this. Her grandfather had believed Captain Owen to be a reasonable Adult. But the Adults' reasons were distorted, corrupted by a cruel god. Genome is love, they kept saying. But his love only ever engendered hate. Genome did not love life—he hated it. Genome meant love of death. And Phoenix hated him to death.

She laid her grandfather's head gently on what was left of an entire species. The fire-butterflies were all gone. As far as Phoenix knew, they lived, they existed only here. Now they were gone.

Standing, looking down through her flowing tears at her grandfather and the other Elders of the City Council, she saw that the Adults would make all Agles, all Rodents as extinct as the butterflies.

And for what? For not being Adult, or being in the way of the Adults and their power-crazed, jealous god.

The light was still fading. The bodies of the Elders looked blank now, featureless silhouettes against a very dim background. Phoenix did not want to leave her grandfather here, like this, but she had no choice.

She had to turn and run back the way she had come. Her feet crunched across the butterfly bodies, throwing up broken bits of wings, showering her ankles in cold sparks.

Now she knew. Captain Owen had wanted her to see this. He was as cruel as any Adult, as Genome allowed them to be. There was no fighting against such godlike power. The only thing to do was spit in the face of such a god, to never again bow down before it.

Phoenix dashed back, running uphill all the way, oblivious to the catches and scrapes against her shoulders and arms on the rocky walls. She almost flew up the metal ladder and out of the cover in the pavement of the street.

She knew they'd be there. And they were. Waiting for her, Captain Owen and his band of Adult brothers-in-arms, killers, every one. Phoenix leapt out into the light. Her tears were still streaming. She ran at them. "You can kill me now! I don't care!" The soldiers seemed to stall. They watched.

As she drove towards them, all Phe could see was Captain Owen, the guilty commanding officer.

"Kill me too!" she screamed.

The soldiers moved aside to let her through. They allowed her to dash to the captain, to throw herself at his hard body armor, pounding at the shell of toughened skin.

"I hate you! I hate you all! You killed them—you killed my grandfather! Kill me too, why don't you? Why don't you just kill me now? I know you're going to!" She was lashing out, hurting her hands against the unflinching face of the captain. "Go on! Do it! I demand you do it!"

He stood there, taking her blows, neither moving nor speaking. It was as if he were not real, but some kind of plasticated creature manufactured of machine parts and powered by electricity.

"I hate your god—I hate Genome!"

Phoenix screamed at him her hatred of everything he and the other Adults were. This, surely, would get a reaction from them. Any reaction! Anything at all—because whatever they did, these cruel worshippers, must show them for what they really were.

"Genome disgusts me!" she screamed in Captain Owen's face, pounding at him. "He is Hate! And so are you! You are made out of Hate! So hard!" And she thumped and thumped at him. "Hard! Hardened Hate! That's all! That's all you are! You and Genome! That's all! That's all!"

And, at last, as Phoenix was running out of energy, her hits growing weaker and weaker, her tears falling wilder, as she started to drop to the ground in despair and exhaustion, she got a reaction.

Captain Owen caught her, but gently. She cried. She hung her head. "We're beaten," she said. "Every one of us."

"Take her," Phoenix heard him say.

If she'd had any energy left, Phoenix would have tried to fight, to force them away. But she had nothing now. She was empty. Hopeless. Completely hopeless.

"You are wrong," she heard Captain Owen's voice saying, "Genome *is* love," as they led her away.

# 63

The first thing he saw, on the other side, was her face. "You really *are* an Angel," Gabriel said. He was looking up into Alice's eyes as she smiled down on him. "Am I dying?"

"Dying?" Alice said. "No. But you're going to feel really sick in a moment or two."

As soon as she said that, sure enough, Gabriel's stomach tensed and he retched.

"Lie back," Alice soothed him. "Just relax. You'll be fine."

Gabriel looked around at the place they were in. It was a room. It was cool and calm. Then he saw Jay-Jay in a bed, still asleep.

"Where are we?" he asked.

On the other side of the room, Gabriel now noticed that there were two Rodents and an Elder female Ground Agle, all watching him. He was lying back, resting against his wings. They were still unfettered, spread out on either side of him against the floor.

As Gabriel looked again at Alice, her wings flexed involuntarily, unfolding behind her. Gabriel sat up. His head was spinning. "What happened? You were shot—I was shot!" He was looking to his side where he had felt the bullet hit him. A red mark was the extent of his injuries. "How come?" he said.

"A tranquillizer dart," one of the Rodents said, the female.

"They knocked us out with an injection," Alice said. She nodded at her brother in bed. "Like Jay-Jay, only not so strong."

Gabriel was staring at everything, everybody. "What—why?" The Elder Agle he now recognized as Phoenix's mother. "You, here? Why? What's going on?"

"I don't know," she said. "I only wish I did. I don't know where my daughter is, or my father. The soldiers came for me and brought me here, that's all."

Gabriel looked at the two Rodents. But before any more questions could be asked of anyone, the bolts on the doors were being shifted. Gabriel jumped up, his wings perturbing the air. The door opened and the armed Adults came in, followed by one of the army captains—not FitzRoy, the other one. Captain Owen. He had someone with him.

"Phoenix!" her mother cried, running to her.

Gabriel watched the soldiers stepping back to allow the female Ground Agle through. He looked at Captain Owen. But the captain was watching the mother and daughter.

The captain was allowing the Ground Agles to embrace. He was waiting for them. This was the first time Gabriel had seen an Adult waiting for anything. Waiting was not their way. They took whatever they thought they needed, immediately. Usually with threats of violence, if not with violence itself.

But Captain Owen waited, looking on, saying nothing.

# 64

Totally had been taken along with her distraught foster mother. Grandfather was out all night and now Phoenix was missing too. Then the soldiers came for them and they knew it had to be bad. Totally's mother had not stopped blaming herself for letting Phoenix go.

But then Rap Rodent was in the back of the truck before them, with tears all over his face. His hands were shaking. "What have we done?" he was saying. "They took off the Air Agle's wings! Why do they want me? What have I done?"

"You haven't done anything," Totally's foster mother said, holding the Rodents. "Don't worry, you haven't done anything to them, they won't do anything to you."

Totally knew she didn't believe what she was saying. Gabriel hadn't done anything to the Adults, but there he was, lying unconscious on the floor with the other Angel, the lovely Alice. And Jay-Jay, irreparably damaged, also unconscious, in a bed. Who had done anything to these Adults? And yet look at what they did, for nothing!

Then Alice woke and was nearly sick. Then Gabriel, the same.

"What's going on?" Rap kept whispering.

Totally just shook her head. All she could do was hold onto Rap, watch, and wait. "We'll find out," she whispered back to him.

We will find out, she was thinking, as the doors opened and the soldiers came in. They would find out, she knew, as soon as she saw Captain Owen and then Phoenix.

Phe's face was set hard as her mother rushed to hug her. She was not crying but had been. She was still overwhelmed at seeing her mother there. But Totally could see, over everything else, the anger emanating from Phoenix, a frightening, rage-like hatred thickening the air all round her.

"I should leave you," Totally was surprised to hear Captain Owen say.

But Phoenix turned the dense air-cloud of her stare towards him. "No!" she cried. "Don't go anywhere! Tell us what's going on."

The only one not standing now was the comatose Jay-Jay. Totally and Rap were still holding each other nervously. The two Angels had backed their precious wings into the wall as if to protect them.

"Don't go away!" Phoenix had turned to shout into the captain's face.

"You've collected us here," she was shouting, glancing at everyone else, including the Adult soldiers, "for some reason. What are your reasons? Why have you murdered my grandfather?"

The words, like Phoenix's anger, thickened the air with clouds of meaning and consequences.

"Why have you murdered my grandfather?"

"What?" said Phe's mother. "What?"

Totally was moving forward, catching her foster mother as she stumbled, about to fall. She fell anyway, taking Totally with her.

"They've murdered them all," Phoenix was raging over them. "The Elders—the City Elders! They're all dead! The rat runs are dark and poisoned. Your runs Tolly—your place has been poisoned! Its halls and its rooms—they're gas chambers now! And all the butterflies and the City Elders and—and Grandfather—gone! Forever!"

# 65

The deep eyes blinked under the huge armored forehead in the captain's face. "Genome is love," he said. "You must believe me—"

"Why should we believe anything from you?" Phoenix couldn't help but say now.

"Have you killed my father?" Phe's mother looked up and asked the captain directly.

"You must believe me," he persisted, "I had nothing to do with that. You had to find your grandfather," he said to Phoenix. "We couldn't get down there. If I could have found him for you, I would. If I could have saved him . . ."

"But you didn't," Phoenix said.

"He was poisoned?" her mother was saying. "Poisoned?"

"Carbon monoxide," Phoenix said.

She exchanged a glance with Gabriel as she said that—almost as if she were admitting something to him. Her knowledge, her learning, affirmed that she was no flier, that she was a Ground Agle, so she knew these things. Gabriel caught her look and returned it. He understood that too.

Phoenix got up, leaving Totally on the floor comforting their mother. "Pumping the rat runs full of exhaust fumes, poisoning everything, shooting Air Agles, cutting off their wings, destroying their identities, taking their lives from them—this is what Genome does in the name of Love."

"No!" the captain said. "This is what we do—this is what human beings do in the name of Genome. But Genome speaks to us all in different ways."

"Yes!" Phoenix said, looking at and feeling the grief of her mother on top of her own. "*This* is how he speaks to us."

"That should not be," said Captain Owen. "We have done this, human beings, not Genome. We are responsible. And we are wrong."

Phoenix turned away from him, returning to what was left of her family.

"And what's a human being?" Totally said, looking up from the floor.

"An Adult, as you say," Captain Owen said.

"No," said Totally, "I mean what sort of *thing* is a human being?" She looked at Jay-Jay, at the terrified Rap, at her foster mother in grief, at Phoenix. "What kind of thing can do all this? How can it ever look another species in the face without shame? Tell us—how can human beings do this?"

## 66

All day they had waited. Jay-Jay was awake, pale, silent. An Adult came in to give him more medication. Jay took the injection as if he wasn't aware a needle was going into him. Phoenix kept looking at Jay as Alice tried to get through to him. Alice wanted to hear that her brother was all right, but it was as if he was still unconscious with his vacant eyes open.

Night came outside. It was time to leave, the captain entered to tell them. Now, Phoenix noted, it was as Totally had said—he could not look another species in the face without shame.

The others were nervous, still suspecting an Adult trick. But Phoenix was able to assure them. . . . Grandfather had been right about this captain and his handful of close followers, armed Adults that they were.

"Grandfather knew," she said, to her mother. "We should respect that now. We should go with Captain Owen."

"I can't go, not now," her mother said, with so many tears it was as if the room was awash.

"But you must!" Totally tried to insist, picking up her foster mother's hand in both of hers. "We can't go without you."

"We won't go without you," Phoenix said.

"Yes, you will," said her mother. "I have to stay. I have to see to your grandfather. Tell me where he is. I can't leave this place. You have to go—you have to go for me."

"No, Mother! Please!"

It was time to leave. Phoenix and Totally had to get into the back of the truck without their mother. But they leapt back out.

"We didn't tell you what we overheard," Phoenix said. "Captain FitzRoy and the priest are going to destroy everyone. They think they can do that."

Her mother looked at Captain Owen, who looked away. "We won't let that happen, will we?" she asked the captain.

"No," he said, quietly, without looking up.

Phoenix felt his lack of conviction, the falseness in his single-worded answer. But it also said that he would try—he would, at least, do that.

"We'll come back," Phe whispered to her mother. "We'll get help. We'll come back and get you—all of you."

"Yes," her mother said.

Another one-word answer, empty with lack of conviction and disbelief.

# 67

Gabriel and Alice were keeping a hold on Jay-Jay as the truck bounced and rocked wildly.

"We'll be staying off the roads," Captain Owen had told them. "We'll be traveling without lights. Hold tight. It's going to be a rough ride."

It was, Phoenix thought, a very rough ride. All the way through everything that had happened, up to her grandfather's death and the leaving behind of her mother—almost too rough to bear.

Phoenix looked round in the back of the truck. An electric lantern, swaying madly, threw their moving shadows aslant like drunks, adding to and exaggerating their motion. She looked at Gabriel as he kept glancing at Alice. Alice was fixed on her brother, while Jay-Jay's concentration peered into the middle distance as if nothing were happening round him. Totally and Rap were tightly together in one corner. Phe was jammed into a corner of her own, on her own, alone with her thoughts. Captain Owen had told her he'd wanted to bring a friend for her, but that friend, he said, was already there.

Gabriel looked at Alice again. And Phoenix, holding onto herself in the corner, looked away. She felt very, very alone here, trying to keep upright, trying to keep her thoughts together. The truck bounced and knocked them all sideways. Phe hit her head on the side. It didn't hurt. So she knocked it again, on purpose, to try to feel some pain because—because she was in pain. Earlier, she and Tolly had held and comforted each other. They had cried for their mother. But Rap was breaking down, coming to pieces with his own grief at leaving his family. He was afraid. Only Totally could help him.

Phoenix sat on her own. She hit her head again to try to empty it of some of the things she had seen and would like to forget. Her grandfather, lying on a bed of crumbled fire-butterflies. . . . The truck jolted again as the electric light blinked and glowed brighter for a moment. Then it went out. Their space was filled in with absolute darkness in an instant. Rap cried out.

Someone seemed to return the cry from outside. The truck lurched and jarred, throwing them violently.

Phoenix heard someone fall. She felt the air movement of Angel wings. Another shout came, before an unmistakable roar.

Raptor!

Raptors, outside, their kill-cries from the forest. A shot rang. Another. The roars receded.

The back of the truck flew open. "Out! Everybody! Quickly now!"

In front of the truck, another, smaller car was slewed at an angle. In front of that, a Green Raptor, lying dead in a mess of broken feathers.

"I tried to miss him!" the Adult driver was saying, to anyone who would listen. She was female. And she was disturbed by what had happened.

"It can't be helped," Captain Owen said. "We must move, now!—Don't fly!" he shouted at Gabriel, whose wings were disturbing the foliage all round them.

Phoenix could see, even through the dim light of the cloudy night, that Gabriel was not about to take off. Neither he nor Alice would leave Jay-Jay.

But, "don't fly!" the captain called again. "Stay together, all of you. Keep round them!" he ordered his few troops.

"Keep in! Night vision, now!"

The soldiers donned special goggles, but it was Phoenix who could see more clearly now—she could feel the fear from these soldiers, nearly all female as they were. As heavily armed and as impregnable as every Adult soldier, still these special few felt afraid. But not for themselves. They were afraid for the Ground Agle and the Angels, for the Rodents. And they were afraid for—not of—the Greens roaring from the undergrowth.

Shots were fired, always into the air. Great tongues of fire shriveled the forest growth to harmless cinders, or soldiers hacked with flashing blades. In the midst of the assault on the dangerous forest, the party of Agles and Rodents were escorted through. A massive Green Raptor appeared like a statue in the light of a flame. More shots rang out. The Raptor ran.

Phoenix peered about her. The undergrowth in every direction shook and crackled. Dark green shadows flitted through, one after another lit by the flare of a flamethrower.

Now, Phoenix saw, Jay-Jay was walking unassisted, shoving away his sister and his friend. His face was sweating, his movements jerky and unnatural. An Angel's every movement was always weighed against the sway of the wings, balanced and graceful. But Jay staggered and sloped, slanted, half-crouched or falling away without the counterbalance of his extended back and shoulder muscles. He jerked from one position to the next, gazing out here, then here. Once, with the flare light of a flamethrower blazing, he staggered sideways to what looked like a Green in a bush. It was just a bush, burning.

"Where are we going?" Phoenix was trying to ask.

Nobody answered. But she soon knew. Everywhere led, eventually, to the sea. The forest suddenly gave way to the strip of sand that was the beach.

"Don't move!" Captain Owen ordered.

They had stumbled out onto the edge of the land. The sound of the sea met them, along with its smell. But they couldn't see it.

"Don't move a muscle," said the captain.

They could not see the sea. There should have been boats.

All they could see, in front, to the sides, appearing from the bush behind, Raptors. Nothing but Raptors.

# 68

"Don't move!" Gabriel heard Captain Owen's voice. "Stay right where you are."

Gabriel was trying his hardest to do that. Suddenly surrounded by Raptors, his wings wanted to take over, his instincts, the flight reflex snapping as if to attention. Alice suffered in the same way. But between them, the Angel with no wings, trying to crab-crawl across the sand to get at the Greens. Gabriel and Alice held hard onto Jay-Jay. He, sick and weakened, unable to struggle free of their grip, gnashed and cried, falling to his knees in a bubbling mess of mixed emotions and end-of-tether desperation.

Jay would not survive much longer with no wings, Gabriel knew. But then, bunched between the band of allied Adults, covered in every direction but up by Raptors, none of them looked likely to escape with their lives.

"You Raptors!" Captain Owen was speaking loudly and with authority. "All of you—I want you to clear this place. Do you understand? Go from here, now!"

The young male Greens had never understood a single word of Rodent. And now they were a leaderless rabble, uncertain of what to do or who to follow. They backed away from the sound of the Adult voice booming at them over the noise of their disparate, uncertain clicks. Ruffled as they were, they glanced at one another, Gabriel noticed, all waiting for each other, looking for a new leader.

"Step away," Captain Owen ordered, stepping forward.

Not one Raptor tried to disobey him. They clicked and swayed, looking at Jay-Jay, the killer of their leader Spartan, as Jay flopped forward on the sand. They swaggered as they moved, but every Raptor stepped backwards away from the confident Captain as he advanced among them.

"Go home, please," he said.

The Raptors fell away, dispersing round the captain as if dissolving from the power of his presence.

"You have done well to track us here, but now you must leave."

The Greens were darkening, fading into the background, back into the trees.

"Good," the captain was reassuring them. "Very good. You have achieved much. But now it is time to—"

A scream!

The captain looked round.

Gabriel had been doing nothing but observing, along with almost everyone else, enthralled at Captain Owen's control, his calm authority and his strength of character. Gabriel had been watching the flattening feathers as the Raptors retreated until . . .

Until the scream.

At Gabriel's feet, Jay-Jay cast himself forward, crying out at his nightmare shapes in the shadows. "Murderers!" he screamed. "Filthy scum!"

He was staggering across the sand, shouting and flailing his fists before Gabriel and Alice or any of the soldiers could get to him. He ducked, throwing himself forward. He staggered to his feet, with Angels flying from his shoulders.

"I killed him, that filthy murderer! I got him, Spartan! It was me! Do you hear me, Green scum?"

Now only those closest to him, only Gabriel and Alice could hear him over the roar of the returning Raptors. The Angels tried to lift him from the sand into the safety of the air, but Jay, slippery with sweat, twisted free again.

"Come on then!" he railed at the Raptors. "End this now! Do it now!"

The tongues of fire licked at the overhanging canopy of the forest, with stuttering automatic gunfire ripping through the leaves. But Jay was shaking all over, furious with his fists, head swaying, desperate for a fight, challenging the Raptors. And all the Greens could see now was the killer of their leader. They wanted justice. The old Raptor code, the Rule of Claw, demanded that they exact revenge for Spartan's death.

Gabriel grabbed Jay by the hair. Jay lashed out at him. But Alice managed to grip him by the wrist and they got him off the ground as the Raptors closed in. The Greens were leaping, snapping beaks, appearing and disappearing into the confusion below.

The Angels could not keep hold of Jay-Jay. He was struggling free under them. Guns were firing. Bullets were fizzing through the air.

Gabriel still had a hold of Jay's hair, but Alice, he felt, could not maintain her grip on her brother's arm. He slipped free. The weight dragged Gabriel down and down, into the milling mix of species on the beach.

The Greens leapt. They snapped and fell. Their feathers flew out of the night, expanding, crackling, fading into their fall. But Gabriel was falling after them, with Alice scrabbling at Jay's thrashing limbs.

They fell, all of them.

Alice swooped and gathered her brother's feet just as a huge Green appeared from below, all feathers and beak, his hands grabbing and touching without catching hold.

Gabriel tried to fly under Jay, to better take his weight. As he did, another Raptor rose, thrown upwards by his friends from below, turning in the air as he came. As Gabriel looped under Jay, the Raptor came up feetfirst, talons first, tearing through the air and ripping clean through the taut stretched flying skin of one of Gabriel's wings.

The Raptor slit his wing in two. Gabriel saw it go, the nightmare talon passing clean from one side to the other. There was no pain. Only horror.

He turned. He tumbled. Jay and Alice were spinning with him, all dropping down, spiraling away across the beach. The sand broke their fall. But the Raptors were running, crazed with rage now, bearing down on the three Angels.

Alice went for the air, the only one now able to fly. All Gabriel saw was green, rampaging across the sand at him.

Jay stood, ready. Gabriel was not ready. He would not want the Raptors to end him for nothing, like this, with one torn wing and no hope of a last and final flight.

## 69

Phoenix saw the Green turning a slow somersault, thrown up from the beach. The glint of his extended, super-sharpened talons flashed back in the lick and flicker of a flame.

But through the flamethrower light, a pale wing was shown sliced and the Angels slowly fell, turning and turning in a widening gyre, their frightened faces screaming out unheard over the battle raging on the beach. Phoenix watched them fall. She made to move, but an Adult hand held her back just before she was thumped in the face by heat and light and sound.

An explosion sent them staggering back. Above their heads, forcing Alice out of the air, driving them all into the sands, a firebomb blast like a low sun over the breaking sea. The report, the force of light and heat ripping through the air, broke in waves up the beach, crashing into the trees behind.

"Now stop!" cried a single, huge and able Adult voice, sweeping outwards from the battle's center. "Everyone! Stay exactly where you are!"

But Jay-Jay's voice came back at him. "Let them come! I'm ready! Let them come!"

"Shut him up!" the captain ordered the other Angels.

Two soldiers moved across to help Gabriel and Alice hold Jay down. He was still fighting, shouting out between his sister's fingers as she tried to stop his mouth. He would not be stopped.

The battered Raptors, shaking the shock and sand of the explosion from their feathers, were able to regroup, beginning to grind forward, heads asway, ticking malevolently.

"You Raptors!" the captain was trying to order them. "Stay! You are ordered to stay!"

But now they were not listening to the sound of Adult words or heeding Adult threats. They wanted an end to Jay-Jay, as much as he wanted the end to himself. Forward they swayed, as one, condensing the effect of gathering green towards the epicenter, contracting like the iris of a green eye focused on the middle of the target.

Jay, in the middle, Jay as the epicenter, the focus, stood, shaking off his restraints, turning to face the oncoming Raptors.

Gabriel and Alice could not do a thing. The soldiers could not stop the Raptors now. Even the captain's voice, even his authority had dropped below the level of Green threat ticking like a primed time bomb. No other explosion would blow them all off their feet like the one timed to go up at the end of tick, tick, tick and tick. On they came, advancing, Green.

"Back I say!" yelled the captain, from somewhere too far away.

"Stop them," Phoenix heard Rap saying to Totally. "Oh, stop them."

"Please stop them," Tolly said, as if to Phe.

"Speak to them!" Phe shrieked at her. "Come on!" She took Totally and the shivering Rapacious and bundled them towards the epicenter, towards Jay-Jay and the Angels. "Tell them!" she was shrieking. "Tolly—you tell them! Tell them who their enemy really is! Go on! Rap! You too! You can speak Raptor! Tell them about the Adults—tell them about Captain FitzRoy. He'll kill us all—the Raptors too. Tell them what the priest will do to them in the name of Genome."

And Tolly was flailing wildly, clapping where she could not manage the Raptor-click sound.

"Tell them, Tolly! And you, Rap!" Phoenix pushed him at the Raptors. "Tell them about Genome. Tell them what he's going to do to them—to us all!"

He told them, crazily, jerking out the message, the good-news gospel according to Genome's Holy Ministry, his Trinity of Hate through mother and son and ghostly whole administration of priestly doom, through their love which is not love but twisted and wrong reason.

"It's true!" Phoenix cried at the top and the bottom, at the full stretch of her voice. "Tell them, Tolly, Rap! Tell them the one they're looking for is here!" She shouted, pointing towards the one Adult she trusted, the *only* one she would ever fully trust in her life. She trusted him *with* her life now. She had to. So did they all.

"This is your leader now!" Phoenix called, pointing to the captain. "He is the only hope you—or any of us have! Tell them, Totally! Tell them this Adult, this human being is their only hope of survival!"

"Oh," the Raptors seemed now to say, "he is, is he?"

They seemed to say that, because one amongst them spoke in Rodent-Agle language, using the voice of another Adult.

"Their only hope, is he?" the voice said, as the Green crowd separated and he was standing there, his eyes glinting with grim, malevolent satisfaction.

# 70

Totally clacked out what Phe said, because she was right to tell the Raptors. Tolly and Rap spoke to them as they had been taught in school. Captain Owen was their only hope. But then he was not the only captain there on the beach. The other, the officer of no hope, their nemesis, the bringer of extinction was among them, with his armed guard at his back. They appeared glistening in the broken moonlight and disappearing under a cloud.

"Your only hope stands there?" he said—the other captain, FitzRoy, glimmering in the half light on the beach.

Captain FitzRoy signaled. From every angle, his troops poured, flowing over the beach like a sea of darkened turtle shells, taking up patterned positions on the sands, in the shallow waters, in and between the trees.

"Do not try to get away!" FitzRoy's lone voice took control, with everyone looking for and failing to find a way out. "Genome is love!" he said.

"Yes!" Captain Owen bellowed back at him. "He is love! He is the love of everything that lives and more than that—he is the love of everything..."

"That is blasphemy!"

"No! It is Truth!"

"Captain Owen, you are suspended from duty immediately. I am arresting you for heinous blasphemy and for treason. Your actions are anti to our Holy Ministry. You and your—your misled followers—

will be taken from here and dealt with severely. As will every blasphemous mutation. All wings will be removed before extinction. It is for your own good!"

Totally saw Alice's wings snap to.

"Restrain the mutation! It is for your own good. You will all be dispatched to the Other World. There you will face Genome. You will affront him with your stigmata, the evil of your—"

"No!" Alice screamed. The soldiers had taken hold of her and of Gabriel, with his torn-in-half wing. But Alice was screaming for the other Angel, the wingless one, as he dashed braying up the beach towards Captain FitzRoy. "Jay-Jay! No!"

"Go!" shouted Gabriel over her. "It's time! Go, Jay! Go!"

# 71

And so Jay flew, his bare back working as it would with wings, picturing himself flying forward, pitching swift and sure through the air, sweeping across the beach for one last flight, his final and most glorious scream-swoop—but flying, coming off his feet despite everything stacked against him. And, for a moment, yes, flying like the Angel he was—Jay-Jay, full of flight and fight and beauty and doing the one thing the Angels were designed for.

He met the blast, the bullet-bite, head-on, driving at it every bit as much as it fired forward at him.

Gabriel ducked out of the handholds of the soldiers guarding him. He saw Jay fly, for one last, most sacred of seconds, the Angel in the air like the most perfect of species most perfectly adapted to what he must do.

Jay had to meet the bullet from the blast set off by Captain FitzRoy. That Captain's arm was raised, the flash, the bang, the smoke emitting as if from the officer's hand, the kickback, the drive forward of the lead missile meeting its target.

It killed Jay-Jay on impact. One second he was flying, the moment at the eternal end of that second he was gone. A true Angel! The utmost!

"The Skymost!" Gabriel gasped.

Alice was wailing. "No! Jay-Jay! No!" She ran to the body, her wings flapping wildly across the beach.

A burst of automatic gunfire lit the ripped-through air and a hundred or more Raptors were illuminated in attitudes of panic and fear and raw aggression.

With the first shot, with Jay-Jay's fall, with Alice's frantic Angel burst across the beach, Gabriel after her, with the gunfire exploding and everyone suddenly on the move and the war-cry Raptors raging and the soldiers fighting forward and back with Captains on either side shouting orders to troops unable to hear—it was suddenly a battle, full-scale, all out and utterly chaotic.

Gabriel tried to fly to Alice, forgetting how badly his wing was damaged. He had to run, covering her as she fell on her dead brother.

"He's gone!" he could hear her screams under him. Alice was almost out of her mind, scrambling over her brother's body. "Jay-Jay! Please! Jay!"

Gabriel, trying to get her up, saw Alice's face in the light of a sudden flare that looped glowing red over the beach battle. Alice's features, scarlet and black, a demonized Angel face, looked at him with wild eyes.

"Kill me," she said, too calmly, just before a hard-bodied Adult hefted her into the sand.

## 72

Captain Robert FitzRoy fired, hit and finished the ruined Angel in a single shot.

Phoenix watched it happen. She seemed to see the bullet fly, hit home. All was chaos in an instant as the factions of the Adults turned on each other with the enraged Raptors going for everyone and everything, not knowing who or what not to attack.

She ran. Somewhere here, her sister and Rap and the other two Angels. But she could see nothing, until a red flare bloodied the whole scene and Adults shot Adults and Raptors, and Raptors tore Raptors and Adults. There was no way out.

"Here!" Phoenix heard a voice shouting close by. "Follow me! Now!"

Captain Owen, wearing his night vision goggles, was gathering them to him, his friends, his allies. Totally and Rap were there already, clinging to one another. Gabriel dragged at Alice. She, wild-eyed, would not leave without her brother. "Kill me now! Why don't they?"

From one side, from the other, Green Raptors attacked. Captain Owen's guard stunned them with electrical charges. Everywhere else, Raptors fell shot, dead and dying, killed by FitzRoy, with his troops following orders, destroying the enemies of Genome, which meant everyone and everything.

In the red and violent flare light, Phoenix saw Captain FitzRoy shouting and pointing. A hundred, a thousand lethal weapons homed in on them.

Alice's voice still sounded through. "Kill me now! You have to!"

Phoenix turned as Captain Owen's hard hand landed across Alice's face. The Angel fell stunned from her hysterics to the ground.

Captain Owen and Gabriel dragged Alice across the sand to where there were boats waiting. Two boats, one tied to the other.

A shot whistled by. One of Captain Owen's troops fell. The captain faltered, for a moment. In that moment, a Green Raptor leapt into the center of their group, lashing out with his huge lizard legs. Rap Rodent was sent spinning, throwing out a spatter of flying blood.

A stun gun felled the Raptor. Phoenix ran with Totally to collect Rap where he squirmed in pain on the slope of the beach. "I didn't want to come!" he was saying. "I didn't want to come here."

Together, Tolly and Phe dragged the injured Rodent to the water's edge. Captain Owen was there, throwing everyone aboard the biggest of the two boats. The smaller one was full of boxes and bottles, supplies and medicines. "Push them off!" he ordered his few remaining guards. Phoenix caught him by the arm, as two bullets whined by, one each, two close misses. Captain FitzRoy was bellowing in the background. "Hold fire! Hold fire! I want him alive!"

The shouting stopped. The sound of Raptors started up.

Phoenix was eye to eye with Captain Owen. "Come with us," she said. His eyes were deep. It was almost impossible to read them. "Please."

He shoved the boats from the beach, all the while looking at her. Phoenix felt the swell of the sea under her. They were floating away. "The motor!" she heard Captain Owen calling. "Start the motor!"

Phe was standing at one end of the boat. She looked. There, fixed to that end, an engine and some kind of steering stick. She looked up. Captain Owen was standing in the shallow water. He lifted his hand, as if to wave good-bye, when the FitzRoy soldiers fell on him and he was hefted sideways, falling into the water.

Everyone was splashing in the surf. Phoenix looked to the boat engine, pulling at the starter string. It spluttered and stopped. The others in the boat cried out at her. She looked up once more. The sea was Green, raging with Raptors. Captain Owen was being dragged away. Soldiers were firing at the boat. Raptors were falling, hit. The water was turning red.

Phoenix dragged at the motor again, again. It sputtered, died. She pulled. A great Green leapt from the sea onto their supply boat. He reached forward with his foot and took a grip of the rope tying the two boats together.

Phoenix dragged once more at the starting string. The motor guttered and seemed to catch hold, driving the biggest boat forward to the length of the rope tying it to their supplies. The first boat slowed, dragged almost to a halt, tautening the rope between the two.

Shots were rattling over. As the rope tightened, the Raptor dragging at it fell back, shot, his talons slicing straight through.

The rope was cut and the first boat freed to drive out to sea at speed, leaving behind their supplies and their medicines, leaving behind Captain Owen at the mercy of Captain FitzRoy on a beach foaming with Green rage and red blood and Jay-Jay, dead, lying face down in the sand.

# 73

The steering stick at the back of the boat seemed to work the wrong way about. To turn right, the stick was pulled to the left, and vice versa. But Phoenix, holding tight, soon had it fixed dead center, with the front of the boat pointing away, away, out to sea.

Behind them, the roars and rattling shots, the flame flares, disappearing. They were leaving ASP Island. No Agle or Rodent had ever done such a thing. Even the Angels only ever skimmed along the strand of the sandy beaches. There were too many massive seabirds and flying sea-lizards over the water, too many multi-toothed stripy zebra-sharks and seatiger-sharks in among the waves.

"We'll get help!" Phoenix was shouting out loud, as if she was calling to the Agles and the Rodents left behind. "We'll find others to help us!" she was calling, without knowing who she was supposed to be telling. She was so confused and afraid. Jay-Jay was gone, forever. Phoenix did not know what other injuries the rest of them were carrying away, out to sea, where nothing was known. And now they had no supplies or—or anything. But all she could do was keep the boat pointed towards the unknown, as the known was too hostile to survive. They had only this one slim chance left.

As they moved away from their home, with the motor of the boat churning away behind, the farther-out, deeper sea started to dip and rise. The cloudier sea-skies hung black over the dark vacancy of the ocean. The land and the battle-screams of war were lost in the hills and valleys of the growing waves. Only the drone of the engine sounded unlike wind and water.

Phoenix had stopped shouting. Her cries into the night had given over to the voice in her head. The move from speaking or shouting to thinking had not been a conscious one. For some time she had believed herself to be talking when suddenly she came to, to find herself as silent as everyone else in the boat.

Even Rap had quieted, sinking into the dipping, diving darkness. He had been weeping hysterically, in pain, crying for his family.

Gabriel, who was also injured, with the vicious tear in the skin down the center of his wing, said nothing. Alice was unconscious.

Totally had stretched out several times from farther down to touch Phe's hand with her own. It was the first of these touches that had brought Phoenix back from the call-cries in her own head, when the motor drone had seemed to click back on and the warm wind started blowing back through Phe's hair with the motion of the boat.

"We'll get help," Phe said, into the darkness, if only to test her speaking voice. She felt herself—her arms, her legs—to be sure she was not carrying any injuries.

Hours passed. Or minutes. The unchanging engine elongated every inseparable moment. Breathing was like counting to infinity. The night, impenetrable. Darkness was in the air, it was upon and in the sea. There was no difference. For hours or minutes, for ages or for no time at all, they slipped through the crease between air-dark and water-dark, skimming between as if through thick black sheets.

Phoenix began to long for the interminable string of elongated moments to bore her, to feel too stable, to find her feet fixed to the firm pavement land of her city home. How often she had wished to escape. And now, almost as soon as she had, she wished herself back, to feel solid things around her. She wanted school, her friends. She wanted her mother. She wanted Grandfather.

Why, she asked herself, when she was wishing herself away, wishing wings on her back, did she never envisage what it would be like not to have her home round her? How had she become so dissatisfied?

"Where are we going?" she heard Rap's frightened voice coming out of the darkness.

Phoenix felt somehow surprised that voices would still work out here. "We're going to get help," she said, without much conviction.

"Are you all right, Rap?" she asked, wanting to keep sounds going, to break time off in chunks from the eternal drone.

He did not answer. He let out a cough. He sniffed. Some time after, Phoenix felt Totally sliding closer. "He's bleeding," she said. "He doesn't know how badly." She slid away again.

Phoenix wanted Gabriel near her. He wasn't. He was sitting over Alice, with his wings covering her. It was too impenetrably dark to see him, but Phe could feel his care, the covering love of his extended wings. But one of his wings had been spoiled, slashed in half by a Raptor talon. Phoenix felt ripped apart like that, her feelings torn in two, left hanging uselessly.

The night went on and on across the waves. The sound of the engine began to disappear. It ran on, unchanging, while the ears lost contact with it, picking out instead the smack and splosh of the waves against the prow of the boat.

There was no knowing how far they'd have to travel. None of them knew where they were going or what they might find. But they knew enough about Evolution, the world-wild force of Nature, to know that it would be unfamiliar and strange, beautiful, savage and very, very dangerous.

# STRANGERS IN A STRANGE LAND

# 74

A crash, a metallic wail! The motor was screeching as the boat turned in a tight circle.

Phoenix bounced awake. She had slumped onto the steering arm, shoving it to one side, turning them round and round on what looked like a disk of bubbling sea.

"What is it?" she murmured.

Rap Rodent was hanging half in and half out of the boat with his arms dangling into the water.

"Help me!" Totally was shouting, trying to drag him back. Rap seemed startled, struggling to get into the sea.

Phoenix went to help, but the steering arm flew to one side again, flipping out of her hands. She tried to haul it back. It was snagged.

"Help me!" Tolly said again, more loudly. "His arm's in the water—he's bleeding into the water!"

"Here!" Gabriel was shouting, helping to drag at Rap.

"Don't!" Rap was struggling. "What are you doing? I'm going home! Stop it!"

Then another crash sent them all sprawling. The steering rod came flying out of Phoenix's hands. The engine screamed. Another huge crunch, and the boat rocked from side to side.

Alice stood, suddenly wide awake. She was looking about wildly when the next crash came, knocking her backwards, sending her somersaulting over the side.

"Fly!" Gabriel was shouting down at her. But Alice was in a panic, thrashing at the water with her wings. Circling round her, round them all, huge striped crouching-tiger-sharks, attracted by Rap's blood in the water.

"Get her out!" Gabriel stretched down, taking Alice by her grasping hands. "Help me!"

Rap had fallen back, sitting dazed in the bottom of the boat, while Totally picked up a long heavy stake from the side and thrust it out into the water by Alice. A great saber-toothed tiger-shark champed down on the flat end of the stick, showing its furry striped head. Phoenix could see its eye staring up at Totally as it thrashed and tore. The end came off the stick.

Phoenix let go of the steering rod and ran to help, grabbing the other long wooden, flat-ended pole from the other side of the boat. A tiger-shark leapt from the water next to the wailing Alice. Gabriel was heaving-to to try and drag her out.

"Get hold!" Phoenix was screaming.

Everyone shouted at everyone else.

The tiger-sharks closed in, more and more of them, circling, making runs towards the boat. They were huge, with massive clamping mouths and orange and black-striped bodies. Gabriel and Totally pulled Alice to the side of the boat. They dragged at her. A shark's great tiger-shark face appeared. Phoenix whacked it in the eye with the pole.

Alice's soaked wings were opened across the surface of the sea. "I'm too heavy!"

But Gabriel stretched down farther and dragged up on her wings. Up she came, with a sucking sound from the surface of the sea. Alice was scrambling into the boat and Gabriel was pulling on her with his ripped wing still slowly bleeding.

Phoenix was hauling back her wooden stake when the saber teeth of a tiger-shark bit down on it and tried to drag her over the side. She let go of the wooden pole. All round the boat, a mass, a pack of tigers. Then, from farther out, the base-boom of a lion roar. In they came, these even bigger predators, massively thick-maned, a pride of sea-lions on the attack, tearing at the tiger-sharks. They thrashed and turned in the water, rolling over and over to tear off lumps of tiger-shark meat. The sea turned red in bubbling patches all round the boat.

Vampire birds came swooping in to sip at the darkest patches. More roaring lions homed in on the feast and the spreading red brought in more vampires.

The boat was knocked and pummeled as the feeding frenzy stepped up and up. Phoenix tried to hold on to the steering pole but it was thrashing from side to side too wildly. She had to hold on to the side, like everyone else, while the boat bumped and rollicked and felt as if it would be broken into pieces.

Great squirming, rolling and turning bodies frothed the red sea to pink bubbles. Tentacles and flashing fins appeared, vanished. The turmoil waters extended as far as the horizon in every direction. The little boat bobbled on the surface, as if sailing over an ocean of broken rocks.

The motor attached to the back of the boat began to shriek, as if something had done it great harm. Smoke started to pour from it. A monstrously toothed head reared out of the red waves to bite on the metal, to twist and tear it away. Both huge motor-eating head and the engine itself disappeared in a last blowing bubble-froth of smoke and blood.

# 75

Then it was all over. The sea settled round them, smoothing off, growing calm. Here and there, certain dislocated body parts floated. Seagles came and swooped in for their share, clearing up. They took the odd few languid pecks at those sheltering under arms and under wings in the boat. But the pickings left in the sea were too rich to bother with living things.

Phoenix looked over the side. As she did, a dozen knives flew out past her head. "Down!" she yelled.

Flying swordfish stabbed out of the surface, lancing seagles, falling back with them. Every falling seagle formed a little island of frenzied swordfish. For a while, the air whistled with living missiles. And then all was still once again. Everyone in the boat sat stunned, waiting for whatever might come up or down at them next.

Rap started wailing. "I'm too hot! I'm burning up!" He was trying to get back into the cool of the seawater.

Phoenix and Totally held him on the bottom of the boat while Gabriel, with one torn wing flapping and gently bleeding, dipped bits of torn fabric into the water to douse Rap down.

Alice sat dazed, looking to the horizon in every direction. "What are we *doing* here?" she kept saying.

They had Rap lying on the rough tarpaulin cover for the boat that had been thrown into the bottom. He was still bleeding profusely from two very deep cuts.

"He needs to be stitched," Totally said. "He needs medication."

"What are we *doing* here?" Alice said, yet again.

The sun was climbing quickly. Phoenix caught a glimpse of sunshine reflected from the sea between the falling flaps of Gabriel's ripped wing.

He, holding up the wing, looked at it, then at Phoenix. His face was even paler than usual, his lips quivering as he stumbled over what he wanted to say.

"What are we *doing* here?" Alice seemed to say for him.

"What *are* we doing here?" Gabriel asked Phoenix.

She could not answer.

# 76

The sun went nuclear white. Everywhere they looked, the colors bleached from their eyes.

Gabriel watched Phoenix and Totally binding Rap's injuries. He laid his damaged wing on one of the flat sitting surfaces in the boat, carefully positioning together the membranes of skin. The tear had bled steadily for a while, before the healing process had begun. It would heal quickly, but would not be strong enough for flight for weeks yet, maybe months. The danger was that the two flaps would not knit together but heal separately, leaving his wing permanently dysfunctional. He had to position the pieces neatly together, to constantly hold his wing there, checking it every few minutes.

He would have liked Alice to help him. Gabriel would have loved that. She didn't. She stayed away, sitting in the front of the boat looking out, always, or else up into the sky. Gabriel watched her flexing her wings.

Then the helicopters came. "Stay!" Gabriel called to Alice, as she snapped into her take-off position at the first sound of the stuttering flying machines. Gabriel's own wings had flexed instinctually, the damaged skin flaps flinging apart.

Rap, still lying on the blue tarpaulin with his bound but still viciously open wounds, started awake at the sound from the sky. "Water!" he exclaimed. "They've got all the water!"

Gabriel just managed to catch hold of Alice before she could take to the air.

"They'll catch you," he said. "Stay!"

"Cover the boat!" Phoenix was shouting. "Get the cover. Spread it out."

They picked Rap up, and Gabriel and Alice dragged the tarpaulin from under him and spread it out over the boat. They all climbed under.

Rap was crying out. Under the cover, his voice filled up the space with panic and dread. "Water! Water!"

"Make him stop!" Alice was demanding of Gabriel.

"You stop!" Phoenix shouted at her.

Together, but nobody really together, they crouched or lay under the heavy blue cover. Outside, overhead, the Adults clattered by, searching for them.

"They've got all the water!" Rap shouted. "They've got it all! There's none anywhere else! There is no water anywhere else!"

Nobody could look at anybody else, because they had to listen to what Rap was shouting out, and they all knew he was right.

# 77

Totally knew they'd not be able to hold it together with Rap growing ever more hysterical and delirious. The heat was building under their thick canvas cover. There was no air movement with the sun bearing down on the sea blue fabric.

"We'll get some water for you," she was whispering to Rap. "We'll get water, soon."

But the only water for miles was saline, heavy, thirst-making seawater, thick with weed particles and plankton. Between the chopping blades searching for them in the sky, they could occasionally hear the sea sloshing where something out there turned or leapt. The ocean was a living thing, souplike and laced with swimming creatures, of all sizes. The cloths they had wet to dab Rap's face dried to a crisp with thousands of minute animal bodies dying of the dryness.

"Shut him up!" Alice cried from the other side of the boat. "Can't you shut him up for a little while?"

Totally touched Rap's face. He was soaked, with his skin excreting something like seawater, thick and oily. All his moisture was leaking away.

"Who's there?" Rap was saying, looking up at nothing, speaking as if to the Adults above. "Who is it?"

"It's me," Totally said. "It's only me. Rap, you'll be fine. Hold on."

"I'm cold," he said.

Totally touched his arms, his chest. His drenched flesh shivered. "I'm so cold. Why am I so cold?"

"Make him stop!" Alice was wailing.

"You stop!" Phoenix shouted at her.

Totally had to sit and listen to them. Through it all, the Adults crossed and recrossed the sky, the sound of their machines chopping the air, cutting the voices under the boat cover into spiteful little pieces.

"Who's there?" Rap was asking again. His eyes, in the shadows, were popping wide apart. "Who is it?"

"It's me." Totally crouched by his side. She put her face on his. All his moisture was running away, as salt as the sea. But the sea couldn't replace it. Totally could do nothing but touch him. "It's me, Totally," she whispered close, under the tarpaulin, under the skittering skies. "Rap, it's your friend, Tolly," she confided, under the anger and the fear and the aggression in the boat with them on seasick waves under the endless sun. "Rap, it's me, Tolly. Do you understand?"

He nodded. His eyes calmed as he turned slightly, looking at her. "Tolly? It's you. I thought it was someone coming to get me. Tolly, can you hear me?"

"Yes, Rap, I can hear you."

"Why have you brought me here? It's so cold!"

"It's not, Rap. It's hot. You're too hot, that's all. It's confusing you. We'll be away from here soon, don't worry."

"How is it so cold?" he said, staring into her. "I didn't know what it was, cold—till now. Tolly, are you my friend?"

"Yes, Rap. Of course I am."

"Then why? Why do this? Why would you? Listen, I can hear them. It's them! They're coming to get me."

"Yes. It's them. They're looking for us."

"The water! They've got it all!"

Suddenly, Rap was struggling to get up.

"No, Rap. No!"

"Why are you doing this? They're here. I've got to go. Get out of the—let me go!" And he was falling from the wooden strut on which he'd been positioned, fighting to get up, turning over and lashing out.

"Stop!" Totally couldn't hold him. "Help me! Help! Hold him down—Rap!"

But Rap was screaming to be let go. He was hysterical, running with sweat. It took all four of the others to hold him down. He fought them, reopening his worst wounds. Their hands were bloodied.

"Knock him out!" Alice was screaming over Rap's cries. "He'll kill us all!"

Totally fell on top of Rap, holding him down with her body. Beneath her, his struggles began to subside. His bubbling breath started to slow slightly. Totally felt the others take their wet hands away.

They all listened. It was silent. No helicopters, no sound of the sea lapping. Nothing. Totally could hardly bear to lift her body up to look at Rap. When she did, she was relieved to find him looking back at her. But he was staring too hard, breathing too shallowly, not shivering continuously now, but shuddering all over, violently, again and again.

## 78

"They've gone," Alice was saying. "Get this thing off us. I can't breathe under here."

"Wait!" Totally turned to say.

Phoenix stopped, but the others were already dragging at the blue tarpaulin, letting in the air. Letting in the sunlight. The bare heat hit Rap in the face.

"Cover him," Totally was shouting at them. "Leave it here. Cover Rap."

Phoenix dragged the tarpaulin away from Alice.

"Start the engine!" Alice was throwing out orders to everyone.

"What engine?" Phoenix had to say. "There is no engine. We lost it."

"What?" Alice's wings were beating.

Rap turned his face slightly towards the source of the air movement. Phoenix and Totally noticed how it revived him a tiny bit, allowing him to focus and listen.

"What?" said Alice. "No engine? What did you do?"

"Me?" Phoenix said, confronting her. "A shark took it. What was I supposed to do?"

"Oh," Alice thumped against the side of the boat. "Oh that's just great!"

"Keep it," Gabriel was trying to pacify her. "It wasn't Phe's fault."

"No," Alice was flapping, lifting off in anger, "it never is, is it! Like—like Ember wasn't her fault either—that wasn't her fault either, was it!"

# 79

Gabriel kept looking at Phoenix, trying to help her. He wanted to tell her it wasn't her fault, no matter what Alice said, but she wouldn't look at him. She was, she said, trying to keep a lookout on the horizon, for land, for Adult search parties. But Gabriel could see her hair moving, picking up the animosity out of the hot sea air. He was trying to calm Alice down, to keep her down. If she flew now, she'd almost certainly be spotted and picked off by the helicopters.

"Help me, please?" he asked Alice again, still trying to keep his weeping wing in one piece. "Alice, I need you. I need you here."

Alice, like Phoenix, was constantly looking away. She stared up at the sky, taking in the great free blue dome of above, while the boat in the sea below fell still and too silent.

Sounds carried too easily across the empty spaces between them. Gabriel could hear Totally whispering reassurances to Rap. He could hear the soft rustle and the air-snap of Alice's wings as she barely resisted the urge to take flight again.

"It's all right, Alice," Gabriel was saying, trying to steady his voice. "Alice, don't go. It's all right. It's all right." He reached out to touch her.

She shoved him away again. "Don't!" she said.

"Alice," he said, softly, "it's all right."

She went for him. "It's not all right! Nothing's all right! It's not!"

"Come on," said Gabriel, taking hold of her, trying to soak up some of her pain. "Alice, it's *me*. I'm your friend."

"Friend? There aren't any friends here! You're all—I hate you all—don't! Let go of me!"

"No—Alice, no! Come on—let it out. This is about Jay-Jay. I know it is."

"Of course it is! Of course it's about Jay-Jay. He's dead! Everything's about him—because he's dead and so will we be soon. All of us! Look at this—look at us! We're never getting away now, never! We're all going to die here, right here, in this horrible, horrible, horrible place!"

Alice was crying, thumping against Gabriel's shoulder. He tried to exchange a glance with Phoenix, but she still would not look at him.

Neither would Totally. She was looking down at Rap. And Rap was looking up, steadily, at nothing.

# 80

The breeze came back up as the sun dipped and started to fall closer to the ocean. On the boat, everyone sat listening to the sun—as if, at the backs of their minds, they could hear it blazing. Nuclear reaction, fusion was going on above them and they suffered it in silence. Or crouched out of it under the tarpaulin, trying to listen for Rap's breathing, trying, at the same time, to pretend not to notice that they couldn't hear it.

"I can't do this!" Alice was suddenly decrying. She had her wings and was instantly up on them, hovering over the boat. Directly over Gabriel, who sat nursing his own badly damaged wing. This time he didn't jump up to try to bring her down. Phoenix saw that he just did not have the energy left with which to care that much.

"I can't just sit and wait!" Alice was shouting down, at Gabriel in particular but at them all in general. "The helicopters have gone, they've given up. I can't just sit here—how can I, when I can fly?"

Gabriel nodded up at her, momentarily. He went back to looking down at his splayed wing, placing the separated sides together.

"You wouldn't sit there, if you could still fly!" Alice was raging at him. "Don't try to tell me that!"

"I'm not," Gabriel said, quietly, with a slight, sorrowful slant of his head.

"Then don't try to stop me!"

"I'm not," he said again, just as sadly.

"Nor any of you!" she cried. She stared at Totally, at Phoenix. At Phoenix, for the longest time.

Then, with a few flaps of her magnificent and pristine wings, she was on high, not much more than a speck against the nuclear blue white arch of the sky. Gabriel, Phoenix noted, would not, *could* not look up at her. He tended his wing carefully. Phoenix looked at him as Alice turned and tumbled with no helicopters coming for her, outflying the screeching seagles, looping and dropping almost onto the sea's surface, skimming over it faster than a flying swordfish, as if to smash into the side of the boat. She pulled up short, on the side where Gabriel sat. Alice stopped in an instant, rising into an air-standing position.

"I can see for miles," she said, as if to Gabriel. But Phoenix well knew that Gabriel would not need to be told that. He was the original Arch Angel, the Archetype, by far the best flier, with unparalleled, precision, long-and-short distance eyesight.

"There's nothing," Alice was saying. "No land. Nothing. We're stuck here—*you're* stuck here," she corrected herself. "I can go, find out. I'll find land. I'll come back."

"Yeah," said Gabriel, without looking up.

"I can't stay here," Alice said. "I just can't."

She waited. Alice, Phoenix could see, wanted Gabriel's approval, badly. But he could not fly. If Alice found out which way to go, how *could* they go that way? Even the rowing sticks they'd started out with had had the ends bitten off by crouching tiger-sharks.

"I'm going," she said. She waited again.

Gabriel pushed the damaged flaps of his wing closer together. "'Kay," he said.

Through her hair, or more through her every sense perception, Phoenix could feel Gabriel's reluctance to say good-bye. He felt, she felt, that saying it would be somehow allowing it to happen. Good-bye would be like saying go, because you can, and I can't. Go, without me. Gabriel could not do it.

Phoenix watched him, feeling his pain with him. Her heart was breaking, along with his. She would not see him like this, if she could help it, even had it meant saying good-bye to him herself. That, she would have done because he would have to go with Alice, if only he could. And Phoenix would have preferred that to this.

Alice lingered another few moments in hope. Then she turned and stepped through the air, tilting her body. Her wings held her parallel to the horizon for another moment. Then she flapped away, slowly at first, then more and more quickly, gaining height as she went. She was following the sun, looking to prolong the day, pursuing the evening light over the surface of the water. Then she was gone.

Phoenix wanted to go to Gabriel. But he did not want her to. That much she knew, without bothering to feel it through her hair. She knew he did not want her, not now, especially.

# 81

Darkness did not come. The sun went down and the light dipped for a while before a fish jumped out of the sea. It emerged in a burst, a shower of falling, liquid light.

Phoenix was so thirsty it was difficult to resist the urge to drink the sea. She had been looking at it for hours, spying on the sun through its reflection, dreaming of a long, long cool drink of clear water, some fresh, juice-dripping fruit and her bed at home.

As the tip of the sun's nuclear eye dipped below the horizon, as darkness was about to come, the fish jumped. The sea lit up.

"Did you see that?" Gabriel was asking Phoenix. "Did you see the light?"

A scatter of small fry, a shoal of baby fish leapt like sparks. The water glowed and flared in splashes with phosphorescence, as small creatures swam and leapt and drifted. Suddenly, all those on the boat, with one exception, could see everything that moved around them. Tiny, microscopic algae glowed with iridescent blues and yellows, reds and greens. With the sun gone from the sky, the temperature dropped slightly and a breeze blew into the faces of the watchers on the boat.

"It's beautiful!" Totally said, looking all round with awe.

The surface of the sea glimmered and glowed everywhere, as the creatures that lived in it came gamboling to the surface as if to celebrate.

"They're swimming in light," Gabriel said, standing next to Phoenix, as was Totally. "It's as if," he said, "they're flying—light-flying, like Angels do. Like we do." His voice was full of regret.

"Gabriel," Phe said, "your wing!"

It was hanging, separated, the torn halves healing singly. "I might never fly again," he said.

Farther out, a furred, multilegged creature came floating to the surface on the currents of light. Its legs were so long it had no control over them. They floated, the fur full of the tiny phosphorescent animals. It looked like a wheel of colored light turning against a background of shimmering rainbows.

Phoenix felt like crying again. The sea scene was so very beautiful, in such stark contrast to her drastic thirst and her emotional condition. Gabriel might never fly again! The beauty of what they were seeing brought it home all the harder, their perilous situation, the tragedy of ending up here like this.

"Rap's gone," Totally suddenly said. She had been feeling what Phoenix felt. And further than that, Phe could sense her Rodent sister's grief moving through not just her hair, but her heart.

"Oh, Tolly," Phe said, turning to her.

"Gone?" Gabriel was saying. "Gone where? How gone? Is he gone?"

Phoenix took her foster sister in her arms and watched while Gabriel stammered for better understanding.

"Hours ago," Totally was whispering. "He's been gone hours. I couldn't say anything." Totally was not weeping. She was whispering, as if this were a secret finally shared.

"You didn't need to say anything," Phoenix said, knowing now the feeling in her heart, the grief she had over and beyond her own had been emanating from her sister.

"Look at this," Totally said, staring out across the soft glimmer light show of the slow ocean. "Just look how lovely it is."

"Rap's gone," Gabriel said again, looking over at the body under the tarpaulin as the Rodent and Ground Agle sisters looked instead to loveliness.

Phoenix wiped away the salt water silently flowing down Totally's face. Her own tears reflected the colored light, as if the ocean were leaking from her eyes.

"If we finish up here," Totally said, still looking out, "I hope it looks like this. It's not so bad," she said, "to be a part of this, forever."

"No," whispered Phoenix. "It's not so bad."

And they stood, the Ground Agle, the Rodent, the Arch Angel with the mutilated wing. Together, they gazed out as a million creatures mixed the phosphor glow of the water into a blazing soup, a living liquid in which Evolution brewed new species from old in a geological moment.

"You can feel the extinction," said Totally. "I can feel it happening—extinction and adaptation. Nothing stays the same."

"The Angels always knew that," Gabriel said.

"The Angels were always right," said Phoenix. She felt Gabriel's gratitude and affection as his arm went round her shoulder. But Phoenix kept hold of Totally, who, Phe felt, was wondering what it would be like to slip into the warm extinction of the lighted sea soup.

"Help me," Tolly said, moving away.

Phoenix and Gabriel watched as she went to Rap. She stood over him for a moment. She looked up at them. "It's not so bad," she said, bending to start to lift him, a single tear falling from her face.

So the three survivors raised Rap's body and rested him on the edge of the boat. Without another word, they lowered him into the still water. The light shone out all round Rap's body as he floated away, sinking gradually, his colors disappearing into the swarm of life that swallowed him gratefully, with slow dignity. He turned in the water and, for a few minutes, appeared to be looking down into the depths of the future.

Then he was gone and all there was, was color and motion, which was life over death, always changing but going on, indefinitely.

# 82

"Land," Totally said.

She hadn't slept all night, watching the luminescent glow of the sea fade as the sun came up on the other side to where it had gone down. Totally looked away from the first glare peeking over the edge of the earth and there it was. For a few moments, she couldn't believe what she was seeing, and she hadn't thought they were drifting that rapidly. But there it was, the edge of an island with the seabirds and the sea reptiles flying, cawing and croaking above it.

"Land!" she cried. "It's land! We've made it! Look. Oh, look!"

Phoenix and Gabriel leapt up under the tarpaulin, struggling out, blinking in the low morning sunlight. They turned. Their expressions changed. Land! A pebbly white shore, with some kind of vegetation growing on a little hill.

Totally watched Phe and Gabriel hugging each other. "I can see things growing. That means water—that means a drink of water."

"We're drifting away!" Phoenix exclaimed. "Come on. We've got to get there."

Gabriel was looking up into the air, looking for Angels, finding none. He looked down into the water. Without a word, he jumped.

"No!" Phoenix was shouting down at him. "There could be anything in there!"

"Throw me the rope!" Gabriel knew nothing about the sea. It was just as much a surprise to him as it was to the others to find out how good he was at swimming. He'd just watched what the flying swordfish had done and copied them. His wings, even with one so badly torn, were like huge flippers when half folded away, half out. He was able to hold onto the rope with his hands and fly through the water. Emerging onto the white shore, he pulled the others close enough for Totally and Phoenix to jump out and help him drag the boat onto dry land.

All at once, they sat down on the shoreline, just to feel the stability under them. But it was too uncomfortable to stay there very long, studded, as it was, this new, somehow leathery country, with hard, clinging shell creatures.

"These are all from the ocean," Totally said, trying, and failing, to pick one off. She looked back into the encrusted land. "The water must come up here."

"It's the tides," Phoenix said.

"Tides?" said Gabriel.

"The sea's in love with the moon," Totally said. "It follows it."

Gabriel laughed. He turned away, as if he was thinking they were trying to make a fool of him. Totally shrugged at Phoenix.

"Come on," said Phe. "Let's go up there. I want to see where those things are growing. I can't tell you how much I want to drink."

Totally and Gabriel followed her up the small hill towards the line of dark, upright vegetation. They were all desperate for water. So far, this island looked as salty as the sea. The shells cracked underfoot. Totally and Phoenix walked on as if along a pavement on their hard-skinned feet, while Gabriel jumped from one flat surface to another, his flier's tender feet suffering over the sharp crack of the shells. "Help me."

Totally stopped and held out her hand to him. Together, they turned and looked up to where Phoenix stood touching shoulder-high, single-stemmed plants.

"They're like," she called back to them, "I don't know. Giant hairs? And they're only growing on the edge of–it looks like some kind of slit in the ground. And the land here, it looks like–hey!"

Totally stopped with Gabriel holding onto her. They watched Phoenix stepping away from the dwarf trees, if that was what they were. "They–they're moving!" she cried out.

And so they could see it, looking up the hillock as the sides started to draw away. The row of plants separated into two as the skin of the hillock slipped back and Phoenix fell into the gap. Totally and Gabriel were brushed farther back as one of the rows of dark plants swept towards them. They stumbled on the shells and fell.

Totally looked up. The hillock had opened and Phoenix was slipping and sliding on what lay beneath.

It was an eye. A giant eye had opened and focused on the sky. Phoenix was sliding down over it, through a pool of salt tears. The land, which had seemed so stable, was rising, rapidly.

The boat slipped, scraping back into the sea, as it came up–a leviathan creature fully encrusted in sparkling shells like wet jewels. Totally and Gabriel found themselves falling into the water near the boat with the thing growing out of the sea like a building, like an apartment block, no, two–now many buildings–like a village of high-rise houses quaking out of the sea. Rivers of water were cascading, splashing from the megamonster's body as it grew and grew, with a tiny Ground Agle bouncing out of its eye and sliding across what must have been its massive face.

Waves of white water washed the Rodent and the Angel, along with their bobbing boat, backwards, away. Phoenix seemed to be rapidly getting smaller as she struggled like a disappearing speck picked up and projected upwards on a torrent of water exploding from where she had slipped on the mountain creature's back.

Totally and Gabriel could make no headway against the current washing them away. They turned in a terrifying whirlpool with their boat, with a thousand other swirling sea animals drifting up from the deep. Totally looked up. She saw Phoenix, like a dot, high in the sky.

# 83

If he could have taken off, Gabriel would have had time to fly up and collect Phoenix. Enough water to overfill a large lake was sent sparkling into the air. All kinds of creatures were flying up in it, dropping down into the splashing sea below. Above the noise of the falling sea there came the sound of some kinds of voices, as the bodies of the various species splattered back.

The huge monster-beast began to sink again, leaving the diverse shapes of other animals flailing, floundering down on a cushion of sea-fall, turning on the swirl of the mix of displaced water and seabed sand and swimming species.

"It's her!" Gabriel heard Totally cry. But he had already seen Phoenix, struggling as if trying to fly, dropping down and disappearing under the torrent from above.

Together, Gabriel and Totally tried to swim over to her. The surface splash and undercurrent of the sea swept them round and round. They lost sight of Phoenix. Something flashed by them in the water. Gabriel saw it; he hoped Totally had not. He wanted to keep calm.

"Did you see that?" Tolly said. "Something touched me on the foot. Look, another!"

Gabriel felt it too, now. Something forced him against the current, holding him in one place. He reached down into the water, expecting to be bitten. Whatever it was holding him shrank away into the deeper water below. He looked up.

"It's Phe!" Totally cried out. "Phe!"

"Tolly!" Phoenix was calling back. "Tolly! Gabriel!"

She seemed to be moving too steadily across the surface, as if gliding. "What is it?" Gabriel called as she sailed up to them, coming to rest gently in the calming waters.

Phoenix spluttered, coughing for breath, trying to speak, but Gabriel couldn't catch what she was saying. The flying sky-hunters came, diving into the sea all round them, bickering and fighting and screeching as they battled for each other's catch. The skies were darkening with so many more sharp-faced, spear-headed birds and beasts flocking into the fray. As they dropped like knives falling they impaled each other, twirling in their stabbed and stabbing death throes in the busy, chaotic waters. Then the flying swordfish came, flinging up at the flying down hunters, hunters hunting and being hunted, mayhem and death everywhere.

"The boat!" Gabriel was trying to shout through the caw-cries and the thrashing of the living-dying ocean. "Where's the boat?"

Nobody could have heard him above the noise, but the boat seemed to respond to his voice, floating very quickly towards the three. In a few moments they were scrambling aboard and hiding under the old blue tarpaulin away from the flying daggers and the reptile teeth on the wing.

"I could hear them!" Phoenix was insisting as they hunkered down. "I couldn't believe it. They were . . ."

"You're all right!" Gabriel found Totally shouting along with him. "Phe! You're all right!"

"I'm all right!" she laughed. "Yes—I am! I don't believe it!"

"You're safe," Gabriel laughed, almost hysterically.

Phoenix shook her head in wonder, but not at what Gabriel had just said. "You wouldn't believe what it was like," she said.

"We thought you were going to be sucked under," said Totally.

"So did I," Phe said. "I thought it was the end, the end of everything—until I heard them. I heard them!"

"Who?" Gabriel asked. "Who did you hear?"

"I don't know. In the water. The Agles in the water."

"Agles?"

"They sounded like—they were laughing, like Agles."

# 84

Phoenix looked up into the now-clear sky and tried to feel good about her narrow escape. But she had swallowed salt water, so much that her thirst had been magnified, throughout her body. She could feel the thirst in her fingers and her toes. It seemed to move through her, affecting her cells like some kind of wild virus. Even breathing was becoming difficult.

They might die here, all of them, with the cruel sun so high over their heads. The sea round them was still, growing ever more salty in the pounding heat. Soon they'd be bleached white, a few broken bones and strips of sodden wood on the floor of the ocean. And still Gabriel scanned the sky, constantly hoping to spot an Angel on the horizon.

"Wouldn't she be back by now," Phoenix had to ask him, in the end, "if she was coming?"

He didn't say anything. He turned away and went and sat under the boat cover in the shade.

Angels' eyes allowed them to see a long, long way. Phoenix tried to imagine how far, when they were floating like specks in the sky. Alice would be able to see around the curve of the world, to distant island countries like other worlds. If she were coming back for them from there, Gabriel would have spotted her, long ago.

She glanced at Gabriel again, watching him still trying to patch together the halves of his torn wing, knowing that he was really trying to patch up whatever might remain of his life.

Totally had insisted that Phoenix had imagined the sound of laughter she'd heard while dropping out of the sky. It must have been, Tolly said, the thing she'd *wanted* to hear. Phoenix had to agree. She did want to hear laughter, if she could, at the end of her days. But Gabriel, as he peered out at nothing from under his cover, holding his wing, looked as if he might never laugh again, however long he lived.

None of them could go on very much longer, anyway. Phoenix, listening out for faraway laughter, heard only the sun. It blazed audibly, buzzing in her ears. The earth moved noisily round the sun. The sun drew it in continuously, loud with effort. The solar system cranked and creaked, its physical laws, its dizzying rotations grinding through Phe's head, just behind her eyes.

When she had thought she was about to perish, her head had redounded with laughter. Now, as the sun drew her, particle by floating particle, into itself, Phoenix caught again the same sound, snatches of laughter coming to her as if from outside the portals of her ears. As she tried to look up, the light threatened to pluck out her eyes. The world, the universe was thumping, beating at the very limits of Phoenix, trying to get in, to take her to pieces more thoroughly than any Raptor. Phoenix was disintegrating, evaporating and distilling in the high heat.

Then the sun came even closer. Phoenix tried to stand up to it. Phoenix was going to cry out or to join in with laughter of her own, but her lips and her tongue, the sides and roof of her mouth were all welded together.

"I can hear them laughing," she would have said, if only she could speak.

Totally spoke for her. "Can you hear that?" she was saying.

Then came Gabriel, running out from under the thick tarpaulin. "What is it?" he said. "Who is it? Who's there?"

Phoenix turned, spinning like the world around the blaring, blazing sun.

"They're laughing like Agles!" Tolly said. "It's like—like you said, Phe—laughter! Look, the bubbles coming up."

"Bubbling up!" Gabriel said, smiling now.

All round them, out of the sea, the sound erupted in bursting shouts, breaking the sea's surface. Phoenix turned, spinning on the world's axis, listening to the laughter at the end of her life.

"Bubbles of laughter!" Gabriel laughed, fading into the dark distance as the sun sloped quickly away, disappearing into the far corner of Phoenix's brain as everything slipped from her side.

# 85

Rodents never laughed. They swayed, doing a botblag, as they called it. Agles made that sound, when they were amused or happy, the exact sound that burst in fits on the surface of the sea.

"Bubbles of laughter!"

Gabriel was laughing too, as he spoke, as they all looked over the edge of the boat trying to see what might be down there making such a noise.

As they looked, Phoenix went, staggering and crashing to one side. Her legs went from under her and she was down. Totally ran to her. Phe's eyes were disappearing into her head, as if to look at her own brain, leaving only the bare whites showing. Her mouth was flecked with some kind of dense foam, nothing like normal spit.

"She swallowed too much seawater!" Totally cried out. "She needs a drink—she needs a drink!"

Gabriel was next to her. "Now I'm losing Phe too," he was saying, with his whole and damaged wings dangling desperately. "I'm losing everything—everything!"

"We need water!" Totally cried out, as if to someone, to anyone who would give them some. "We need water!" A lump of heavy seaweed thumped into the bottom of the boat at Totally's feet, followed by much laughter. "What's this?" she said, looking up at Gabriel.

What had sounded like laughter turned out to be just that—Agle sounds, amusement, fun, joy. Totally dashed to the side of the boat over which Gabriel was pointing. She could have looked over any side. They were everywhere. Less than half in, more than half out of the water, long-faced fishlike beings stood as if on their tails.

The tails flapped back and forth under them, holding them aloft while they laughed.

"Water!" one of them called, dipping into the sea, lobbing another lump of the dense seaweed into the boat.

"Water?" Totally said, looking at the weed, looking back at the happy, long-nosed face grinning at her. "You speak Rodent? You say water?"

"I speak Old Porpoise—so do you!" He laughed, the creature speaking from out of the sea. "We are the Porpoise People!" As he said that, a dozen of them leapt and laughed, splashing into the sea, reappearing, standing on their strong tails, their flipper arms flapping.

"Porpoise People!" Totally said back to them. If she could have smiled, she would.

They leapt at the sound of her voice, laughing, always laughing.

"We need water!" Gabriel said. "You don't seem to understand—water!" At which, more of the heavy deep green seaweed flopped into the bottom of the boat from the Porpoise People's flippers.

"What's so funny?" Gabriel demanded to know. He looked red and angry.

"He's worried about Phoenix," Totally said, pointing down. "My sister."

One of the Porpoises, the one so far doing all the talking, leapt from the surface, diving back in with barely a splash, his horizontal tail slipping into the water behind him, only to reappear in an instant hanging onto the side of the boat. He peered down at

Phoenix, looked up at Totally. "She doesn't look like your sister," he said.

"Look!" Gabriel stepped up to the Porpoise with all the anger of his worry in his face. "She needs water—drinking water! Don't you get it? Not seaweed! Water!"

The Porpoise looked at Totally and laughed. "See those?" he said. He hoisted himself up, so that he was balancing, all of him, on the edge of the boat.

Totally could now see how fishlike he was. But farther down his body, his legs seemed to have been fixed together, with his flat feet flying out from the ends on either side to form the tail flippers. And there were his fingers, all fused together, with four fingernails and one little Agle stump of a thumb stuck to one side.

"Don't look at me," the Porpoise said. "Look at the bladder wrack—yes, there, the seaweed. See the little sacs, the bladders? Tear one off."

Totally did as he said while Gabriel watched with suspicion taking the place of the aggression in his face. "This?" said Tolly, holding up a kind of soft green pulpy bubble.

"That," said the Porpoise. "Now, put it in your mouth."

She glanced at Gabriel. He shook his head slightly. "It'll be salty," he said. "Salt will kill you without fresh water."

"Please," the Porpoise smiled. "What's your name?"

"Totally."

"*Totally*?" he laughed, looking round. "Put it in your mouth, Totally," the Porpoise said. "You'll not die. Go on. Try it." He watched her place the bubble on her tongue. "Now," he said, "bite it."

Totally glanced at Gabriel once more before positioning the bladder between her teeth and champing down, ready to spit it all out. But it flooded her mouth at once, clean, pure, cool, perfect. "Water!" she exclaimed. "It's water—fresh water!" And she was tearing off the bladders from the weed and bursting them and drinking it all down. "Gabriel! It's water—it's—it's . . ."

But by now he was cramming them into his own mouth, drinking and drinking as the hysterically laughing Porpoises bombarded the boat with more and more bladder wrack. "It's real water!" Gabriel cried. "Quick, Tolly. Help me."

Between them, they held Phoenix with her face up, her mouth hanging open. Gabriel bit on one after another water-filled bladders and transferred the cool reviving fluid from his mouth to Phe's, as if he were giving her the kiss of life.

# 86

The kiss soon began to work and Phoenix stirred, coming back to life, blinking at Gabriel as he kissed her.

Phoenix jumped. "What happened? What's happening? Who are—what's going on?" She was looking round at the lined-up row of Porpoise faces. Their laughter was erupting, bubbling into the boat.

"You were taking the ride," the first Porpoise said. "We saw you riding the water jet over Gargantitude."

"I heard you!" Phoenix said. "You were laughing and you were—Gargantitude?"

All the time, Porpoises were falling back with mirth into the sea, only to be replaced immediately by more long, smiling faces. But the first one stayed, doing the talking for them. "Gargantitude," he said. "She's a giant mega-walrus whale. She's great. There's nothing else like her in the world. Did you enjoy the ride?"

"I—I don't know." Phoenix was stumbling, still dizzy and confused. "Ride?"

"Drink some more," Gabriel said, holding onto her.

"Drink?" She was looking about for the water. "Drink what?"

Totally showed her.

"And eat the rest of the bladder," said the first Porpoise. "It has everything in it you need. That means all your food and drink in one go."

"Who are you?" asked Phe. She bit into a bladder. "Hey! This is—it's wonderful! Oh! Look at it all."

"The sea's full of it," said the Porpoise. "My name's Ha-Ha. And this is Ha-Ha-Ha, and this is Ha-Hey, and this is Ho-Ho, and this is—"

"You're all laughter!" Phoenix said.

"Laughter?" The Porpoise laughed. The others made a similar sound back at him. "That's a new word—not a Porpoise word. What's laughter?"

"Are you the Elder?" Totally asked. "Are you the Elder Porpoise, Ha-Ha?"

"I am the Origin, yes. It's a long, long time since I have spoken like this. I thought I'd forgotten this ancient language, but no—it all comes back to me now. Where did you learn such an archaic, dead tongue?"

"This is Rodent language," said Totally. "It's how we speak."

"All the time," Phoenix said.

The Porpoise spoke in laughter and his species laughed back. "You're all Rodents, then?"

"Totally's a Rodent," Phe said. "I'm Phoenix, a Ground Agle, and this is Gabriel. He's an Air Agle."

"Air?" Ha-Ha said, looking at Gabriel with interest. "You can fly?"

Gabriel held up his damaged wing. "Not at the moment," he said.

Ha-Ha turned and said something in Porpoise, at which one of the young ones round him flipped back into the sea. In a moment he was back, throwing some other kind of seaweed into the boat. A tangle of thin white strips.

"Take it," Ha-Ha said. "Gabriel, put it on your wings, along the tear. Let it dry."

"Why?" Gabriel said.

"Come on," Phe said to him. The water coursing through her grateful body and the feeling in her hair allowed her to trust these smiling Porpoise People. The white weed was getting sticky, it was drying out so quickly. Phe and Tolly laid Gabriel's wing out and plastered it together, with the weed blending into the Angel's pale wing skin.

Phoenix sat and ate more bladder wrack. Every bit tasted different, sometimes sweet, sometimes nutty, always delicious. She and Totally shook flippers with the laughing People round the boat.

"Ha-Ha," Phoenix said, "can you help us? Can you get us to land?"

"Land?" he said, surprised. "Why would you want to go on land?"

"Our mother's there," Totally said. "In great danger."

Ha-Ha blinked, slowly. "There is danger everywhere. There are boats—not like this, but big, with weapons. There are harmful species in the world, floating from the land. Not hunters—not like the hungry hunters of the sea. We stay away from weapons. We stay away from species on boats. But you," he said to Phe, "taking the ride on Gargantitude. You're different."

"My mother," Phoenix said, glancing at Tolly, "our mother's waiting for us."

Ha-Ha glanced at both of them. "You live on the land," he said, "but he doesn't."

Phoenix and Totally turned. Behind them, an Angel, startlingly beautiful with full, wide wings, was hovering over the boat. The disturbed air blew into Phe's face as Gabriel rose. All heads, Ground Agle, Rodent, Porpoise moved up with the elevating flier, watching as he tested his newly repaired wing, flapping only pensively at first, then with more and more vigor.

"You should leave it longer," Ha-Ha tried to call up to the Angel.

Gabriel let out a cry, at once all pain and anguish and relief and joy mixed together. His voice bounced off the surface of the sea and he flew, up and up, glorying in the sky and in his born-again freedom. His lithe body was like a fish, silver against the blue, and he flipped and dived and swooped. He was crying. He was laughing. These good Porpoise People had given him back his flight, his life.

"He's not like you," Ha-Ha said to Phoenix.

Still watching Gabriel, she wiped her eyes. Phoenix had never seen Gabriel quite so happy. "No," she said, "he's not like me. No, he isn't."

"But he should have left it longer," Ha-Ha said, as Gabriel tumbled, first in a controlled roll, then in an undignified clatter as his wing broke apart again, and he tipped onto his back in a splat against the flat smack of the sea. In a moment, the other Porpoises were with him, lifting and skimming him back to the boat with more tangles of white weed to effect another repair.

"No," said Ha-Ha, watching Gabriel clambering over the side of the boat, "he's not like you—not like you at all."

## 87

This time, land was as they recognized it. Totally stood on the sandy strip of the beach waving at the Porpoise People. From a distance, for a while, it had been possible to catch a glimpse of great flying things hovering over the other side of the island to which Ha-Ha had brought them. "There is too much danger here," he had said, with his permanent smile tainted by fear. "We cannot go any nearer. Our place is out there, away from the islands, where all we have to run from are the ocean hunters and sea scavengers. We do not feel safe here."

Totally stood and watched until the Porpoise People were out of sight, far from land, where the sun was beginning to set into the sea. The forest, when Tolly turned from the red stain of the sun across the sea, looked dark and forbidding. The shadows of the trees brought night on early inland, with midnight at dusk deep inside the woods under the sun-grabbing canopy.

"You can't fly," Phoenix was retelling Gabriel, "not for three days. Your wing will tear again."

"I know," Gabriel was saying, as if in a sulk. He was folding his wings back into rest position. "I was just stretching."

"Well don't," Phoenix said. "We'll walk. We have to find out what this island's like and who lives here."

Totally was listening to the creatures in the darkening trees as they bickered and started to screech. A shiver ran through her. "We need to do nothing," she said. "It will be dark soon. We have to stay here for the night."

They had dragged their boat half out of the sea onto the sand.

"We have water here," she said. "Seaweed water and food. We won't want to be stumbling through the forest in the dark."

And as if in warning, the sun seemed to dip, glowering at them over the edge of the world.

"Let's get back in the boat," said Totally.

Something rustled in the undergrowth, whistled and then shrieked. Suddenly, the three were running for the cover of their tarpaulin in the boat. The darkness dropped like another blanket over them. Every bush along the edge of the beach cried out as some creature lost its life to another. All round them, extinction. The lesser evolved were giving way to the greater, screaming as Evolution ran wild through the trees and surfaced in the sometimes blood-red shallows of the sea.

In the dark, Totally lay listening to the struggles for survival, the wildly mutating offspring of species turning on and devouring parent and ancestor. She tried to think of her lessons at school, or her teacher trying to tell the Adult soldiers, through his nervousness and growing despair, how geological studies showed that once, before the Legendary Ash's time, it took ages, millions of years to evolve new species. But now it took one hungry generation. The world outside, this new island, was not likely to be anything like the world they'd left, by the night sounds of the extinctions happening all round them right now. Things would be very different here.

"This," she heard Phoenix suddenly say, probably from reading Tolly's feelings, "must have been how it was for Ash and Laura and the other first Agles in the Old Stories. They lived on a beach, like this. It must have been this way for them."

"Scary, you mean," said Gabriel.

"No," Totally listened to Phoenix saying, "not just that. Unknown—with something terrible out there, something they felt but—just something they felt!"

Totally shuddered as she felt the dread emanating from Phoenix, as if Tolly had the sensitive hair of her sister and Phe was suddenly Rodent and very frightened, like Rap had been, wanting only to go home.

# 88

Phoenix leapt out of sleep with thunder in her ears. The rain was driving down, thudding against the tarpaulin. There came another crash as Phe opened her eyes. She felt the motion, the movement of the sea. "Quickly!" she called. "Wake up!"

Phoenix threw aside the tarpaulin. The rain hammered against them. They were drenched in an instant. The wind in Phe's hair felt like the high emotional anger of the world and its weather.

The boat was being carried out to sea by the wild water. "Now!" Phoenix shouted at the other two as they ran back and forth along one side of the boat. She jumped into the shallow water. "Come on!" she called. The sea sloshed into her face, filling her mouth with very, very salty water.

"No!" she shouted up at Gabriel as he started to try to take off. The wind and the rain ditched him into the sea in a moment and soon the three survivors were struggling to bring the boat back to the beach. But the storm currents were too strong for them.

They struggled out of the surf and looked back at the little boat as it dipped and was washed over by a huge wave. That was the last they saw of it. The boat went down.

On land, the multicolored forest wavered in the wind like another ocean. The survivors took one last look out to sea, at each other, before plunging into the shelter of the trees.

Everything changed in a moment. The wind tangled above in the canopy, throwing down leaves and twigs and the ruins of nests. But the air was quite still among the hanging vines and the slippery trunks of trees.

The rain never reached this far down. The glutinous blobs dropping from the canopy overhead were thick with sap and pollen mixed, so that they set almost solid in the hair and the clothes and on the skin, until Phoenix felt she was being set in some kind of jelly.

"This is horrible," she heard Totally saying. "If this stuff sets on us . . ."

Phoenix was glad she stopped there. None of them needed to hear about the insects that would surely come when the sun came out above the forest canopy and the heat rose. They all knew they'd be thick with this stuff, no matter how hard they tried to rub or scrape it away. Soon they were like walking syrup-sticks, so sticky they hardly dared blink for fear that their eyelids might become fixed together.

As they trudged through the low, clinging undergrowth, slithering things slinked away from their feet. Eyes peeped out from the other side of tree trunks, from inside shuddering bushes.

"Look out!" Phoenix jumped as Totally shouted.

A deep red bush speckled with blue had seemed to rise up, dragging its roots from the ground. It launched itself at them, tumbling over the undergrowth with its poisonous leaves breaking and flicking venom all the way.

They jumped out of its path. It trundled by, leaving a trail of dying plant life in its wake. The tree it collided with started to wither and drop its leaves in a few moments.

"We've got to get out of here," Totally kept saying.

Phoenix was behind Gabriel all the way, helping hold down his wings, trying to stick them to his back with the gluey mess she harvested from her hair. Great sticky-buds on tendrils were being released, swinging at them from the branches overhead. Every time one hit home, they were bespattered with more dense, cloying glue. Round their ankles, the low-lying plants oozed. Soon there was no need to hold Gabriel's wings to his back. They were all so sticky, so weighted down and heavy it was getting difficult to walk.

Phoenix was breathing heavily with the effort, as if she'd been running for too long. "It's trying to stop us," she gasped. "The forest's trying to stop us."

"If all the island's like this," Gabriel said. He didn't bother finishing what he was saying. They wouldn't last long here.

"We should go back to the beach," Totally said. She turned. "This way."

Poison-leaf bushes were rolling towards them. Thick, sticky sap bombs were swaying out of the trees. A plant grew green at their feet in seconds and seemed to turn towards them. A mouth opened in its flower face in which needle teeth clicked and gnashed.

"We'll still go back," Phoenix said, stepping round the snapping toothed flower. Another sprouted in front of her. Behind it, another, another. The first one lunged for her leg. All the way back, furious flowers grew, gnashing at the air.

Phoenix turned again. "They're following our trail," she said. "Come on. Keep going."

Behind them, flowers, snapdragons, clipping after them. They ran. The sweet and sickly glue plopped down over their heads. Rows and rows of writhing worm-plants squirted white fluid that stank like dead animals. Right behind them, every quick step, the dragons snapped.

"Keep running!" Phoenix shouted at Gabriel. She shoved him in the back to hurry him along. He had his wings, but Phoenix had her bodily strength and her vitality. With all the good seaweed food in her, she was the strongest of all Agles, the fastest along the ground. Without her there, Gabriel would have fallen behind. Phoenix had no doubt that, once surrounded by snapdragons, that would be the end. But she was strong, stronger by far than Gabriel and Totally. She kept them going, tearing through the forest of glue, her heart beating harder, her legs and arms working like never before.

"We need to find a way out!" Totally was panting, growing desperate by Phe's side.

But Phoenix could run! She could run like this, holding onto Gabriel, taking Tolly by the hand, running on and on, forever if necessary. There was no stopping her. The forest tried to, spitting and dripping, flinging sticks and rushing towards them, but Phe was too strong, too fast. She had never felt like this in her life. She had never known so much about herself as she did now, how powerful she was, and how determined.

"Keep running!" she ordered them. "We don't give up! The forest will give in before we do! I know it will. Believe me! I know it will!"

# 89

Totally believed her sister. She had to. The toothed plants were growing, gnashing faster in their wake, the evil milk white worms squirting. The sticky mess of the hostile forest stank. It reeked to death. The forest was nothing but an organism to kill and to devour, steeped in viscous venom, growing and thriving on decay. Totally had to try to believe that there was a way out of this. They had no means of escape from this island now. She had to hang on to something. And Phoenix was it.

It was getting harder and harder to move. But Phe was running them faster and faster. Totally and Gabriel were gasping, while Phoenix seemed to be dragging strength up from the soles of her feet.

"Keep going!" she was shouting from behind them, shoving both Totally and Gabriel forward. "Run! Run! Do it!"

The more they ran, the farther they penetrated the island's clogged heart, the more the trees, the plants, the worms threw at them. They became caked in glue-like sap and worm spit, covered in dead leaves and sticks and bits of bones from dead, devoured animals. Every step was growing heavier and harder. Totally felt as if her legs were going to give way under her, her heart burst inside.

"It's getting worse!" Gabriel kept trying to call behind, to where Phoenix shoved at his back.

Phe wasn't listening. Totally believed in her, even more. She heard her sister shouting from behind. There was a grim and tough determination in her voice. "Move yourself! Don't think about it! Don't think about it! Just run!"

They just ran.

Somewhere above the canopy, the sun had broken free of the earlier storm clouds. The temperature was rising. The runners thought, first of all, that it was just their increasing body temperatures. Until the humming sound grew too loud.

Then they knew. It was the sun. And with the sun, the insects.

# 90

"Oh no!" Gabriel said, spitting out in front.

"No!" Phoenix, from behind. "No! Don't! Heads down! We don't stop! We never stop!"

*We never stop!* Phe kept saying that to herself. The rasping buzz of the blackening clouds rose to engulf them. Almost immediately, they were covered in winged insects, stung and bitten, with pin-prick legs penetrating their hair, into their clothing and their ears, prying open their eyes.

"Clenched teeth!" Phoenix gritted. "Breathe through clenched teeth."

There was no light. Phe kept a tight hold of Totally and Gabriel, running on into the hell-sound of eardrum buzz. The noise went straight into the brain. They were in a black cloud, like death coming down on them. It felt like it. It looked like it. That was how it sounded. But still Phoenix fought back, struggling through, shouting, crying out. She would not give in. Never!

She'd been through too much. They all had, but she had only just found out about herself, what she was like. She had only just discovered a sense of her own worth. She was not about to give it up to darkness, to the nothingness of insect bite and slow, stinking decay.

Phoenix screamed. So did Totally and Gabriel as they tore through the catching thrash of the low undergrowth, with countless flying creatures gathering over and round and on them.

On they crashed, clutched at by the branches of trees, the spiteful thorns of bushes. It was like running farther into the depths of bad dream-sleep, driving themselves into the middle of the nightmare, with no waking way out.

Phoenix drove herself farther and harder than she'd ever have thought possible. She never knew who or what she was until now. Now she was something, something real and valuable in the dark, thrashing for a way through. There was a way! This way! With Phoenix driving towards it, believing in herself, wanting to live, wanting to live and to one day love as a Ground Agle, glad to be that, profound and beautiful.

She tore through the darkness at the evil heart of the new island, pushing Rodent and Angel before her, one subspecies providing strength, giving its power up in a desperate struggle for survival.

She almost fell. Had she, they'd all be finished. They were three different types, the only hope for the future of their separating species. Phoenix couldn't let go. It would have meant extinction, for them all. She would not give in, even as the darkness bit into her, driving directly into her buzzing ears, up her nose and in her mouth, prickling into her eyes. Nothing could stop her. She was never going to give in—never!

Even as she fell, which she did eventually, dropping over a precipice into another world, she shouted and flailed and fought. Squirming through thin air as the other world came up from the depths to take her, she called out until the moment closed over her head, engulfing them all entirely in a different, freezing darkness.

# 91

The contrast took the breath away. To go from the prickling black heat of a million-million nip-stinging insects to the cold of the underworld, turned the senses inside out, tipping the universe upside down and shaking up everything in it. From every direction, the cold raged at them.

Then Totally suddenly shot out of the surface and the air hit her lungs again and she gasped. Nearby, Gabriel and then Phoenix came popping out, biting bits out of the air. Totally cried out in relief, crying with joy. "It's a river!"

The quick, cold waters were rushing them through the island's forests, with the black mass of angry insects on one side, and a clear vista of transparent air and giant tree trunks on the opposite bank.

"Swim for it!" Totally called to the other two. She turned and started to paddle for the far steep bank. Behind her, Phoenix was calling. Rodents could swim, instinctively, paddling through the deepest waters with their bodies submerged but their sloping noses held high and dry. But Ground Agles were built only for the ground. Totally turned again to help her sister as she struggled against the current.

She needn't have worried. Gabriel was there, flying through the rapids as if riding a westerly wind, his water-supported wing strong enough to act as a fin. Totally watched him collect Phoenix before she turned again for the other side of the river. But Gabriel was flying again, very nearly back in his element, picking up the Ground

Agle and the Rodent too, driving them quickly through the rushing waters.

"You did it, Phe!" Totally had time to call to her sister. "You got us through."

In a few moments they were all three scrambling up the mud of the far bank, slipping back into the water, finding a handhold and foothold, hauling each other out. Now they were soaked and covered in mud, but at least the cloying sap and the insects had all been washed away.

Totally sat shivering on the high riverbank, staring across to the other side. The whole of that half of the island seemed covered in a dense dark cloud of loud and crazed insects. But they stayed where they were, as all kinds of beautiful, many-colored birds patrolled the river itself, picking up and eating any small flying thing that happened to try to cross. The insects seemed to know, to understand that they'd never make it. The river was like a natural border, cutting the island in two.

Phoenix was coughing, still trying to clear her lungs of the river water she'd breathed in.

"Would you look at this?" Gabriel was saying.

Tolly looked over her sloping shoulder. Gabriel was standing with his back to her, staring up and up. The giant trees disappeared into a faraway canopy, way, way up towards the sky. Their great trunks were as big as city buildings, but far more permanent. They had been there for ages upon ages. Their hugely gnarled bark spoke of time passing, of changes occurring in the world. And yet, these trunks looked steadfast, impervious to time and to the wildness of Evolution. This part of the island was dominated by these strident giants, by the flowers that grew in perfumed profusion across the forest floor and climbed some way up, giving the first third or so of the soaring trees the look of a high-rise garden. Humming birds and insect lizards flitted between the blooms. Butterflies glided, like the ones Totally knew from the rat runs but more brightly colored. Here and there, brilliant poison frogs sat in full view, deadly if touched, but so effective at catching flies the pure air looked clear and breathed cleanly and easily.

"Oh," Totally heard Phoenix exclaiming. "Oh, are we in the same place?"

They all looked back across the river at the same time to see the blackened, buzzing, angry wall of insect life.

Turning back again, they had to blink, to look down at themselves and at each other to be sure they could believe that they were really here, together. They were dotted with bites and stings and caked with mud from the riverbank. They were confused and disoriented. But they were smiling, those that could. Totally was swaying with relief. She watched Phoenix and Gabriel start to make the sound they called laughing. Tolly felt their laughter, forcing herself to sway into bot-blag all the more.

"Look at where we are!" Phoenix said, still smiling broadly. She ran from one tree trunk across to the next. Big, brilliantly painted butterflies flapped and sailed off as she went. A yellow and green snake curled away from her, slowly, unthreatened and unthreatening. "Look at these trees! The flowers!"

Gabriel flapped his wings in pleasure. He only just managed to prevent himself from taking off for a flight around the high, high treetops.

"And look!" Phoenix grinned. "This is to eat!" She picked some red and ripe fruit, biting into it. "It's delicious. This place is like—this is made for us. We could live here, easily—easily!"

Totally had to turn away. She gazed back across the river at the thousands of tiny birds picking at the wall of insects. Behind her, she could still hear the other two, the Agles as they celebrated, as if they were certain that they had arrived somewhere safe, somewhere they might one day call home. Totally did not want to spoil their happiness. She kept her back towards them as the tears ran down her face. But then Phoenix was by her, looking at the side of her face. Being a Ground Agle, Phe's supersensitive hair soon let her know what her sister was feeling.

"Oh, Tolly," Phoenix was saying.

"I'm on my own here," Totally said. "I'm all alone now."

"No you're not," Phoenix said, taking hold of her. "I'm here with you."

But Totally could feel that Phe sensed what she meant. "Rap was my only chance," she said. "He was the only hope for the Rodents. At least you're an Agle, and so is Gabriel. At least you two are Agles, together."

# 92

Totally felt alone in the world, maybe the last survivor of her kind. Extinction was staring her in the face now. It was this hurting Tolly so much, the sheer loneliness of leaving nothing of yourself behind when you died, of disappearing forever, to no effect in the world.

It was hard. Too hard to take. And Phoenix could barely stand it either. She held her sister and felt what Totally was feeling. But she too was feeling it, for herself. Gabriel, she saw, was always looking up to and beyond the sky-leaves in the cloud of the canopy to where Alice might still be in flight. That was where Gabriel most wanted to be, and that was what Phoenix wished for him.

The loneliness was overwhelming. They were the three survivors. Of what? And *for* what?

"We're not done yet," Phoenix said. "This isn't it! This place is lovely and we could live here. But I think—I think it belongs to someone, or something else. It's not right to think that any place is your own, because—because it's just not right. Someone else might have more claim to it, someone formed from this forest, someone made for it. We're not Adults," she said, "taking everything we see."

"No," Gabriel turned, "we are not Adults."

"I've felt," Phoenix said, with her antennae hair prickling, "since we landed here, some kind of—I'm not sure what it is. There's some kind of suffering here. Some kind of Agle or Rodent suffering going on. I didn't want to say anything, but we have to find out what's been happening. Because there *is* something," she said, setting off, stepping through the New Forest, feeling beyond what she saw. "There is something here we need to know about, something that will be important to us all, Tolly, Rodent or Agle."

They wandered on, taking in the simple green of the trees and the bushes, the brilliant colors of the flowers and the little creatures. There was nothing here to harm them. "But," said Phoenix, "I can feel something else, something in this place that isn't *of* this place. There's always been peace here, it's in the green of the leaves and the slow comfort of the creatures. See, how nothing's afraid of us?"

"Why should anything be afraid of us?" Gabriel asked. "I've often wondered that back home."

But Phoenix stopped short. The blood drained from her face. "That's one reason why," she said, pointing between the trees. "Because of that." Her hands were shaking.

Totally and Gabriel peered through at what Phoenix was seeing. As they looked, as they too saw it all, the reason to be afraid, the sound started up. Helicopters, flying war machines chopped the perfect peaceful air into frightful chunks. Through the trees, the forest was burnt away. On a great, newly blackened plain they stood, the massive, familiar constructions of incarceration.

"There's always a reason to be afraid," Phoenix said, as the three gazed upon huge, black-barred cages full of tall, dark-skinned Aglelike people, with Adult army helicopters clattering over their heads.

# PART SIX

# WARS AND RUMORS OF WARS

# 93

"Adults!"

Phoenix felt their presence. She had, right from their first step on the island, mistaking the sensation of their proximity for fear of a strange land. Now Totally and Gabriel were ducking in dread behind bushes while Phe stood staring down the length of her own arm at her shaking index finger.

"They've found us!" Gabriel was saying. "How have they found us here?"

"Who have they got in the cages?" Totally asked. "Who have they locked away this time?"

"Agles!" Phoenix said, with certainty. Since her first glimpse, she had remained standing there in full view with her arm and index finger extended, pointing at the Agle-people in the cages.

Now she could see the guards, the fully-armed Adults with their splatter-threat faces glowering as before, their tiny dead eyes. They looked, they felt exactly as before, except for some kind of sign, some insignia on bands around their thick upper arms.

"We've come all this way!" Gabriel was exasperated. "How will we ever be free of them?"

"We never will be!" Totally said. "They, and Genome, are everywhere. All over the world. Genome will never let us go. They're right, the Adults, Genome sees everything. He's everywhere, in all our thoughts. He sees everything. Everywhere we go, Genome will be there. There's no escape from him and his . . ."

"That's not right!" Phoenix shook. "I'm never going to accept that. Genome? What is he? He doesn't exist, if we don't let him. Don't let him in and he can't do anything. He's what the Adults have done, what they do. We mustn't let Genome do it to us! We can fight him! I can fight him! I'm never going to let him into my heart and mind, never! Because I'm what I am without anyone to tell me but me. I know it now! Genome's nothing if you're yourself for yourself and for where you are and for everyone you love. That's what I am! I'm that! Not Genome! Never! He doesn't exist! He never has! And he never will!"

94 And from the bush they came, as if broken free from the cages, running at them with dark faces painted green and orange, with long glistening limbs, wielding ferocious carved sticks. As Phoenix shouted out denying Genome, the bushes broke around them, seeming to explode with dark lithe bodies.

In a moment they were under attack, in another, overwhelmed. Totally just about managed to see Gabriel's extended wings grasped and held before she was taken down. Phe's voice stopped as the sirens started.

Guns were going off, bullets whistling in, clipping through the undergrowth, smacking into the trunks of trees just over their heads.

Totally had lost sight of Phoenix and Gabriel. She felt herself dragged down and pulled along. They tugged at her, pushing her head down again, again, as they forced her to run.

*Genome does not exist,* she had been listening to her sister insisting. Well, now they were under attack again and Genome seemed only too real as the sound of automatic gunfire ripped through the peace and tranquility of the forest.

By her side, a body fell. Others pushed Totally away. She was powerless to resist. Every time she fell, which she did often, strong hands were at her, pulling her up, pushing her on.

They did not stop. The gunfire began to recede at their backs as they ran, heads down, over one of the giant trees felled like a bridge across the river. In a moment, Totally's eyes and ears and nose were refilled with insects as she was shoved into the swarms on the opposite bank of the river. Now, washed clean of sticky tree sap, the bites and the stings were on the skin, scratching and tearing away at her as she fell back through the black, airless, clicking buzzing cloud.

# 95

Now Phoenix did not know what they were fighting. She was on the ground, scrabbling to get the insects out of her mouth, from up her nose, and there were hands slapping at her, dragging her own hands away. Something stank of acid, dizzyingly strong.

As the smell grew even stronger, the insects just seemed to fall away from her and Phoenix found that she could suddenly breathe again. She fell still, lying on the ground as the hands stopped slapping and the buzz in her ears moved several steps into the background. She was able, she found, to open her eyes again.

The dark, painted faces floated over her. She scrambled away. Totally and Gabriel were there with her on the ground in the firelight under a dome of seething angry black insects.

"Don't be afraid now," one frightfully decorated green and orange face mask veered forward to say. His head was framed in firelight. Above the burn of torches, a ceiling seethed, black with insects. No, the insects *were* the ceiling, nothing else over them, round them.

Phoenix crawled backwards to make contact with Totally and Gabriel. "Who are you? What do you want?" Her back was pressed against the other two. They were looking out here and here and here at the camouflage of the bright forest painted onto dark Agle faces, their decorated orange hair in long plaits, each pooled in the heat and smoke, in a house of acrid air in an underworld of maddened insects.

"Take your time," the first face said. "You don't need to be afraid. Not of us."

Phoenix felt Totally and Gabriel huddling harder at her back. "Who are you? Why have you brought us here?"

She glanced around as she said "here." The dome of the insects wavered in torchlight, stiflingly hot and thick with the smell of burnt acids. Dead insects were constantly falling from the living walls and ceiling, dropping like black rain onto the crunching ground or flaring for a moment in the open fire of the torches.

"What is this place?" Phoenix heard Totally asking. "You brought us back across the river."

"Who are you?" Phoenix asked the first face again.

"I am Aspect. Here is my brother, Foresight. We are Bright." He said this from the darkest Agle face Phoenix had ever seen, but with the brightest and saddest of smiles. The contrast of what she saw and what she felt converted inside her into a feeling of warmth and trust. She relaxed and smiled back at the brothers. "You *are* bright," she said. "Yes, you are."

"We are Bright," Aspect said, indicating to his left and right with his carved staff. The Bright lit up, all smiling softly, gently, at the three friends in their midst.

"Are they–'kay?" Gabriel said.

Phoenix could feel he was still afraid, surrounded by very tall and dark Agles with sticks, surrounded still further by the black chaos of the insects.

Phoenix turned to Gabriel. "We don't need to be afraid. They are Agles—Bright Agles."

"We will allow you to," Aspect said, with a twitch of the staff in his right hand, "to gather yourselves. We have startled you."

All round them, the Bright were dispersing, assembling again into groups sitting on the ground among the insect bodies, oblivious to the dying falls and the flickering firelights and the smoke and the terrible smell.

Phoenix watched Aspect and his brother Foresight as they moved a short distance away. The little groups of Bright, all apparently male, sat cross-legged on their carpet of dead insects or tended to the fiery torches, pouring on some kind of oil to be burnt. The Bright were very long, dark-limbed Agles with beautiful white teeth and plaited hair thickly smeared with orange oil. Everything about them was graceful and gentle, while everything about this place, this acid-smoke insect cavern, was brutal and desperate. Phoenix felt more and more the Bright's pain, the cause and source of their sadness.

"What do they want with us?" Gabriel was whispering at Phe's elbow.

Totally was by her too. "What is it, Phe?" she said, looking at the undulations of her Agle sister's scalp. "What do you feel here? This is a terrible place, isn't it? Why have they brought us here?"

"They're suffering," Phoenix said. "This *is* a terrible place, and they're suffering in it, just like we are."

# 96

The others watched as Gabriel went to the wall. His limbs and wings were smeared in the thick orange oil. As he approached the seethe of the insects, the black wall moved away from him. It was like a mirage or a rainbow after a heavy storm, continuously keeping its distance.

"We collect the oil, from the forest," Foresight was saying. "We burn it here, we wear it."

"And the insects can't stand it," Totally said. She and Phe were crouched with Aspect and Foresight as Gabriel went running at the insects, laughing as they, in their hundreds of thousands, fell away from him.

"This is how you stay here," Phoenix said. "You create this space here and live in it."

The two brothers, without their forest-colorful camouflage now, blinked back at them, with slow grace. Every single movement they made was deliberate, smooth and unhurried, and very beautiful. When the Bright walked, it was something to be watched. Their skin was very, very dark and glistening, with stretched, perfect muscles always moving just below the surface. They smiled slowly, carefully. The sadness always showed through. And yes, they were all male. And yes again, they were in pain, every one.

"But you don't belong here," Phoenix said, glancing, grimacing slightly at the ugliness of being surrounded by insects. "You belong in the forest, don't you? I can feel the forest in you."

Aspect and Foresight laughed. Whenever they did, they lit up.

Phoenix could sense that Totally felt it, the breakthrough of the brothers' laughter, the potential they showed for great, for the greatest happiness. It was all there, inside them. The Agle and the Rodent sisters felt it in the Bright brothers and in what was left of their tribe.

"We saw," Phe said, "many like you, many Brights—"

"No," interrupted Aspect, "we are Bright. That is all, always. Bright."

"Many Bright are being held in cages. We saw them. And we saw who was holding them—Adults!"

"Human Beings," Totally remembered.

Across the other side, the Bright were holding out and marveling at Gabriel's wings. He, soaking up their admiration, smiled very nearly as broadly as they did.

"They call themselves Human Beings," Phoenix said. "But we call them Adults. They are an army, a fighting force for Genome."

"The Army of Genome's Republic," said Aspect.

Phoenix and Totally looked at each other. "That's . . ." said Totally, hesitating.

"That's a different army," said Phe, "the one they were always afraid of. But they're the same! They're all Adults—we've seen them! They're exactly the same!"

"The same?" the brothers asked, trying to understand.

Phoenix and Totally were trying too. "We have come from across the sea to escape from the Adults. Adults—the same as the Beings here. They look the same, they carry the same weapons."

"They build cages—"

"To lock the Bright away!"

"To lock us all away," said Phoenix. "They do the same there as they do here—they burn the forest, they erect their metal huts, they drive their machines through, they fire weapons and they lock up anyone not like they are."

"Yes," breathed Aspect, "they have locked the Bright away. That is why we are here. We have to hide, those of us left out of the cages. I think—we think they will kill us all."

Phoenix and Totally nodded, reluctantly. They could not help themselves. The Adults would surely kill all the Bright, as they would every other species they had so far incarcerated or enslaved.

# 97

"Yes," Aspect breathed again, seeing the knowing expressions on their faces. "They have locked up our mother and our father," he glanced at his brother, then around at the other Bright as they gathered, still admiring Gabriel's wings. "They have put our mothers and fathers in cages—our sisters, brothers too. First of all, when they brought in their machines and burnt the forest away—before the cages, they knelt us down and told us to believe."

"They knelt you down," Phoenix said, "and their priest—"

"Their parson-person," said Foresight.

"Priest, parson-person—he told you to believe in Genome and bow down and worship him."

"With our faces to their false floors," said Aspect, "and our ears full of their furious writings from the black book about Genome making the world for Human Beings, for Adults, in six days and giving it to them, making them in his image and giving them these words for their book that makes everything else a lie. That's what they do—they make everything else a lie. They have these words—abomination!"

"Stigma," Phoenix whispered, just out of earshot of Gabriel.

"Blasphemy," said Totally.

"All these things make lies and terrors of us," Aspect said. He turned to Phoenix. "When we heard you speak—you'll never let Genome into your heart, he does not exist! We knew then. They'd want to kill you too, the Beings."

"They've already killed our grandfather," Phoenix said. "They murdered our Elder Elders. They call it 'cleansing'—that's what they say."

"That's how they think." Aspect nodded. "They think they're Genome, or Genome's them. They were created in his image—that makes them the creators of the world. But really, they're the destroyers. Their book promises them another life after this one, in another place—a life that goes on forever—eternal life."

"It doesn't make any sense," Totally said. "Eternal life? It's like some kind of horror—it would be pointless, hopeless. It would be unbearable, because it would never, ever end."

"They believe Genome loves them and wants them to be with him forever. *Nothing* goes on forever. They call that place Paradise, but how would they recognize it when they got there? Would they see its plants and trees, its animals? No, they'd destroy them. They don't know where they already are," Aspect said.

Phoenix glanced at Totally before she spoke. "And where are they?"

"They're already there—in Paradise. This is it."

Phoenix shared another glance with Totally before they both looked towards the moving, miragelike walls of the overheated dead air insect hall. "This—is Paradise?"

Aspect and Foresight smiled. Sadly. "Here? Yes," Aspect still smiled, quite beautifully. "Here, as well as everywhere. We are still alive. To be alive is to be in what the Beings should recognize as Paradise. Life only has a point, a purpose if it begins and if it ends."

"And if it has a middle," Totally smiled. "If it has some life to live between the beginning and the end."

"Yes," Aspect smiled more broadly still. He looked as if he were about to shuffle off melancholy.

Phoenix knew that Totally believed he looked happy, at this moment—but Tolly could not feel through her scalp the mixture of profound emotions of the Bright, as Phe did. She loved the way they felt everything to such extremes, so passionately and so considerately.

"This Paradise," Aspect said, "it exists—only the Beings have failed to see it when they're in it."

"And you don't belong here," Phoenix said, with the dead, dropping insects plopping from above. "Not here," she said. "You belong out there. The forest, that's your home. *That's* Paradise, isn't it, Aspect?"

"It is Paradise," he smiled. "And it is the first thing the Beings destroy to make way for their wars, to make way for their Genome."

"Everything is energy," Foresight leaned forward to say.

Phoenix felt his profoundly intelligent emotions delving deep inside her. At the same time, she could feel herself hanging on to his every word, taking them into her mind and holding them there forever.

"The energy of everything is the same," Foresight said, staring at Phoenix as if to give her his words to keep. "Look out into the sky—the sun, the stars—that's what we all are. We—the Bright—we can feel this. We are always part of everything. And everything communicates with us."

"But the Beings," Aspect took over, like the other side to the story, "they are given to believe that they are *outside*—that they aren't really a part of everything. Their Genome has given them that. But it is their error. They look for the Truth but ignore the evidence closest to them. Their Paradise, *their* afterlife separates them. It makes *this* life nothing—nothing but a war to impose their mistakes, their terrible errors on everything else that lives. They will impose their will, or let nothing else live. Believe or die. And if you look like that," he said, pointing momentarily at Gabriel flapping his wings, "you will die no matter what you believe. We have seen their hatred of him."

"Of him?" Totally said.

Gabriel's head turned. He looked over quizzically.

"The Beings have captured one like him. As if his sister."

# 98

*Alice!* The Bright had seen her! The Adults, the Beings had her. Tied up, she was, they said. Adults everywhere would be afraid of and disgusted by Arch Angels. They would torture and degrade them, as Gabriel knew only too well. They'd remove their wings and hang them up to dry.

Alice was suffering! She'd be thinking of what her brother went through, even as she was suffering herself. She'd be thinking there was no one here to help her.

"Where is she?" he demanded.

Aspect and Foresight were standing with Phoenix and Totally. They reached for Gabriel. The other Bright were gathering close in the smoky, dirty insect-littered light.

"Show me where she is!"

"Gabriel," Phoenix was saying. "Wait a moment. Calm down."

"Calm? You know what they do to us. You saw Jay-Jay. They'll do the same to Alice. They'll do terrible things to Alice. I've got to help her."

"Where is she?" Phoenix turned to Aspect. "Please, can you show us where she is?"

Aspect exchanged a glance with Foresight. "There isn't any way you can get there to see her. It is too dangerous. Believe us."

"There is a way!" Gabriel insisted. "You think there isn't! There's a way. I'll find it. I'll find Alice, and nothing's going to stop me."

# 99

He hovered over them in his own insect annex that he appeared to have carved out of the ceiling. Nothing was going to stop him. Phoenix felt the rip, the tears and the burden of his love for the other Angel. Only death would prevent him from being with her again. He was willing to risk everything.

"They'll destroy you!" Totally was screaming up at him, using the words that Phoenix was only thinking.

"They'll destroy Alice," he said, looking down, with such sadness in his face as would match the emotions and the inner pain of the Bright.

Phoenix stared up and up at Gabriel while he gazed down and down. His eyes were on her, asking her for understanding. She, understanding more than he would ever know, wanted that he would not go—not for herself, but for him. But she knew he would, whatever she said or did.

The insects moved away from Gabriel's orange-oil smeared wings, making as if a hole in the black sky where the blue showed and the sun shone through. She watched as Gabriel seemed to be taken up, and Phoenix could not help but think about the Paradise that the Adults lived in hope of, and how it shone here, in the insect underworld—how, as Aspect had said, it was here already and just to live was to be in it.

"Go," she said, quietly, with her Rodent sister all aquiver by her side. Phoenix smiled. Gabriel broke through from the dark under-belly of the world back into the light. For a moment, before the buzzing black hoards closed back in, it was possible to see right through, to see and feel Gabriel's flight-sensations as he tested his wing, as he looked up to the sky. The buzz blacked him out.

"He's gone," Totally said, with sheer hopelessness flattening her voice.

But now Phoenix had seen through. The light shone from the other side. For so long she had wanted to fly. Now she understood fully what it meant to stand with her feet firmly planted on the ground.

"It's time for us to go, too," she said.

Aspect and Foresight and the other remainders of the tribe Bright had gathered closely round Phoenix and Totally as if to protect them.

"Go?" Totally said. She was shivering as hard as she had from the cold of the fast-flowing river. "Go? How? *Where?"*

"I know what I'm doing now," Phoenix said to her sister. "Trust me, Tolly," she said. As she touched Totally's arm, her shivering stopped.

Phoenix turned to Aspect.

"You will go to him?" he said, glancing up as if Gabriel still hung there between the two extremes of outer and inner atmosphere.

"We will go to him," Phe said.

"But—" Totally shuddered again.

Phoenix gripped her arm.

"It is very dangerous," Aspect said.

"That is why you must not come with us," Phe said, smiling up at him.

As he gazed down at her, Phoenix felt his beautifully gentle suffering all over again. "You—didn't fight them," she said, looking round at the able bodies surrounding them, the strength these young Bright bore with such languid grace. "You didn't fight the Adults—the Beings. You didn't, because you couldn't kill them, could you."

It was not a question. Through her extra senses, she felt the Bright conviction that everything that lives should never be killed by them. Aspect did not say anything more about it to her—he did not need to. He knew she read him more accurately than words ever explained. He, through his open face, through his soft smile, told her of his Truth—that everything that lives, that everything inanimate too, was *greater* than the concept, the bad idea that Genome represented. Genome, Aspect's expression said, was love of self gone awry, love twisted and distorted, love spoilt. The Bright lived their love, far deeper and further reaching than any god worshipper was ever capable of imagining.

"We love our friends, the Arch Angels," Phoenix said to Aspect, taking Totally by the hand. "We have to go."

"Then we will show you where," Aspect nodded, looking at his brother, at the brotherhood of the Bright.

They turned, those tall and graceful people. Their passing produced a tube to travel through the insect air, illuminated by flickering handheld firelight. As they went, the Bright smeared their faces and their bodies with green and yellow and orange, the better to blend into the vibrant background colors of the forest.

Totally went to take some of the staining oils when Foresight offered them to her. Phoenix stopped her.

"But they will see you," Aspect said. "The Beings will see you—they will catch you."

"Yes," Phoenix said. She did not stop.

Aspect faltered, uncertainly, for a few moments.

Totally wanted to wait with him, but Phe moved them on. To be marked, to be identified with the Bright, as much as Phoenix might have liked to be, was wrong at this moment.

"What are we doing?" Phoenix heard Tolly asking her. She did not answer as she balanced on the log of the felled tree back across the river.

In the clear air, the Bright blended into the foliage, almost as if they had simply disappeared. Totally ducked down with them, while Phoenix walked, her grounded Agle feet, surer than ever, fixed to the forest floor, her head of undulating hair held high.

"Phe!" Totally hissed, following on after her.

Phoenix stopped. She gazed through the trees to where she could make out the vertical bars of a cage. Moving on the other side, many more of the Bright. "I can see your mother and your father and your sisters and brothers," she said to crouching Aspect and Foresight.

Totally was shivering in the undergrowth. "I hope you know what you're doing, Phe."

"They will see you," Aspect said again, watching Phoenix take her Rodent sister by the hand.

"Stay out of sight," Phoenix said to the Bright. "It's time for us to go."

"But what—" Totally started to say.

Phoenix stopped her. "Just answer all their questions, when the Adults ask you." She turned again to Aspect, to Foresight. "Thank you," she said, leading her Rodent sister through the Bright Forest towards the burnt black camp and the stench of Adult exhaust fumes.

# 100

"I'm here!" he cried for her from above. Gabriel saw Alice's head come up. She had heard him, even above the crash-clatter and scream of the helicopters all round them.

"With you!" he shouted down. "With you, lovely Angel, forever!"

But her head fell and Gabriel was soon netted and brought down in a tangle of steel wire. He crashed, thumping up a cloud of dark dust. They were on him, round him, over him in a moment. As before, the Adults screamed in his face. "Where are you from? Who are you? Speak! How many of you are there? Speak!"

"Speak!"

"Speak!"

But with the guns in his face, with the slaps about the head, the punches, the threats with long knives, Gabriel said nothing until they strung him up in the hard sunlight next to Alice. Signs were hanging round their necks. "I had to be with you," he said.

She smiled for him, too weak for words. She smiled and her head fell forward, releasing two precious tears.

"Alice!" Gabriel called to her.

From here, Gabriel looked down upon his captors. From there, below him, the splatter-plate soldiers glanced up again and again, barely able to control their urge to take up arms and attack and disfigure and destroy.

"What are you so scared of?" Gabriel cried down towards them, willing to speak now that he saw them so clearly. "So afraid—why so 'fraid? That's what he's for, is he—Genome? You're all so scared—scared that this is it—this, here, now—and you're just you and I'm me and that's what you're so scared of!"

With the new but self-same Adults milling enraged below him, with Alice falling away by his side, Gabriel shouted all the louder.

"So you make Genome so he makes more of you—makes you into something other than what you are—the scaredest thing in all the world—scared of everything you see and everything that doesn't look or feel like you feel. Genome's *fear*—not love! I can see it all, from here! Fear—the hatred that comes out of fear. Genome's fear—that's all he is! That's all! He's nothing but fear!"

And all at once, from the anger, the hatred, the fear amassing on the ground below, half a dozen raised rifles fired. The smoke obscured the double-cross of the two Angels. But the rifles would not, *could* not miss from there. Six soldiers shot Gabriel. Six bullets tore right through him.

A burst of gunfire and Totally and Phoenix were as if under attack.

"Down!"

"Down!"

"Face down on the ground! Now!"

Phe and Tolly fell. The rifle fire had sounded from some distance away, but the guns here were in their eyes, the bootlike undersoles of Adult feet pressing hard against the backs of their necks, forcing their faces into the charcoal grit of the ground.

"Who are you? How many are you? Speak!"

"Speak!"

"We come as friends!" Phoenix was spluttering up at her captors. "Your enemies are our enemies!"

Totally lay trying to breathe by her side.

"Enemies? Who are you? Where did you come from? Speak! Who are you?"

"We're from over the sea!"

Next to Totally, Phe was spitting out words with the blackened bits from her mouth.

"We have news for you—you need to listen to us. It's most important!"

"Speak, then!"

Totally felt the heel press harder against her neck. She was scared speechless, hanging onto every word that her sister spoke. Phoenix was different now. She seemed to have found her way.

She seemed very brave. Totally hung on to Phe's new bravery, as she would have drowned in this dry choking dust without it.

"Your enemy—the Army of the Holy Ministry of the Immaculate Mother and Son—your true enemy—you are in great danger—they will overcome and destroy you if you don't listen to what we have to say."

Totally listened. She was listening to nothing. Nobody said a word. By her side, her Agle sister breathed hard, but not desperately. Phoenix knew what she was going to say. She seemed to know what they were going to do. It would probably get them all killed.

"We must speak to your commanding officer," Totally heard Phoenix saying. "It is imperative."

Totally hardly recognized her sister in the words she was using now, in the way she was speaking. Phoenix probably would get them all killed, but not, her words and her voice were saying, without a fight.

# 102

"We are Mutations!" Phoenix was saying. She and Totally stood in another cool office faced with another cold stare. This time it was the Supreme Commander of Genome's Holy Republican Army—Commander Huxley—a different title, another army. There were no real changes. The machine eyes of the Adults beamed black, anti-rays of evil light-matter. Their ears listened zealously, picking up any anti-Adult, Genome-blaspheming inference.

But, by now, Phoenix had better understanding of these Human Beings, feeling her way back to their past, seeing through their hatred and their fear to their own mutations. Yes, the Adult species, in their plated skin and hardened helmet heads were not as they once were. Phoenix understood that in olden times, in the legendary Ash's day, not so very long ago, the Adults themselves would have stood very differently than they did today. But the Adult, the Human Being, was by its nature, a denier of reality. Claiming to hold the utmost Truth in a black book in its hard, mutated hand, the Human Being was at heart the biggest liar on the face of the earth.

"Yes," Phoenix was saying again, facing-off the leader of this other army, "we are Mutations." She was not telling a lie, not yet—she and Totally were mutations, and so was Commander Huxley and his army, and so were the other army, as was everything that lived and breathed in the entire world. Nothing stayed the same, especially now, Phoenix knew. She had not been as clever or attentive at school as her Rodent sister, but this much she did know.

"But we were always willing to throw ourselves on the mercy of the Lord Genome," she lied. "No, more than that," she went on hurriedly, trying to disguise the reaction she was getting from her sister beside her, "we wanted to take Genome into our hearts, to throw ourselves on his mercy. But Genome's mercy had to come through them—through the Army of the Immaculate Mother and Son."

Commander Huxley's unblinking eyes were just like Captain FitzRoy's, taking everything in, taking everything with the same hungry intensity.

"They showed us no mercy!" Phoenix hurried on. "Even after we told them everything they wanted to know about our technology, they didn't stop in their cruelty towards us. They killed our grandfather and all the City Elders. They locked up our teachers and our scientists."

"Scientists, you say?" He spoke, for the first time.

Phoenix and Totally had been hustled into position and the officer informed of their capture and their request. He had so far listened to Phoenix dispassionately. Only now did the flow of the zealous light flicker for a moment deep inside his head. As soon as he spoke, Phoenix could begin to feel that she was having an effect upon him.

"Our scientists," she confirmed, "yes. We were willing to tell them everything about our energy technology, but still they took our teachers and our scientists and they—"

"And," his voice came again, in a question issued like another order, "what is your 'energy technology'? What is so unusual about any technology from a race of Mutations like you?"

Phoenix remembered the conversation between her grandfather and Captain Owen. "It's nuclear," she said.

# 103

Totally watched the commander almost spring out of his seat behind his big metal desk. It was a lie, of course. But a very effective lie. Commander Huxley had to check himself, taking a moment and a deep breath. "So," he exhaled, "you have—nuclear capabilities?"

Totally was trying not to shiver. She had to listen to the lies coming out, to her sister leading the army commander on. On to where? She wasn't at all sure.

"We have nuclear power from our reactors," Phoenix was saying by her side.

"Fusion or fission?" the commander blasted his question at them.

"I don't understand the difference," Phoenix stumbled. "I don't—but my sister does. Don't you, Tolly?" And the Adult officer's eyes moved smoothly from Phe's face to Tolly's, his human machine-head flicking from one position to the next.

"Well?" he beamed at her. "Fusion or fission?"

"Fission," Totally said, struggling to get the word out. Her throat was dry. She couldn't breathe properly. "It's—" she started to say. "Can I have—some water?"

Commander Huxley peered at her, then snapped away in a moment, nodding at one of his soldiers. The soldier went to a machine. Water came from it, into a plastic beaker. Even their water came out of machines. The water, when Totally tasted it, was colder than ordinary water should ever be, almost iced, with a metallic tang, as if iron was dissolved in it.

"Tell me about nuclear fission," the commander said, watching Totally gulping down lumps of near-solid, cold, hard water.

"We use plutonium," Totally said.

The black beads of the Adult's eyes fixed on hers, giving nothing, taking, demanding. Totally was lying. His eyes suspected it. She drank more water. The ASP City society had never used nuclear fission, but they had always understood it. Totally and Phoenix had both been taught about it, and Tolly had been particularly interested in atomic reaction, the fission of nuclear decay as unstable atoms came apart, of fusion, the fusing together of atoms, the very process that drove the sun and stars.

"The nature of plutonium," she said, remembering her school, her teachers, friends, her family, "is unstable. The atoms decay into simpler atoms naturally. A piece of plutonium is always warm as the nuclear energy is being released. We merely take this material and hurry the process along." She paused.

The Commander had sat back in his seat, listening with all the dark intensity of his nuclear eyes.

"If we heat plutonium to a sufficient level, the molecular structure is opened and further destabilized and the atomic decay is accelerated. Accelerate the decay enough and the release of energy inside—I mean the decaying atomic structures will destabilize other fragile atoms and they will in turn destabilize others and a chain reaction is set up. In other words, there is a massive release of energy. We harness that energy and use it to—for our energy."

"And," the commander came in, with much deliberation, "tell me—what happens if you do not harness and use that energy? What happens to that chain reaction?"

Totally's throat was dry again. She had run out of water. She opened her mouth, but Phoenix spoke instead.

"It explodes," she said. "It's a nuclear bomb."

# 104

"A nuclear bomb!"

It was as if one had gone off. The room went silent, but energetically so, with the reaction of what had been said clattering like a chain through the deeply protected brains of the helmet heads of the Adults.

"And *they* understand this now," Phoenix went on, providing more fission fuel into the explosive nucleus. "They have our technology and our plutonium. Lots of it. We were so afraid—they are an army of ruthless terrorists. They think they have authority—supreme authority over—"

"They are blasphemers!" leapt the reactive commander. All round the room his radioactive troops were ticking and cracking, glowing with inner heat and aggressive passion.

At last, Phoenix could feel—sensitive hair or not—the emotions driving this deep, darkly insensitive species. She had tapped into the fear at the machine heart of the Being, causing a series of explosions she knew would crash on through from atom to Human atom.

"But they believe in the total authority of the Immaculate Mother, given to her by Genome."

"Immaculate Mother? That is the grossest blasphemy! Where is your community—where are you from? Where? Speak!"

"We're from ASP Island."

*"Where?"* Tell us where that is!"

"I can't!" insisted Phe. She wanted to reach out for Totally as Commander Huxley came at them, raging towards them.

"You dare! You will tell me where the enemy of Genome lies, where you have given the Devil his means to power! You will tell me where!"

"I can't! I don't know where!" Phoenix was afraid now, more than ever. But she shouted back at the advance of the commander and his armed and ever-ready guard.

"We escaped!" she screamed to the whole room, and further, to the back-up and beyond. "We got away from them in a small boat! We drifted, under the sky. You must believe us!" Phoenix was breathing heavily. "We were lost, for a long time. We lost all sense of direction. We don't know the way back. But there are those that do know."

"Who?" he raged. "Who knows? Where are they?"

"They are strung up like crosses from tree to dead tree! The fliers! The flying Mutations! They know. They have seen it all from the air. You need them to show the way."

"The winged ones? Those with the mark of the beast? Those, you say?"

"They are Stigma!" Phoenix said. The word stuck in her throat, but she spat it out anyway, as if at the army commander. "They are Stigma—but they know the way back."

"We can find your island ourselves," the commander said, but thoughtfully.

"Not in time," Phoenix said. "Our enemy is upon us. She is armed with the most powerful weapon ever created. The Immaculate Mother and Captain FitzRoy will not hesitate. You haven't a moment to lose, Commander. Or all will be lost, forever."

# 105

Blood seeped slowly into the six holes in Gabriel's wings. He looked towards Alice. "I wish they'd shot me properly," he said, as if she could hear him.

Alice's head was down, her eyes closed.

"How did you manage to miss me?" his eyes said, with a crazed smile crossing his face.

Gabriel's voice cracked and he broke down.

The soldiers took no notice. They were too busy with their weapons, cleaning and lubricating them.

Gabriel must have blacked out, turning off the sun for a while. It came back on suddenly, with a jolt of his head, flashing from rifle long-knives.

A soldier with a naked blade fixed to the end of his rifle went glinting behind Gabriel and Alice. Gabriel looked skyward, bracing himself. He had hoped that death would take him before this. He'd have preferred to be shot than cut, to die than to lose his wings. He gritted his teeth as the soldiers gathered round, expecting the first bite of the blade against his back. The next thing he knew, the air was whistling through the holes in his wings as Gabriel fell back down to the ground at the soldiers' feet.

## 106

Totally had never seen her sister like this. Locked in a back room together, Tolly watched, saying nothing while Phoenix pulsed and stamped and sparked. She was so full of energy it seemed to be flowing from her hair. This was a brand-new Phoenix.

When Totally went to speak, Phe put her hand over her mouth. Phoenix looked about the metal room. Tolly watched her shake her head, her mouth resolutely pressed closed. Phoenix tapped her ear and pointed round the room as if to say that somebody might be listening in.

As soon as another Adult entered in his rich robes, flowing through the door at them, Phoenix threw herself to the floor at his feet. Totally followed, holding her head facedown in case the lies showed through her eyes.

"You are the priest!" Phoenix crawled closer to him, touching the hem of his long gown.

"I am the parson," he said, with grim determination. "I am Genome's first servant and he is my Master."

"We are Genome's servants too," Totally heard her sister saying. "He is the Master of us all."

"He is our only savior!" insisted the parson.

"Our only savior!" Phoenix chanted.

Totally joined in. She had to. "He is our only savior!"

"And you accept Genome into your hearts?"

"We do."

"Yes, we do."

"And beg his forgiveness for the sins of your vile, mutated flesh?" The parson's nose and chin and forehead and cheeks were thick with dense skin plates, his hard lips bumping out words one after the other. "Beg! Beg his forgiveness for the sins of your vile and mutated flesh."

"We beg forgiveness!" Totally shouted, cowering at the parson's hidden feet, clutching at his rich and holy robes.

"Forgive us our trespasses!" Phoenix was chanting, scrabbling next to her sister.

"You are sinners!"

"We are sinners!"

"Only through Genome will you find retribution and the chance, the possibility of everlasting life. How will you meet your maker, when you die?"

"With humility," Phoenix said, straightaway. "As a sinner. I beg his forgiveness."

And with that, the parson halted. He placed his hands on the sisters' heads.

"You have learned your lessons well," he incanted. "There is hope for you yet. Hold onto that thought. Genome will never desert you, as long as you are true to him."

But Totally felt, even through the hard and hefty weight of his hand, the true correlation she had with her Agle sister, which was not through the parson-person's connection to fear of sin and death but through joy of life, as Phoenix now felt it and passed it on to her loving, ever-grateful Rodent sister.

# 107

It didn't take long. Phoenix could feel the urgency ramping up outside. The room she and Totally were locked in was pretty well soundproof. But there was too much going on outside, and it was all too frantic not to be felt through young and tender Ground Agle hair.

Then, as if to prove the point, Commander Huxley burst in, the wide open door slamming against the wall, his army primed and ready for action just outside.

"They do not corroborate your story!" he blared into Phe's face. "Your fliers—your Stigma—they know nothing of any nuclear capabilities!"

Totally had fallen away, stepping back from the assault by the senior soldier. Phoenix tried to hold firm, setting her face in position as the Adult attacked her.

She took a breath. "They are our servants," she said. "They are our slaves."

The Commander glanced at Totally. "There is no truth here!"

"They bring food into our city," Phoenix hurried on, grabbing back his full attention. "How should we discuss such secrets with their type? Would you?" She paused, for a moment only.

"They fly for us. We tolerate their—their offensive form because they are of use. That's all. They are slaves. They are nothing. We use them. As you should. As you must. We don't have any more time. Please understand me, Commander Huxley—we suffer a common enemy. They will learn about our nuclear capabilities, adding them to their power—their Revelation!"

"What?" The commander seemed to stagger. "Their—what?"

Phoenix's hair bristled hard. At last she had him, remembering what Captain Owen had said. "The Revelation Element!"

He was trying to steady himself. "The Revelation—they have the Element?"

"Yes!"

"You've heard them say this—the Revelation Element?"

"Yes!"

The commander allowed himself another moment, another, two moments to scan the Agle and the Rodent faces, before sweeping away with a slam of the door.

Phoenix shared a long look with Totally. From what the commander had said, it meant that Alice and Gabriel had been taken down and revived enough to be questioned. The look between the sisters was one of at least partial relief.

Then, when the door flew back again, they saw that their look, their relief was well founded. Commander Huxley exploded into the room, but with his armed guard just outside, two Angels, their hands bound and their wings clipped in much the same way as they had been in the other camp.

"You!" the commander raged at Phoenix. "You will come with me! You!" At Totally now. "You will remain here!"

He turned to Phoenix again. "Don't for a moment forget," he said, "that your—that *she* will be here, as will he," he pointed to Gabriel, "under armed guard."

Gabriel was hustled into the room while Alice, still worn and dazed beyond fear, was held outside. Phoenix avoided any eye contact with Gabriel.

"We will be holding this one, and this one," the commander said, pointing at Totally and then Gabriel, "until we are victorious. If we do not prevail, we all lose. When we win—well, we shall see."

"But we will win!" Phoenix said, stepping forward without another glance at Totally or Gabriel, presenting herself as ready, as an important part of the campaign against a common enemy. She walked away into the military might on the move outside the door.

Phoenix did not look round again. She moved forward, with Commander Huxley by her side, not quite knowing whether to treat her as an ally or his prisoner.

# 108

"I need to speak to the flier," Phoenix demanded. "I need a word alone with her."

"No!" the commander stated. "I cannot allow that."

Phoenix was still demanding respect. She wondered how far she could push him before the commander would turn on her. For the moment, she—through the advantage of her secret scalp and hair—knew he was too weighed down with what she was telling him. His army was on the move. He was going to need all his energy just to keep control.

"We will remain in sight," Phoenix said. "The Mutation needs to hear her instructions from me. She may try to trick you. But she will recognize my authority."

Alice was still bound, hand and wing, when they were allowed to meet on a cleared space on the Adult plain. The soil was burnt and black, as ever, with the vast stumps of tree trunks like wooden platforms hacked away at ground level. Phoenix stepped onto the tree base on which Alice waited. Soldiers stood behind their weapons all round, their tiny eyes blinking on and off and on again.

"What do you think you're playing at?" Alice said. Her face was thin and very pale. She still looked like suffering, her features fixed as if in lingering pain.

"Don't, Alice," Phe said. "You would have died, tied up there in the sun. So would Gabriel."

"Yes, but now I'm supposed to show them," she nodded at the firearms of the guards, "to show them the way home?"

"It's the only way. Don't try anything stupid. Just show the way. It's our only chance."

"Then we don't stand a chance. They shot Gabriel's wings, did you know that?"

"No, I didn't. Is he—"

"They shot him. And they'll shoot us all, when the time comes. They'll kill everybody—oh, no, that's not what they call it, is it? You know them. They call it cleansing, don't they? They'll cleanse the earth of everything and everybody. I've heard them talk—when they've done enough, then Genome will come again and they'll all be taken up—and we'll be taken down. They have to do it—for Genome! He'll make them! Sooner or later, they'll destroy us all."

Alice was breaking. She'd been through too much. She was still in shock.

"Listen," Phoenix tried to say. She would have taken the Angel in her arms, she would have helped her to cry, to assist her across the emotions that were crowding in on her, building up and ready to burst. "Listen to me, Alice."

"Listen to you? Why should I listen to you? You? I hate you! I've always hated you! I always will!"

"Alice, it doesn't matter what you think of me—"

"No! It doesn't! It doesn't matter what Gabriel thinks of you either, does it? Does it? What are you doing, trying to get me killed so you can—"

Phoenix slapped her, hard. She wanted to hold her, to help her see her own way through. Instead she had to lash out and clap Alice round the face.

The Angel stepped back. There was no pain on her face suddenly. Shock still, yes, but no pain. Anger welled up in her. "My hands are tied!" she snarled through gritted teeth. "If my hands weren't tied!"

"That's it," Phoenix said. "That's right. Your hands are tied. Don't forget it."

"If I could fight you now!"

"Well, you can't! And even when they release you, you still can't. Your hands will still be tied. They've got Gabriel and they've got Totally. So you just do as you're told and you'll get the chance to fight me later. I promise."

"I'll be looking forward to it!" Alice called after her as Phoenix turned and started to walk away.

The soldiers had all seen the slap, heard how hard it was, how meaningful. They'd never guess its real meaning, not from the look of consummate hatred on the young flier's face, or the way Phoenix turned away, having hit her. Phoenix would not let anyone see the effect the hit had on her, keeping her face down, marching away with Alice glaring at her back.

It looked exactly as Phe wanted it. Her head came up, now that her face had cleared and would not betray her. Commander Huxley was waiting in an open-topped vehicle, watching carefully.

Phoenix gauged the glint in his far-distant eyes. She saw from the nod he gave his guard to close in and take the Angel, from the flick of affirmation he threw out to his closest officers, from the activity, the gunmetal clank and the chorus of machine roar that they were go—Go! Go! Go!

And that now there was no stopping them.

# 109

The beaches were littered with metal and plastic. The Adult armies dropped waste wherever they went, scarring the land and spoiling even ancient environments forever. Nothing seemed able to survive them. They ruined the very air they left behind, permanently altering everything in their wake.

Phoenix saw all this as—held fast under armed guard, with Alice restrained even more tightly some way off—she looked around at the beach and across the sea to the waiting ships. All the trees were down and smashed into the ground, the soil and the sand and the water churned into one dirty, indistinguishable mess as the army vehicles drove on through to the beach boats. Helicopters flew back and forth overhead, with supplies and arms, with great guns and massive shells ready-made for maximum destruction. Hundreds upon hundreds of soldiers, every one seemingly the same in size and arms and uniform and intention, stamp-marched in terrifying unison into the landing craft ready to be transported to the ships.

This beach, Phoenix could just tell, must have been beautiful. But, being once beautiful, its charred and trodden remains were even more tragic, even more painful to look upon. The Adults noticed nothing. But Phoenix, looking all round between the bodies of her heavy guard, felt appalled.

Without firing a single shell, without one flamethrower on fire, the destruction by these Human Beings was absolute here. They behaved as if they were the only truly living things on the planet.

Looking back at the beach from the deck of a ship, Phoenix could see the extent of the damage to the land on this side of the Bright's beautiful island. All the way from the coast the forest of giant greenwood trees was down, with the logs tossed in stacks, and a great charred track striping the natural slope to the island's center. There had grown the metal town, the home of the military forces of the Army of Genome's Republic. Adult Town—a false place of clanging floors and cold walls, chilled air and tainted water. To look back at what was left behind was like being able to see all at once what the Adults were. The character of their species was written into the color of the air they lived in and breathed, its transparency lost among the particles of dust and the smoke of ever-present fumes.

Phoenix saw the effect they had on the island, the effect they would impose on any country. She could see, as if her hair and scalp looked into the past, that the wild instability of modern Evolution was caused by what these Beings did. The change, the acceleration of Evolution had and did depend upon the Human Beings in their machines and their false environments. Again, Phe felt, she knew, that the Adults were afraid of the world outside their own making. They were the most unnatural of species, isolating themselves, considering themselves above, while looking down with utter contempt and disdain.

Suddenly, Phe felt someone behind her, looking down on her, with all his contempt and his disdain. She turned and looked up into the eyes of Genome through a holy ghost. All Genome's jealousy of the world and everything in it was contained in the ambitious black light blinking under the parson's heavy eyelids.

"You," he said, very slowly, with every bit of his authority evident in the weight of the one word he had said. He stopped there.

Phoenix felt the weight of his conviction, the burden of his belief. The parson believed that when he closed his eyes, Genome's world disappeared entirely. Nothing really existed with him, not without his superior consciousness assisting his god with its creation.

"You," he said again, after Phe had felt these things filtering rapidly through his mind, "have seen the one they call the Immaculate Mother?"

Under Phe's feet, a vibration through the big ship, a vast motor turning, ready to drive them forward. "Yes," she said. "I have seen her. And her son."

"So—they exist, the mother and the son? They are not just—figments? Figureheads?"

"Figureheads? No. They exist. I have seen them. We have heard them speak. I mean, we and our Elders have had to listen to them asserting their authority. We have suffered their blasphemies, all of us."

"Yes," he said, "*blasphemies*. You were right, my dear, to come to us."

"Commander Huxley is a good soldier," Phe said.

"Undoubtedly," agreed the parson with a severe nod. "Indeed. But we are all good soldiers for Genome, are we not? It was—it must have been the superiority of our faith, the—the *assurity* of Genome's true ministry in our authority—that must have been what you were seeking, was it not, my child?"

"Yes, Father," Phoenix agreed, immediately. "It was just that."

The other ships in the huge fleet—dozens of aircraft carriers, landing craft, battle cruisers—were vibrating and belching more black smoke into the already spoiled skies.

"See," the parson pointed with a weighted, steady index finger, wearing an expression of weighted, steady pride, "see how she flies, your mutation? She flies for Genome, now."

"Yes, Father," Phe said.

"Now, at last, she is blessed."

"At last," Phe said. "Yes, Father—at last we are all blessed."

# 110

The Commander's ship was positioned at the head of the fleet. Phoenix stood somewhere along the landward side. From the front, a single, winged being flew up between the hovering helicopters, her wings blowing away the billows of ship and flying machine fumes.

"Your slave, the Stigma!" The commander stood next to Phoenix, on the opposite side to the parson.

"Yes," said Phoenix, watching Alice breaking through the blackening billows, turning and turning to get her bearings.

Alice appeared confused and sickened, flying through the opaque air. She did a complete circuit of the ship, watched by a thousand soldiers, hardly any of whom could resist the urge to point a gun in her direction. She seemed, for a while, to be challenging them to shoot her down, to put bullet holes in her wings as they had Gabriel's.

"She'll not disobey you?" the commander turned to Phoenix.

"She's a slave," Phoenix said, with a dead certainty she by no means felt.

"And you," he said, "no tricks?"

"No tricks," she repeated, turning away to watch Alice again.

"The spirit of Genome is in her," the parson leaned forward slightly to say to the commander. "I would swear to it."

The Angel swooped, with the pointing guns following her graceful movements. Then she turned away from the island and flew some way out to sea. There she waited for the fleet to turn and follow on.

"The spirit of Genome is in me," said Phoenix, relieved to see Alice waiting to show them the way.

"And the Immaculate Mother and her son," said the commander, "what do they look like? Tell me what the mother looks like."

"She carries a wand."

"A wand, you say?" said the parson, glancing at the commander. "That contains the very Revelation Element itself."

"Perhaps," said Huxley. "But what does she look like?"

Phoenix turned her face to the horizon, towards home. "Oh," she said, "she—she and her son—they're deformed—grotesque mutations. They're devils—like the devil himself."

She heard the parson breathe in, a heavy breath of deep satisfaction. "Just as I thought," he exhaled. "You see, Commander? It's exactly as I said—they are like unto the devil himself."

"Yes," Phoenix said, standing between the parson and commander, speaking first to the rock and then to the hard place, "but like a devil with Genome's Revelation in her hand."

## 111

Alice could fly faster than the ships could go. But not for long. The battle cruisers, the personnel and armaments carriers turned and their black-burn smoke billowed ever harder until all the ships were slicing out to sea after the Angel. In their wake, the churned ocean released torn bladder wrack seaweed and sliced-through dying animals, while the fumes fell from above in rainbow slicks of spoil. Even across the sea the Human Adults left the discernable line of their destructive progress.

The air came fresh into Phe's face as they cut through following the flight of the Angel, but fell exhausted behind the fleet. Everything that came into contact with this species just dropped away, dying, or drastically damaged and altered forever.

Phoenix was allowed to walk where she would around the deck of the command ship. The commander was forever watching her, with doubt etched hard into his plate-face. The parson gazed on her too. Phoenix felt his faith burning, the pride of his passion, his mighty strength and certainty.

She was allowed to inspect the fleet following behind, to feel the speed and the power they were able to maintain, this massive fighting force. Phoenix watched Alice flapping through the air out front as she tried to outfly the speed of the fleet cutting through the water. She could not. The forward thrust of the big ships was too constant, the churn behind too destructively powerful. The Adults went wherever they wanted, when they wanted. At this rate, they'd be there, on ASP Island, in no time, bringing this new, terrifying menace to Phe's home.

But a sudden volley of gunshots broke Phe's thoughts of home, crackling along the other side of the ship. Running to see what it was they were shooting at, Phoenix could not get near enough for the soldiers hunched there with their primed weapons at the ready, firing whenever they felt like it, aiming into the water over the side.

"Grant her viewing room," she heard the parson's voice. "Make way there, in the name of Genome!" he flared at the soldiers nearest to Phoenix.

In the space the parson made for her next to him, Phoenix determined the shapes in the water far below. More shots rang out. "Why?" she shouted at the parson. "What's the point?"

But the soldiers were firing hard at the shapes flying just below the surface. They cheered. They were jubilant as soon as blood was spotted and one permanently smiling Porpoise face floated into view. The Porpoise People swam around the dead body of their friend. The celebrating soldiers clapped each other's shoulders.

"Rid the world of abominations!" the parson passed along the line, clapping and congratulating. "We shall cleanse Genome's creation back to purity!"

Phoenix turned towards him, hurt, angry. But the commander's eyes were fixed on her, gauging and testing her, again and again. She turned away quickly, clenching in secret as more shots rang out.

"They will have their sport," she heard Commander Huxley's voice close to her ear.

Phoenix peered over the side, trying not to gag. The sickness she suffered felt worse than using a sick-stick—much worse! The

Porpoise People were dying just down there, dying of Adults, but because Phoenix had brought them here.

"They are trained to fire," the commander leaned in even closer, almost whispering in Phe's ear. "It is right—and it is righteous, this cleansing, is it not?"

"Yes," was all she was able to say, meekly.

Just then, a great shout went up. Farther out, away from the ship a supremely massive form was erupting, breaking the surface of the deep ocean with a huge, sky-high spout of water jetting up and slapping down behind. Hundreds of creatures swam away, having been on the ride of a lifetime.

"Oh, no," breathed Phoenix, very quietly. "Oh—no!"

The guns were immediately trained away from the Porpoise forms under the waves and onto the giant body still erupting from the sea like a new land forming.

"Gargantitude," whispered Phe.

Nobody heard her. The soldier shouts were too loud, their rifle fire too extensive. Gun smoke drifted away. Phoenix shuddered as another volley of bangs fired out across the water at the giant creature.

Gargantitude must have sensed the danger. She was trying to dive, but something as massive as she could never have changed direction in time. She was still rising slowly out of the sea, her mountainous back arched in fear.

The firing was continuous now. The bullets were disappearing into Gargantitude's side, lost in her thick, dense layers of blubber fat.

Phoenix was desperate not to cry out, to scream for the life of the leviathan, the innocent sea creature, to shout and spit in the faces of her tormentors. All the time, the continuous heat of the black lasers of Commander Huxley's eyes bore into her back, into the side of her face, testing her, inspecting Phoenix for signs of her true emotions. And all the while, Phe kept her feelings trapped inside, suffering behind a stick-on grin as Genome's holy parson encouraged the Republican Guard to set up their shoulder-held rocket launchers, as Gargantitude fought against her own size and weight, collecting more and more bullets in her side, turning slightly as her many, many wounds gathered and started to take effect.

The Commander was looking for tricks, for hidden emotions, for ulterior motives in what he could see of Phoenix's face. She showed him nothing. But on her head, in her hair, the movement of despair and fear and pain for Gargantitude flowed in thick waves. The Commander missed the significance of her scalp, while Phe had to peer over at the Porpoise Ha-Ha as he surfaced for a moment in the water next to Gargantitude. For a single second he appeared there, not long enough to be aimed at accurately and shot. But long enough to seek out the only Agle face on the ship and exchange a look with it.

Phoenix would never forget the expression, the pain and the accusation on Ha-Ha's Porpoise features. She would never now forget how it felt to have to hold out, to maintain her own look of impervious neglect, to offer him in exchange only a smirk of disdain. He did not, Phoenix was sure, have time to examine and understand the obvious Agle message on her shifting scalp. Ha-Ha was there for that one moment of his agony before the first of the rockets fired, trailing a winding track of sparking smoke from the ship to the blast-burst on Gargantitude's humped back.

Ha-Ha had to leave her, disappearing with the Porpoise People, their laughter left a long, long way behind.

Gargantitude took the first blast with a shudder. Through the holy smoke of the rocket, the parson leapt in worshipful joy. The soldiers cheered. Their commander moved in more closely.

Phoenix, with her eyes full of the first red spurt from the gentle giant's side, cranked up her false smile. Her head was sore with the motion of the hidden emotions across her scalp. She was being pulled apart.

Gargantitude was being blown to pieces. Another rocket exploded in red spate, opening another gushing crater in the wretched creature's body. Phoenix thought she heard the giant walrus whale cry out in pain. Phe's mind shuddered to imagine the level, the amount of agony such a massive and magnificent beast might expect to suffer.

On the deck all round her, Phoenix felt the wild excitement of the soldiers as they aimed and fired, aimed and fired—as the rockets they launched shot across the gap every one plunged into Gargantitude, just a broken second before the next bloody explosion after the next, until she was leaving great island chunks of herself behind in the stained water.

Time and again they hit her, hit her, hit her, hit her—until Phoenix felt that she too was about to crumble. Then the sound came. From Gargantitude's mountain back, a gurgling rush, a blowhole bellow as she exhaled on her own lifeblood and the reddest spout, the highest blood-gush the world had ever seen splattered upwards, as if all over the sky.

The soldiers cheered!

Phoenix cried out. Then she checked herself, with the commander so close by, watching the leviathan breathe her very last.

The rich red fountain failed at last and the first ship in Huxley's fleet left the leviathan turning slowly in the crimson waters with the rest of the ships flowing by still firing, while the first of the tiger-sharks appeared below with the seagles falling from above.

Phoenix watched Gargantitude fade. She had been the only one of her kind. The Adults had made her extinct for nothing more than sport, for fun. She turned her face away. Huxley—there staring at her.

Phoenix fixed a smile of pure amusement on her features, while inside she swore revenge upon them—on every single one of Genome's special creation, his chosen ones.

## 112

"Now," the commander set himself before Phoenix as she secretly, smilingly swore, "it is time to tell me more. Where will we find them—this devilish mother and her son? When we reach your island—ASP Island?—where will they and their center of operations be situated?"

"You will need to penetrate the heart of the city." Phoenix smiled, her face aching under her still-sore hairline. "You will find all you're looking for in our Old Royal Palace."

"Royal? You have royalty—a king?"

"No, not now."

"You are a Republic, then, as we are."

"I suppose—yes. But the Royal Palace is a special place for us. It is important in our history."

"Your history is not important!"

"No," agreed Phoenix, immediately. Her hair told her what to say. Through it, she played the Adults' game so much better than they ever suspected. "Genome has made our history—irrelevant," she said.

Words were coming at Phoenix again, their meaning almost outside her understanding. But words like these worked on the Adults. Out of her mouth they fell, whenever she wanted to give the commander or the parson a little more of what they wanted to hear.

"Only Genome matters now," she said. "His holy writings were given to us all for our redemption."

"Just so," he glowered, his every motion like the threat of an attack.

Phoenix had to defend herself against him in her every reaction. "Yes," she said, in self-defense, "we *are* like you—a Republic. We do not accept the wishes of kings or so-called Immaculate Mothers and their weak and whining sons."

"The son is weak, you say?"

"And whimpering. A fool."

The Commander seemed to falter, stepping back half a pace. He pondered for a few moments more. "But you are sure they have taken residence in your Old Royal Palace?"

Phoenix nodded. "That is why it is such an insult. They behave like royalty over us. They insist on their supreme authority through Genome. It is an affront and a blasphemy."

"So you decided to escape and come to me—to us?"

"I came to Genome's true word, his Republic," she said. "I came knowing of you. They are afraid of you—your army and your own holy authority. I came knowing that you will not rest in the face of this—this terrorism," and the commander flickered darkly, "until we have cleansed the earth of this blasphemy."

From the last ship at the rear of the fleet, a cannon boomed across the water as Phoenix and Huxley turned to see one more of the red explosions splattering back down in a frenzy of blood-bespattered seagles.

Phoenix turned back to Commander Huxley. Now she wanted to see *his* blood splattered, his bare skeleton crunched and consumed. "So be careful," she warned him, unable to keep the hint of threat from her voice, "because they'll be coming for you."

Staring back at him, it looked as if Huxley had finally seen through her. His laser-light eyes might penetrate anything, eventually.

A sound started up, or perhaps just the forefeeling of a sound from somewhere just over the curve of the world. Phoenix picked it up, mistaking it for the hair-judder of feeling Adult enmity emanating from Huxley. But it was not that.

"They're coming," Phoenix said.

He peered out through the space between empty seas and skies as his ears caught the early warning vibrations in the apparently peaceful air.

"Gunships!" he said.

He stepped away. "Prepare for battle!" he bellowed across the deck.

Phoenix looked to the horizon. "Prepare for battle, you Humans," she breathed. "Prepare for battle."

# 113

From over the edge of the world they came, breaking through the seam between the ocean and the sky. Phoenix watched Alice as she dropped down, skimming just over the sea's surface. The helicopter gunships in a triple line flew towards the oncoming fleet without noticing the one tiny Angel form flitting below.

They came on fast, maintaining formation, flying in low, lower, lower still, firing off a first volley of rockets that were either met with return-fire rockets or else fell bursting in the waters nearby. In an instant, the air was punctuated with fireballs, the sea sent blasting into the fiery air. One, two, three lines of helicopter gunships skittered over the fleet in waves.

Phoenix found herself crouching against the side of the ship, shielding her ears from the blasts and the engines. The explosions were so close, she tasted them afterwards. The soldiers were firing indiscriminately with automatic rifles and with rocket launchers. Everyone was shouting.

Commander Huxley was to be seen at the front of the ship gesticulating and roaring at the top of his voice. "Hold fire! Hold fire! They're too far away! Hold fire I say!" Some heard him. Most did not. At the first sign of action, Phoenix was heartened to witness the chaos of Huxley's control failure.

In the air behind the fleet, the three ranks of gunships were reforming, on the turn, flying back towards them. The winding smoke from their rockets striped the air. One of the ships farther back was hit. The lick of a flame leapt out of the ship's stern, just before the report thumped home against the inner ears of everyone on the decks of all the ships.

At once, the air carried so much smoke and shells it seemed to be setting solid above the darkening sea. The helicopters swooped away, one chased by a rocket that looked, to Phoenix, to just clip its tail. The whole thing went up in flames in front of them, taking two other gunships with it. One exploded, the other two spiraled into the sea. What was left of the first wave of the attack continued flying back towards the skyline from which they had appeared.

On deck, Huxley's soldiers were raging in their ecstasy. "Genome is great!" they roared. Some danced, with their holy black book in one hand, an automatic weapon in the other. "Genome is great!"

The parson-person passed among them in full ceremonial garb, grasping the good book to his chest. He gesticulated, and he cursed the carnage of the enemy's destroyed helicopters as the ship sailed on past them towards ASP Island.

Guns were still going off, fired into the air in jubilation. All the while, the victory cries from soldier and parson, venerating the greatness of Genome.

Phoenix watched them. Some Adults had died in the downed helicopters, others had probably lost their lives in the hit ship behind. Commander Huxley was trying to assess the damage. But Human Beings died and Human Beings celebrated. Genome was fighting hard from both sides, just as Phoenix had hoped.

"You fools!" Commander Huxley appeared by Phoenix. He bellowed at the celebrating soldiers, at the blessings of the holy parson. "That was just a reconnoiter!" he raged.

The parson held up his hands, as if conducting the chorus of the soldiers. He lowered his arms slowly. Their voices followed him.

"Prepare yourselves for the real battle!" the commander yelled. "Most of you have never been in action until today. And let me tell you, that was only a foretaste. By the end of the day you'll be just about sick of the flavor of it. Prepare yourselves!" He glared for a moment at the parson. "You will require all your faith, your resolve. Genome will require much of you today. Be sure you are worthy of his asking!"

"Genome is with you!" the parson suddenly yelled out, spinning round, his exquisite robes flailing outwards. The soldiers nearest took a touch of his holy hems.

"Genome is great!" they cried.

In the air, in a thousand Adult high-held hands, the black books, the rifles. In Commander Huxley's eyes, as Phoenix looked at the old soldier, a thrilling glimmer of doubt. It was Phoenix who was thrilled to detect doubt where before there seemed to exist only zealous pride and the certainty of faith in Genome.

"Land!" came a cry from above, breaking into Phe's concentration. "Land, ho!"

And there it was, a line on the far horizon—ASP Island.

# Baptism By Fire

# PART SEVEN

# 114

The helicopter gunships did not sweep across the water at them as before. They were launched and prepared, waiting for the attack of the Republican fighting forces to come to them. Most of the soldiers at sea were positioned now in landing craft, ready for the first assault on the beaches.

Phoenix was being held close to the commander on the biggest battleship. From where she stood, she could see the strand of the beach. It was a beautiful afternoon. ASP Island looked perfect under the high sun, its shallow approach waters pale blue to white, glistening and clean. Phoenix felt the ache, the pull of homesickness, like regret for a time she had let slip through her fingers.

Then it began. From nothing, from a brilliant, glistening blue afternoon, the battleship seemed to lurch and bounce under Phe's feet. The great guns over her head, one after the other, sent a massive shell screaming across to the land beyond the beach. One after the other guns boomed above, the decks bouncing below, with ASP Island throwing up a line of trees and flying soil.

With the signal given and understood, the landing craft were released and began to trammel forward while all the other ships sent shells wailing through the air. Phe's island home was flaring up along the line beyond the beach.

In little more than a moment, the clear air was filled again. Helicopters crisscrossed, firing on each other, hitting home almost every time. Down they span, exploding in the darkening seas.

Phoenix ducked behind the metal wall of the ship. But from the other side they came. The guns were firing, like explosions deep inside the head. Phe's ears were ringing. She cried out, but her voice was lost in noise.

Other ships, enemy battle cruisers, had edged round the curve of the island to attack the Republican forces. The commander was on his communications equipment in the ship's metal cabin, peering out, bellowing into a handset.

Phe peeped over the side. The island was being taken apart. Everything was dirty. In seconds, air was just noise and filth, water just filth and metal and broken boats and dead soldiers. The sea raged, as in a storm. The helicopter clouds rained down from above.

Everyone but Phoenix, the commander and the parson was firing at everyone else. They all wanted so much for the others to die. Phe's own close guard were aiming at the helicopters above. The choppers flew in, launching their rockets at the landing craft, veering away—sometimes into other helicopters. They exploded in midair. Nothing was left of their pilots, nothing at all.

The rockets blew mostly into the sea, spraying dirty salt up over everything. Then they'd make a direct hit, dead center of one of the hundreds of forward-driving landing craft. Phoenix watched one rocket flying into the open-topped boat full of Adult soldiers. The explosion was redder than ever, blowing them all to pieces, knocking out the sides of the craft.

Adults were in bits, floating in the dark, choppy waters. Oil leaked and caught fire. Between the ship and the landing craft, the sea blazed. Soldiers falling overboard screamed and thrashed in the hot sea. They disappeared. And still the battle raged. Still the skies were black and the ocean burning up towards it.

In among it all, the strangest sight—like a big, flightless bird flapping one way, then the other, past Phoenix, in and out of the commander's cabin, flinging away aft, charging to the fore—the wildly excited specter of the parson. Up and down the deck, his robes in the smoke, his blessings sanctifying the heat and blaze of battle.

Holy and ghostly, fighting his good fight, he railed into Phe's face as she took to shielding herself against the metal wall of the bulkhead. "Genome is great!" he spat at her. His eyes were like death rays, smoke-dark, as if ready to fire.

"Genome loves you!" he screamed, his voice crossing the gap between them like a guided missile. "You are the bringer of Truth! Genome has brought you to us!"

He and she, the priest-parson and the Ground Agle, were surrounded by their own guards. One fell, hit and mortally wounded by shrapnel, the sharp, white-hot pieces of metal from rockets or blown from the body of the ship.

"Rejoice!" the parson blared down at the downed soldier. He dropped over the dying Adult, his death-black robes fluttering in the battle wind. As the soldier's life drained away, it looked like death diving to greet him, darkly flapping, smoking and stinking of heat and gunfire.

"You will be welcomed at the gates of Paradise by Genome himself!" the parson insisted, as the Adult faded at his feet.

"Rejoice! Rejoice! The Kingdom of Heaven is come! Genome will never desert you!"

## 115

Landing craft were reaching the beaches, their entire front opening up to spew forth their cargoes. As more boats opened and soldiers were seen like insects crawling up the slope of the long sweep of the beach, another new wave of helicopters came in, sinking low in a line over the forest. They dipped to strafe the soldiers as they ran, the fiery lead of their bullets pounding in the sand.

Phoenix watched them fall. The line of latest choppers threw off a final few rockets at the ships as they flew over Phe's head. The small, fast battle cruisers of the opposing army of the Immaculate Mother turned away and left the scene.

The beaches were littered. Metal, glass, plastic, oil slicks. And dead soldiers. But the first battle was over and Phoenix felt her guard closing in round her again as Commander Huxley left the shelter of his metal command cabin.

The parson was leading a cheer. The black book of Genome was held on high.

"Prepare to land!" the commander bellowed.

Along the side of the ship the parson leapt and turned, spinning his robes outwards, taking up space, expansive and jubilant in his victory. "We fight the good fight!" he cried, as he stumbled over the body of the dead guard. He fell with a wet smack onto the deck. He looked like a tentacled sea creature, just recently landed. His book slid across the metal flooring on a slick of the soldier's lost blood, and came to rest, bumping against Phoenix's feet. She kicked it away. The commander watched her all the while, but she turned from him.

Crossing the shallow sea to ASP Island, Commander Huxley's eyes were fixed on Phe's face. Helicopters still buzzed overhead, carrying arms and supplies to the shore.

The parson, at the bow of another small landing boat, stood with his book tucked under his arm, his stained garments hanging limply, drying off in the dirty breeze. He faced forward, lost in a mystical haze of righteous purpose. Every now and then he held up the book. His soldier guards responded with a roar, with a crackle of gunfire. But the parson-person was all for facing forward, onward with Genome's soldiers, fighting the good fight, with all his might.

The commander, meanwhile, with the shore approaching rapidly, looked more and more quizzically at Phoenix. "We have always tried," he said, slowly, "to disbelieve the rumors—the Immaculate Mother and son—but now, you say, they exist. You say they have nuclear materials—plutonium. But plutonium is a by-product of another process. It is a by-product of uranium fission, is it not?"

Phoenix tried not to stumble over her ignorance of the nuclear processes. "I—I don't—my sister knows—"

"But you do not—you do not know. And you weren't expecting me, a mere soldier, to know, were you? You did not anticipate that I was once a scientist."

Phoenix was trying, but failing, not to look too surprised.

The commander's eyes bore ever more deeply into her. "You have lied to me, I think," he said.

Phoenix opened her mouth, but no words would come.

"Do not think," the commander did not wait for her to speak, "never for a moment think that you have fooled me. I am in control—I am in command here. You have lied. There is no nuclear threat. But you *have* heard about the Revelation Element—you have come across this term."

Phe nodded. Still no words.

"And the Immaculate Mother and her son?" he went on. "What do they look like, again?"

"I said," she said, feeling more and more exposed and uncomfortable under the steady state of the commander's glare, "I told you—they're like—like devils."

"Yes, but what does that *mean*?"

Their craft was coming to the shore, the deathbed of sand scattered with so many fallen soldiers. Phoenix heard, for the first time, the many moaning voices of the injured and the dying.

"What does it mean?" Commander Huxley was pressing her ever harder. "Tell me—exactly—about the Immaculate Mother—tell me what her son really looks like."

While soldiers groaned and cried, the parson flapped at them, like a harbinger of doom as they died. He seemed to love and admire them more when they were no longer there.

"Tell me," the commander leaned in, blocking out the sight of the flying parson, "what is he like, her son?"

The military machine was assembling round them, with the Republican Guard standing to attention on the strand of the beach. But Phoenix still crouched in the boat, shifting under the gaze of the commander, unable to escape his eyes. She wanted to set her feet back onto her homeland, to feel its stability under and supporting her. But he would not let her go. He kept her with his expectant gaze, demanding so much from her.

"Well?" he said.

Here, crouched leaning against one edge of the little boat, the commander did not appear to be so very big. In Adult, or in Human terms, compared to the tall attentive guards, he was smaller, with ever so slightly grey skin plates.

Now, as Phoenix studied Huxley with the Immaculate Mother's son in mind, there was something . . .

Phoenix opened her mouth to speak. But the sound of guns spoke for her, suddenly ripping open the edge of the near forest, cutting down most of the line of guards waiting over the boat. Soldiers fell, knocked face down in the sand, writhing there, or face up to the sky, still. Dead still.

# 116

"Small arms fire!" rallied the commander. "Return fire!" He leapt up.

Phoenix collapsed into the bottom of the boat. The bullets whined and whistled past. If the commander got hit now, it would mean a massive blow for the Republic. Phoenix turned over and looked up at him as he threw out his arms and his orders. But there must have been many soldiers surviving the onslaught, as the return fire hammered loud nearby and the bullet spray from the bushes diminished and then stopped altogether.

"Forward! Advance!" roared the commander. He turned and reached down, dragging Phe out of the boat.

"I'll want my answer from you!" he yelled, tossing her at the remains of his close guard.

They ran towards the nearest bushes, those soldiers in the advance wave up the beach. Here, so close to the sea, the forest was green. Then the nearest green leapt up at them, snapping into the Adults' faces.

Green Raptors had been positioned in a line at the edge of the forest. Young Male Greens leapt like roaring bushes, only to be cut down in a spray of bullets. Another line of Greens came at the soldiers. They did not get far.

Phoenix turned her face away.

The battle-crazed parson jumped onto green-feathered bodies, his frenzied face a picture of delirious exaltation. "Today Genome will be triumphant! He is come! The time of Revelation is at hand! His Kingdom will be established here on earth! Genome is great!"

Then his voice was lost in the sound wall of small arms fire splattering through the trees into the forest. Soldiers with flame-throwers cleared the edges close to the beach, exposing the woods beyond. Raptors tried to run away. Phoenix had to watch them mowed down.

"Advance!" bellowed the commander.

Phe's nerves were jangling. The Raptors had been her allies, once. But baby Greens had always been headstrong, suffering with so many aggression-making, uncontrollable urges. Now they were dying, afraid, alone, without their mothers to tell them what to do, with no clue how to get out of this suicidal war.

She had to turn away from their burnt bodies. Commander Huxley's eyes were on her again. She had to march forward, before dropping to the ground once more as the barrage of bullets splattered again, as the Raptors roared.

Phoenix dived, with her ears ringing as the machine guns cracked and the flames were thrown and the machetes hacked through, through bloodied Green bodies, through the burning bush. Any dangerous weed or sucking bog was destroyed in moments by angry flames. The forest and everything in it fell away, its balance broken, another ancient environment damaged beyond repair. Whatever happened here in the future would be very, very different from everything before. As the Adults cleansed the world, they dirtied it forever.

Marching on without mourning losses, with the parson celebrating death all the way, rejoicing at the destruction of every species, including his own, the Republican Army forced Phoenix ever closer to her home. She stumbled with them, despising them in so many different ways. They set no value on each other, or anything else. They showed no love, no mercy.

The bullets ripped again, on reaching the other side of the forest. But this time, the assault soldiers of the Immaculate Ministry were running away from the cover of the woods across the open plain. The Republican Guard gave chase, firing and bringing down their enemy as they went, until a last line of bushes turned into Raptor and the Guard ran directly into them.

At last, Greens took them down. The soldiers were too close. The Raptors had sprung as if from nowhere into the Adults' shocked faces, snapping at their heads before the soldiers could even shout.

Phoenix watched the fight. She heard the commander roaring above the Raptors for the next line of Guards to drive forward. The front-line forces were being crushed, ripped apart by beak and claw. But Phe could see, from where she stood, that these Greens were different. They were older. There were females as well as males, and they were all, every one of them, tethered. They were chained up, their shackles fixed to the ground by metal stakes. These Raptors had been captured and placed here, and now they had to fight for their lives. Ever since ASP City had been taken, the mature Greens had been held in fear by their hateful and manipulative enemy—so now, of course, given the chance, they killed. They took revenge. They killed Adults.

# 117

"Next line forward!" the commander called on his troops, always expecting replacements, never disappointed.

The troops advanced, quite prepared to die, even as they saw their friends and comrades ripped to pieces by Raptors. On they ran, firing as they went, shooting down the Greens and accidentally killing injured allied soldiers at the same time. No matter! Death was like life to this misguided missile-species. Paradise beckoned. They fell for it in monstrous numbers.

Phoenix halted. She watched the chained Raptors dying. She and the commander stood on the edge of the forest looking out across the plain. Huxley's own guard, overexcited to see the enemy on the run, had given chase, had fallen as the Raptors rose.

The commander called for ever more replacements. The heavy vehicles bringing up the rear had to trundle slowly through the ruined forest, knocking tree trunks out of the way as they came. Helicopters overhead carried big guns, giant ammunition.

"Guards!" the commander called behind. "Where are the—" Something stopped him.

Phoenix felt the Raptor before she saw her. Commander Huxley saw her first. The female Green had lain like another bush at the edge of the forest, allowing the attack soldiers to rush by.

But Huxley had stumbled through too close, shouting out too loudly.

The Green Raptor would not have understood what he was saying. She thought he was shouting because he'd spotted her there.

She jumped up, silencing him in surprise. Phe felt the surprise silencing the commander.

The Green Raptor leapt at Commander Huxley, clanging to a halt as she dragged at the limits of her restraining chain. Huxley fell back, fumbling for the handgun in its holster on his leather belt. He drew the gun. The soldiers fired from the front, the machinery of war crunching through the forest from behind, slicing through the air above.

Nobody else heard the Raptor as she thrashed and battled to get away. The Commander's gun was leveled at her. She was terrified.

So was Phoenix. "No!" she screamed, dashing at the commander, throwing herself into his side.

He stumbled, catching his foot in the tough low undergrowth. The gun flew from his hand as he fell into the chain radius of the Raptor.

"No!" Phoenix shouted at the Green as she snapped at the retreating Commander. Phoenix fell onto the gun. Huxley had scrambled back to safety, with the female Raptor still snapping at his ankles. Phoenix watched him kicking back, looking round for his gun. "Here it is," she said.

His eyes flickered into her face, to the gun, back to Phe's face. She had the pistol pointing at him, at his heart.

The Raptor stopped thrashing at her chain.

"Give me the gun," said Commander Huxley, starting to get up.

"Stay where you are," Phoenix ordered.

He halted, noticing, for the first time, the shift of her hair. His eyes bore into her. He could finally see what she was thinking.

Phoenix couldn't avoid showing him. She had shuffled off fear again, into hatred. She had wished Commander Huxley dead, many times. Now she could kill him. One pull of the trigger and he'd be gone. No one else would hear, with the many other guns going off and with the machinery on the move.

"What are you doing?" asked the commander, although Phe could see he knew the answer.

She was going to shoot the leader of the Republican Guard. Then they'd be undermined, severely weakened. Phoenix was going to shoot him and run, making her own way into the city to find what was left of her family and friends. All she had to do was pull the trigger.

The Commander had sat back, relaxed, glaring straight at her, almost challenging Phoenix to shoot.

She was going to! Her hand flexed. Huxley was going to die, now. Right now!

Phoenix was trying to concentrate, to remember the death of her grandfather, the maiming of Jay-Jay, the passing away of Rap Rodent. The Adults had damaged and destroyed everything. They deserved to die.

The gun was heavy in her hand. All she had to do was squeeze—all she had to do to achieve at least some kind of justice. It was right. It was right to kill . . .

But then—as if he had never gone from her forethoughts—Aspect, his gentle face, his brother and all the other Bright were there. It was as if Aspect were beside her now, speaking to Phoenix in his soft and gentle tones. Aspect would not kill.

Human Beings, every single one would pull the trigger to end an enemy. But the Bright would not.

So then . . . what should a Ground Agle do? Kill, or not kill? Should she be more Human, or Bright? Which was it to be?

# 118

Phoenix could not do it. She went to drop the gun, still fully loaded, but it was lifted roughly from her grip and she was shoved aside. The Green Raptor never stood a chance.

"Be gone, sub-Human mutation!" the parson-person wailed as he discharged the commander's pistol, as the female Green collapsed backwards. He shot her again and again, pulling at the trigger until the chamber was empty of bullets and the Raptor lay still and lifeless.

As the parson leapt on top of the Raptor's body, the commander went at Phoenix.

"Genome is merciful!" the parson was yelling, raging from the top of his kill. He kicked out the green feathers, as if wading through them.

"I saw what you wanted to do!" the commander glowered down at Phoenix. "I am going to make you wish you had the courage and the commitment to do it!"

The parson still waded and thrashed through crackling green feathers, wild with glee.

"Now," the commander shouted into Phe's close face, "now I want my answer. I asked you a question and you haven't answered it. Answer it! Now! Right now!"

The parson's voice was crazed and crowing, but the commander's was growing more high-pitched, ever more like a scream. It was strangely familiar, that voice, with the parson's in the background—a sound Phoenix felt she had suffered from somewhere before.

"You'll answer my question, right now!" that hysterical voice was shrieking. "I asked you what he looked like—I asked you what the Immaculate Mother's son looked like—and now I'll have my answer! Now you'll tell me! Tell me now—what does he look like? Tell me now! Tell me! TELL ME!"

The parson had halted at last, stepping down from the Raptor's body. "TELL ME!"

"He looks," Phoenix said, now that she was sure, "he looks—and he sounds like . . . like you."

# 119

"Like you!" Phoenix stared at the commander.

"What did she say?" the parson was approaching.

The Commander stood there saying nothing as the wail of a rocket came winding in from behind, from over the forest to slam into one of the helicopters above. The chopper had been carrying a big gun, a cannon, which fell spinning from the explosion.

Phoenix stood face-to-face with the commander. Behind him, the cannon dropped from the sky and smashed barrel first into the ground.

The Commander did not flinch. His eye contact with Phoenix did not waver, while the parson, running away across the plain to the safety of his guard, praised Genome in his infinite mercy for sparing him from the fall of the great gun.

"Guards!" the commander yelled out, still looking into Phe's unblinking eyes.

"Don't let her out of your sight for a moment! Keep her close to me."

Above them, the enemy helicopters were flying in again.

"She will show us the way to the Royal Palace," he said, "where we shall see for ourselves."

# 120

Phoenix was continuously looking, searching for signs of Agles or Rodents as they marched into ASP City. All she saw was Adults and chained, helpless Raptors. It was becoming clear now that the Republican Guard were more in number and better equipped. The other side were falling fastest, taking the Raptors with them. Phoenix hoped that everyone else had fled or taken to the rat runs for shelter against the air raids. And on they marched, with destruction. The city behind them lay in ruins, burning, the buildings in front under constant attack.

Phe noticed that all the drains had been sealed, cemented over. Every entrance to and exit from the runs was blocked off—to defend the runs from attack? She wondered about that only for a moment. The Agles and the Rodents would never have had the chance to build blockages. They were defenseless—Phoenix knew that, only too well.

Phoenix cried out to see the fifty or more trucks pumping motor-belch, pushing smoke into the rat runs. The entrances, the exits were all sealed! It could only mean one thing!

Carbon monoxide!

She knew instantly just exactly where the Agles and the Rodents had been put.

"They can't do that!" she cried aloud. She tried to run.

"Stop her!" ordered Commander Huxley.

"No!" she screamed. "You have to stop them! There! Bomb them! Those trucks—bomb them! Now! RIGHT NOW!"

The guards held her back. Huxley peered across at the group of driverless vehicles with their engines running. He too saw the flexible pipes disappearing into the ground. He looked more closely at the effect the sight was having on Phoenix.

"Well, well," he said, with the doubt immediately wiped from his face, "what do we have here?"

"Please," begged Phoenix. "Please, Commander Huxley. Please."

He glanced again at the trucks, the pipes, again at Phe. "How very interesting," he said.

# 121

Phoenix pleaded with him.

"Those trucks," he said, as if about to issue an order. He pointed them out to his officers. Phoenix breathed with relief. "Defend them! Keep them running!"

"No!" On the instant she was breathless again, her heart pounding. "No! They'll all be killed!"

"The Royal Palace!" the commander leaned towards her. "Show me where it is!"

"Destroy the trucks first!"

"Show me first! Defend those vehicles with your lives! Rocket launchers! You, there! You are to keep those engines running! Now!" He turned back to Phoenix.

She struggled and ran. But the Guard and their Commander shot at and attacked her, dashing with her through the ruinous streets towards the Palace. The parson flapped just behind Phoenix and the commander, blessing the new progress they were making in the name of Genome.

Phoenix, cursing quietly, breathing loudly, trying not to be sick, ignored the bullets whining by, the cries of the close hand-to-hand combatants she weaved around. She outran the armored vehicles booming destruction into the buildings behind. She ran through the falling dust and debris from bombed, collapsing walls under helicopter bombardment.

Her plan to bring the other Adults here to war now seemed insane. She had never worked out how she was going to rescue anyone from the cages or get them away from the island. And the winners of the war would still be with them, always persecuting them, as Adults, Human Being believers in Genome forever would.

There was no escaping the Humans now. Genome was truly everywhere, omnipotent and everlasting.

Phoenix ran until she was sick. Then she swallowed what she'd burped up and ran some more. Her head was thumping. She saw the Old Royal Palace through pounding eyes, under hot and throbbing brow.

"There!" she screamed, pointing to the high blank walls. "Up there–the gates!"

Phoenix ran them along the wall, with machine guns stuttering Genome's will, crackling like laughter into the brickwork behind, above, before.

The parson prayed. The bullets did not appear to veer away. The parson ducked for his life.

Commander Huxley, waving wildly, advanced his troops through the streets behind them. His helicopters gunned down the avenues. The lines of trees were felled, blown down and smashed up.

The forces of the Immaculate Mother were fierce and strong, but they were outnumbered, outgunned. Genome's will was might. It was sheer force and ugly, naked aggression.

The Royal Palace lie at the heart of the city. The Republican Guard were everywhere now, with their tanks and big guns rolling up the breaking streets. A few enemy helicopters tried to fly away. They did not get far. Snipers left alone in the shells of shelled buildings picked off a few more lives before losing their own.

The forces of the Republic were gathering in the center of the city, condensing round the periphery walls of the Palace. Losses had been heavy on both sides, but the battle winners didn't bother stopping to count. They eliminated the opposition. They were still alive, although diminished, while the others were not.

Only the Palace remained, the last stronghold of the Ministry of the Immaculate Mother.

"Let me go now!" Phoenix was screaming. "It's here—you've won!"

"No!" the commander snapped, dragging her to the huge wrought iron gates in the massive stone walls. "Rocket fire!" he bellowed.

Phoenix tried to run as the gates were blown through. But Huxley reached for her, tugging her from the hold of his guard. "Show me where!" he roared, dragging her through the open space in the wall.

The gates were destroyed entirely. Phoenix was shoved through into the grounds beyond. She had been there many times. It was always green. As now it was—green—Raptor green.

Hundreds of them. Thousands. All tied, chained. Female Green Raptors in their thousands were chained together, a living Green moat round the huge, majestic building floating like an island in the middle.

# 122

Behind the Raptors, before the great house, inside a bristling ring of arms, what was left of the Army of the Ministry of the Immaculate Mother. The terrified Raptors raged and battled against the tether of their chains. But the soldiers stood, prepared to battle to the last for their beliefs.

On the steps of the Palace, speaking into the amplifier system, Phoenix caught sight of him again, where she had seen him before. This hatred of that voice was not new to her.

"Hold fast!" Captain FitzRoy was saying, calmly, steadily. "Prepare yourselves. They are the true enemy of Genome. You will all be martyrs now, with a martyr's reward in Paradise. Take as many of their number as you can. You are still and will forever be the guardians of Genome's Immaculate Ministry on earth. Prepare to die in glorious martyrdom!"

There was no time left. Phoenix went to move forward, but Commander Huxley caught her by the shoulder. "Wait!" he said. "We wait for the full force of the Republican Guard."

Phoenix felt as if she could taste the carbon monoxide in the air. She felt light-headed, out of touch with reality, above danger. "No! We move! Forward!" she raged.

The commander dragged her back. Phoenix, twisting free of his grip, smoothly swiped his handgun from its holster on his belt. The guards round them prepared to shoot her dead on the instant.

Huxley waved them down. The gun was pointed at him. "I know you can't do it," he said.

"We can't wait." Phe's breath was labored. She was sweating. Carbon monoxide would kill her too, like this, before very long. "We move, now." And she started off. Her head was spinning. She felt everything through her hair as usual, but more than that—she remembered everything, all at once, her whole life coming back to her in an instant.

She made a sign. A Raptor signal. Until now, she never thought she had learned any of their language. But now Phoenix could almost read the thoughts of the terrified female Greens. Now suddenly she could speak to them.

Phoenix passed among them as Captain Huxley and his guard stood gazing on. She saw Captain FitzRoy noticing the change in the Raptor behavior.

"I am the Ground Agle Phoenix!" she signaled, turning, clicking and nodding, speaking Raptor for the first time in her life. "And I have returned to free you all!"

Huxley's Republican Guard were shooting away the chains, on the commander's order, from the legs of the Greens.

"Fight for your lives!" Phoenix Raptor-roared.

"You!" she heard FitzRoy's hated voice blaring through the speaker system. Phoenix looked over at him. "I knew it was you!" he raged, his voice screaming from the speakers in the trees. "I knew it!"

Phoenix glared up at him. She had faltered and failed to pull the trigger of a gun pointed at an Adult. But this one did not hesitate for a moment. He aimed at her. He pulled. The gun fired.

# 123

He fired. But he was falling forward.

Phoenix stood with her ears ringing from the near blast, from the bullet whistling by, hot against the side of her head.

Captain FitzRoy staggered, spinning. Something had dropped on him from the roof. He twisted wildly, trying to hit upwards, tripping down the Palace steps with the winged being on his shoulders clinging to his face.

Alice went down with him.

Phoenix cried out to her, but the commander and the parson collected her from the lower steps and ran her towards the big wooden doors of the Palace.

"Alice!" Phoenix was screaming, dragged backwards into the big building, while the Angel scratched at the Adult her brother Jay-Jay had hated most. "Alice! NO!"—with the Raptors closing in, lashing out with razor talons as they had on the plain that other terrible time, when Ember had been taken to pieces in a similar frenzy of Green fury.

# PART EIGHT

# NUCLEAR REACTION

# 124

"We need them alive!" Commander Huxley was in her face. "The mother and son! We must take them alive! Where will they be?"

But Phoenix was lost, spitting and crying, breaking down. "I can't save anyone! I'm finished with all this."

"But we've won!" the parson rejoiced, with the guns still cracking outside. "Genome is victorious!"

Against the wooden doors of the Palace, great thumps were pounding. The Raptors were raging on, soldiers still soldiering.

"It's not over," the commander said. "It is not over until—until you show us, now, what we've come here for. Where will they be—what's the safest place here? Where would you put someone if you wanted to keep them out of the way?"

"I don't know!"

"Think! Where are they? Quickly, before it's too late! We'll lose everything if you don't think!"

Phoenix was beaten. What else was there *to* lose? "In the old tales," she said, tearfully, "in the stories of Ash, our Legends—she was kept in the cells, locked away, but protected. In one of the rooms downstairs!"

They were standing in the huge hallway, with a staircase rising, going only up. "Where?" the commander blared. "Show me where!"

So Phoenix took them there. She showed them the way to the other steps at the back of the house, the ones that went down and down. She descended with them, with the commander of the victorious army and the parson minister of Genome's Republic. In a daze, with her head throbbing and her ears ringing, she thought she was delirious to see a shadow rising up towards them. But they all halted as the apparition peered up at them.

"Get behind me, Devil," it said, the anti-light effigy of the Immaculate Mother's priest, hovering funereally in darkened robes like Death on the stairs.

# 125

"The Devil is with *you*!" The parson blared down the stairs. "In Genome's holy name, be gone, you dark forces!"

Phe watched the priest ascending, holding up his copy of the black book, the dark book of Genome, while the parson descended to confront him, his own copy of the self-same words as justification for the fight.

"Genome is great!" the priest leapt up.

"Blasphemer!" bellowed the parson, flying down in a rage.

Phoenix stood still with Huxley as the priest and the parson prepared to do battle in Genome's name. They waved their books, thrusting them in each other's face, shouting out quotations, as if firing them at each other.

*"And the angel said to the immaculate virgin: you shall conceive in your womb, and bring forth a son!"*

*"But he utterly destroyed all that breathed, as the LORD commanded!"*

Somewhere in their dark, drastic book of many writings, Phoenix remembered now, they had both been instructed to love their enemy. But the book was full of contradictions and Genome's many justifications for war.

*"And he made us to be a kingdom, to be priests unto his glory for ever and ever!"*

*"Genome shall bring a nation against you, from the end of the earth, a nation of fierce countenance which shall not regard the old, or show favor to the young!"*

Phoenix stood and watched them fighting, flapping at each other, robes and holy quotes. And she felt their frightened need, their childlike desire to be the one closest to their "father"—like two baby Agles they vied for prominence, for favor in the eyes of their most esteemed and potent parent.

"Genome is great!" they railed at each other.

"But Genome is greatest on the side of the victorious!" the parson screamed, with the full conviction of his righteousness. He was right because the Republic had killed more, had all but annihilated the argument against them.

Phoenix felt the full force of Genome, his unstoppable progress in the world. Genome would always be proved right. The greatest force would be his victory always, forever. He could never lose. In one guise or the other, Genome's holy war was always won, his will done on earth, as it would be in the repressive terror of his heaven.

"Genome is great!"

The parson's words were ringing in Phe's ears. She felt the force of them as the priest did, pushed backwards, falling away from the advances of the Republic. His holy book flew fluttering and fell into the stairwell and the priest dropped down after it, thumping onto the back of his head and lay splayed in dead black robes under the shock of the electric lights.

# 126

"Genome's will be done," the parson turned to Commander Huxley.

The Commander was the first to move, leading Phoenix downstairs, stepping over the rasping, groaning priest. "Where?" he was demanding of her. "Where are they?" He was shoving her and shoving her, every time with more ferocity. "Where? Show me where they are!"

"Here!" she shouted back at him as he hustled her through the door she had indicated. "In here! Oh!" she said.

"Oh!" a high-pitched and terrified voice said, as Commander Huxley and the parson entered. "Oh, Mummy! What do they want? What are they going to do to us?"

Phoenix was pushed aside by Commander Huxley. He stood filling out the doorway with the parson making holy signs by his side. Huxley appeared to be struggling to breathe.

Inside the open cage built against the back walls of the stone room, the boy Adult tried to wriggle farther into the swirling skirts of his mother's dress. She, the *immaculate* one, stood tall, staring back at the commander, her head up, her breathing steady. There they stood, all of them, without a word spoken, for what seemed to Phoenix like an age. This, for Phe, was the time of carbon monoxide—the poisonous time, ticking like an engine turning over. The doorway was blocked by the body of the commander. He and the parson stood together, aghast, gazing.

The Immaculate Mother pressed her little son closer to her. She held up the ornate wand she always carried.

"Hello, Thomas," she said, in a calm voice, to Huxley.

The parson's glare shifted from the mother to the commander in disbelief.

"I knew it was you," the commander said. "I always knew it was you."

"Mummy," the boy Adult cried, cringing under the flitting eyes of the commander, "Mummy, who is it? What does he want?"

The immaculate Mummy said nothing. She was staring too intently at Huxley. He, looking from the boy to his mother then back to the boy, said, "I am—I am your father."

# 127

"Mummy! What does he *mean*? What does he mean, Mummy?"

Phoenix could not take her eyes from the boy and his mother. "I always knew it was you," she heard Commander Huxley's voice.

The boy was cringing, crying. "But Genome is my father! I'm the son of Genome! Mummy, I'm Genome's son on earth, aren't I?"

"No!" snapped the parson. "You are born of sin, of the temptations of the flesh—and your mother is like any other tempter!"

"But," the commander seemed to trip forward in a daze, mesmerized by the boy-Adult, "how are you still like this? After all these years? How still a child? Surely," he said, looking to the boy's mother, "he is fully grown?"

As the commander stepped forward, Phoenix moved towards the doorway. Only the parson stood there now, not looking at Phe, as his eyes flashed from mother to son to Commander, mother, son, commander, more quickly, more quickly still.

"He is fully grown!" the commander stated.

The boy cowered before the Adult claiming to be his father. The mother breathed in, facing Huxley, defying him. "He is not a mutation!" she said. "He is different. I had to protect him." The boy huddled ever closer, crawling into his mother's skirts. "And I will protect him!" she said, holding up the wand.

"But you do not still have it?" the commander halted. "The Revelation Element? It was destroyed, all of it."

"Not so," she said. "I created it. I kept it. Better deliver my son to the open arms of the Lord than give him up to you and your evil empire."

Phoenix sidled closer to the door. She could just squeeze behind the parson and run out before—then she stopped.

"But you'll destroy the world," Commander Huxley said.

# 128

Phoenix stopped.

"The Revelation Element will destroy the world!" Commander Huxley said.

Phe turned back. She, like the parson, looked: mother, son, Commander. *Mother.*

"Yes," she said, holding up the thin black-and-white wand. "Then Genome will come and my son and I will live in Paradise with the Father forever."

Phoenix sensed the parson might explode at any moment.

"You will not harm my son," the mother was saying.

The commander shifted, still moving slowly towards them. "I will not harm him," he said.

"He has no sin!" The boy's mother held him tightly against her. "He is pure. There is no sinful mutation here."

"No," the commander said, softly. "He is my son too. I will protect him."

The boy peeped out. He disappeared again, just his back showing in the deep folds against his mother.

"If only you understood him," she said.

"I shall," promised the commander, reaching out to them. "I will work to understand him, and then, by Genome—"

"By Genome!" roared the volatile parson. In a single explosive movement he had picked Phoenix from the floor and thrown her into the cell. She fell against the commander. He stumbled. The mother clutched her squealing son to her body.

Phoenix just had time to look up to see the parson swipe the wand from the mother's hand before he was back outside the bars of the cell, clanging closed the door and turning the key.

The parson stepped away as the commander flew across the cage at him. Through the metal upright rods Huxley's hands were clutching at the parson. He grabbed nothing but the air. In the parson's hands, the key and the Revelation wand. He threw the key into the far corner of the room.

"I have it!" he trembled, holding the ornate stick in both hands now. "Genome's Revelation has come at last!"

"Don't do it!" yelled the commander.

"What will it do?" Phoenix asked, speaking for the first time, because she was afraid. The cell was full of dread now. But it was not the fear around her affecting Phoenix so profoundly—it was the excitement, the fervor, the lost, maniac longing in the eyes of the parson.

He raised his face to the ceiling, as if glorying in the light from the bare electric bulb overhead. "Genome is great!" he repeated his mantra once again, "Genome is truly great!"

"Don't!" Huxley commanded him. "Parson! Genome does not want you to do this!"

But the ordained Adult lifting the magic wand to the roof was unable to hear. "He is here!" he was saying. "Genome is calling!"

"No!" the commander crashed against the bars of the cage.

Phoenix felt the fear again, as the little Adult wailed against his mother, as she tried to comfort him. "It is Genome's will," she said.

"His will be done," spluttered the parson. His face was thrashing from side to side. Saliva flew out of his mouth. "The time of the Revelation is at hand. The world will come to an end and Genome will return to gather his people–his chosen ones! His will be done! On earth, as it is in heaven! Amen!"

"No!" cried the commander, one last time.

"Genome!" screamed the parson. "Take me! I am ready!" And, taking the wand in both hands, he snapped it.

Phoenix flinched as it broke into two unequal halves. She felt the mother's lurch of despair beside her, and Commander Huxley's gasp. But nothing happened.

Everyone stopped. Silence thundered into the inner eardrums.

Phoenix had expected some kind of explosion, but there was nothing, not even a pop of release from whatever had been contained in the wand. She watched the parson's fervent expectation drain away. Phoenix watched him peering into the hollow wand, looking up left, right, for something to reveal itself.

"There's nothing in there," he said.

The mother's son was crying. She held him. "Oh, my boy," she said. "We should not be afraid. Genome will care for us." And as she held him, the commander went to them. Together they stood as a family.

"There's nothing," the parson said. "The Revelation–it's nothing!"

Phoenix looked at the commander and his family. They had seen something. The parson, no, but they had. "What is it?" Phe said.

"It's the end," said another voice, from inside the cell, as if from nowhere.

## 129

The hairs on the back of Phe's neck stood on end. She turned to look to the rear of the cell, from where the voice seemed to have come. In the darkness, from a pile of blackened rags, the voice came again. "You shouldn't have come back," it said.

A face appeared. Adult, Human, very nearly, but distorted. The face Phoenix could not recognize, but she knew the voice. "Captain Owen!" She ran to him.

"It's all nothing." The parson was still grieving, outside the cell, peering dumbfounded into the empty hollow wand. "All nothing."

"No," Commander Huxley was heard to say. "Not nothing."

The boy, the fully grown boy-Adult, was still to be heard, his stifled whimpers as if from a long way away.

Phoenix sat down by the beaten and distorted face of Captain Owen. She took his hand. "Oh, what did they do to you?"

"You shouldn't have come," he said softly, his one unclosed eye focusing on Phe's face.

"I had to," she said. "I had to try."

He exhaled mightily.

"All—nothing!" bemoaned the parson.

"I would have understood," the commander was saying to the mother of his son.

"The Revelation Element," Captain Owen whispered to Phe, "it is out now."

"But there's nothing," Phoenix said, with a glance at the distraught parson.

The captain's head shook slightly, painfully. "No. It's in the air now. It is air. It is oxygen. But it's an isotope—its atomic structure has changed—it will alter the air, every atom affecting every atom round it. Now they've let it out there's no stopping it. It will explode outwards from here with nuclear reaction."

"Wait!" the parson said suddenly.

Phoenix looked up at the sound of the urgency in his voice.

"I can see . . ." he said, the parson, looking up, with the light of religious fervor clicking back on in his eyes.

"Now it begins," exhaled Captain Owen.

"Yes!" said the parson, dropping the broken wand to the floor. "Yes—I can—yes, Lord—I can hear you!"

Phoenix noticed Commander Huxley and the mother closing in more tightly on their eternally baby son.

"It will crash through the atmosphere of all the world," Captain Owen hissed. "Faster and faster—enveloping us all. All of us! Everything that lives and breathes—"

"My Lord!" the parson threw up his face and his arms.

The captain was speaking more and more urgently as the commander and the mother held tightly and close together. "The Revelation foretold Genome's return to the earth when the end comes—these fools think that if they bring about the end, then Genome will come."

"He comes!" screamed the parson, falling to his knees, face and arms up. "Praise be!"

"He's coming," Phoenix whispered to Captain Owen.

He gripped her hand too tightly. "No," he said. His hands were starting to shake. Phoenix was beginning to think he was going to break her fingers.

"It's not him," the captain said.

But the parson screamed out. "The Lord! He comes! He—the Lord is here on earth. Take me, Lord! Take me!"

Phoenix watched with horror the parson quivering madly as she felt Captain Owen begin to convulse. Commander Huxley dropped to his knees with a desperate sigh. The mother of his son stood only a moment longer. She too gasped, falling forward.

"Lord Genome!" the parson screamed.

"Where is he?" Phoenix heard the hysterics of the boy-Adult's voice. "I can't see him! Where is he?"

Then the screaming parson let out his loudest wail. His holy book flew out of his hands as he fell, screaming, convulsing on the floor.

"Genome!" he screamed. Then he *screamed.* In horror. "Genome—why have you forsaken me?"

# PART NINE

# REVELATION

# 130

Anything they had to say to each other had been exhausted ages ago. Shut away in a box of a room where the air was brought in, cooled, from the outside, it was impossible to keep track of time.

Totally had slept. When she had awoken, Gabriel was asleep. They had no idea how long they had been kept here, what time or what day it was. All they had inside their four grey walls was a pile of ripening fruit and some nuts to eat, a water fountain, a little toilet out back, and each other.

They had talked so much . . . so much of what they had said was about Genome. Even when they spoke of other things, the changes in themselves, the massive changes in Phoenix, Genome stood over them like a grim specter, listening to and watching them, ready, as ever, to punish. Genome was a jealous god. They could feel his envy, his vindictive greed everywhere here, locked up with them in the town of the Adults. He was there in the hiss of the air through the vent, in the coldness of the electric light, the headache-inducing static of the atmosphere, and the metallic tang of the water. Genome was present in the sound of vehicles moving by outside, in the urgent Adult voices snapping out orders. Genome's purpose was evident in all the false and Adult, Human things.

"Listen!" Gabriel said, breaking Totally's train of thought.

"What is it?"

"I heard—wait! Listen—there!"

From far away, a cry. An Adult in agony. Then another, closer scream.

"What's happening?" Totally said.

They looked at each other in fear as the cries multiplied outside, increasing in number and volume until the Adult town had become another city of screams.

Then, as it had begun, so it stopped. Totally strained to hear. Nothing. Silence. "Not even the air hissing in anymore," she said.

She and Gabriel exchanged another look. Then the lights went out.

# 131

In the impenetrable blackness under the Old Royal Palace, nothing but the boy's voice, wailing in the wilderness. "Mummy! Where are you? What's happening? What is this place? I'm so scared! Mummy! Where are you? Where's Genome? I hate it here! Help me! I'm so scared!"

Phoenix crouched with Captain Owen's motionless hand in hers. She was still here, she was sure, in the same place, untouched. Then Phoenix heard the boy fall. He had been trying to move, desperately seeking help. But he tripped and fell down. His hands, Phoenix heard, were scrabbling through fabric. His mother's skirts! His fingers, she sensed from the rush of emotions gushing from him, had found his mother's face.

She was dead. Everyone else was. Just Phoenix and the boy left.

Why *them*? Why weren't they all dead?

# 132

"What's happened to them?" Totally was whispering.

Gabriel didn't say anything. Tolly heard him moving, the rustle of his folded wings. Then she felt him, sensed his excitement as he clung onto her.

"Can you feel it?" he rasped. "Can you feel the difference? He's gone. Genome's gone."

# 133

"Listen to me!" Phoenix cried, prying Captain Owen's fingers from hers. "Boy!" she shouted through his wailing screams. "Listen to me!"

"Who are you? What do you want? You're not Genome!"

"No, I'm not," she said, suddenly sure of one thing. "Genome's gone!"

## 134

They waited in the darkness. Their ears and heads ached with listening so hard. The temperature started to rise, very quickly.

Totally guessed that it was around midafternoon, judging by the intensity of the heat coming in from outside. These metal-box Adult houses were cooled by technology, by electricity. The water was pumped in under pressure. Now the heat was intensifying by the moment, the last of their water supply dribbling away.

No sound outside. Nothing stirred.

"We're all alone," Totally heard Gabriel whisper close to her ear. "They've gone. Genome's taken them all away."

# 135

Then she heard it. A voice, calling to her. "In here!" Phoenix cried.

Almost immediately the door was barged open and lights flashed through like tears in the fabric of the darkness.

The boy cried, "Genome!" once more. But then she flew in, silencing him—a torn Angel with ribboned wings flailing through, followed by two ruffled Green Raptors.

A scream greeted them as the boy scuttled away to the far corner of the cage.

"Alice!" Phoenix rushed to the bars, reaching through with her arms. The Angel Alice, with wings ripped and flesh bleeding from a multitude of scratches, hesitated for a moment. For a moment only she stayed away. Then she rushed to Phoenix, the two clutching each other through the bars.

"I thought you were—" Phoenix was saying, breathless. "I thought you'd been killed."

"Not me!" Alice said. "Not without that fight I promised you."

Phoenix laughed. She burst out. It turned into a cry.

The boy-Adult was trying to scuttle even farther away as the Raptors approached.

"Thank you!" Phoenix clicked to them.

"What's this?" Alice was saying, looking over at the boy.

"I can't explain now," Phoenix said. "There's no time. We have to move. The key—it's over there. Quickly!"

Alice retrieved the key from the other side of the room and unlocked the cage. "What about him?" she said, as Phoenix dashed by.

Phe turned back. The boy was tying himself in knots as the two huge Female Raptors bore down over him. "Bring him," she clicked at them.

He screamed louder than ever as they laid their Agle-like hands on him. He kicked, he cried for his Mummy. She, beside his father, lay face to the ceiling, staring with glassy eyes at nothing.

# 136

The door opened; it did not crash wide but moved aside steadily. Totally stood with Gabriel. They were both holding their breath. The daylight leaked in from another doorway farther away.

Framed in leaking light, a dark, decorated, tall figure. His face lit up as soon as he saw them standing there. "You are safe," he said. Totally ran to hug him. "Aspect!" Behind him, as ever, stood his Bright brother. "Foresight!" Tolly said.

"We are all safe, now," Foresight said.

"You must come and see," said Aspect, still holding onto Totally while stretching out for Gabriel's hand. Gabriel reached for him. Aspect led them out into the light.

# 137

Phoenix ran out of the Palace basement and up the staircase with Alice close behind her. Farther back, Phe could still hear, the boy was being brought out by the two Raptors. He was beyond hysterics.

The frightful sound he was making faded as Phoenix ran out into the huge hall at the Palace entrance. The doors had been blown away. Outside, all was in ruins. Crashed helicopters lay burning. Between them, the bodies of killed Raptors and Adults. There were many Raptors. There were many more Adults. Female Greens still stood here and there. As if stunned, they looked about them. Fallen Adults lay everywhere, in attitudes of agony, as if they were still writhing.

Not one had survived. No—*one* had. One only. He was being brought upstairs behind her, Phoenix could not help but hear.

"Quick!" she said, running out across the wrecked lawns, taking Alice with her. "Hurry!"

"Where are we going?" Alice asked, with her torn and shredded wings flapping uselessly behind.

Phoenix was running too hard to answer her. She was moving too fast for Alice to keep up, weaving round the wrecks of flying war machines, the still and silent armored cars, leaping over the endless bodies of the agonized Adults and between the green islands of the Raptors.

When she reached the vehicles she did not pause for breath, dragging away at the stacks of pipes still pumping the poison underground. Phoenix heaved and dragged at them, but they had been fixed and would not give.

"Get the trucks!" she shouted as she felt Alice approaching. "Turn off the trucks!"

"Come out of the way," Alice said, coolly.

Phoenix looked round. She ran.

Alice, with an Adult rocket launcher on her shoulder, hit the trigger button. The missile fired, flinging her back.

Phoenix watched it wind through the air and explode in the nest of pipes, blowing them all to pieces. She looked back at Alice, as the tattered Angel was picking herself up from the ground.

"I watched them do it enough times," Alice said, shrugging.

Phoenix wanted to hug her again. She ran to the tangled opening to the rat runs, dragging away bits of bent and broken metal and plastic. Her hands were being burnt.

Phe did not care. She pulled and pulled until she and Alice cleared the entranceway and peered into the gloom below.

"Hello!" Phoenix shouted down. Her echo, only, answered. She was about to clamber into the hole when Alice stopped her.

"Don't go down there," Alice said. "You'll never come back."

"I must!" Phoenix said. "They're down there, all of them!"

"Wait!" Alice ordered her. "Don't do this now. You're just trying to sacrifice yourself."

"Get out of my way!" Phoenix shoved her.

But Alice shoved back, harder. "I told you I was going to give you a fight. Stay where you are!"

"Get out of my way!"

"No. You'll have to go through me."

The Angel was standing tall in front of the Ground Agle. Alice stood much taller, while Phoenix was stouter, stronger.

"You'll never stop me," Phe said, staring at Alice's scratched and dirty face.

"Try me!"

Phoenix glared at her. She imagined, for a moment, the fight they were going to have. But then a tear slid from the Angel's big green eye. It tracked down Alice's face, leaving a slightly cleaner stripe over her perfect cheek.

Phoenix felt her legs begin to give way as all her resolve, all her fight excitement drained away too quickly. She staggered backwards slightly, as if about to collapse.

Alice was with her again, holding on. "I don't know what you did," Alice whispered, "but you've won. You've beaten them. You did this." She was speaking directly into Phe's ear. "Don't sacrifice yourself. Not now."

Phoenix was watching, blinking over the Angel's shoulder as they held onto each other.

"There's no need," Alice whispered.

"No," said Phe, over Alice's shoulder, watching the first stirring of the life that was beginning to scramble from the ragged hole in the pavement. "There's no need," Phoenix said, as the first one, a Rodent, started to climb out, blinking her huge pink eyes in the glare of the afternoon sun.

# 138

The afternoon light was too strong in Gabriel's eyes. He peered out from under the hood of his hand. He could not believe what he was seeing.

The Bright, hundreds of them, freed from the cages, were walking slowly and with great respect between the bodies of the Adults. All the Adult machines were silent, as were they.

"It's a miracle!" Gabriel said.

"No," corrected Aspect, immediately, turning to look at him, "there are no miracles. There never were. Something has caused this—something that can be explained. There are no miracles. That is Human thinking—that is Genome. Be very careful."

## 139

Then out they came. A few, at first. Following the Rodent, a young Ground Agle. Then another. One following on, Ground Agles and Rodents, all very young. They scrambled up, a trickle, then a steady flow, blinking and crying, looking for family, for friends. Many hugged Phoenix—Ground Agles, mainly. They felt, through their scalps and their hair, just what she had been through. They knew she had saved them.

They were all so young. There were no Elders. None survived. Not one.

"Did they not send any Elders down with you?" Phoenix asked.

"Yes," came the reply.

"Was it the exhaust fumes?" she asked them.

"No," they all said. "Something else. We were with them. They just went. We couldn't save them."

"And there were no Angels?" asked Alice.

"No," they said, even more sorrowfully. "The Adults . . ." And they turned away. There were no Angels. They were too late to help them.

Phoenix went to her. "Alice," she said.

Alice could not speak.

"There is another," Phe said. "Don't forget him. He's still there. And he's waiting for you."

# PART TEN

# WILD EVOLUTION

# 140

He was waiting on the sand. Gabriel wished he could be as certain as Totally seemed. He had his doubts that he would ever see Phoenix again. Alice, he was sure, had gone forever, or she'd have shown up by now. But he stood on the shore with Totally, hoping.

The Bright remained farther back, keeping their distance. Their island had altered. The huge trees were all dead, with their leaves dropping. Most of the insects had disappeared.

Gabriel looked back at the green profusion of the island's undergrowth. It had run wild in the sun with the disappearance of the canopy overhead. Nothing would ever be the same again.

"There!" he heard Totally say, by his side.

Gabriel swung round and gazed out to sea. He expected to have to look far, to use his perfect, long-distance eyesight to spot a little boat bobbing over the horizon. Instead, an Adult landing craft sliced through the surface, speeding towards them.

They had to hurriedly step back as the metal boat slammed up the beach with its front falling open and—

And—oh, yes! Phoenix was bounding out at them. She leapt.

They all went down into the sand, screaming and crying, with Phoenix almost hysterical on top of Gabriel and Totally.

"You did it!" Totally was shrieking at her Ground Agle sister. "I don't know how you did—but you did it!"

They were crying.

Gabriel picked himself out of the sand. He had seen her, the other figure alighting from the landing craft. She was even more beautiful than he remembered. Her face and arms were scratched and bruised, her wings a patchwork of white seaweed repairs—but she was infinitely Angel—the utmost—the skymost!

Alice moved slowly towards him, with more Ground Agles and Rodents and a few female Green Raptors stepping from the boat behind her. She was shaking, looking at him. She halted. Everything about her was atremble. Her magnificent green eyes were fixed on his.

Gabriel took a step or two towards her. "I love you," he said.

She should not attempt to fly, with her wings so badly damaged, but Gabriel saw that she was powerless to resist. Her wings snapped to and she was off the ground. As was he.

Gabriel flew to Alice, even with the holes in his wings, sweeping her up, flying with her, up and up, high above the scene on the beach with the landing craft spewing Ground Agles and Rodents and Green Raptors and what looked like one small Adult. But Gabriel did not look down at them as they all looked up at him. He looked at Alice.

"They're all gone," she wept, as he swept her away. "All those beautiful Angels. All—gone!" He flew with her along the line of the shore and back, swooping low over the Bright as they waved from the furious foliage.

"We're the only ones," Alice said.

Gabriel smiled. "Then we are the origin of our species. Look," he said, peering down, "Evolution's running wild. And we'll run with it, over it and in front of it. Nothing will ever again stop us flying."

Alice held out her own wings, despite their patchwork of repairs. She felt the air, the altered air move them in the same old way. "No," she smiled. "Nothing will ever stop us."

# 141

"It was an isotope of oxygen," Totally said.

Aspect and Foresight turned their soft gazes towards her. Phoenix nodded, telling Tolly to go on with her explanation.

"The Adults, the Humans found a way of altering the atomic nucleus of oxygen. They made a different type of air that affected every other oxygen atom in the world. The effect was nuclear, like a bomb or a series of bigger and bigger bombs going off."

"Our old," Aspect said, "our Elders as you say—they did not survive. Neither did yours. Our ancient trees have all died."

"Only the young have survived," said Phoenix. Totally watched her glancing towards the exceptional Adult, the apparent boy huddled on the ground under his Raptor guard.

"Evolution has moved us on," Tolly went on. "When they made their—their Revelation Element, it would have been death to everything. But Evolution has made us all immune. At least for now."

"For now?" asked Aspect.

"Maybe our DNA, our genes will switch over later, when we're older. Maybe we'll all die of the Revelation later on. We don't know."

"What we do know," Phoenix said, glancing over at the boy-Adult hunkered down over his precious copy of the big black book, "is that Genome's gone. So we should get that book from him and collect all the other books like it and build a fire on the beach on ASP Island and burn—"

"No!" said Foresight, speaking for the first time. "That's the wrong way."

"But Genome's gone and we must—"

"Genome will never go away," said Aspect. "Don't be fooled. He lives in the misguided mind. Sooner or later some species will look out at the complexity of the world, of the moon and the stars, and they'll gasp in awe. Then they'll make the eternal mistake of thinking that complexity must have a maker—and a purpose! And thinking like that, they'll make *themselves* the purpose, the center of the universe, and they'll give praise for their chosen and special position and they'll worship their maker and they'll make it like themselves and call it Genome—or something! It doesn't matter what they call it, Genome will come again. We must watch out for him. We must never allow him in again."

"He doesn't exist," Foresight said. He pointed to the boy. "Except in their minds. And that's how he comes."

"So what do we do with him?" Totally asked the Bright brothers, glancing towards the boy.

"Leave him here," Aspect said. "We will teach him against the book. Only in that way can we close Genome's door into the world. Burning books will never achieve that."

# 142

"Will you not change your mind?" Aspect was asking her. "Will you not stay here with us, Phoenix? Your city is destroyed and your island is—"

"Our island is just beginning," she interrupted him. "We have to go home. I'm sure you understand."

Aspect smiled. He nodded, with slow grace.

"I'm glad I met you, Aspect," she said, moving closer to him.

He bent, so that she could kiss his cheeks.

"I'm glad we met the Bright," she said.

He nodded again, closing his eyes.

She turned before he could open them again. Phoenix walked onto the Adult landing craft and waved her signal to close up the front. As the boat backed away from the beach and started out to sea, Phe made her way to the bulkhead at the back.

The Bright were on the beach, waving them off. They were decorated in their full forest flower colors, holding their sticks in the air. Above the boat as it accelerated away from Bright Island towards ASP, two Angels flew high in the sky, following on.

Phoenix felt Totally beside her as they took a last look at the Bright on the beach. "We'll live by the sea," Phoenix suddenly decided. "We'll live as Ash and the other survivors used to—simply."

"But," Totally said, "we'll keep our library and look after it and add to it."

Phoenix, catching a last glimpse of the one surviving Adult as he stood squat beside his Bright keepers, remembered the look of sheer hatred, the religious light still glinting malevolently in his eyes.

"Yes," she said, turning towards the front, facing the future across the sea of Wild Evolution. "Because next time," she said, waving to the school of Porpoise People leaping and laughing in front of and alongside the boat, "next time we'll know what we're up against. Next time we'll understand, all of us."

## About the Author

John Brindley's previous novels include *The Rule of Claw, Changing Emma,* and *Rhino Boy.* He lives in southeastern England and has two grown-up children. He enjoys music of all different types and plays squash and trains to stay fit. He likes to draw ideas and inspiration from all aspects of life, especially the people he meets.